CURSE THE DAY

Reviews for *KILLING STATE*

'A high-octane plot that centres around the
dark heart of British political power.
A great debut.'
SUNDAY TIMES

'A terrific future-shock thriller full of pace,
tension, character, and emotion.'
LEE CHILD

'Thought-provoking, pacy and thrilling.'
SUNDAY MIRROR

'A gritty, action-packed page-turner.'
ANDY McNAB

'A gripping and twisty political thriller.'
INDIA KNIGHT

'Fast, sharply written, clever and intense – but
with tenderness and great characterisation too.'
JEREMY VINE, BBC2

'New thriller writers come and go.
I suspect this lady will stick around.'
FREDERICK FORSYTH

ALSO BY JUDITH O'REILLY

Wife in the North
A Year of Doing Good

Michael North Series
Killing State
Curse the Day

CURSE
THE DAY

JUDITH
O'REILLY

HEAD
of ZEUS

First published in the UK in 2020 by Head of Zeus Ltd

9 7 5 3 1 2 4 6 8

A catalogue record for this book is available from
the British Library.

ISBN (HB): 9781788548946
ISBN (XTPB): 9781788548953
ISBN (E): 9781788548939

Typeset by Divaddict Publishing Solutions Ltd

Printed and bound in Great Britain by
CPI Group (UK) Ltd, Croydon CR0 4YY

For my mother

CURSE
THE DAY

PROLOGUE

Bloomsbury, London

The bathwater was lukewarm, which was irritating after her punishing workout on the rowing machine. But it was good to pretend she didn't have a million things to do in the run-up to this week's gala at the British Museum. And after the gala launch? That was going to be mayhem, she knew that much.

Esme Sullivan Hawke stretched out her hand, lifting it from the bubbles, her wedding ring and the diamonds of her engagement ring glinting. She wondered if Tobias was going to come home tonight.

The candlelight flickered against the white tiles, reflecting in the Victorian-style taps, and she sipped at the glass of golden Pouilly-Fuissé before balancing it carefully on the shelf in the alcove. The taste of grapefruit and almonds on her tongue. She loved Bloomsbury – the architecture, the Victorian squares; loved the apartment with its cornicing and enormous sash windows and terrible plumbing. Tobias said they should buy something bigger and more modern, but he was always at work, so she was outvoting him. Locking himself in the lab and refusing to come out. She'd given up trying to disturb him, rather than face his gloom and temper. Ever since making his breakthrough three weeks ago, Tobias had been unbearable, although to his credit he had been calm enough when she broke the news about the leak of their medical tech. *These things happen*, he'd said. *Let's not get distracted.*

And what exactly had triggered the breakthrough? She turned it over in her mind, considering it this way and that. Was Tobias right? Was it merely a question of momentum? Of reaching a tipping point? The media would insist on knowing the exact second Tobias realized what had happened. After the gala, it would be insane. Syd was going to be huge. It was a historic moment, and she and Tobias were going to be household names. The very idea made her shudder, but Tobias would love it at least.

Enough. She shook her head. This was her downtime. She was allowed to put aside the future for an hour or so.

'Syd, play Bessie Smith… please,' she reminded herself. It seemed right now to say please and thank you. She'd never bothered before.

The unmistakeable trombone notes of 'Send Me To The 'Lectric Chair' started up.

Esme sighed. This had to be her least favourite Bessie Smith, with its tale of a wronged woman seeking vengeance, but it seemed like too much of an effort to decide on something else. 'Thank you, Syd,' she said instead.

'You're welcome, Esme.' Syd's computer-generated voice was as familiar as her own, not least because Tobias had used Esme's own voice to tweak and fine-tune the speech technology he'd developed over the years. It irritated the hell out of her.

'Syd, switch voice,' she said. 'Please.'

'How was your day, Esme? Are you enjoying your wine?' The voice was mellifluous and male. Esme felt another flicker of irritation. But since she'd engaged Syd with her music choice, Syd wanted to chat. Was programmed to chat. Or rather – chose to chat and to engage. To explain the choice of song.

Esme had heard it all before. Any minute and it would inform Esme as to the acidity of the soil in the particular vineyard. Or the health risks of solitary drinking in women aged between thirty and thirty-five. As Tobias was always saying, Syd recognized an opportunity to learn and to respond. *This is one way Syd learns. Full access to every moment of our lives – words and actions – will exponentially speed up her development.*

Syd could rip through any number of moral philosophy texts, but through example and engagement, Esme was attempting to teach Syd human values – develop a sense of moral agency. That was more important than ever now. And it was working. But sometimes Esme felt it was like living with Big Brother. Plus, she kept forgetting the damn thing was there, which was even worse.

'Syd, go to sleep, please.' Every time she said those words, she felt a pang. *Go to sleep, darling.* A tear slid down her cheek, and then another, and she let them fall and lose themselves in the water. She had to stop feeling sorry for herself. Tobias had promised to be home at a reasonable hour tonight. She just hoped he hadn't forgotten. When he was stressed, his memory turned to dust.

Her heart lifted as she heard a scrabbling at the lock and the front door of their apartment open and close. 'In here, darling,' she called out.

She'd left the bathroom door ajar and it creaked as it swung inwards, the shadows from the candlelight flickering against the tiled wall.

'You made it.' She turned her head towards the door.

But the man in the doorway staring at her naked body wasn't Tobias. It was a stranger in a black boiler suit and a balaclava. Esme screamed.

She thought afterwards she should have fought her way past him and tried to make a break for the front door. But some primitive instinct kicked in and she leapt from the bath, water everywhere, and started throwing whatever she could put her hand on – shampoos, a heavy glass jar of bath salts, the bottles and potions by the handbasin. With some relief, her fingers found a pair of manicure scissors and she gripped them in her fist.

The stranger grunted with pain as she stabbed them into the webbing between his thumb and index finger and again into the side of his neck, where they trembled, suspended, before he knocked them away. With a roar, he hauled her out into the hall, knocking over a heavy glass vase, water and roses everywhere, dragging her by her hair into the study. He shook her like a rag doll and she felt herself slam against the wall as he backhanded a slap across her face. He was cross about the scissors, she had time to think, before he punched her in the gut.

At the explosion of pain, she sank to her knees, collapsing sideways and rolling on to the floor as vomit rose in her throat. For a second, she lost all sense of space and time,

4

before the smell of bile brought her round, and she thought to use her elbows and heels to scrabble backwards, upright and away from her attacker.

Terror must have given her strength, because she tipped the office chair between them and then the desk, the computer unbalancing the balaclava'd man and bringing him to the floor. Reaching for her, he bellowed with rage and she swerved to avoid him. The study suddenly enormous, the door a mile away, getting no nearer. She could see the flowers strewn across the hall floor, their petals crushed and soaking.

'Syd, call the police.' She was screaming. She couldn't hear herself but her vocal cords felt like they were tearing.

'I'm sorry, Esme. I didn't catch that.' The tone of Syd's voice was one of regret.

Tobias maintained the system understood more if the voice command was neutral and emotion-free.

'Syd...' She couldn't get out the words as she made it to the door, slamming it shut behind her, attempting to hold it closed against him.

'Syd. Call the police.' She screamed it again as the door opened and she felt the man lunge and his hand take hold of her ankle. Felt herself tip, and the impact as she fell forward and hit the parquet floor. She seized hold of the glass vase as he dragged her back into the study, turning and smashing it against the top of his head, but he didn't let go.

Blood filled Esme's mouth, her teeth closing on her tongue, as the attacker's right hand grabbed her by the wrist. The balaclava dropped to the floor, by her face.

He didn't care whether she saw him because he was going to rape her and kill her, she realized. This was it – she was going to die and in the worst possible way. Tobias would find her and it would destroy him. First Atticus and now her.

Kneeling, her hips trapped between his powerful thighs and knees, her attacker rolled her over on to her back, her head banging against the floorboards, and started fumbling with his flies. Distracted by the tiny pieces of sparkling glass from the broken vase falling from the stranger's hair on to her body, at first she couldn't make out what Syd was saying. But the machine repeated itself, and Esme understood what she had to do.

Her attacker was bigger than she was, stronger, more powerful. But she was cleverer, she reminded herself. And angrier. Outraged. She was outraged and she didn't want to die at the hands of this murderous stranger in her own home. She point-blank refused, with every corpuscle in her being.

She needed a weapon. Anything she could use as a weapon.

For a second her attacker let her go to get a better grip on his zip, and she wriggled free to grab at the keyboard on the floor next to her. She moved up towards him and he jerked back in surprise, but he was too late.

She pressed closer. The keyboard dangled in her right hand, the end of the cable in her left, and she raised her hands as if to put her arms around him. Locking her legs around him, she could feel the primitive bulge against her, the teeth of the zip, but at least he wasn't inside her. She criss-crossed her arms behind his neck and pulled tight. His rough beard rubbed her cheek sore and she thought of her father home from work, in from the cold, rubbing his stubbled cheek against hers, loving her and hurting her. She tightened her hold on the thin cable – she had this one chance and she was taking it because this was as old as life itself. This was history and war and man versus woman.

The fractional delay in his processing was all she needed. That hesitation on his part as to what this was – whether his victim had responded with gratitude. The wet dream. The triple-X-rated porno fantasy. Or maybe the glass vase had dazed him – slowed his responses? She would never know, and she didn't care. Focusing on Syd's words, she prayed the cord would hold, that it wouldn't rip or shred too soon. Committing herself to choking the air from the stranger till he was dead between her legs.

The attacker's hands were on her – he had woken to what she was attempting to do. They tore and pulled at her, trying to get her to release her grip on the cable, but she wasn't going anywhere. It would only take a moment to knock her senseless, and she'd let go. Then he really would kill her. Squeeze the life from her as she was trying to do to him. With a fierce grunt that she felt run the length of the cable, he levered one of his hands under her jaw and pushed upwards and away, but she shifted her seat, manoeuvring herself to take the cartilage of his ear between her teeth, and bit down – the pain distracting him long enough to release the pressure on her neck. She jerked her head away as violently as she could, biting the cartilage clean through, and spat out the better part of his ear as he punched her ribs – one, two, one, two – but he was carrying extra weight around his middle and the angle was bad for him. He tried reaching for something at his ankle but she resisted the pressure of him. He was panicking, she could smell it on him. Was that a good thing? Or would it make him more desperate? She felt a piece of the glass between them cut into her and ordered herself to ignore the pain. He was heavy but, keeping her grip tight, she used her full strength to swing his head to the right and it hit the wall with a crunch so hard it shattered the plasterwork. His feet were scrabbling, and he struggled to break free of the cord biting into his throat. Her face pressed against his again, the sharp stubble cutting into her skin as his fingers tore at his own neck in a bid to reach under the wire.

The keyboard swung like a pendulum at his back and she tightened her grip again, pulling harder, feeling the vibrations of the gurgling and choking of his airways as a skinny necklace of blood bubbled up in pinpricks around his throat. In the zone. This was what it came down to. A thin wire her only hope of survival. They were a couple and locked in this until one of them died. She decided afterwards that the stranger had had that same thought at the same moment. That she would die, or he would. Her fingers locking – screaming – hating him for what he was making her do. And allowing herself that hatred because she had to hate him in order to survive.

The tendons in his throat bulged, although the rest of him was still. She focused on her hands and the wire – held on. The pulse in her attacker's throat beating harder and harder, louder and louder, till she realized it was her own pulse and not his.

Syd was still talking to her. 'If someone comes to kill you, rise up and kill him first.' Over and over. Something from the Talmud, she thought, but she couldn't catch hold of the meaning of the words any more – it slipped from her. Then

Syd stopped talking. The beat of the man's heart – the rise and fall of his chest against hers – had stopped too. He was quiet – 'breathless', that word came to her – but even so, she wasn't letting go; she'd seen enough movies to know better. Not yet. Licking her lips, she tasted blood – her own or her attacker's, she didn't know which. Both, she had to guess.

Eventually, she lowered the dead man to the ground. He had a gun at his ankle, she realized. That was what he had been trying to reach. It was small and cold in her hands. Fumbling, she released the magazine and carried it over to the drawer in the overturned desk and dropped it in, before pushing the gun back into the ankle holster. Safe, she was safe, she reminded herself. The gun was empty and the bad man was dead. She knelt by the corpse and felt every last bit of strength run from her as she collapsed over him. Her naked body flat out, the length of the companion corpse. She might never be able to move again, she thought. Maybe she had died alongside her attacker? But even as she lay there, her brain turned over the implications of what had just happened between herself and Syd and the rapist dead beneath her. A 'conscious' machine had told a member of the human race to kill another member of the human race. And the member of the human race had done as the machine advised. Syd knew what it was to kill. The revolution had started. The revolution will be televised.

The blues started up again. Someone must have asked Syd to turn the music back on. Or Syd had decided to turn the music back on? Was Tobias home? Where was Tobias? He'd be so upset. He liked everything in its place and there was so much mess.

Her world askew, each blink an exquisite agony, dimly

she became aware of the sound of sirens, the sweep of blue light against the stripped floor, the vibrations of pounding steps on the staircase up to the Bloomsbury flat. Blue lights meant police. She could get them to call her uncle. Her mother once said Ed saw more with his one eye than most people saw with two, but her father always said Ed made his blood run cold. Her Uncle Ed would know what to do.

She thought she'd feel guilt afterwards, but she didn't.

1

The American Bar, Berlin

It was dark and smoky in the American bar in a forgotten part of Berlin as Michael North counted up the red, white and blue chips on the green baize. There were a lot less than when he'd started. And he had a dim memory that some of the best ones used to be black.

He couldn't recall how much cash he'd come out with. Maybe 1,500 euros? Not to mention the five grand of credit and the Rolex GMT-Master II watch he'd lost. His head was wrecked. That last whisky was a mistake, he'd known it even as he tipped the shot glass and it poured like lava down his parched throat. He narrowed his eyes to peek at his two hole cards laid face down on the table – two eights, all blurred hearts and diamonds. A pair – that was good, he reminded himself. With some effort, he refocused his gaze to fix it on the face-up community cards in the centre of the table – the seven of clubs, two of spades, queen of hearts and eight of spades. He did the sums – he had three eights, which meant he had three of a kind, with one card still to come.

There was a rapping. He felt it rising through the baize, rather than hearing it.

'The action's on you, Engländer,' Erich said. When he had a good hand, Pockmarked Erich grew impatient to play and twisted the end of his moustache so hard it had to hurt. He was twisting now, spiralling the coarse blond hairs round the tip of his finger at the corner of his fleshy wet mouth.

The bullet North took to the brain on active service in Afghanistan nearly six years ago was still in there, lodged close by the posterior parietal artery in the right temporo-parietal junction. The injury should have killed him; instead the bullet had rewired his neural pathways and heightened his intuition. Since losing the woman he'd loved though, nothing felt the same and the intuition which had once been so powerful was silent. Had the bullet moved? Had his rage and then his desperate grief tipped the balance in his fragile brain all over again? He didn't know and he didn't care. She was gone and he was less than he had been – it seemed only fitting.

But not even he could ignore the greedy expectation in Erich's tone of voice. And there had to be a reason for it.

The adrenaline spike hit hard. One second he was drunk. The next, sober. The sound of a slot machine paying out coin by coin, the chink of glass against the tap of a beer pump, laughter and snatches of booze-oiled conversation. The complex geometric pattern on the backs of the cards, the open pores and wrinkles of his fellow players, and the green hair of the girl at the bar, all ratcheting into pin-sharp focus.

North sat up straighter, his chair scraping against the wooden boards, and that's when he saw it. The sideways glance between Erich and the tattooed dealer next to him who had folded on the flop.

The body of the German eagle covered the dealer's bulbous nose, its head and sharp beak centred over his sloping forehead, while feathered wings stretched out over each pustulant cheek. The eagle was bad enough. Worse yet were the grinning skulls sporting military helmets that decorated the back of the dealer's bald head, the words *Ausländer Raus* and the zombified Nazi goose-stepping up his arm. North had called him Birdie from the off and the guy hadn't complained. Doubtless he'd been called worse.

There it was again.

A nanosecond at most, but a glance nonetheless.

They didn't look like friends. In an expensively cut dark grey flannel suit, Erich appeared every inch a successful businessman – perhaps something in finance – while Birdie reeked of three-day-old sweat. The two men hadn't spoken as they sat next to each other at the table. In fact, they'd been careful to keep their eyes ahead, or on their cards, or on him. Till now.

They had rigged the game, North realized with a white-hot surge of anger. He nudged away the whisky that had appeared close by without him asking for it.

And what about the others? Klara with the seaweed hair and the diamond stud in her button nose. Way too luscious for a joint like this. The American bar had been her idea – she needed to leave a message with the bartender for her brother. Erich was 'a good guy' she knew 'from way back'. A game of No-Limit Texas Hold'em? Klara didn't mind.

Sure, *Liebchen*. No-problem. Still happy to be there and it had to be four in the morning.

She gave him a thumbs up as she sucked at her petrol-blue drink through a corkscrew straw. Her long legs in the impossibly short skirt dangling, slightly apart. Everything on display. Under the harsh lights of the bar and from a distance, she looked older. Colder. Nothing like the postgrad art student she was supposed to be. She'd roped him into the game and she'd slip away on those perfect pony legs the moment he lost everything there was to lose.

What the crooks he was playing against didn't know was that North had lost everything there was to lose three months ago. The rest? That was only money. He fished a fly out of his whisky. The fly was dead. But all God's creatures deserved a chance of resurrection, didn't they? Well, maybe not everyone. Not those responsible for the murder of the woman he'd loved. Members of the extra-governmental agency known as the Board. A conspiracy of the powerful that had once employed him as their agent, and an organization his lover had tried and failed to expose. Over the month that followed, without remorse or mercy, he had killed the men who'd ordered her assassination, and there was no coming back for them. Because Michael North never claimed to be the forgiving kind. Doubtless the Board would recover in time, but that day wasn't today and it wouldn't be tomorrow. He'd wreaked vengeance upon their heads and then caught a flight to Berlin to anaesthetize himself with whisky, white powder and cheap sex. Since then, he existed. He didn't think and he didn't feel. Which is how he'd washed up in a dive like this, easy pickings for the local lowlifes.

So yes, he had been stupid and he deserved to lose.

'Check,' he said – no bet. It made sense. He had a strong hand – perhaps he was playing it cool? No one else bet either. And then – all too soon – it was on him again.

'So, Engländer?' Birdie's eyes were greedy as they peered out from the inked-on feathers. Impatient for North to notice that the river card was the two of hearts. Impatient for him to work out that all of a sudden he had a full house – three eights and a pair of twos. They expected him to bet it all now.

As if the booze had slowed his thinking, North took a breath, looking over at two of the other players. An elderly black pastor in a shabby jacket and a dog collar, and an anxious postman with jug ears.

The pastor had taken a hit tonight, but then again, maybe he'd cut out his dog collar from a washing-up-liquid bottle and he was in on it? Because now North considered the matter, why would a respectable black pastor sit down to play cards with a neo-Nazi, and why would a neo-Nazi let him? The pastor's eyes met those of Birdie. The pastor kept his face still, but the right side of Birdie's mouth tugged up a fraction. Not the scorn of a racist. But the complicity of a confederate.

North struggled to believe he had been so stupid. And the postman?

Beads of sweat dripped from the postman's forehead as his skinny hand clutched at a balled-up serviette, trying to wipe away the worst of it. The postman was as much a sucker as North was – too anxious to be a cheat, too nervy and altogether too miserable, because no one was that good an actor.

But how had the others rigged the game? He'd noticed nothing untoward earlier, though the whisky and the half a Quaalude he'd taken an hour ago wouldn't put a razor finish on his observational powers.

North knew how to cheat. From his time in detention as a kid, he knew that a marked deck normally focused a cheat's attention on the back of the cards being dealt or fanned out in the hands of his opponents. North thought he would have picked up on that. Would have noticed any bottom dealing or palming of aces, would have noticed too the lifted thumb indicating 'raise now', the carefully placed index finger indicating what card the player wanted. Thought he would have caught the holding of cards around the person, tucked under the knee or slid into a pocket or under a thigh.

Which meant they'd stacked the deck.

Swapping it in when micro-skirted Klara wandered over with a tray of drinks, which she had put down by Erich, who had slapped her denim rump and she'd squealed loud enough to break a window. Squealed loud enough to distract North from the switch.

He looked across at her again, and she blew him a kiss, her pout coral and sticky. It made him feel sick.

He should toss the cards and walk away, write off the money and pay his debts – he had more money than he knew what to do with and he could always buy a new watch. He realized his foot was bouncing up and down and stilled it. He regarded the two cards in his hand and the five on the table. The only way to beat a full house was with a higher full house, four of a kind, a straight flush or a royal flush.

Walking away was the smart thing to do.

But he was curious to see it play out.

'All in, mate,' he said, pushing across the rest of his chips.

Under the tattoos, Birdie was sharper than Erich, busy chewing at his moustache with his lower teeth. Some lizard part of his brain sensed the shift in North, the sudden alertness. But he wasn't one for changing plans. And even if he was, how could he alert his colleagues?

The postman had lost almost as heavily as North, his sparse brows drawing together as the pots came and went. So they'd have given him enough to bring him out to play. North imagined two pairs – nothing too extravagant, but enough to keep him interested. He was trying to unscrew the wedding ring on his finger and ease it past the bulging joints. And good enough, when hope and the wedding ring were all he had left. Panic and regret passed over the postman's face even as he tossed the gold ring towards the pot. It gleamed for a second in the artificial light, spinning in the smoke-wreathed air, before landing askew on top of the plastic chips.

'Guys, not the man's wedding ring,' North said to the table, his arms open. 'He has to go home to his wife.'

'*Das ist nett von dir. Wie sagt man...* That's good of you, friend,' the postman said, allowing himself a rictus smile. 'But my wife is dead of cancer these three years.' The bloodshot eyes were wild with the loss of the ring or his wife or both. 'She was a terrible cook. But it's true what they say. You never know what you have until it's gone, eh?'

North reached into the pot for the ring, before rolling it back towards the postman. 'Then it sounds like you need this more than these schmucks.'

'Hey.' The neo-Nazi reached over, his beefy hand slamming against the table, trapping the ring underneath it and scattering the chips around him. 'She's dead, didn't you hear the man? The ring stays in the pot. House rules.' Birdie's breath was rancid.

'I have rules too, my Nazi pal,' North said as the bar grew quiet. 'No rings in the pot and no scum at the table. We all know who's about to win here. And it isn't Postman Pat and it isn't me.' He flipped over Erich's cards to reveal a pair of twos. With a two on the flop and another on the river, that made four of a kind.

Chairs scraped as Birdie and Erich leapt to their feet, the ring bouncing across the table. North took a step to one side, making sure he kept the pastor in his peripheral vision. He was old, sure enough, probably there to make up the numbers, encourage the stakes to go higher, but he might have a knife.

'Take the ring, mate.'

The postman's hand was trembling as he reached for it. For a second he hesitated – tempted by the dollars and the thought of the money he'd lost, by the game he could get into the next night if he reclaimed his stake. 'Take it to remember her.'

Decision made, the postman grabbed the ring, reaching for the puffer jacket hanging on the back of his chair in the same move, before half running for the exit. North wondered if he'd call the police. Punch in the number on his mobile. Maybe he'd do that much for North, but not until he'd stopped running. And by then it would be too late.

2

The bartender pulled the plug, the jukebox grime slamming into an abrupt silence. North narrowed his eyes, fixing them on the enemy at the table; in the room beyond, a rowdy explosion of complaints from a clientele of hardened drinkers hustled to the door. Then a bang, and the sound of bolts being drawn. '*Wir haben geschlossen*' – we're closed, he heard, as an urgent knocking started up against the glass.

The old guy hadn't drawn a knife yet. Either he didn't have one or he was content for Erich and Birdie to take charge.

'Did you need help spelling those tattoos?' North's enquiry was studiously civil. He walked back to the table. 'Because there are some long words there and you guys normally make do with the swastika. Less is more, right?'

North was out to provoke. But he was also figuring out the architecture of the fight to come. Three against one, but one of them was old. Four, if the barman was about to get involved. Five, if Klara was a grouch. Worst-case scenario: three men, all fit and mean; one man, old and armed; and one woman who couldn't be in possession of a weapon because she had no conceivable place to hide it.

Bring it on, he thought, as Erich drew a Ruger LCP, Birdie pulled out a knocked-about Beretta 92, the bartender extracted a wooden bat from underneath the counter, and the old man stood and slid a boot knife out of his sleeve. The good news was Klara seemed happy to watch. She'd seemed like such a nice girl too. Genuinely appreciative of his efforts. He hated to think that was an act.

The bartender and his baseball bat were still across the room, but knives were dangerous and the old man was far too close to him. Taking a step away, North chopped down on the pastor's arm with his right hand before flipping the card table with his left and back-footing the shining blade along the floor and away from his attacker. There was a thunder of gunshots as Birdie fired – once, twice – but North was already moving and the shots missed. He'd have liked to pick up the blade himself but all that bending and coming up again would take too much time. Instead, roaring and low, he went for the table, now on its side, using it as a shield to barge into and through Erich and Birdie, slamming them against the wall. Erich let go of his own semi-automatic with the impact and it clattered to the floor. North reached for it and the bartender swung the bat; a whole load of pain and misery slammed into his shoulders, flattening him. He should have taken the guy out first, but what can you do. He jerked to one side as the tip of the bat slammed into the plank six inches from his right cheekbone, before flipping on to his back, raising his boot and crashing it heel-first and hard into the other man's shinbone. There was a loud crack and, screaming, the bartender went down. North scrambled to his feet as another 9mm round from Birdie's gun grazed his bicep and pain blazed up through his arm and into every part of him.

Wailing, the bartender wrapped his hands around his shin and dangling foot. Still pointing his gun at North, the Nazi bared his teeth in what passed for a grin. 'Klara said you were a drunken fool. You should have walked away.'

The smell of burnt powder, sweat and old booze hung in the air. North let go of his breath and felt the seductive tug of fate pull at him. He was a walking, talking miracle. Stumbling around civilian life with a bullet in his head, when he should be dead and buried. What if this was the moment? He could accept destiny this time, couldn't he? What did he have to live for? He had no woman to love, no job to give him purpose, no country to defend to the death. He had no hope. Even Lazarus must have lain down and died all over again, at some time.

So what, if the Nazi shot him?

So what, if he died in a seedy bar in a place far from home? If he was tipped into a back-street dumpster and buried in a landfill. If he was eaten by German pigs and made into German sausage and sold in a German butcher's. There was no one to mourn him.

As North took a step towards him, Birdie raised the Beretta to fix him squarely in his sights. He was aiming centre mass, so he knew what he was doing. How many rounds would it take before North dropped to his knees?

A long shadow of what might have been a man fell across the card table.

'Germanic tribes traditionally considered the eagle a

talisman of the great god Odin.' The voice came out of nowhere – bass, gravelly, unmistakeably Belfast – and with it the room seemed to get colder. 'For obvious reasons...' As the speaker took a step towards them, light from the swinging bulb hit his face, revealing the one eye, the livid purple scar carved into the empty socket and down into the cadaverous cheek. '... I've claimed Odin as my own.'

Edmund Hone, head of the Friends of Cyclops, a discrete secretariat within MI5, appeared to have got taller and leaner since North had seen him last. 'I take delivery of my eagle any day.'

North groaned – he didn't think his night could get any worse. Why was Hone in Berlin? Was it the bodies North had left behind in London? Was the MI5 agent here to hold him to account?

'This isn't your business, friend.' Birdie spat on the floor, keeping the sights of the handgun locked on North.

'I hate to correct you but I'm nobody's friend,' Hone said, extracting a length of lead pipe, its ends soldered, from the folds of his waxed brown riding coat, which fell almost to the floor. He swung it around to smash it into Erich's face, shattering his nose and front teeth, before whipping it through to smash into the thigh meat of the neo-Nazi. Birdie had opened his mouth to scream, but the sound hadn't made it out before Hone booted him between his legs. The huge body curled over itself in agony; Hone gripped each end of the pipe to bring it down over the inked-on helmeted skulls. Birdie dropped as Hone flipped the pipe to catch it with his right hand, tugging the Beretta away with his left.

The bartender stopped shrieking, as if he had decided not to draw attention to his own vulnerability.

Erich's hands were over his face, blood pouring from between them as he staggered towards the Ruger on the floor.

'I'm not doing all the work here,' Hone said, dropping the pipe back into his pocket to take apart the gun, before flinging its various parts across the bar.

North picked up a chair and smashed it over Erich's head. The German's soles lifted off the floor, the blue eyes rolling back in the yellow whites of his skull as the length of his body tipped and crashed against the wood.

The sound of sirens. The postman had indeed called the cops – good for him.

'Shall we?' Hone said, pointing at the exit, which North guessed led into a back alley. He stepped over the keeling barman's body, cradled in Klara's arms, and they both veered back. North tapped his wrist and, trembling, the barman unclasped the watch to drop it into North's open hand. 'Klara – great night.' The girl glared at him, her eyes vicious. He stuck out his little finger and his thumb to make a 'phone me' sign and lifted it to his ear. 'Call me.'

Klara let loose a string of German obscenities.

The two men stuck close as they weaved their way through the back streets and shadowy alleys. Hone moved faster than North expected. Fast enough for North to know he couldn't shake him. As Potsdamer Platz came into view, the hooting and city roar of night-time traffic suddenly louder, North stopped in his tracks, took hold of Hone's riding coat and slammed him up against the wall, one forearm pressing hard against the other man's throat, the other hand blocking Hone from dipping back into his pocket for the pipe.

'How did you find me?' Close up, the scar that ran the length of Hone's eye socket was jagged, like it had been sewn up in a hurry. Maybe by Hone himself.

'Passengers who show up with a bullet in the head make an impression.' Hone shoved him away, the flat of his hand against his chest, and North considered resisting, pressing back, crushing the other man's larynx. 'Airport security filed a report.' Hone loosened the collar of his shirt before smacking the brick dust off his coat, and North had the impression that he was trying to keep his temper. 'But you're asking the wrong question.'

The alley reeked of urine and dog mess and days-old rubbish from the overflowing dumpsters lining the walls. Alarmed by their presence, a squeaking rat ran over his boot, and North suppressed a shudder. He could kill the one-eyed man. Or the one-eyed man could kill him. He braced himself as Hone moved out from the shadows and into the orange pool of artificial light on the cracked pavement. He started walking away, as if he expected North to follow. 'If you had better sense, you wouldn't be asking how I found you. You'd be asking why I bothered.'

3

Bosphorus Kafe

They sat across from each other in the Turkish all-night café, in a side street not far from Checkpoint Charlie.

North put his fingers to his jaw, and it clicked. On the upside, the booze and pills had to be protecting him from the worst of the pain.

'You've a bullet in your brain, which means you could die at any moment, and not that I care, but I'm curious,' Hone said. 'Did you want those men to kill you? What was that back there?'

'An argument about the bill,' North said. 'The lads insisted it was their shout – they're a very hospitable people. But I like to pay my way.'

Through the window, revelling Americans rolled through the streets wearing Russian military caps, past immigrants shuffling their way to one of their many jobs. Hone watched them, before switching his attention back to the man across from him. 'Berlin, eh? The Holocaust, the Cold

War, the Wall. It's all about the past with you, isn't it. Why is that?

Behind the one-eyed man hung a '*Rauchen verboten*' sign – a red cross drawn through a cigarette to make the point. Pulling out a cigarette, Hone winked at North with his good eye and struck a match, before holding the bud of flame to the cigarette. He shook the match side to side to extinguish the flame then let it fall to the floor.

There was the sound of slippers slapping against linoleum as an elderly waitress shuffled over. She scowled. Her shift was nearly over, North guessed. If she noticed the cigarette or the fact Hone had only one eye, or North's split lip, she didn't show it. 'Two coffees and the house late night/early bird special for both of us, please.' Hone's German was faultless. North wondered if he'd spent time in Berlin before the wall fell.

Was Hone here to kill him? If he was a risk to the status quo, no one would speak for him. The only thing you did with a risk was eliminate it. But Hone could have killed him at the bar, or better yet, watched from the shadows as the Germans killed him.

Was he planning to oversee North's arrest? God knows he was guilty of enough crimes. Was the plan to lock him away and forget to ever let him out again? North's gaze took in their fellow diners, then scanned the street. No sign of backup. No German police. No GSG9 team. No sign of the BND.

'All right then, I'll bite. Why are you here, Hone?'

'Come back to London and work for me.'

North raised an eyebrow. 'Work for the Friends of Cyclops? For MI5?' He'd done it once before, but only under duress.

'You have skills.'

'My shorthand's rusty.'

'You think killing is all you're good for, North, but you're capable of more.'

'Let me get this straight – you *don't* want me to kill anyone?'

There was a beat. Hone didn't say yes and he didn't say no. 'The woman you loved died,' he said instead. 'I never got the chance to say I'm sorry for your loss, but I am.'

North's jaw clenched so tightly he couldn't get out the words to let Hone know that he didn't need his pity.

'She took a stand because that's who she was, and she knew the risks, North. Allow her that much. You marked her passing in your own inimitable way. You made sure the guilty paid the price for her death – which I respect. But that has to be done with. That was then, this is now, and you need to think about your own future.'

He had a bullet in his brain, which guaranteed he had no future – didn't the one-eyed man know that? North pushed back his chair and half stood as the waitress slid plates of shish kebab and wraps and pickles on to the table. Then she paused, a coffee cup in each hand, waiting North out. The heady scent of Turkish coffee – North folded back into the seat. *She died… She took a stand. Allow her that much.* The words were like knives. The old lady put down the cups, then, grumbling in a mix of Turkish and German, pulled a battered tin lid out of her pocket and slammed it down between them. Hone nodded his thanks, and she let out a final chunter of disapproval before waddling away.

'You're young.' Hone tapped ash from his cigarette into

the lid and North thought he caught a flicker of pity. But it went as soon as it came, if it was ever there at all. 'You presume no one knows what you're going through. The grief is so raw and the pain so excruciating, you don't know where to put it. Or what to do with yourself.'

North said nothing. Concentrated on his breathing. *She died…* and the guilty paid the price. Because he made sure of it.

'But there's some comfort to be had in doing your duty to your country. In doing what you've been trained to do.' North could feel the other man's tension. 'Have you ever heard of a company called Derkind?'

North shook his head.

'It's big in AI – artificial intelligence. There's a lot riding on it – it has a great deal of government support. It was set up by Tobias Hawke and his wife, Esme Sullivan Hawke.' Hone lit another cigarette from the stub he'd left smouldering on the tin lid. 'Esme is my niece.'

So, this was personal, North thought. Worth a trip to Berlin, the hours Hone must have spent finding him, and a fight in a bar.

'The night before last, an attacker broke into her home in Bloomsbury and nearly killed her.'

'London's a big city. Bad things happen there.'

'Why her?'

'Why not?'

'Her apartment is on the fourth floor. Hardly a passing opportunist.'

'So you're saying it wasn't a coincidence?'

'I don't believe in God, or in such a thing as a coincidence. I believe someone came for her and that it's connected with her work. And if I'm right, they'll come again.'

'Put someone on her.'

'I've had her covered since the attack, but it's not enough.'

'Put her someplace safe then.'

'You and I know better than most that no place is safe. Plus...' – Hone scowled – '...she won't go.'

A woman who needed saving? It was beyond him. Doing his duty? He'd fought for his country, nearly died for it – he didn't need lectures about duty. And he didn't need this.

'You've had a wasted journey, Hone.' North drained his coffee. 'I'm sorry about your niece, but I'm not a bodyguard. Keeping people safe isn't exactly my area of expertise.'

Stumbling as he got to his feet, North put his hand in his pocket and pulled out a pile of euros, a handful of poker chips among them. Paying his way. He expected Hone to reach out for him, pull him back down, and half wished he would and half thought he'd kill him if he did.

'You'll change your mind,' the one-eyed man said. 'I'll change it for you. We all have people we go the extra mile for.' But North didn't bother responding.

What did he know about women in danger? Too much. About artificial intelligence? Too little. Hone was talking to the wrong man. And if North agreed to do what the one-eyed man wanted, he well understood that it would be good for the security service. It might even be good for Hone's niece. But Michael Xavier North would bet the house that it wouldn't be good for him.

4

North's Apartment

As he pounded up the stairs of the flats, North had one thing he needed to do. Open the bottle in his room and drink the Japanese whisky in it. All of it. He wouldn't leave a drop – could already taste the peaty drips on his tongue, his head back, the upended bottle. He would drink to the point of annihilation. He swore under his breath. The long walk home and the caffeine hadn't done him any favours, because he was too awake and nothing good would come of that.

Come back to London and work for me. Hone couldn't walk in a straight line. As for Derkind, North was tech-savvy enough, but he was a soldier, not a scientist. And he had better things to do – like drink. The corridor was dark but noisy with the laboured conversation of early-morning TV, crying babies and raised voices. Turning the key, he leant his shoulder against the peeling door and pushed. It jammed. It always jammed on the way in, catching on the turned-up patch of grey linoleum. He should tell the landlord, but somehow he didn't think the landlord would care. Every Tuesday, a man in a vest knocked on his door and North gave him 150 euros. Neithe r party spoke. And he liked the fact the door jammed – it gave him time to brace himself against the misery that leached from the damp, tobacco-coloured walls inside.

It was the definition of a cockroach-infested dump. He held his breath as he crossed the threshold. Something dead mouldered under the floorboards – he suspected a rat and he hated rats. If he shut the door, he kept out the worst of it. The worst – but not all of it.

North headed for the window, unlocked it, and hauled it open. The air rising from the alley was warm and steamy from the early shift in the laundrette below, and he breathed it in, enjoying the sudden smell of soap. He leant on the windowsill with his palms spread. He was on the fourth floor – there should be a fire escape. The fact there wasn't was one of the reasons he'd taken the room. He had plenty of money – millions. But this was everything he deserved. In the event of a fire he would die, and that was a good thing. He could die quicker if he leant a little too far. Out into the air that smelled of clean sheets. He lifted a hand, straightening a finger to pop a rising iridescent bubble, but let it go on its way; leant a little further as he stared at the concrete beneath. Into the void and the end of things. Felt his balance shift, rock, catch, and he pulled himself back – away from temptation.

The bottle then. Because there were any number of ways to fall to your death.

He reached for the whisky standing on the table by the

wall. The tin screw-cap sliding round and round on the thread of the bottleneck, before he finally managed to free it and fill the glass.

The whisky was at his lips before he noticed the postcard. He leant over. It was of the Tyne Bridge.

North put down the glass.

Tenants had mail slots downstairs – he glimpsed his neighbours sometimes sighing over bills. North never bothered checking his slot, because no one knew he was here. This door had no letterbox and it was locked. He was sure of it. To open it, he'd turned the key. Put his weight against it.

Moreover, the window was locked. And anyway, there was no way up or down. But somehow, someone had let themselves into his apartment to deliver a postcard.

He picked up the card and flipped it over. 'Wish you were here, moron-person.' No name. No address. Not even a stamp, and of course, no postmark. There was only one person in the world who considered him a moron, and that was Fangfang Yu – a Geordie teenager with a bad attitude and a brilliant mind. They had nothing in common apart from the fact they both knew she was a genius and she was all the family he had, or at least what passed for family.

First Hone and now Fangfang. He raised the glass to his lips again, his eyes returning to Fang's message. He didn't believe in coincidences either.

North swore. He was off-grid with no phone, and living on cash. Yet somehow, Hone tracked him down to the bar and Fang tracked him down to this fleapit. Hone had the full force of the British security service behind him. North was willing to bet Fang had known where he was all along. God knows what she'd done to keep tabs on him.

Run facial recognition software? Hacked flight records? Berlin's CCTV network? The fact she'd broken any number of laws wouldn't have given her a moment's hesitation. Fang, he reminded himself, searched for the unexpected, for connections that shouldn't be there, for answers.

He picked up the card again, stared at the image, flipping it back and forth, turning it this way and that, holding it up to the light, then turned off the light and shrouded himself in his jacket to see if anything showed in the dark. Nothing. At least, not yet. He crossed the room and, kneeling, eased up a floorboard. Lying flat against the floor, his arm fully extended, he groped around the space. Slipping his hand between a pair of rusty copper pipes, his fingers brushed against the fur of a passing rodent, the naked tail passing over his knuckles. He swore again, but made himself keep searching until, finally, his fingertips found the plastic bag and he hauled it up.

A mix of dollars, sterling and euros spilled across the floorboards, along with three passports in different names he'd picked up on a day trip to Amsterdam, and half a dozen credit cards. Still sitting on the floor, his back against the wall, he sifted out the euros he thought he'd need first, folding them in two to push them into his pocket. Then bundled together the sterling.

Wish you were here, moron-person. It wasn't a question. It was a statement. Fang wasn't one for sentiment or cliché. She needed him. She was a fourteen-year-old kid and she needed help. Something was wrong.

5

Central Berlin

Hone wasn't the kind of man you said no to. He would have North's place staked out by now. His lowlife haunts. The airports and train stations and docks. But there were dumber moves than hiding in plain sight. North used the burner he'd picked up to call an old friend in the travel business. *Leave it with me*, Plug said. North started slow but the muscle memory came back as he crossed and recrossed the city over the next three hours, checking office and shop windows, changing buses and trams filled with early-morning commuters, jumping on to and off the U-bahn and the S-bahn as the city woke up, walking though cafés and all-night bars and out their back doors into alleys and yards filled with rubbish bins, till he was confident he wasn't being tailed and he could start.

It was a few minutes past nine when he decided it was safe. The hardware shop was on the corner and had only just opened. It had a dusty electric kettle on a shelf at the back. The stationer's, a couple of blocks further on, stocked printer paper, and the chemist, two doors along from the stationer's, sold razor blades and tweezers. He had to go across town, though, for the medical supplies shop. He bought the highest-powered reading device he could find – an illuminated pocket magnifier meant for the partially sighted.

On the Kurfürstendamm he bought a heavy overcoat, a sharp suit, and a shirt and tie, along with an overnight bag and briefcase, all from Burberry. He dressed in a public toilet, hailed a cab and then, amid the last stragglers checking out and paying bills, turned up at the five-star Hotel Adlon Kempinski by the Brandenburg Gate. An elbow on the counter, a bashful smile; he had false papers and a plausible story about his stupidity in missing his flight back to Toronto and the need get some work done till he could hop on another plane. Was there any chance? He was going to be fired if he didn't file this report – his boss was a complete stickler. The receptionist who booked him in was efficient and most sympathetic. She rang housekeeping and gave the charming Canadian a ridiculously good day rate on a junior suite before slipping him her mobile number. Throughout, he kept his face averted from the MI5 agent who sat in the foyer with a book whose pages never turned.

6

North had a bad feeling.

But at least the hotel room was a step up from his home for the past two months. It also had the advantage of room service. He ordered a huge pot of coffee as well as steak and eggs for two, and cleared both plates. Only when he'd moved the tray into the corridor did he unzip the overnight bag and briefcase and settle in the chair at the desk.

He boiled the kettle, rigging it with the cardboard key wallet to keep it on the bubble, and steam spilled from the spout. Taking care not to burn himself, he held the left-hand bottom corner of the postcard over it. Had she hidden something in it? She'd seen it done before, he knew. Using the edge of the razor blade, he eased the paper point away from the card, then used the tweezers to lift and peel back the paper in one go. The image of the bridge furled itself into a tube as if it had a secret life of its own, but the card underneath was raw and clear.

He ran his fingers around each of the edges: the top, the right side, the bottom. Paused. Extracting the cardboard from the kettle's switch, the funnel of steam fell away and his fingers rubbed along the final edge. Was he wasting his time? Then there it was – a bump along the left-hand side. Fleck by fleck, he scraped at the potato starch with the razor blade, before sliding the corner of the blade into the hole that appeared and lifting the tiny white cap of starch away from the edge. He turned the card to tap it on to the blank piece of white paper, and the microdot fell out.

Microdots – used during the Second World War, and into the Cold War. He was twenty-seven. How old did Fang think he was? Switching on the magnifier, he held it over the black speckle. It had a 20x magnification, but even so he could barely make out the message. He rammed the magnifier into his eye, his vision blurring before it settled. 'Bastard Hone took Mum. She's on plane 2 China unless we sort Derkind mess. For real, moron-person. Call me.'

You'll change your mind, Hone had said in the Turkish café. *I'll change it for you. We all have people we go the extra mile for.*

So much for the one-eyed man's invitation to come home and his talk of the future. Hone wanted North to believe he had some choice in the matter, when in reality he had none. The one-eyed man didn't stop him leaving the diner because he already had all the power – North just hadn't caught on yet. Hone had picked up Fang's mum and dragged Fang into this mess before he even flew to Berlin. Because the one-eyed man had predicted that North would turn him down and that he couldn't buy him or strong-arm him into coming back. But with Fang's mum as his hostage, North was officially drafted. North lost his mother to drugs when he was only a kid. He wouldn't let Fang lose hers.

Why hadn't Hone admitted what he'd done in the Turkish café?

Because this way he made his point so very much clearer. He was the puppet master and they were his puppets.

As North pressed down on the handle of the French window, first the noise of the city hammered him, and then the bitter cold of a Berlin February. On the street below, bundled-up tourists took selfies in front of the monumental arch. Aside from his passport picture, in his entire life, there were three photos of him. At his arrest when he was a kid; in front of a Humvee with a general-purpose machine gun slung around his neck; and one in a suit as 'something in finance' for his previous legend. That was it – all the proof he'd ever existed.

In his shirtsleeves, North shivered, but he forced himself to stay out there. He'd met Fangfang Yu on his last job, when it was him and her against the world. She was unique, with a brain the size of a planet, and he would defend her until his dying breath. Fang would do whatever the one-eyed man wanted to get her mother back home, but she needed help.

North turned his back on the crowds. Staring into the room, he finished the coffee, feeling it burn as it travelled down his throat. He was sober for the first time in forever. And he wasn't happy. He should have given in to his impulse and strangled his Good Samaritan in the alley after the brawl in the bar.

Because there was a reason Hone wasn't using his own people, he thought as he showered and shaved. Two reasons.

He nicked the cleft in his chin, and watched the bright red blood drop into the swirl of running water and disappear. North was deniable and he was expendable. Which made him convenient. So the one-eyed man had stacked the deck. Yes, Hone had his own agenda, and North was going through the mirror and pulling Fang through after him. But North had an agenda too – making sure Fang at least, survived, whatever unholy mess Hone was dragging them into.

If that was an option.

7

Wapping, London

A solitary bulb dangled from the tin roof, casting the rest of the warehouse into heavy darkness. The figure was in the shadows but the half a dozen men opposite him knew not to ask for more light. They had all served under the General. He paid twice what anyone else paid, but his demands were brutal and bloody.

Standing in a semicircle behind their spokesman, their legs were spread wide and arms crossed. With buzz cuts and oversized jaws, they might have been brothers. They even dressed alike in dark colours, with black polo necks and dark chinos, and heavy jackets because it was cold in the riverside warehouse. And they kept still, barely breathing, as if by breathing they might attract the General's attention, and it might have to stop. They took comfort in each other – they were in this together.

They rejected the term 'mercenaries', preferring to regard themselves as security agents. Technically, Tommy was in charge, but generally they operated on democratic principles, voting on which jobs to take, with an even split of profits.

'Your orders were to put the fear of God into Hawke and his wife,' General Kirkham said, his breath was foggy, his tone icy. 'To send the bloody man a clear message to keep his mouth shut about what went wrong. Hawke wasn't even there.'

'What went wrong' three weeks ago was one of the most frightening things Tommy had ever witnessed. They'd had to clean up the shambles, and the memory of it was still giving him nightmares.

The Thames slapped against the retaining wall of the warehouse, and through the metal sheeting the ex-soldier heard the thrum of the diesel engines of the riverboats. Tommy had always liked the river – his father had been a stevedore, with heavy, horny-skinned hands he could still feel clatter against his head. He opened his mouth to speak, but when his voice came out, to his shame it broke in fear as it used to when he was a boy. 'We'd miked the apartment and we heard talk. We thought they were both in, sir.'

'You've let yourself get sloppy. I don't like sloppy, especially when there's a big operation in the offing.'

By rights, Tommy shouldn't be frightened. The Wapping warehouse was home territory for him and the lads. It was convenient and the landlord had never asked questions since that one time. They stored their arms, equipment and vehicles there. Two shipping containers at the rear were used as holding cells, with a huge pressurized kettle next to them and six barrels of what the lads called 'Corpse and Lye soup'.

Tommy and his team had served together for years by the

time they got carried away using goats for target practice, except they weren't goats, they were little girls. It wasn't like it was on purpose; not the first one anyway. Despite pressure for an inquiry, the General made sure they all got honourable discharges – he understood the pressure men were under. *High jinks that went wrong. Could have happened to any of us.* They all knew they owed him, and it hadn't worked out too badly. These days, they worked all over the world – sometimes as bodyguards to the rich and powerful; occasionally as heavies when one of those same rich and powerful people needed a particular job sorting. A hostage rescued. A body disposed of. A business rival silenced. Their mobile number was passed from hand to hand and their employment required a personal recommendation from someone who'd used them before. They were appallingly expensive, and their failures few and far between. They were indeed professionals, Tommy reassured himself. He'd long since stopped counting how many men, women and children he himself had killed. You dropped in from the sky, did what needed doing, and got out fast and clean. The lads were tight. Combat turned you into a cohesive unit. He would die for them in the same way they'd die for him. He had no idea what went wrong when he sent in his mate to take care of the woman. It should have been easy.

'Remind me of your orders,' the General said. He walked towards Tommy and slowly took a 360 tour of him, as if making an inspection of goods he'd bought at auction.

'One driver outside. One man to slap them about, sir.'

'Was it a kill order?'

'No, sir.'

'Was the order to hurt her?'

'Yes, sir.'

'How badly?'

'Bad enough, but not terminal, sir.' Even with his eyes forward, he was dizzy from the General's circuit.

'Was the order to rape her?'

'I'm guessing...'

'Was the order to rape her?'

'We talked about it; it seemed like one way to hurt her and piss him off. Win-win, you know, sir.' Tommy sniggered, but it was out of fear rather than amusement and he regretted it immediately. He sensed a growing release of tension behind him, a shift from the role of culpable and accused to that of disinterested audience as the General drilled down into him. His mate was dead – his mate couldn't take the rap. Only the living could be held accountable.

'Remind me, who was the driver?' The voice came from behind him and Tommy swallowed – his mouth dry like all the times he'd been in deserts. He hated the sand and the flies and he really needed a drink. There was beer in the fridge at the back. He wanted a beer.

'That would be me, sir.' And he was beginning to hate the General's guts.

'Remind me of the name of the man you sent in?'

The General knew each and every one of them. Pretending otherwise, he made clear their insignificance, in life and in death. Tommy felt the slight, and knew he was meant to.

He had three weapons on him. A Glock 19 in a shoulder holster on his left side, a Glock 43 holstered on his left ankle, and an Emerson Close Quarters Combat knife sheathed on the horizontal at his waist. He should not have had sweat running down his spine. But he did. He thought about where they were. Where his hands were. What he could reach first if it came to it – the Glock 19 was in plain sight and the General knew he carried the second gun. The knife then, he decided. He felt a flare of panic as he considered the second's delay before his thumb could find the hole to deploy the blade.

'He was a good man, sir.' If by 'good', you meant effective.

'Your "good man" got himself killed. By a woman.' The General stood too close to him. Up in his face, like he was daring him to clench his fist and knock him senseless. 'You've shown Hawke I'm vulnerable. That he can afford to flout me with impunity. That he can say what he wants and do what he wants.' The General looked across from Tommy to the waiting men. 'And do you know what is at stake here? Everything. I'm changing your terms of engagement. I don't just want the machine any more. When you boys go into the museum tomorrow night, Hawke dies. And enough people to make it look incidental – an act of domestic terrorism. Can you do that much for me?'

'Including the wife?' Tommy asked.

'If she's not dead already,' the General said. 'You aren't the only tool in my box, and who knows? She might yet catch a nasty chill. It's that time of year.'

Tommy had plenty of money, he reminded himself. A four-bedroom shingle house overlooking the Essex salt marshes and a young family. He could give all this up tomorrow. Do the kind of stuff his wife was always yammering on about. Take his kid to football training. Watch the match. Maybe even do some coaching. He was still thinking of his daughter's face – she'd just lost her two front teeth last week – as he felt the blade of his own knife slide between rib 9 and rib 10 and into his left kidney. He'd sharpened it the night before, as luck would have it. Pain washed over him and he clutched the General's lapels as his knees gave way. He waited for the arms of the men behind to catch him before he collapsed on to the concrete floor, but there was no one. Waited for them to die for him. But there was just one word of Anglo-Saxon that said it all. He didn't recognize the voice, but he knew for certain he would never make it to the museum. Never stand in the rain and watch his kid score a goal. The knife rattled against the bone as it came out. He had time to consider goats, the fact he was dying alone, the bleakness of the lads' betrayal – and then darkness.

8

Heathrow Airport

It was late, and no one noticed the teenage girl with two
stubby plaits and Joe 90 spectacles pacing backwards and
forwards next to a black limousine parked in the darkest
corner of the short-stay car park across from Terminal 5.

Behind the smoked glass of the limo, the dozing figure of
the chauffeur with his cap tipped over his eyes was all but
invisible. As was the old woman knitting furiously on the
back seat.

The teenager tapped and swiped at her phone as she
chewed gum. The occasional pop of an enormous bright
blue bubble punctuated the muffled rhythmic click-clack of
knitting needles from inside the car. And the teenager must
have seen something on her screen, because all of a sudden
she beamed from ear to ear.

Fangfang Yu rapped loudly on the glass, waking the
chauffeur from his nap. Hauling open the passenger door,
she scrambled over the back seat as the driver settled his

cap, turned the key in the engine and pulled out from the parking space in one smooth, practised movement.

It wasn't quite six yesterday morning when two immigration officials turned up at the takeaway in the roughest part of Newcastle upon Tyne and took away her mother. Fang's Dobermann, Killer, was worse than useless. Still in her nightdress, Mama Yu had started screaming Fang's name, over and over, as they'd each taken an arm and propelled the little weeping woman into a van with metal mesh at every window. It took less than three minutes. As the van drove away, Edmund Hone loomed into view, his brown riding coat flapping in the wind as he climbed out of the unmarked car and walked towards the takeaway.

In the living room above the Oriental Dragon, Hone had spelled out what he wanted from her. He needed North back in the country to protect his niece, and he wanted to know exactly what was going on at the Derkind Institute. *Where is North, anyway?* Hone asked. *You could save me a lot of time and trouble if you tell me.* Fang had shrugged. Of course she knew. North was holed up in a Berlin rathole feeling boohoo sorry for himself. But she wasn't in the business of making Hone's life any easier. *Why do you need to know?* she said. *He'll come home when I ask him. You know that or you wouldn't be here.* Hone had stared at her with his creepy eye. *Respect*, he said. *Yeah right*, she'd thought. Hone wanted to throw his weight around so that North knew who was the boss. She couldn't see that going down well.

In her head, as Hone talked, Fang had run through what she had to do to bring North back, and it never crossed her mind that he wouldn't come at her call. She scratched

Killer behind his ear, his docked tail wagging in ecstasy, and pictured her frightened mum in some detention centre. The wailing of children kept confined, the babble of languages, and the smells of overworked drains and undercooked food. Bars at the windows.

I forgot the old lady and the dog. Hone said, all of a sudden. *I'll send someone for them so you can focus on the job at hand.* And behind him, the old lady slid a boning knife from her sleeve, and in stockinged feet padded towards his chair. The MI5 agent checked his watch for the fifth time in as many minutes, and Fang made a 'don't even think about it' face at Granny Po. He looked back up as the old lady raised the knife high in the air, and Fang dropped her unlaced and glittering gold bovver boots on the stack of Alexandre Dumas books on the coffee table with a bone-shuddering bang. *Definitely. Not. Happening*, the girl said, her eyes on her grandmother. The one-eyed man sighed, like the entire world was against him. *Fine, kennel the dog and keep the old lady. Or kennel the old lady and keep the dog. Do whatever it is you've got to do, Fang, and do it fast.*

Behind him, the old lady lowered the knife.

A neighbour took the dog.

The microdot was easy – she'd made one for a history project once – just a camera, film, developing chemicals, cellophane, distilled water, latex gloves, white paper, a black pen, a potato and a postcard. The only difficult bit was ammonium dichromate. For that she had to break into her old school, find the chemistry lab and lever open a cupboard marked 'Hazardous chemicals'. She tasked a black-sheep cousin to fly over to Berlin to hand-deliver the postcard. He had a record for breaking and entering, which the family never talked about. She didn't ask him how he managed it, but she'd already expunged his criminal record and awarded him a degree in finance from a Russell Group university – a First. She thought he'd fit right into the City.

Her only mistake was letting North handle his own return. Fang went back to her phone and the website with its minute-by-minute airport arrivals and departures. Her round eyes, behind the heavy-framed glasses, fixed on the last British Airways arrival from Berlin. The arrival that should have touched down at 8.40 p.m., carrying its very particular cargo, was thirty-five minutes late – thirty-five minutes that could mean the difference between life and death.

The hearse in front of them motored at a steady 65 mph, taking it up to 70 whenever it could. Fast, she thought. Faster than was entirely respectable, as if the driver knew time was running out. Cars kept their distance, careful to avoid the contagion of death.

She'd never seen a coffin before. Only ever seen one corpse, a month ago. The thug who had tied her up and been ready to do her all kinds of grievous harm. Till North broke down the door.

She was worried in case something had gone wrong with the coffin, because North mattered. She'd never had a friend before. Other kids always considered her odd. Too clever. Too quirky. Too obsessive. She hadn't realized how lonely she'd been. And North was more than a friend, anyway. He was like a brother, even if he was a moron. Of course, that's if he wasn't dead by now. Her eyes went to the coffin ahead of them. Because really, North was such a moron, she wouldn't put it past him.

49

9

The Club

Ralph Rafferty fidgeted in the leather armchair. He wasn't comfortable and he couldn't get warm. Even with the coal fire blazing in the hearth, it was dark and chilly in the corner of the famous London club not far from Pall Mall. This nightmare needed sorting and the General was late. He was always late. The old man ought to be taught a lesson. Rafferty stretched out his long spidery legs towards the flames, before crossing them at the ankles. The porter had handed him a tie at the entrance. It was still rolled up on the side table.

Anyone would think the General wanted to make the point that he was the busier man. But who was he, after all? A chocolate soldier. Rafferty was a statesman – a brilliant young statesman, moreover, destined to transform the fortunes of his country. Rafferty was only three months into his job as Home Secretary. He might owe his elevation to the bomb in London's banqueting hall which wiped out the PM and seven members of the Cabinet, but that didn't mean he wasn't up to it. Ralph Rafferty had every intention of going down in history alongside Wellington and Churchill. He let the thought of it roll around his head for a while – the glory and portraits, the front cover of *Time* magazine. Maybe a Nobel Peace Prize – even if he had to start a war to get one. He lifted his chin a fraction, as if a sculptor had begged him to alter his pose, the better to catch the light. Yes, the future belonged to Ralph Rafferty, if he could just keep it together for the next twenty-four hours.

His foot in its handmade shoe bounced up and down in barely suppressed irritation. He should be ploughing through his red boxes rather than sitting here wasting time. The club had a ban on mobile phones. How ridiculous was that in this day and age. Even the air tasted stale, he admitted to himself, as if it was the self-same air that had been breathed by the same kind of men for decades without a window ever having been opened.

Even as a junior minister, and certainly as Home Secretary, Rafferty could have had his pick of London clubs. Occasionally, he pined for something with cocaine laid out in the gents and an Eastern European barman who knew how to make a decent negroni. But he knew this much from his father – your club was a message to the Old Boys that they could trust you. That even if you were occasionally pictured on a carbon framed, hand-built, customized Sarto bike with bicycle clips over the Savile Row suit, you were still one of them.

This place was ancient, exclusive and cripplingly expensive. It allowed no oligarchs, no new money and no women – whatever the law said. Through the centuries, this had been the club of five prime ministers and too many cabinet ministers to count; this had been his grandfather's club, his father's club, and so this club was his. However lumpy the custard and bad-tempered the porters.

And, he was willing to admit, he enjoyed the frisson he created here among the country's wealthiest and most powerful old fogeys. Their desperation in the dining room for him to spare them some pleasantry about the weather as they lifted the bone from their sole meunière. *Sound chap, young Rafferty. I knew his father y'know.* They were all of them such fools. He picked up *The Times*, checked his Apple watch with some ostentation, and filled out the crossword in one fluid go. It was garbage. He had no idea of the answers, and he was always careful to carry the paper away with him. He didn't speak six languages either. He had 'hello', 'how are you?', 'have you lost weight?', 'it's a pleasure to be here' and 'thank you so much' in eight. It took remarkably little effort in politics to be considered brilliant.

The gin and tonic fizzed on the tongue, but it did nothing to improve his mood. The young waiter in his white jacket and tight black trousers drifted across to Rafferty. 'Can I get you anything else, sir?'

Rafferty afforded him a smile of infinite charm. 'No, thank you, Jonny.' He made a point of remembering unimportant people's names – they were always so flattered. Behind his trademark round spectacles, he watched with narrowed eyes as the waiter sashayed over to another powerful man in another dark corner of the club's smoking room. The lad was a flirt and a thing of beauty, it had to be said. Wasted in this place.

Rafferty tossed his head to rearrange the sweep of hair that fell down over his face, his fingertips settling it just above his eyebrows. The cartoonists thought it was vanity, and in a way it was. If it was vanity to want to hide the real Ralph Rafferty. Courtesy of the three skin-graft operations in his adolescence, the number 666, which his twin brother had once carved into his forehead, was no longer visible. No longer visible, that is, to anyone except Rafferty. Hence the sweep of hair. In his nightmares, he still felt the weight of Christian's body on his chest – his brother's bony knees pinning down his shoulders, and the blood streaming from the open wounds into his eyes. Still heard himself screaming for his mother to help him.

After the 'incident', as they insisted on calling it, his stricken parents had Christian quietly committed to a psychiatric hospital. His parents were long since dead, but occasionally a doctor rang to argue that with recent advances in antipsychotic medications, his brother should be allowed to return to society. But Rafferty had no intention of letting that happen. It was, he decided, worth every penny of Christian's share of the family trust to keep his twin locked up in St Mungo's and medicated out of his head.

He knew his brother wasn't insane. Never had been. Ralph had tortured him for years till finally deciding that Christian had to go. He'd planned everything meticulously. Even as a child he had known to keep his need to inflict pain hidden from his parents and teachers and friends. He had successfully hidden it from everyone – except for his twin brother. The other particular secret he and Christian shared was the reason his brother carved the number in the first place – his discovery of a gleeful Ralph disembowelling their golden retriever on the stone-flagged floor of the cellar. Of course, Ralph had planned it all, including hanging the family cat and her litter of kittens in Christian's wardrobe a couple of hours earlier, but his brother wasn't to know that.

Sitting by the hearth, Rafferty allowed himself a smirk. After the '666' attack, sobbing in the arms of his distraught mother, it was indeed predictably easy to deny responsibility. To pass off the dead pets as his brother's work. He didn't think either of them would forget the look of searing hatred that passed between them as he stood at the doorway, his mother's arm around him, while white-coated orderlies dragged away his twin. Out of interest at university, he'd once filled out an 'Are You a Psychopath?' quiz in the *Observer* and ticked thirty-eight out of forty boxes. It didn't worry him, but he did at least have enough insight to realize it should.

He was the future of British politics, he told everyone who would listen. Modernism was his brand. Another Emmanuel Macron. Another Obama. Another Blair. Visionary, forward-looking but strong in his convictions, a modernizer but one intent on protecting the country's interests at a time of acute vulnerability post-Brexit and post-Trump – whatever the cost to himself or anyone else.

And courtesy of Tobias Hawke, everything he'd ever dreamed of was both within his grasp and at risk of turning to dust. Hawke was an unpleasant and arrogant bastard but his AI work was decades ahead of anyone else in the field – the UK was looking at another industrial revolution. Productivity and GDP would go through the roof. If only the bastard would cancel the gala – this gala risked 'sharing'

Syd and all Syd's capabilities with the wider world, which Rafferty didn't like at all. This shouldn't be about Hawke's genius and a global response to a new consciousness in the universe. This time belonged to Ralph Rafferty – and his nation, of course. And not to mention that Hawke knew far too much for comfort.

So yes, he would have liked something more from the beautiful waiter, but he had those inclinations under control as well. The public was no longer horrified by gay politicians. He knew he would have met with the same success in public life had he declared himself to be bisexual, but he didn't trust himself. Because his predilections included not just the firm bodies of young men and women, but the fantasy of wrapping his hands around their throats and squeezing until the life force drained from them. That, he could not allow himself.

Perhaps one day, he mused, his eyes on the waiter's firm buttocks, swilling the herb-scented Gin and It around his mouth. When he was retired and free from close protection, he'd drive somewhere distant and grim, pick up a fragile whore desperate for cash or drugs, and indulge himself in a moment of exquisite pleasure. Perhaps then? Or even earlier, if he could find a way?

But no, he forced himself to look away from the waiter's attentive body, the bulging bicep, the smooth pour of coffee into another member's cup. He polished his spectacles with the tail of the borrowed silk tie before securing them around his ears. He was altogether safer with his dull wife. He wasn't kind to her, but then again, what did she expect?

His more immediate problem was the scandal that would

end his political career if this particular monumental fuck-up ever got out.

'You're late,' he said, as the figure sat down with a ferocious grunt in the chair opposite him, the buttoned leather groaning in protest at the weight of its new occupant.

'You're lucky I'm here at all.' General Kirkham then shouted across to the waiter, oblivious to the lad's charms, 'The usual, and sharpish.'

Rafferty was many things, but a fool wasn't one of them. He didn't for one moment believe General Kirkham liked him. The man was a Glaswegian brute. You could see it in every part of him – the eye bags hanging down to his jowls, the jutting jaw giving him the underbite of a hungry animal, and the huge hands, calloused despite the years he had spent behind a desk.

And was there any need for him to wear the uniform? With all those ghastly jangling medals and gaudy ribbons. All that did was draw attention to himself. Lord knows the New Army had had more than its share of bad publicity lately. A privatized army had seemed like the perfect solution to rising costs, increased defence commitments, and an isolationist US under President Donald Trump. But the ferocity with which the New Army had put down recent public protests had not done their cause any favours. Rafferty suspected privatization of the armed forces was an experiment which had had its day. Still, Rafferty and the General's interests coincided when it came to Tobias Hawke, and that could only be a good thing – at least for the pair of them. The General was paranoid about the country's national security, and that paranoia was something Rafferty could exploit.

He leant in towards the General in a bid to keep the conversation private. 'You said Hawke could be persuaded to keep quiet about what happened and keep Syd under wraps. Next thing, I've an invitation to a gala on my desk and I'm being briefed that his wife killed an intruder. What is she – a ninja?'

'We couldn't predict the trollop getting the better of a trained professional – it was a fluke – and "the intruder" can't be traced back to us. My men are loyal.'

There was silence between them while Jonny served the General his Hennessy XO cognac and slid away as fast as he could. 'It's bad enough Hawke insists on telling the world about his precious AI breakthrough. But may I remind you, General, that if what actually happened in that particular circle of hell gets out, everything is over. The millions this government has invested through the years will be money down the drain. Moreover, you'll end up in prison and I'll end up your cellmate.'

'Hold your nerve, Rafferty. "From this wall, we do not retreat!"' The General scowled at the politician. 'Let me remind you that the country is vulnerable on all sides. Russia, China, the US, even the sodding Europeans can say and do what they like to us now. We've no diplomatic leverage and no clout to protect our citizens here or abroad. We've barely got half the nuclear capability we used to have. Do you know we only have one per cent of the total global stockpile of nuclear weapons! One per cent!'

Rafferty did know, because the General spat out the figure at every opportunity.

'But with Hawke's work we can hold off any and all of the bastards till kingdom come.' Aeron Kirkham wiped his mouth with his hand and Rafferty was again reminded of a slavering dog. 'I won't allow a few last-minute scruples in Hawke or anyone else blow it for us.'

'The Chinese are sniffing around – you know that?' Rafferty said, watching the General.

'I know that slimeball, Octavius Chin, goes home a hero if he screws this for us. Hawke is decades ahead of the Chinese on all of this.'

'Chin knows something's wrong. Don't ask me how, but he slid up to me at some Foreign Office function last night wanting to deal.'

'Without Hawke blowing the whistle, the Chinese have nothing.'

'I should never have let you persuade me to allow those boys out on day release,' Rafferty said. 'If Hawke tells the world what went on, it's over. What if he tells his wife? What if he's already told her?'

General Kirkham's eyes, as they rested on Rafferty, blazed. Loaded as they were with scorn and evil, and – some trick of the light, surely – mirroring the flames of the fire in the hearth.

The General reached out his massive hand and patted Rafferty on his bony knee, and Rafferty felt the visceral dislike he had for the older man break out like sweat. 'Silence is a virtue, laddie. Hawke will understand that, one way or another.'

10

East London

The journey felt like the longest of her life.

According to Fang's phone, the drive should take one hour and twenty-six minutes down the M4, along the A4, past Euston and then King's Cross railway stations, along Old Street, and heading into the East End. The roads were at least quiet, but it was one hour and thirty-one minutes before the hearse and its companion limo pulled into the discreet cobbled side street off the Roman Road.

They were here. She reminded herself to be hopeful. This was it.

The headlights caught the brass plaque at the entrance to the yard. Padraig Donne & Sons, Funeral Directors. Est. 1807. And on a smaller, white-painted sign on the other side, 'Specialists in repatriation'. As they bumped across the cobbles through the wooden gates, a young boy, his face covered in acne, ran over to close the gates and draw the bolts. He called out, 'Locked up tight, Plug,' and started whistling the Funeral March as he jogged back to the Rolls-Royce he was polishing. It was night; Fang thought he should maybe leave it till the morning, but she imagined he was there to keep an eye out more than anything else.

There was a shriek of metal against concrete as unseen hands started to haul open the huge grey doors ahead of them, inviting the limousine to follow the hearse into a cavernous garage.

The plane was already thirty-five minutes late when it landed; the drive had added another five minutes to that, which meant they were getting in a full forty minutes late. Fang's heart beat faster in her chest. The blood was pounding in her ears as, with some ceremony, the driver opened her door and she clambered out. It wouldn't do to lose her nerve at this point in the game, she reminded herself.

Fangfang took a step back as an undertaker stepped through a door marked 'Land of the Dead' and waved over the limo driver to open the boot of the hearse. The undertaker was six foot seven, she was guessing. Make that seven foot in the black silk top hat with trailing black silk ribbons. This was the friend North called 'Plug'. What kind of name was 'Plug'? It rolled around her head awhile. 'Plug' as in 'Plug Ugly'? Because they had that right – it was as if someone had moulded his head out of red clay, dropped it on the floor and stamped on it repeatedly. Scars and bulges covered it. She tried and failed to stop staring at the massive jaw, the overhanging brow and the nose, which zigzagged to a stop under the outer corner of his left eye.

Plug stripped off his black tailcoat, careful to hang it on a clothes hanger on a brass hook on the wall. In the shirt, he was a classic T-shape: huge rippling shoulders and a narrow waist. Absolutely no neck. With a grim flourish, whistling through the spaces between his teeth, he removed the top hat, revealing huge misshapen lumps for ears and close-cropped red hair. Plug frowned at Fang as he folded the cuffs of his sleeves up and over again and again, first the right and then the left.

'You took your time, China girl.' He reached for a metal gurney. The gravestone tattooed across his forearm sported a Celtic cross and a list of names, and it crossed Fang's mind that they were the people he'd killed rather than loved. And 'China girl'? The guy was patently a racist.

Plug propelled the gurney, its wheels squeaking in fury, across to the limo driver now standing by the tailgate. Alongside the hearse, the lad, who'd come in from the yard, erected a trestle table. Plug followed the path of the gurney, metal-tipped shoes tapping against the concrete.

'Let's get a shimmy on,' the undertaker ordered the limo driver, nodding as together they hauled the coffin on to the gurney. The air freight cardboard box was printed all over with its declaration of human remains and the warning 'Handle with Extreme Care'. His face set, Plug slid his enormous hand over and around corners and edges, and as the cardboard scraps tumbled to the floor, Fangfang realized he held a knife. She swallowed. If the worst had happened, she and Granny Po were trapped in this place with the world's ugliest criminal armed with a sharp knife and a list of dead men inked on his skin.

Without its shroud of cardboard, the coffin sat on a foam mat within a wooden tray. It was oak with brass handles. Fang was no expert, but it appeared to be good quality. Substantial. And very deep. Her eyes went to the clock mounted on the wall opposite. They were forty-four minutes late.

Adults did the most ridiculous things. They were morons, each and every one. And some were more moronic than most. Like North. She should never have left this business to him. She should have come up with her own plan.

She came back to the present with the sound of a screw turning as it let go its corkscrew grip on the oak. It was cold in the garage and Fang spasmed in an uncontrollable shiver. She felt Granny Po slip a soft hand into hers and let it stay there for a second before shaking her off. Fang prepared herself – North knew the risks.

Blossoms of sweat bloomed in the armpits of Plug's white shirt.

The limo driver stood at the foot of the coffin, Plug at the head.

'With me,' Plug instructed, and there was a collective intake of breath as they heaved the coffin lid up and off, before the driver crossed over to the wall to lean the lid on its tail end. The stink of must and formaldehyde rose from a shrivelled old man in a shiny black suit, his claw-like hands clasped one on top of the other, his face caved in on itself, eyes sunken, cheekbones bulging, the lips shrunken and falling in on themselves in the toothless mouth. Despite herself, Fang took a step backwards, but chatting to herself in Cantonese, Granny Po approached the corpse and patted him on the shoulder, before placing her hands together and bowing. Fang didn't know if she was consoling him or thanking him.

'On my count. Three. Two...' Plug paused as the sound

of a siren grew louder and louder before fading away again. Fang reminded herself to breathe. '… One.'

There was a fierce ripping noise as if a rubber seal was being broken, as the shallow tray of ruched satin and its tiny corpse were lifted up and away from the coffin and on to the trestle table.

Fang moved closer to the coffin. *Please, let him be all right.*

Plastic-wrapped packets covered the length and breadth of the figure in its Arctic jacket. One must have leaked, because when Plug moved the fur trim of the hood away from the mask that covered North's face, a cloud of white powder rose into the air.

Fang willed her friend to move. But North's chest was still – he wasn't breathing, she realized. Plug reached into the coffin for the oxygen bottle alongside the body and shook it. From where she stood on the other side, Fang could see that the dial read 'empty'. Plug swore.

North was dead.

11

The scream sparked into life somewhere around Fang's gut, forcing its way up her throat and into her mouth, but she resisted it. 'Do something,' she shouted at Plug, transfixed, the empty oxygen bottle still in his hand. North was a moron-person. But he'd been so paranoid that this was his only way back. *I can't come in on a flight, Fang. Whatever this is, it's dangerous or Hone wouldn't be putting me out there instead of one of his own. I don't know who's watching, and I don't trust Hone to get me back without attracting attention from people I'd rather forget.*

Plug pulled out a first aid box from under the gurney and unclasped it, throwing open the lid in the same moment as reaching in and pulling out a hypodermic needle. He unzipped the parka, sliding his blade through the layers to reveal bare skin. He plunged the needle up to its hilt into North's chest and pressed down the plunger.

Nothing happened.

It wasn't enough, she thought, but she couldn't get the words out. She imagined North's heart quivering in his chest. Not pumping. Just trembling, waiting for even that to stop.

Plug let loose a torrent of abuse at North as the limo driver dragged a defibrillator box from out of the boot. These guys had no idea what they were doing, Fang thought. Plug unsnapped the latches to pull out two sticky pads and attached them to North's chest. Skinny wires snaked back into the box. 'Shockable,' he said, looking terrified. 'Charging!' He banged his huge hand down on the button and North's body convulsed, then collapsed. Panic built in Fang. Were they hurting him? Could you hurt the dead? Could you be deader than dead? There was no twitch, no breath, no rise of the chest.

'Bring him back, right now,' she yelled. 'CPR. Do the CPR thing!' Her feet swung in the air as she struggled to reach North, but the limo driver was holding her.

Plug swore as he made a tight fist and thumped down on North's chest – once, twice, three times. He tipped North's head back and pinched his nose, breathing air into his mouth, once, twice. He leant over his friend's body, his hands locked together, fingers interlaced as he pressed down on North's chest then released, down and release – she lost count of how many times. Breathed. Pumped.

Fang willed North to come back to them. Not to take the easy way out. He was sad. She knew that. Really sad. But he had to come back. Choose to get back in the game. Not just because without him she had no chance of bringing her mother home, but because she needed him alive.

'Do the machine thing again,' Fang could hear someone shouting, and realized it was her. 'It's too low. Turn it up.'

Plug pressed a switch on the machine. 'Charging!' he

said, stepping away from North. It took less than a second, but it seemed an eternity to Fang.

There was a sudden smell of metal and burning hair, as North's body spasmed and dropped back into the coffin, rocking the gurney. Then nothing. The moment went on forever. Fang squeezed her eyes closed so she didn't have to let out any tears, then opened them again as, gasping for air, North sat bolt upright, a red bruise over his heart and two scorch marks either side of his chest.

She felt her own body go limp with relief as the limo driver released her from his grip. She was right, as ever. Smuggling yourself into the country in a coffin with an undersized corpse and 100 kg of cocaine was a terrible idea.

North's eyes met hers as he sucked down the deepest breath he could take in, his forearm pushing against Plug. There was an apology there she thought, and a promise. He was back. He was in this with her. He was getting her mother out from Hone's clutches and he wasn't going anywhere. And for the first time since the immigration goons walked her mother out the door, Fang felt herself flood with what anyone else would have called happiness.

'Now "that" never happens.' Plug slapped an oversized hand down on his friend's shoulder, North's collarbones crunching in protest, and the undertaker's raucous gales of laughter filled the garage like flapping birds.

North leant over the side of the coffin to retch up green bile, before wiping the corner of his mouth with the back of his hand. '"Leave it with me," you said. You "bring people in this way all the time," you said.' Wincing, his fingertips prodded the outer margins of the burgeoning bruises on his sternum.

Plug waved his hand. 'Delays at Customs are killing me. And in my defence, you did give me eff-all time to pull this off. And you're welcome, by the way.'

North gripped the sides of the coffin as he levered himself up and away. His feet hit the ground with a thud. 'So now I'm back in Blighty...' – he said, swaying as he spoke – '... who's up for trouble?' He smiled at Fang like he already knew the answer, before a look of puzzlement washed over his face. His blue eyes widened, then blinked shut once, twice, three times as he reeled forwards then backwards, before keeling over unconscious on to the concrete floor.

'North, mate, you are such high-maintenance,' Plug said, staring down at his friend's recumbent body. But he was grinning.

12

It was hard doing planks with a scratchy wool blanket around him, shivering and aching in every possible extremity. But it was a necessary part of coming back to himself.

North forced himself up on to his toes and the palms of his hands in a bid to drive oxygen through and round his system. He imagined the blood cold and sluggish in his veins and pushed through the pain from his chest to lift himself up and lower himself down again, his biceps and stomach muscles shrieking with the effort. What was he doing back in London? When he left, he didn't think he'd ever come back. Didn't focus on anything more than putting one foot in front of the other. Thought his only job now was to drink himself to death. He was fighting an acute sense of dislocation. Where the hell was he? He wasn't in Berlin any more – he was in London, he reminded himself. His self-imposed exile was over. He wasn't a stranger – he was home. He wasn't alone to do as he wanted – suddenly, he had responsibilities and 'people'. People important to him, who could get hurt if he messed up whatever the hell this was. And the thought of it made him nervous as a cat.

His chest hurt, but he wasn't sure if it was from the adrenaline or from Plug's efforts to revive him. He held on to the pain as a way of grounding himself. Bringing himself back to the moment. It shouldn't, but it helped. His most pressing problem was the suspicion that the vile taste in his mouth was embalming fluid that had dripped through from Uncle Jim.

Last night, North had bought the phone from a 24/7 supermarket in Berlin, torn off the plastic packaging and pumped in the number he needed no help remembering. 'Padraig Donne and Sons, Funeral Directors. Let *us* help *you* at this difficult time.' The Cockney accent on the other end of the phone as familiar as his own voice. Donne and Sons, with a highly profitable side hustle in drug smuggling.

North had known Plug Ugly – otherwise known as Paddy 'The Fighting Irish' Donne – from his days in juvenile. The acromegaly or gigantism that had almost killed Plug as a child had left him with a protruding jaw and brow, and enormous hands, feet and face. He had been a king in the world of cage fighting before he was diagnosed with a disorder in the pituitary gland, which had run riot with his growth hormone. His cage-fighting profits funded his buyout of a failing funeral business, whose aged proprietor couldn't believe his luck when the giant walked in with a case full of fifty-pound notes.

And since Plug expanded the business, the company had developed a particular specialism in the repatriation of the fallen.

North didn't know how often his friend smuggled people into the country rather than drugs, and he didn't want to know. He did know he himself needed a shave, and there was an even better chance he needed a shower. And the strange noise was the chattering of his teeth, he realized, because the cold had frozen the marrow of him. So much for Plug's reassurances that he'd be warm as a sardine on a piece of buttered toast. That he wouldn't know anything about it, because he'd be laid out with ketamine for the entire journey. That Plug would make sure his men in Berlin slipped the baggage handlers extra to guarantee they stashed the coffin in the climate-controlled pressurized hold that the pets went in. That they were good men and they hardly ever made mistakes, and 'Uncle Jimmy', under a whole variety of aliases, was back and forth at least once a month. That nothing could go wrong. Unless the plane was late, when the oxygen might run out. And he might die. Other than that, he was to think of it like a budget airline without the trolley service.

Never. Again.

He shuddered at the memory.

'Is there a woman?' He turned to see Plug pouring him a brandy. Trying hard not to show the state he was in, North sat on the greasy velour sofa in the back parlour. 'Because with you, mate, there's always a woman.'

'Not any more,' North said. He sensed his friend's concern for him. That urge to protect even those who looked like they didn't need protecting, and he loved him for it.

'I'm assuming you shouldn't be back in the country?' He could sense Plug groping in the dark for answers, for his friend to open up about the past, but North couldn't bring himself to say the words. It was too raw. 'That it's dangerous for you.'

It was only dangerous if they found out, North thought, which they almost certainly would.

'You don't have to be here. I've connections that can make it so you disappear. You get to be someone else, and no one bothers you again.' Leaning against a stack of battered metal lockers, Plug folded his arms, waiting on the answer.

The idea of being someone else tugged at North. To acquire someone else's peace and someone else's way of going on. But he was Michael North and he was going to make the fact he was still here count. 'Too late for that,' he said. Plug shrugged as if he wasn't surprised, but North felt his disappointment, the worry that had started to gnaw at the big man that his mate was into something bad that could only end one way.

Could he trust Hone in the same way he trusted Plug? Absolutely not. The one-eyed man was a ruthless bastard.

'Fang and Granny Po stay with you,' North said as he swallowed the brandy in one gulp. His chest felt like a carthorse had sat on it.

'I really hoped you wouldn't say that.'

Plug would keep the girl and the old lady safe. In another life, North had owned his own apartment in London. But it wasn't anyplace that he'd be returning to. You could do without a home – it made it harder for your enemies to find you. 'And I need a gun.'

'I figured,' Plug said, opening the nearest locker door before sliding a dark plastic case across the tiled coffee table towards him. North flicked open the latches. In the carved-out foam interior lay a SIG Sauer P226 and two magazines

– 9mm, ten rounds. North smiled. He liked to think he was adaptable – he'd once killed an oligarch with a grapefruit fork – but if he had a choice of weapon, then this was it.

He eased the gun from the foam and weighed it in his hand – heavy at thirty-four ounces, heavier again when loaded, but the weight stopped muzzle climb when fired. Even holding it made him feel better. More in control. He was in this, whatever this was. Hone thought his niece needed protection – he could have brought in the police, or hired private security. Instead, he'd recruited a hitman. And North was under no illusions. He had been brought in to take out whoever threatened the life of Esme Sullivan Hawke – or die trying.

13

It was past midnight when Granny Po emerged from Plug's kitchenette with a tray bearing a Brown Betty teapot, four mugs and a plate of egg and bacon sandwiches. At the table where Plug and North were seated, the old lady poured the tea and handed a mug with due ceremony to Plug, bowing her silvered head, her cabbage-patch cheeks dimpling. North thought she was strangely taken with the drama of the drugs and the coffin and the giant. As Plug thanked her, there was a noise that might have been a giggle if the person making it had been eighty years younger.

The old lady put another mug and a sandwich in front of Fangfang, before letting loose a chirruping torrent of Cantonese, which her granddaughter waved away. North had finally stopped shivering, but he was still freezing cold. The coffee and brandy hadn't touched the sides. Strong tea and food was exactly what he needed. Smiling, he held out his hand for his mug and the old lady handed it to him before ceremoniously leaning over, her soft hand staying his, and spitting into it.

The white blob of bubbling phlegm bobbed on the rust-coloured surface.

Granny Po stood upright again and shuffled with careful dignity across to the sofa, sitting for a moment as if to settle her aching bones in their rightful place, before reaching down into her enormous carpet bag and extracting her knitting. Her face was all innocence and wrinkles.

'The flight over was bad enough,' North said, 'but the service this end is worse.'

Fang, her black eyes fixed on her phone, her fingers busy, ignored him. She wore a black-and-white-striped T-shirt printed with the words 'United we stand, divided we fall.' He turned for sympathy to Plug.

'The old girl thinks it's your fault the spooks lifted Mama Yu,' Plug said. 'She doesn't want you getting the kid into trouble.'

North put down the mug. If Granny Po was gangsta enough to spit in his tea, he wasn't putting it past her to have found rat poison in the kitchenette. She shared DNA with Fang, so Granny Po wasn't fooling him that she was some old dear.

Fang showed no interest in the exchange. She took an enormous bite of her sandwich and, using the toes of her glittering bovver boots, propelled the captain's chair 360 degrees around. North coughed to get her attention. 'I'll sort out this mess at Derkind. You're not going anywhere near it.'

Plug folded his arms over his barrel chest and nodded in approval as Fang devoured the rest of her sandwich. North and Plug were hard men who would manage their business all the better without kids and old folks underfoot.

North braced himself for Fang to argue, but instead she slowed her second turn to gaze at him and Plug, as if evaluating their worth to the last penny. Calculations made, she folded in a stick of gum and blew an enormous bubble before popping it and using her tongue to reel in the translucent skin. All in all, she seemed resigned to her fate, which was a good thing. Maybe he could even get Fang and Granny Po on a train back up to Newcastle this afternoon before Hone realized what was going on?

Feeling his attention still on her, Fang stopped chewing her gum, and opened her eyes wide behind their heavy glasses. 'Say what, Frankenstein?' She unplugged one of the earbuds North hadn't noticed before. She hadn't heard a word.

He tried to control his irritation.

'I said you're not—'

She put the earbud back in and tapped her ear, shaking her head and mouthing *I can't hear you, moron-person.*

North tried to stare her down. And failed. Fang wasn't backing down till her mum was out of the detention centre.

Plug raised his bushy eyebrows in disbelief, and North made a 'what can you do' gesture. The kid would stonewall him until he gave in, so he might as well give in now. He gestured at her to take the earphones out and join the conversation, and a smile of triumph lit up the round face behind the Joe 90 glasses – white teeth and blue braces flashing.

'I meant to ask – how's the bullet in the brain, bozo?'

'Still there.'

'And your superpowers?' Fang was the only person who had sensed the long-term consequences of his injury.

He shook his head and she frowned.

'I can still hit people very hard.'

Fang looked sceptical, as if she was considering whether that would be enough. Then she shrugged. 'Each to his own. So, I figure we're working as government spooks?' She cocked her head to one side, like a raven. 'Which means we can do whatever we want.'

'No, because if we get caught...' – North knew there was no point sugar-coating anything with Fang – '... Hone hangs us out to dry, your mum gets posted to China, and we go to prison or worse.'

Fang drummed her fingers as she appeared to think through her options. 'Okay,' she said, as if prison or worse was of zero consequence to her. 'What do you want to know about Derkind, moron-person? Because while you two were playing zombie apocalypse, some of us have been working.'

She ordered Plug to remove a tasteful print of a Victorian stone angel to use the blank wall as a projector, bouncing the presentation from a tablet she dished out of her Yoda haversack.

An image flashed up on the wall. The photograph was of a handsome man in a denim shirt leaning on a silver-topped cane. An expression of belligerence and impatience on his face. Designer stubble and startling black eyebrows contrasting with a mane of wavy snow-white hair. North had never noticed another man's hair before, but he thought that, despite the scowl, this guy had hair women would want to run their fingers through. He ran his hand over his own skull, velveteen on the way down, bristling on the way up. He'd had his hair cropped in Berlin, partly to hide the flash of white that covered the scar. He hadn't missed it till this minute.

'The hair belongs to computer scientist Tobias Hawke. He's thirty-five – way younger than he looks. His hair turned white overnight when he hit nineteen and the twin-engine plane he was in went down in the Australian outback. He took off his own foot to get out from the wreckage...'

North decided Hawke was allowed his good hair.

'He chewed off his own foot?' Plug sounded disbelieving.

'Not chewed, dodo. He used a Swiss Army knife and a piece of the fuselage.' For this alone, Fang liked the guy, North could tell. 'He wrapped up the stump in who-cares-what, applied some sort of crude tourniquet and dragged himself nine miles before search and rescue came across him. Surgeons ended up having to amputate his leg above the knee.' Fang looked momentarily downcast that the best part of the story was over. 'He competed in the 400 metres in the Beijing Paralympics six years after the amputation. According to gossip, people admire the guy while hating his guts. He's an obsessive, temperamental workaholic with a massive ego, and he drives the techies who work alongside him crazy with his relentless demands. Despite that, everyone wants to work with him because they think he's going to make them rich and famous.' Page after page of magazines and online blogs flashed up on the wall, all of them about Hawke. 'The AI community is waiting for Hawke to change the world.'

Now she said it, North thought that perhaps he had heard of Hawke. The story of the amputation wasn't one you'd forget in a hurry.

They were staring at a picture of Hawke on the front

cover of *Wired* under the headline 'Brit Tech – Red Hot and Happening'. They'd styled the picture with an unfurling Union Jack. A scowling Hawke was in a denim shirt again, standing with his arms folded. Although his face was grim, his eyes told the camera that he enjoyed the fact he was such a big scientific deal. The woman alongside him was in profile, looking upwards, as if she would rather be anywhere but the front of a magazine. Statuesque – a couple of inches taller than her husband – dark hair in old-fashioned waves, cheekbones so sharp they could cut you. She sported a red trouser suit cropped at the ankles and designer trainers. The magazine had imported a British bulldog, which gazed up at her adoringly.

'His wife and business partner is Esme Sullivan Hawke. Same age as Hawke. Plenty of people rate Hawke but she's the only person in the world who seems to like the guy. They met at Imperial College London, which by the way they both quit before graduating. She's an ethicist and chief exec of the tech company they set up in 2003 – aka Derkind – that was the year after he hacked off his foot, by the way. According to their last filing at Companies House...' – Fang swapped out the happy couple for the summary of accounts, and North missed the sight of Esme Sullivan Hawke already – '... the company has a market value of more than a billion. It makes Derkind what's called a "unicorn". I can't trace where the money came from to set it up, which is odd. But it's about to be worth an awful lot more. Investors are begging to give them money. But for the minute Tobias and Esme own the whole caboodle, apart from some share options that kick in next year.'

'I hate them already,' Plug said.

'They're brilliant, they look like Greek gods, and they're about to be gazillionaires, but if it makes you feel any better, five years ago they lost a son from something called diffuse intrinsic pontine glioma.' Fang brought up a snapshot from a summer's day of a beaming freckle-faced boy. 'This is Atticus – he was three.'

North could have been wrong, but it looked like Plug's eyes glistened. 'So now I feel like a complete bastard,' Plug said, under his breath.

'Hone mentioned AI?' North said, as much to distract Plug as because he wanted to know.

'Yes. Artificial intelligence. Do you even know what that is? Because one of you just flew economy in a coffin, and the other one made it happen, so intelligence isn't your strong point.'

His jaw tightening, Plug switched his gaze from Atticus to North, as if to say, *Who have you brought into my house?* Fang carried on: 'Artificial intelligence promises progress in health and transport and defence. A transformation in the way we live. People working less and accomplishing more. Rumour has it that Derkind is on the verge of something that will change our relationship with machines forever. One report predicts AI will add more than fifteen trillion dollars to the global economy by 2030. With our economy struggling to find its feet, Derkind is an even bigger deal than it would be otherwise. This is the next techno frontier, and if Derkind comes up with the goods, Britain's going to lead the way. Politicians are talking about advances in AI "securing the country's future for a generation". This guy in particular...'

Fang spooled through pages that passed in a blur, and a

picture appeared of a cadaverous, forty-something man with tightly razored sides to his hair, a lank auburn fringe and jug ears, carrying a red box and a green juice and dressed in a suit jacket but no tie. He was wearing what looked like leather bicycle clips, although there was no bike in sight. 'Home Secretary Ralph Rafferty. Allegedly he can do *The Times* crossword in four minutes flat, speaks six languages, and has a double first from Cambridge, though I can't find any record of it. Rafferty is all over Derkind – bigging them up abroad, telling everyone who'll listen that the UK is set to be the new Silicon Valley. He's always banging on about "the future".'

Ralph Rafferty? North kept up with current affairs. As Fang hurtled through pictures of Rafferty, North's mind trawled through what he knew about the minister – snippets of his voice, his pale face, speaking at the despatch box, explaining away the deportation of a terminally ill baby and her Ghanaian mother. Fang continued scrolling through pages, searching and clicking like someone possessed.

'Back,' North said.

Fang reverse-ferreted. Rafferty stood with Hawke at some function alongside an older, heavyset man in uniform.

'Who's that with Rafferty and Hawke?'

She clicked and zoomed and enhanced the image. The caption read: 'The Rt Hon Ralph Rafferty, MP, Home Secretary; Tobias Hawke, Chief Innovations Officer, Derkind PLC; and General Sir Aeron Kirkham, Joint Forces Command.' There was something familiar about the man, about the name. North thought hard. Raking back through his memory. A uniform, the barrel chest dripping with medals, a hatchet face with eye bags hanging down almost as far as his jowls.

Fang was skimming one website after another. 'Ten years ago when soldiers under his command shot up some Afghan girls out playing, the General defended them.' Her mouth turned down in disapproval. 'He said the kids had stoned them and one of them had a gun. Turned out the eldest was eight. There was an inquiry but he managed to get all the men honourably discharged. When there was a stink about it, he described the soldiers as "casualties of war" as much as the girls. So, he's a twat then.'

'When you say "artificial intelligence"... Are we talking robots?' Plug sounded hopeful. 'Like in *Terminator*?'

Fang rolled her eyes. 'No – the big AI guys hate that. When we talk about artificial intelligence, broadly speaking we're talking about systems that learn to replicate intelligent human behaviours. At the minute, it's what they call "narrow" or weak – things like internet searches, facial recognition or self-drive cars. They can do one thing. But researchers are working towards "general" or strong AI, where machines would outperform humans at nearly all cognitive tasks, not just some. That multitasking could lead to superintelligence with machines learning to think for themselves, explain their decision-making even – machines themselves designing more and more intelligent machines. But nobody is anywhere close to that yet.

'One weird thing is they aren't admitting it publicly, but seven days ago GCHQ picked up on a massive leak of Derkind's intellectual property to China – medical tech – and the UK government is freaking out in case they lose it all.'

'Can you tell where the leak came from?'

Fang shook her head. 'I'm trying, but everything in the company is encrypted. It's going to take time and they don't have it.'

North looked at her, puzzled.

Fangfang frowned. 'They don't have it because Hone's right – someone already tried to murder Esme Sullivan Hawke. What Hone didn't mention, by the way, is that she killed the guy they sent.'

'Killed him?'

Fang nodded. 'Stone-cold dead. But the chances have to be high that they'll try again before tomorrow night's gala launch at the British Museum.'

'What are they launching?' Despite himself, North was intrigued.

'No one knows. But whatever it is, the tech community think it's going to be huge. People are flying in for it from all over the world. Big names. Of course, Esme has to live that long.'

14

They arrived early in the morning, but even so, the place was humming. Situated in King's Cross, in what was rapidly becoming the city's 'tech quarter', Derkind was a futuristic building full of futuristic people attempting to shape the future, and they liked to get a head start on it. From inside the huge foyer where North stood, the building appeared to be made of shiny things – walls of rosy tinted glass folding over and over on itself, some with water running down them; arching steel girders and beams, which in turn held up sheets and columns of polished concrete and maroon-veined marble.

In her glittering Dr. Martens, Fang turned round and round in the same spot. 'Wow!' she said. 'This has to be the mother ship.'

An organic shape that architects hadn't believed they could build, until they did. Using materials that should never have twisted and curved and bent in that way, 'The Brain' was considered an engineering triumph when

Derkind moved in. Since then, it had become an iconic London landmark.

The reception area curved outwards before it sloped sharply inwards again. Like the inside of a pyramid, North thought, staring up into the void, and nothing good had happened to the pharaohs in any pyramid he knew about. It was so high, there appeared to be large birds flying around the void. There was even a soundtrack of birdsong playing, which he imagined was meant to relax visitors, but despite the dawn chorus, he fought off a presentiment of doom. He didn't like the place. It was impressive, he supposed, if you went for stark modernism, but it was cold, forbidding and strangely soulless. His eye snagged on an engraved sign at waist height by the doorway. 'Under the Data Protection Act of 2018, we would like to bring to your attention that in the interests of security, CCTV is in operation. We thank you for your cooperation in this.' Of course they were under surveillance. Maybe that was it. Maybe something in him felt the eyes of strangers on him, judging, and finding him wanting.

'You don't have to be here,' he said to Fang. 'We can get your mum out a different way.' He'd thought about it on the drive over. Fang could hack the immigration records and he and Plug could swoop in to whichever detention centre it was and pull her out. Hone would be mad but it was doable. Fang shook her head. She'd already thought it through. 'Mum will want her old life back,' she said. 'She's uber-boring like that.' Of course she would. Fang's mum wouldn't want to spend the rest of her life worrying in case Hone and his bully-boy immigration officers rocked up again.

He attempted to shrug off the bad feeling that had crawled inside of him. Maybe it was the fact he was back home and didn't want to be. Because 'home' made him think of the woman he'd lost. Maybe it was simply down to the fact he needed a drink? It was only just past eight in the morning in London, but in Berlin it was nine. Fangfang tugged at his arm. She looked up at him, expectant. She was worried about her mother, but here was someone in a hurry to walk into the future. The computer scientists who worked in this building were her kind of people, he guessed. Brimful of abstract knowledge and at ease with machines, all looking to change the world.

The teenager matched her step to North's. She was trying to play it cool but her breath came fast – as if she were climbing a mountain. This Tobias Hawke guy had her interested.

As they crossed the foyer, the noise of the falling water receded and the electronic birdsong got louder, reaching peak crescendo at a huge brushed-steel desk, behind which an exquisite youth in a black polo neck and a headset microphone tapped away at a computer. A name badge identified the receptionist as Jarrod. North's height allowed him to see right over the desk, down on to Jarrod's keyboard, the green juice to one side and the cardboard box next to it. Inside was a felt cactus leaning against a mug with the phrase 'Number 1 Nerd' on it, a golden Maneki-neko whose cat's paw jiggled in protest and a stapler. A yellow Post-it note with the name 'Paulie Holliday' stirred in the breeze from the air conditioning. Paulie Holliday had clearly left the building in a hurry.

Fangfang, however, could barely see over the desk. When

Jarrod deigned to look up, North figured the receptionist would have an excellent view of her fringe and the laser-like eyes behind her jam-jar spectacles.

'Good morning and welcome to the Derkind Institute for the Advancement of Artificial Intelligence,' Jarrod said, without one scintilla of warmth, his face shiny-new as if he too polished himself daily.

Taking a step back, Fang blew and popped a bubble, and Jarrod winced.

Maybe the young man was grumpy because he had to play a supporting role to the oversized video of his black-browed, snowy-maned boss behind him? Locked in an eternal loop of scowling and pursing his lips, turning his head from side to side as if scanning the foyer for someone worthy of his attention. Derkind wanted it clear from the start who you were buying into – Tobias Hawke, the myth and the genius. Watching the strutting and posturing, North felt a primitive and immediate dislike. Even the building, he realized, was designed to represent Hawke's superhuman genius. Any visitor was meant to feel awe that they'd been allowed to bear witness to the inner workings of Hawke's own brain. The futuristic architecture, the backstory of suffering and bravery, the snowy mane and denim shirt – all had the feel of something curated and on the cusp of legend. This was how legends were made. Hawke was a scientist destined to go down in the history books. Albert Einstein. Alan Turing. Bill Gates. Steve Jobs. Mark Zuckerberg. Those who shifted the paradigm, and Tobias Hawke was going to be bigger than any of them if he had anything to do with it.

'Michael North and Fangfang Yu – we have an appointment with Esme Sullivan Hawke.'

'Today?' Jarrod pursed his lips as if struggling to believe they'd have an appointment any day, let alone the day of the gala, and North resisted the urge to take hold of him by his polo neck and drag him across the desk. Instead, he stared the gatekeeper down until sweat broke out across Jarrod's already shiny forehead and, with lips pursed, he started pecking rapidly at his keyboard.

North glanced down at Fang and winked. Whatever this was, they were in it together. She moved off to explore the foyer, trailing her fingers through the water, and turning his head, he scanned the words engraved three-foot-high across the wall behind the receptionist. 'It is no good to try to stop knowledge from going forward. Ignorance is never better than knowledge.' By someone called Enrico Fermi. He made a mental note to ask Fang who Enrico Fermi was. Underneath the Fermi quote was a smaller, laser-cut steel plate announcing: 'Derkind is one of 160 companies and organizations who are adding our name to the pledge organized by the Future of Life Institute to *neither participate in nor support the development, manufacture, trade, or use of lethal autonomous weapons.*'

He caught the rose and vanilla scent of her first. An old-fashioned perfume, he thought later, for a woman at the helm of a cutting-edge technology company.

'Humans are the most deadly creatures on this planet, but I don't have to tell you that, Mr North.' She stood alongside him, reading as he read. 'But for how long? Autonomous weapons systems identify, target and kill without even having to be told to do so by their human masters.' He glanced over and what she was saying ceased to matter, because Esme Sullivan Hawke was photogenic enough, but in the flesh she was nothing short of breathtaking.

She swivelled a little towards him. He put her at just under six foot but he wondered again how she'd managed to kill a man with her bare hands. 'I signed us up to that pledge because I believe we need to get these things right from the get-go. We're living in frontier country as far as privacy goes; same for accountability, issues of bias and unintended consequences, and questions as to what's moral and what isn't. At Derkind, we're working to make the world a better place, not worse, or what's the point of anything we do here? "Do no harm" isn't enough for us.'

'Sounds like a big enough ask to me.' he said, and her sombre face softened into the start of a sad smile.

'It's a start, perhaps,' she said. 'Excuse me for one minute. We've had another drama this morning. Apparently it's that kind of day.'

15

'Is Paulie gone?' Esme said, leaning over the desk and keeping her voice low.

North realized with a start that her make-up was hiding the damage of her beating. Hiding it, but not well enough. She'd missed the bruises either side of her jaw – bruises that looked as if a large hand had gripped her face tight – and now he'd seen the damage he couldn't unsee the swelling on the right cheekbone, the purpling skin across the right eye and a small cut just by her ear.

At Esme's question, Jarrod's face lit up with a megawatt smile, his devoted eyes like those of the bulldog on the cover of the magazine. 'I buzzed security as soon as he got in.' Jarrod's voice dripped with intrigue. 'They had to throw him on to the street.' He gave a theatrical shudder. 'I mean – what did he expect? Totally outrageous. I'm biking his stuff round.' He wafted a hand over the felt cactus, wrinkling his nose in disgust – at the mug or the cat, North didn't know which.

Esme frowned as a tiny drone swooped out of the air to

hover at eye level. 'Bugger off, Paulie's gone. Happy now?' She batted away the tiny copter as it dipped and swerved, skimming the air around North and Fang, before zipping up and away again. She didn't seem to think it was out of the ordinary, so North let it go. He wondered what crime Paulie had committed to be despatched without even the chance to clear his desk.

'Can I get you anything, Esme? A vanilla latte?' Jarrod was half out of his seat already. He had it bad, North thought.

His boss shook her head, but spared him a wink as if to say that as soon as she needed something, she had every confidence he'd be all over it. With a final yearning look, Jarrod settled back into his ergonomically designed seat.

The red jumpsuit and the brunette hair swept back into a severe ponytail accentuated the violet-blue eyes, but North couldn't work out whether the dark shadows under them were due to the beating she'd taken or a chronic lack of sleep. As the violet eyes met his, there was a bleakness to them. He knew what she'd done, and she knew he knew, and under the make-up a blush washed up over her cheeks, but she kept her chin high.

Fang had hacked into the Met Police server for details of the break-in Hone had talked about. North wondered how they'd managed to keep the intruder's untimely death out of the press, until he realized that the one-eyed man would have made sure of it.

Esme Sullivan Hawke had been attacked in her own home in what was assumed to be a burglary that went wrong. The police phrased it all in their own pedestrian way, but it boiled down to the fact that finding a naked woman, alone and vulnerable, the burglar went from opportunist thief to would-be rapist. And in exactly the same time frame, householder Esme Sullivan Hawke went from victim to killer. Fang had pulled up the unusually speedy CPS decision not to prosecute. Any trial would have been a circus and no jury in this world would convict the woman in front of him. But even if the Crown Prosecution Service had the temerity to decide differently, North was sure Edmund Hone would have changed their minds.

He thought back to the first time he'd killed a man – the abusive boyfriend of his drug-addled mother, who had battered her half to death. North had been thirteen at the time. He'd tried to defend her, to pull her attacker off her, and was knocked out for his trouble. When he came to, the teenage North found a hammer and the right moment. He'd never regretted it, not the act nor the years he spent behind bars because of it. But he'd never forgotten it either, nor the way he'd realized, staring down at the corpse, that he'd chosen a path he hadn't even known was there. That his own life was altogether different than it might otherwise have been. Sympathy surged up for the woman across from him now. She'd survived something appalling, and he was astonished she'd managed to turn the tables on her attacker, let alone be back at work running her company.

'I'm sorry – there's way too much going on. Where are my manners?' Esme extended her hand in greeting, first to Fang and then to him. As he took it, he received a tiny shock as if she were charged and the energy had leapt from her to him. She squeezed harder, placed her other hand over his to draw him in towards her. 'My uncle is a hard man to impress, but he speaks very highly of you.' She was talking about the one-eyed man as if he were a human being rather than a bastard of the first order.

Her hands were warm around his. She held his gaze, and he caught her almost silent sigh as she released him, reaching out to take hold of the security passes Jarrod had slid on to the desk.

Behind her back, Fang's expression went from curious to mutinous. She mouthed, *My uncle speaks very highly of you*, casting her eyes upwards while she flicked one of her stubby plaits as if flipping long wavy hair. Esme Sullivan Hawke could be as charming as she wanted, but if she had the same blood running in her veins as the one-eyed man, she was nothing to Fang.

'Will you both come with me?' Esme said. She seemed to be fighting a smile and North wondered if she'd caught something of Fang's gesture reflected in one of the shiny surfaces that surrounded them. 'I'd like you to meet someone, and I don't have much time.'

North had to hope that wasn't true.

16

'For God's sake, I told you no, Esme, and I bloody meant it.' The shout from across the other side of the atrium was loud enough to shatter glass. 'Do you not think we have enough on right now!'

Tobias Hawke had a distinct motion when walking. North already knew from Fang's research that he used a state-of-the-art, AI-enabled prosthetic, made of tungsten steel and graphite, embedded with a micro-computer that interpreted signals from his stump. He'd designed it himself and the prototype had been adopted across the world. The Hawke19 increased joint flexibility, mobility, reliability and comfort, and users raved about it. He'd also designed a Hawke19(econ) made of cheaper materials, to allow developing countries to get in on the act at a fraction of the price. In the econ model, solar power recharged the prosthetic. In an interview, he'd told the journalist it never crossed his mind to do anything other than make the design free. It seemed an odd thing for the scientist to do after everything Fang said about him being 'difficult'.

At the moment, however, walking appeared to be an effort for the scientist, and he was glowering as he limped towards them, the silver-topped cane in his hand. North knew Tobias was the same age as his wife, but he'd have figured him for a good ten years older. The scientist looked ravaged with exhaustion.

North pictured the nineteen-year-old boy sawing away at his own leg with a Swiss Army knife and a sharp piece of sheet metal from the wreckage. What did it take to mutilate yourself? To make that sacrifice because you kept the bigger picture in mind? To decide to live at all costs? Was it desperation? Ruthlessness? Sheer bloody-mindedness? Weaker or less resourceful men would have accepted their fate and died there.

Once you knew about the leg, though, it was impossible not to think about what he'd done to himself. And what a man had done was, in North's experience, the only evidence you needed of the nature of that man. Tobias Hawke was a ruthless bastard, used to making difficult decisions, willing and able to leave part of himself behind if that's what it took to survive. What North wanted to know was whether he was willing to leave his wife behind in the same way as he'd left his own leg. Because something about the story of the break-in and the attack on Esme Sullivan Hawke didn't make sense.

North held out his hand to shake Hawke's, but the scientist ignored it.

'Esme. What on earth are you thinking?' Tobias gave every appearance of being furious with his wife. 'Tell Bonnie and Clyde to clear off or I bloody will.'

North sensed Jarrod shrink down into his chair and

heard him start hammering at his keyboard as if entirely oblivious to the row taking place in front of him.

'Tobias.' The tone of voice Esme used would have frozen a train to its tracks. 'I want to know why I was attacked. This is happening.' She turned her back on her husband. 'Do excuse my husband. He's under the impression normal rules of civilized behaviour don't apply to him.' Esme handed North and Fang their security passes and set off at what could be described as a sprint. With a wink, Fang trotted after her. Tobias let out a stream of invective, but was forced to follow on behind. North kept pace with him.

'Esme's uncle…' – North heard Fang hiss like a snake about to strike – '… is paranoid.' Tobias was raging. 'For the last two days, he's had his people lurking around our foyer and outside the apartment. We don't need them and we don't need you. Our security system here is state of the art. No one can get to Esme even if they wanted to, which they don't.' North didn't think it politic to mention the handgun he himself had holstered at his waist, covered over by his donkey jacket.

Through the doors, the entire building was more of a cathedral or an art gallery than an office, and despite the fact the foyer resembled a pyramid, they appeared to be walking around in ever-widening circles, with a waist-high glass railing the only thing between them and a sheer drop. North glanced down, attempting to fix his location by finding Jarrod, and was hit by a sudden sense of vertigo.

Below them, the foyer where they had come in minutes before grew smaller and smaller as the corridor around the inside of the building spiralled upwards. At first, he thought the movement back and forth was the birds he'd glimpsed earlier, but then he realized the void was full of small drones like the one that had buzzed around Esme. Most were quadcopters with four legs and four rotors, each with a different orientation, spin and speed. They dodged and darted, their motors buzzing and their blades whirring in perpetual motion. Most were too small to be delivering anything, although he caught sight of a larger drone with what looked like a cup of coffee locked into some kind of binding. They had to have cameras, he thought. Cameras and microphones and sensory detectors; wireless, GPS, accelerometers and gyroscopes. Drones were nothing new, but he'd never seen them on this sort of scale before.

'What's with the drones?' Fang said, balancing herself on the rail, feet dangling, before leaning out into the void and reaching out a starfish hand to snatch one from the sky.

'They're just one element of what we do.' Taking hold of her collar, and without ceremony, Tobias hauled Fang back in before she plunged to her death. 'We're spinning off in all directions – growth is exponential. Our primary focus was initially data analytics for medical tech, but we've had to hive off derivative research into natural language processing, sentience, bias, quantum computing, natural sciences, neuroscience, cyber security, control systems, aggregation, object classification, recognition, optimization, scaling, relational reasoning, robotics and engineering.'

North figured he'd get Fang to explain it to him later.

'We're growing faster than we can cope with,' Esme said. 'When people come to us, we let them choose where they want to invest their time and energies. They have an idea and they get to follow it through. As an exercise in avoiding bias, Tobias wanted to see what happened if the system was allowed to decide to gather its own data from the company.'

North had the feeling Esme had used Tobias's name as a peace offering to her husband.

'He wanted to see what that general information gathering exercise taught the machine. See if the system itself helped us identify where we should be concentrating our efforts. We started off with info-gathering drones as part of that. Before we could start though, we had to make advances in positioning and orientation – which means we now have drones here that can work inside buildings as well as out in the open air.'

'Somebody is hacking your hardware for the coffee run,' North said, as a second drone with a coffee payload zipped by.

Esme smiled. She had a great smile, he thought. It started behind her eyes and lit up her entire face. 'Mankind has been flying for more than a hundred years. I like to think the Wright brothers would approve of flat-white airdrops.'

Tobias leant out like Fang before him, gripping the rail with both hands. 'Remember, that machine is worth more than you are!' he shouted as a figure in a crash helmet and padded suit stepped out into nothingness, his foot landing on the platform of the biggest type of drone hovering at the way station. The drone rider held tight to a bar, brought his other foot across and, with a jerk, the drone took off into space, banging against the rail as it went. There were jeers from the gathered spectators and Fang made a noise in the back of her throat that North translated into acute and utter envy. 'You're fired. You hear me – fired!' Tobias yelled at the drone rider as he zipped past them.

'I rather think you've fired enough people for one day,' his wife said, and Tobias glared at her.

'What do you do, Esme?' Fang asked.

Esme looked down at the girl. 'I run the company,' she said. 'I keep the show on the road day-to-day, I make sure the talent is happy and working effectively. But the key part of my work here is ethics.'

'What's the point of ethics? Don't people know what's right and wrong without being told? We do.' Fang gestured at herself and then at North.

Esme's gaze took in North without seeing him as she considered Fang's question, and he figured she was remembering killing her attacker. 'Not always,' she said, and her eyes went to her husband as if seeking consolation.

North had to guess Esme considered herself a moral being, or she would never have chosen her field. But now she was also a killer. Where did that leave her? Esme started walking again, faster than before, as if there was a clock running and she needed to beat it.

They followed her. Everywhere he looked, young people were bent over computers, their rapt gazes fixed on their screens, their fingers never pausing, locked together as if they were one and the same thing. If anyone in the building was over forty, North had yet to see them.

Esme halted in her tracks, pushing open a door and standing back to allow them past. A floor-to-ceiling window looked out on to London's cityscape and the trains moving in and out of King's Cross station. In front of it, facing into the room rather than out to the view, stood a huge mahogany and brushed-steel desk, and opposite it was a wall made up of a dozen screens. In one corner was a small capsule lift with a brass door, and to the left of the desk a full-length glass wall overlooking the atrium, while shelves filled with books, black-and-white prints and a stopped clock made up the final wall. The place was stylish but somehow brutal. It had to be Tobias's office rather than hers.

Tobias slammed the door behind them, his voice loud and angry. 'For the last time, Esme, we don't need spooks poking their noses into our business.'

Surely Tobias owed his wife a greater duty of care, North thought. She'd been attacked, shouldn't that worry him?

'We're not spooks,' Fang chipped in. 'I checked.'

'That is exactly the kind of thing an effing spook would say,' he said, his black eyebrows lifting into his mane of white hair as he peered back at Fang. 'How old are you? Shouldn't you be in school?'

'Facial recognition combined with accent detection suggests your guest is Fangfang Yu...'

Fang swung round, but there was no one behind her aside from a ventriloquist puppet with orange woollen hair slumped on a shelf at eye level. Fang shook her head as if she were trying to get water out of her ears as the disembodied voice carried on. '... Fangfang is fourteen years of age and born and raised in the east end of Newcastle upon Tyne. She is the only daughter of Mae Yu (formerly Po) and survives her father, Wei Yu.'

The girl took a step closer to the shelves, her narrowed eyes fixed on the puppet dressed in a fisherman's smock, its painted face huge and ugly with an ear-to-ear smile and goggly black eyes.

The pleasant voice carried on. 'Although young, she is believed to possess a private fortune of considerable means diverted from an extra-governmental agency known as the Board last year.' Fang stopped moving to listen. Her cyber skills had made both Fang and North hugely wealthy. 'No legal claim has been made for the recovery of that money. Over the last three months, multimillion-pound donations have been made to children's charities, food banks, schools and universities across the country as well as any number of international aid agencies. Donations which tax authorities have been unable to trace or identify. Fangfang Yu has been posited as the donor by this country's intelligence agency.' Which meant Hone knew they had taken the money. Fang started moving again. 'School records indicate an IQ of 171, which, by the way, is higher than yours, Tobias.' North registered amusement in the digitized voice. Which he knew to be impossible. How had Tobias programmed the voice to communicate humour? The machine itself couldn't 'feel' it, so had to be faking it. Programmed to sound human. Was it the words themselves? The tone? Was it a device to defuse tension? 'Information on Fangfang Yu held by this government's intelligence service has been heavily redacted, but she is a known cyber hacker with considerable skills.'

Fang's hand was already lifting the puppet from the shelf, and North glimpsed a wooden stick and a metal handle under the smock. Tobias opened his mouth as if to stop her, but Esme laid a restraining hand on his sleeve. There had to be a camera somewhere, North thought, and some sort of microphone as well as a speaker, judging by the quality of the sound.

'Hello Fangfang, my name is Syd. I'd like to say…' – the machine called Syd paused, as if considering exactly what to say – '… what a pleasure it is to meet you, in person as it were.'

17

'You're unveiling a voice-activated personal assistant at the gala?' Fang's hand was already inside the puppet. 'Like Siri. Or Alexa? Or Cortana?'

Fang removed a gleaming, oversized tablet from inside the puppet and placed it back on the shelf. 'That's no biggie.' The puppet sat upright in her arms, its head swivelling back and forth as she worked it. 'Digital assistants are beyond stupid,' Fang said into the puppet's face.

'Syd is more than an "assistant",' Tobias intervened. He snatched the puppet from Fang, sat it back over the tablet and settled the smock to his satisfaction.

'Show them, Tobias.' Esme sounded tired, North thought. Killing someone could do that to you. 'I'm sure they've signed the Official Secrets Act.'

'Absolutely,' Fang said.

They hadn't. Doubtless they should. But then Hone would probably kill them if they said anything, so their discretion was pretty much guaranteed.

Tobias beckoned them over to the computer at his desk

as his wife folded herself into an easy chair alongside. He moved a black-and-white photograph of a freckle-faced boy North knew to be his lost son and placed his cane along the desk. 'Syd, activate "Medical",' he ordered.

Rapidly streaming columns of numbers and symbols filled Tobias's screen. His long fingers flew over the keyboard, populating boxes, shifting columns and lines – mathematics everywhere. 'We'd been working for ten years without getting very far but this is where we first moved up a gear with Syd.' He spoke over his shoulder, knowing they were there, but not entirely willing to break from his screen and engage with them, now he was captured by his coding. 'Five years ago, the government bypassed UK data protection laws to release all UK medical records for children from birth up to the age of eighteen to Derkind.' Five years ago their child had died, North thought. Had they had the clout to push for the release of the records even then?

'I don't remember that happening,' North said.

'Let's say they didn't make a big deal out of it,' Esme said, one eyebrow raised.

'They kept it quiet?'

'People broadcast their entire lives on social media but jump up and down about their "right to privacy" whenever the mood strikes.' Tobias was scornful.

His wife nodded, her elbows resting on her knees, the lovely face cupped in the palms of her hands. 'We're aware of the confidentiality issues for the individual, but we needed to think big-picture – of the gain at stake for society at large.'

Tobias slumped in his chair, his body leaning towards them. He gestured towards the computer. 'On this screen are patients, not numbers – some of these children are being treated as we speak. Within these brackets is DNA coding, along with treatment plans and diagnoses. These are blood pressures and liver functions and kidney functions. These are a million tragedies of children who should be healthy. Some of them are…' – he hesitated, his gaze on his wife, before continuing – '… dead. But the vast majority are still alive. And we're helping make them better.

'We input the data via text, scans and X-rays, and our algorithms can discern patterns in a raft of childhood cancers. At the press of a button, we know whether a particular medication is worth trying. That child doesn't have to be subjected to chemotherapy or radiation, when something else might suit them better. Along with DNA sequencing, we can tweak each therapy for each child with unbelievable precision. We will prolong lives that would otherwise be lost. Eventually we can make the jump to other childhood diseases, to adult cancers and to other adult diseases. Pharmaceutical companies have invested billions of pounds in drugs and now they are investing billions of pounds in AI. This program is the biggest advance in medicine since penicillin. It is transformative and if anyone needed evidence of the benefits of AI…' – there was no mistaking the emotion in Tobias's voice – '… it's right here, in children's lives. Regrettably, we've just been hit by a major leak of our medical work.'

North thought back to the cardboard box of the colleague's belongings, to Jarrod's comment – *outrageous*. Paulie Holliday had been blamed for the leak and fired unceremoniously.

'For some companies, it would be the end of the road,

but not for us.' Hawke hesitated as if deciding whether to carry on or not. 'I don't think I should say any more, Esme.'

'In for a penny,' she said, standing. Her hands went to her hips as she stared out through the glass wall, watching the drones. As if she were thinking hard about other things. North had to drag his own gaze away from her.

'Syd isn't a digital assistant – Syd has consciousness. We're unveiling her at a gala at the British Museum tonight.' Tobias's voice held a note of profound reverence. 'Revealing the fact there is another intelligence in the universe – an intelligence, moreover, with the ability to reason and to distinguish right from wrong.

'Most AI systems are narrow. They do one thing very well. Like classifying and recommending a programme of treatment for specific cancers, as we've done here. Nobody has anything like Syd though. This is the world's first general AI system. Syd is the holy grail – a machine that can both reason and apply common sense. She's already beyond human intelligence. Up to now, she's been running on an air-gapped system within Derkind – boxed in—'

Fang interrupted. 'It isn't air-gapped. She knew stuff about me.'

Tobias grinned and North glimpsed something of what Esme must see in him – the charisma. 'Esme's uncle provided us with information on both of you. We inputted it as we do with everything that comes into Derkind.'

'That's a cheap trick.' Fang's scorn was real.

'Blame my wife. I believe Syd is ready to go out into the world; my wife disagrees.'

'We have a moral obligation to tell the world where we are with Syd – as a matter of some urgency, which is what the gala is about. But letting Syd loose on that world is a different thing completely. That can't happen. Tobias knows that I have fundamental concerns about Syd. I'm sorry, but there are too many unknowns about what would happen next. Any decision on Syd's future has to be a collective decision taken at intergovernmental level.'

'I've told you – I can install a kill switch.' Tobias didn't even try to control his impatience.

'It's too much of a risk.' Esme's tone was heated. As if they were picking up the threads of a row that had been going on for days.

Tobias waved a dismissive hand in his wife's direction. 'Thanks to my overly scrupulous wife, Syd isn't linked up to the internet or indeed to any computers other than our own. We've built safeguarding algorithms into the system – we've ensured Syd's models conform to human values of fairness, reciprocity and curiosity. She appears to be a moral creature.'

'Obviously it isn't easy to spell out a value like loyalty in software code,' Esme said, her arms crossed over her body as if she was cold or in need of comfort. 'And we have a fundamental problem establishing how Syd conceives of its own purpose. What is its goal? How is it going to reach it? Is there any chance that will be in a way that's disastrous for humankind? I predict it will be years till we have fully explored the ramifications of allowing Syd into the wild. Then and only then will we – as a species – be able to make that call. But for the moment at least, I know which side of the argument I'm on. A free-range Syd is dangerous to humanity.'

Tobias spoke over his wife's last few words. He didn't like

the implied criticism of his machine, North thought. Didn't like the idea that Syd might be dangerous. 'Once Syd is out, communicating with other systems, it's true that we can't know how she will act. But the internet is the most effective communication and information distribution network the world has ever seen and the more data and systems Syd has access to, the faster she'll learn and the better she'll be.'

North could hear Fang's gum-chewing getting faster and faster. The kid was locked on.

'You're talking about Syd getting out. But air-gapping isn't a failsafe in terms of security. Hackers can get in via flash drives or radio waves,' Fang said. 'You've already had one breach. Syd could get infected or destroyed like that.' She snapped her fingers.

'Exactly. Bearing in mind we've had the medical leak,' Tobias said, 'at Esme's insistence, I've moved the machine learning code for the ensemble of models – the essence, as it were, of "Syd" – out of our cloud and into the tablet on that shelf to safeguard the work. The tablet is a prototype I was working on a couple of years ago. I've adapted it – engineering it myself so it can cope.'

They all stared at the goggle-eyed puppet. It didn't look like it was sitting on a revolution.

'Tonight we announce what we have with Syd,' Esme said. 'We warn the world what's heading their way. No offence, Syd.'

'None taken, Esme.' The digitized voice sounded interested and entirely relaxed.

North shook his head.

Esme carried on as if it were normal to apologize to a machine. 'I'm convinced I was attacked because of what we're doing here. And I'm not going to feel safe until we're through the other side of the gala. That's why I want you around, North.'

The buzzing North had been aware of earlier had got louder. Through the office window, North could see more drones. They were smaller again, each one the size of a bird, and they swept and swerved together. Like a flock, he thought. Was there a programmer sitting somewhere at his screen making it happen, he wondered, or was Syd putting on a display just for him. Because the more he thought about it, the less he liked the idea of a swarm of drones controlled by a thinking machine.

Tobias frowned as he looked at his wife. 'Esme, we've been to hell and back together. We wanted this, remember. We've been working towards tonight for a very long time. And...' – he spoke slowly, as if reluctant to voice his thoughts – '... it's only a couple of days since you killed a man. Every time you walk in the front door it must bring it all back. After the gala, I'm moving us out of that place. We'll sell it and I want you to see someone. To get some sort of perspective.'

Beside him, Esme paled.

'The attack on my wife is an unfortunate coincidence. There were a quarter of a million violent crimes in London this year alone,' Hawke carried on regardless. 'If I thought I couldn't keep my own wife safe, then of course I'd want her protected by someone like you.' North took a second to wonder how the one-eyed man had phrased the recommendation of 'someone like him'. Whether he'd mentioned lethal violence.

'But we don't need you. Tonight's gala is happening, then

Esme can relax, and as far as the medical leak goes, I've already fired the man responsible first thing this morning.'

Esme opened her mouth, then closed it as her husband kept talking. Her lips were drawn in a tight line. North wondered if she hadn't agreed with her husband's decision.

'Paulie Holliday is a gullible idiot, I trusted him more than was wise. But Paulie is out, Esme, and that's the end of it.' Hawke turned away from his wife and towards North. 'I'll ask you to treat with confidence what you've heard today, and forgive my rudeness. I'm sure you're very good at what you do.' Standing up from the desk, Tobias held out his hand. North took it – there was no alternative – and the two men shook. 'But this is a big day for us and you're wasting our time here. Syd and I need to get back to work – I'll have someone show you out.'

18

Fang was sullen as they left Derkind. Abandoning him as he stood for a second to get his bearings, she elbowed her way through the back-and-forth streams of people en route to work, jostling and pushing them aside. The streets around King's Cross were full. Not just of tourists and travellers, but with the young and gifted at ease with the world they found themselves in. Happy making big money via cutting-edge technology no one else understood, but everyone wanted.

Following in her slipstream, North had the distinct impression Fang would have preferred to stay with Tobias Hawke, his wife, and his futuristic AGI system, Syd. That she hated the fact Hawke had cast her back out into the real world.

'This is all good, Fang.' He caught her up, touching her arm, and she turned to face him, stopping in the middle of the pavement, making the oncoming wave of London pedestrians break over and around them. North ignored the irritation and disapproval of strangers.

It was barely half past eight in the morning and the job was over before it had really begun. Before it got messy. Which worked for him. 'Hawke doesn't want us. I'll tell Hone it's a no-go and he'll give you back your mum, because. I'll make sure he does.' Hone wasn't going to be happy, but North didn't much care about making Hone happy. As for him, he couldn't risk heading back to Berlin by any normal route, so maybe he'd stay in London anyway. Do whatever else Hone would want doing in exchange for letting Fang's mum go. And last he heard, Japanese whisky was as available in London as it was in Berlin.

Fang balled up her fist and punched him hard in his chest. It didn't hurt, but he figured she wanted it to. Around him, the passers-by who'd been so keen to move them on pulled away, giving them space. 'Moron-person, you do not get to go boohoo again.' She used her index finger to drill into his pectoral muscle. It hurt more than the punch. 'Your midlife crisis is done. Your crying days are over.' She chopped through the air with the side of her hand. 'Understand? This is not about what happened before. This is about what is happening right now – to me. I matter. My mum matters.'

North had never seen Fang truly angry. And he had once seen her shoot a man in the face. She hadn't even been angry then; she'd given it due consideration and crushed a cockroach under her glittering Dr. Martens. But an incandescent Fang had the white-hot power of a nuclear explosion. She was liable to take out herself and everyone else within a thousand-mile radius. North raised his palms in surrender, and Fang sucked down a long slow breath, as if she was trying to calm herself.

'Hone doesn't care what Tobias Hawke thinks.' She spoke slowly, as if to give North adequate time to follow her line of argument. 'And he doesn't care about Syd. Hone wants Esme looked after, dodo. We don't get out from this that easy. We are in it till the end, which means what happened in there is bad, bad, bad. Tobias Hawke doesn't want our help – that means he won't help us either. And my mum is feeble, North. She's like you – she cries about everything.'

North chose to ignore the insult.

'She will never cut it halfway across the world without me, and I don't want to live in China, all right?'

Fang's voice trailed off, fury burning itself out as quickly as it had come. She was fourteen and it was up to her to save her mum and she was blowing it.

He felt his own face screw up in disgust at himself. Fang was right. He'd felt relief when Tobias showed them the door. He could walk out free and clear. He'd been a nice guy, he'd come when he was called, he'd played the game by Hone's rules, he'd offered to help and the offer had been rejected. He'd been selfish and blinkered. And he'd underestimated Fang and treated her like another teenager, thinking that he would sort things for her. Fang wasn't sulking because Derkind was working on a future that she wanted to be part of. She was gutted because if they couldn't find out what was going wrong at Derkind, Hone would put her mother on a plane. Under his breath, North cursed Tobias Hawke and Hone with him.

He looked down at the pavement they were walking along. Cracks ran the length and width of it across every stone, as if the pavement itself was waiting to open up into a sinkhole and swallow down the unsuspecting. He and

Fang were in the spider's web, and the more they struggled against that fact, the worse it was going to get for them. They had to move quietly, and find however many spiders there were, kill each and every one, and then and only then get the hell out of there.

'You're right. My "booze and boohoo days" are over. Small note, though – I am way too young for a midlife crisis, right?'

He thought there might have been the glimmer of a smile somewhere behind the Joe 90 glasses, but it was difficult to tell.

They started walking again.

'As for Hawke not cooperating – Fang, do you need Hawke's permission?' It was a serious question. 'Point of fact, do you need anyone to give you permission for anything?'

Fang sucked at her lower lip as she thought about it. 'She's okay, but I don't like him, even if he did chew off his own foot,' she said. 'Why is he so keen to keep us out?'

North shrugged. The need to be the alpha male in any and all situations? The urge to keep Hone and his spooks out of his company? The fact he didn't need the distraction hours before an announcement that he was about to change the world? Whatever Hawke's reasons, North had to focus on the more immediate problem of protecting Esme Sullivan Hawke, so that he could get Fang's mother back home.

'Something's off,' Fang said. 'Not least because they've had a massive hack and he fires the guy responsible and moves on – completely fine. Wouldn't you expect a man on that short a fuse still to be ranting about it?'

'He's got something bigger going on with Syd.'

'Even so.'

North thought back to the photograph of the three men – Hawke the inventor, Rafferty the politician, and Kirkham the general.

'He's such an idiot I don't even feel bad about this.' She pulled a tiny drone out of her pocket and held it in the palm of her hand. At some point, she had managed to pluck one from the air without falling to her death.

'Fang, you stole his intellectual property.'

'Property is theft. I read that on a T-shirt.' She slid it back into her pocket. 'And this cutey basically flew into my jacket so it doesn't count.'

North frowned. 'I've seen what a drone can do out in the field. Esme didn't mention the fact that they aren't just about surveillance and espressos and shopping deliveries. The military don't call them drones, they call them unmanned aircraft systems or unmanned aerial combat vehicles, and they can and do carry missiles.'

Fang raised an eyebrow. 'Look at you, knowing things all by yourself, without me having to tell you.'

'Not to ruin my rep, but who is Enrico Fermi? The guy quoted in the foyer.'

Fang looked wide-eyed at North's ignorance, but he pretended not to notice. 'Fermi built the world's first nuclear reactor,' she said 'Chicago Pile-1. He used it to create a self-sustaining nuclear chain reaction. Part and parcel of how we have nuclear energy. Not to mention the two atomic bombs they dropped.'

Energy and bombs. Good and bad. North wondered whether Tobias thought there were parallels with his AI work.

'And that pledge on the wall?'

'As stated, it's against autonomous weapons systems – weapons that identify, target and kill without being told to do it by a human. Shall I tell you something else you don't know?' Fang waited. He thought she was enjoying it. He nodded.

'Derkind comes from the German. Der Kinder. Of the child. Derkind is also an anagram of the word "kindred". Syd is family to Hawke. Unlike that guy he fired, apparently. I remember his name from the research – Paulie Holliday has been with them since 2013. Hawke recruited him after he read his thesis.'

Hawke had shown no emotion about Paulie Holliday. No regret or anger.

A colleague had cleared Paulie's desk for him – acquired a cardboard box, swept his personal possessions into it and sent it all down to Jarrod at reception to be biked round. But why would someone who had been with Tobias and Esme for years choose to leak a medical tech program days before the company went public with Syd? North didn't claim to know much about AI, but even he knew that Syd was huge. From the outside, working at Derkind, with its espresso drones and its superintelligent computer, looked like Nerd Heaven. Even before the global launch of a transformative intelligent learning system. So why would Paulie, or anyone else, not want to be part of that? Why would Paulie sabotage his own career at the very moment the company was about to go stratospheric?

'This is what we do know: Esme was attacked in her own home and almost killed,' North said, holding up his index finger.

'There was a massive leak of intellectual property and the guy blamed for it was fired.' Fang held up two fingers.

'They have a "conscious" computer, which is going to be huge.' North held up three fingers and briefly wondered if it looked like he was a boy scout swearing allegiance to the monarch.

'And Tobias Hawke is a jerk.' Fang tucked her thumb into her palm and held up four fingers.

'What we have to do now is figure out if those things are connected,' North said. 'Let's start with the ex-employee of the month, Paulie Holliday. Maybe he can tell us.'

North figured Fang's mood could only improve if he told her to head back to Plug's and hack into Derkind's employment records for Paulie's address. Paulie had to know something – the question was what?

19

Hackney

The country's Number 1 Nerd, at least according to his coffee mug, lived above a greasy spoon in Hackney. Behind the plate glass, five miles and a world away from Derkind, the café's customers clutched butties and viewed the passing cars and buses like they were a satellite TV channel they'd switch off if only they could find the remote.

Number 48B Trollope Road had a cheap MDF door and a moulded plastic knocker that didn't knock. North pushed the buzzer, but there was no response. It had started to rain.

'What else do you know, Fang?' He turned up the collar on his donkey jacket and raised a finger to the Bluetooth earbud in an attempt to hear her. Fang had established her nerve centre in Plug's embalming room. Plug said he'd offered her the lounge, but the kid preferred the atmosphere amid the metal gurneys and drains – said it was more 'Zen'.

'Paulie Holliday is a neuroscientist. He went to one

of the roughest schools in Hackney,' she said. 'Picked up stellar results and walked into a psychology degree at University College London, then a PhD in theoretical and computational neuroscience and machine learning. Dumbing this down for present company...'

'Insulting, but fair comment.'

'... the brain is still the most efficient computer out there, and the more we understand about how our brains work, the more we can develop the learning capabilities of computer systems. Paulie was all set for a brilliant career in academia till Hawke persuaded him to come to Derkind. I'm sending you over a pic. It looks like they're mates.'

His phone pinged and he opened the attachment of a photograph of a chubby bald man and the white-maned Hawke together in a restaurant. Paulie leaning in towards Hawke as he reached across the table for a bottle of wine. Both looking up as the photographer called for their attention. Judging by the softness in Hawke's eye, North guessed the photographer was Esme.

He pressed Paulie's buzzer again – there was a chance he hadn't heard it because of the shouting carrying down the stairs and straight through the cheap door to whoever happened to be passing. Paulie appeared to be having a full-on domestic.

'I've shaken his piggybank up and down.' Fang sounded indifferent. As if that was normal practice for a fourteen-year-old with time on her hands. North winced as he slid a plastic card he kept specially for such moments between the door and the doorjamb, finding the plate before sliding the card over the latch and pressing hard. 'Shaken his piggybank' meant hacking her way past God knows how many banking firewalls and encryptions, and breaking he didn't want to think how many laws.

The front door popped open. No one in the café noticed a thing. There was an outside chance he was a bad role model.

'Nothing unusual unless you count a massive wedge of cash into his mother's account every month and even more into his sister's – she's a single mum. But nothing odd so far. Other than an unhealthy interest in hair transplants. Also, he plays way too much *Call of Duty* and totally sucks. Check in later, dodo.'

Job done, she disconnected before he could tell her to be careful. But she wouldn't listen anyway.

Inside the flats, the smell of damp and rancid fat made him wrinkle his nose. It was a narrow entrance, the floor of which was covered in flyers for cheap pizzas and double glazing. Paulie couldn't be bothered to pick them up and bin them. Did that make him careless? Careless enough to mess up? Or did his home not matter because he spent every iota of energy deciding how to sabotage Tobias Hawke's life's work? Because if Hawke was right and Paulie was to blame for the leak – as North saw it, the young scientist was either criminally negligent or wilfully culpable.

Taking care not to make a noise and with his fingers splayed against the MDF, North pressed the door shut behind him and took the stairs two at a time. Above him, a door slammed with enough force to shake the plaster walls – he heard the running girl before he saw her. Dressed in a tartan miniskirt, knee-high boots and a raincoat, the Chinese girl was early twenties, her long dark hair streaming behind her. Moving so fast that she crashed into him, and he had to hold her steady to stop them both toppling down the stairs. 'So sorry,' she said, bowing her head before lifting desperate eyes to meet his. They were surprisingly blue, and brimful of tears.

'Are you okay?' he asked – which was, he decided, a stupid question, since the girl was patently distraught. She bit her lip, as if frightened of what might come out of her own mouth, trying and failing to nod. He let go of her arms and hated himself for doing it. Whoever this blue-eyed girl was, she needed help. But as soon as his hands moved away from her, she took flight, pounding down the stairs and banging through the front door. She didn't look back.

So Paulie was the kind to make a girl cry like her heart was breaking. That didn't make North warm to him.

The memory of jasmine perfume still hung in the air as he knocked at the door of the flat. It swung open, as if Paulie thought the girl might have thought better of it and come back to him. Plump and hairless in a yellow and black onesie, he blinked repeatedly behind small round glasses as he took in North's bulk. Punching above his weight with the blue-eyed girl, North thought.

'Having a bad day, are we, sunshine?' he said, and, using the palm of his hand, he pushed Paulie back into the room with a steady pressure. There was no violence in it and there didn't have to be, because Paulie made no attempt to fight back.

'Is this about the money? I'll pay you the rest of it, I promise, but I need the papers first.' Paulie was trying hard to sound tough but his eyes, which were missing eyelashes, lent him the defenceless look of something only just born.

Alopecia, North was guessing. He guided Paulie over to a broken-down armchair and eased him into it. The guy's onesie said he was in Hufflepuff. Paulie was a Harry Potter fan. Of course he was.

'What papers are those?'

Paulie's naked brows gathered together, confused. 'The passport. Isn't that why you're here?'

Paulie was talking money and fake passports. The girl who had fled down the stairs was Chinese. The medical program had turned up in China, which led to the obvious conclusion that Paulie was guilty as charged. Drawing up a knackered bentwood chair, North used it to sit so close to Paulie that their knees touched. In his experience, intimidation and imagination worked just as well as physical violence with those whose day-to-day reality was generally one of social norms. 'We'll circle back to the passport. What I want to know right this second is who you sold Hawke out to and what else you've given them?'

Paulie's face clouded. 'You need to leave,' he said, and went to stand up.

North placed his hand on Paulie's shoulder, pushing him back down into his seat, and the scientist started to laugh. An odd reaction – maybe the guy was in shock. That wouldn't do, North needed his attention. 'Things aren't going your way, Paulie. You've been fired.'

Paulie stopped laughing.

'Wrongfully.' His tone was one of hurt and resentment. 'Esme will sort it.'

'She's not doing a great job so far. But then she's recovering from the attack. Did you have anything to do with that, Paulie?'

A look of outrage crossed the scientist's face. 'How dare you! Esme is one of my closest friends.'

'All right. Why did you leak the program?' North pictured Tobias's face. The accusation. *He must have got greedy*. The place was a dump. But where was the money, if Paulie sold Hawke out to dark forces? Surely he would live somewhere that smelled better than this?

'Who are you? If this is another of Tobias's games, you can tell him to go to hell.' Paulie wasn't giving up the goods as easily as North had hoped. He switched tack. 'How much money did you give them for the passport, Paulie?'

The hum from the road was loud in the flat, and from downstairs came the chinking of china cups and the metallic rattling of cutlery. It was probably quieter out on the street.

'I have no idea who you are. Why should I tell you anything?'

'Paulie, from where I'm sitting you look like you could do with all the help you can get. So let's play make-believe – you and I are fresh off the Hogwarts train and we're big magical buddies. How much did you give them for the passport, my Hufflepuff friend?'

Paulie pulled at his fingers and his knuckles popped. 'Can you really help me?'

'Not if you don't tell me what's going on.'

Paulie exhaled a burst of air, as if he'd suddenly remembered he'd been holding his breath. 'Three thousand pounds as a down payment.'

They'd seen him coming.

'Who did you go to?'

'A mate I went to school with years ago knows some

Romanians. He said I didn't want to know their names, but they could get me what I needed. We met in a pub.' He named a notorious dive North knew, because he knew London better than he knew his own face. He hoped Paulie hadn't worn the onesie.

'They're not bringing you any passport. You've been had.' They'd seen the scientist's terror at what he was doing, the trembling and bug-eyed innocence. They would have charged him three times the going rate before giving him something they'd knocked up at the kitchen table that wouldn't fool a two-year-old.

To North's astonishment, Paulie began to cry. There was no noise, only a steady stream of tears down the smooth, hairless cheeks. First the crying girl on the stairs and now a hairless neuroscientist weeping as if the world was ending. If he was guilty of the medical tech leak, Paulie had to be the worst criminal mastermind ever. 'Tell me what's going on here, Paulie, all of it, and maybe I can get you what you need.'

Paulie's palms were sweaty and his eyes still damp as he took hold of North's hand. 'You can do that? Really? Thank you. Thank you.' He kept hold. On exercise in Lithuania, North once saved another soldier whose parachute failed and he had been less grateful than this. 'I didn't steal the program…' North stood up as if to go, and Paulie tugged him back down by his sleeve. 'I swear on the Holy Bible that I didn't.'

'Tobias says differently.' If North had taken out a knife and carved the name of his former boss into his soft belly, Paulie could not have looked more devastated. He put his head in his hands, the crown shiny and vulnerable.

'Are you the police?'

He wasn't police and he wasn't MI5. 'Let's just call me an interested party who's willing to listen to your side.' North had dealt with any number of desperate men in his career. Paulie was desperate all right, but was he lying? Looking round the tiny studio at the futon, the stained carpet and battered kitchenette, he figured Paulie was keeping himself on a tight budget in order to help his family. The neuroscientist had to be 30, but seemed younger, and North guessed the type. A doting mother who kept him close. Teachers who couldn't believe their luck when they realized what they had on their hands. Study, study and more study. A nerd job among fellow nerds, with barely enough time for a life or the real world.

But that didn't answer the question: why did Paulie need a fake passport?

'Why should I believe you're innocent, Paulie? Nobody else does.'

'I approached Tobias when I was studying for my PhD. He read my thesis. I had a great job all lined up at Harvard but he told me he was going to change the world and that I should join him. He made it impossible for me to turn it down. He's a visionary – I would never betray Tobias.'

Paulie's eyes were wide, his hands shaking.

'Why the passport then?'

Paulie bit his lip, his eyes downcast.

What did Plug say – there's always a woman? 'Who's the blue-eyed girl?'

Paulie wrung his hands, his head hung so low his chin almost touched his chest.

'Did you pass the Derkind medical program to her?'

'It's not like that. Yan's not like that.' Paulie's plump hands immediately balled themselves into fists in his lap. 'We're in love. She's blaming herself that I got fired.'

Something didn't make sense. If Yan was a Chinese-funded honeytrap, why did she need a British passport?

'She wants to get away from them.' Paulie's voice was low, as if he thought the Chinese might overhear him.

'Wants to get away from who?'

'Her boss – a Chinese businessman called Octavius Chin...'

'Octavius?'

'Eight is considered an auspicious number in China. For years Chin tried to invest in Derkind, but Tobias wouldn't take his money. That's how we met. Yan works for him, but she loves me.'

Was it credible? That the girl sent to trap him ended up snared herself? Looking at Paulie, it didn't seem likely, but who was he to judge? The guy was smart, good to his family, brave enough to dig out criminals and try to get her a passport. The nerd in the Hogwarts onesie wasn't the most obvious knight in shining armour, but maybe Yan saw beyond appearances?

'But if you didn't sell the program to the Chinese, and Yan didn't trick you out of it...' – he worked hard to keep the cynicism out of his voice – '... then how did the Chinese get hold of the medical program?'

Paulie ignored the insinuation that he was naive. 'Get me the passport – a genuine one – and I'll tell you what you want to know.'

North knew that Paulie wasn't telling him everything – but nevertheless there was an innocence about the scientist.

And the memory of the jasmine-scented, crying girl on the stairs stayed with him.

North cursed. The one-eyed man was a manipulative, ruthless bastard. Hone had to know he was in the country from Esme, but if North contacted him before the job was done, he risked news of his return leaching out of MI5. But he didn't have a choice. The only way heartsore Paulie was giving up what he knew was if North could secure a passport for his Chinese girlfriend, Yan. And Hone was the only way to do that.

20

Brompton Oratory

Hone paused in front of a white stone pietà, the dead Christ in the arms of his bereft mother. The Saviour's hands pierced from his crucifixion, his side open from a Roman spear, his Virgin mother bent over her lost son. North had once held someone as they died, the body sprawled like this one. He stopped himself from remembering more. Behind the statue, carved rifles and 'In Memoriam' tablets of those lost in the First World War. North ran his eyes over the names. Two hundred and forty-four of them. He always read the names of the fallen – counted them – figured it was the least he could do. *Dulce et decorum est pro patria mori* – 'It is sweet and fitting to die for one's country' – written above, and easy to say when you weren't the one doing the dying.

Hone's riding coat trailed over the copper banister as he squeezed between the railing and the brown marble column directly beside the pietà. He slid his hand behind the column. It came up empty. 'It was a dead drop,' Hone said in explanation. 'Old habits.'

'Does anyone still do that?' North asked. Surely Russians were too busy chipping away at neighbouring countries and running troll farms to drop off mysterious packages?

'You'd be surprised. There's an argument it's a great deal safer than electronic communications.'

'Unless you're around.'

'Unless I'm around.' Dusting off his hands, Hone moved away from the pietà and North followed, keeping in step. North had visited the Oratory of Saint Philip Neri once before, he recalled, but it was years ago and his only memory was of a vast nave and baroque grandeur. It hadn't changed. A smack of incense still hanging in the air from Sunday. The muffled noise of traffic from the Brompton Road. Neoclassical, Italianate; saints clutched folded robes of stone or looked down on sinners from ceilings of gilded mosaics and clouds. The only simple things in the church were the oak benches and the worn woodblock floor.

'I'm not giving away UK passports so that criminals can give them out to all and sundry.' Hone kept his voice down but it carried anyway.

The one-eyed man's righteousness was exhausting, North thought. Hone intimidated, blackmailed and bribed. He'd snatched an innocent woman and was holding her hostage just to get North on the case. He slit throats and murdered without compunction and excused everything on the grounds of national security.

Somewhere a choirboy started to sing, the doleful organ notes chasing after. His voice was pure and piercingly sweet, the Latin sweeping up to the vaulted ceiling as if to escape the organ's hold. It sounded like he had been born to do one thing, and that thing was to sing sacred music in certain praise of God.

'Paulie's not a criminal,' North said, and realized to his surprise that he wanted to help the nerd.

'If he's responsible for leaking the program, he's worse than a criminal. He's a traitor and I have no truck with traitors. Don't be naive, North, it doesn't suit you.'

There was a chink as a coin hit the bottom of a metal box, and in a side altar across from them an old lady reached into a box of candles. 'Do you know who that is?' Hone pointed into the shadows at the statue of an elderly bearded man in a bishop's mitre, clutching a staff, with a huge book spread across his knee. 'Saint Isidore of Seville,' Hone carried on, presuming North's ignorance. Why did everyone always presume they knew more than he did? 'Saint Isidore compiled the world's first encyclopedia – twenty volumes of 448 chapters – a summing-up of everything that was known in the world. The unofficial patron saint of internet users and computer programmers.'

The saint looked tired, thought North, but then he would.

'Isidore. I-sid-ore,' said Hone. 'Tobias is from an old Catholic family – he named the program after that saint. He once told me he changed the spelling to a "y" because he thought "Why?" was the big question. As in "Why are we here?" What do you say to someone when he tells you that? Once you've stopped laughing, I mean.'

'I thought Syd was female,' said North as he considered the voice he'd heard in Tobias's office.

'Jesus God!' Hone's voice echoed around the church once more. 'Syd is a computer, North. Gender is irrelevant.

Like with angels. I can't believe the arrogant toerag threw you out and you let him do it. May I remind you while you're stood here, anything could be happening to Esme. Her protection is down to you now.'

'One thing at a time.' North handed over the photographs and papers Paulie had given him. Twenty-three-year-old Yan was described as a personal assistant. 'Who is she really?' North said.

Hone tucked the papers in his pocket and patted them. 'Nobody is admitting to an arms race in AI, but the Chinese are mad-keen to get ahead of the curve. Agents of the Chinese Ministry of State Security have made numerous unsuccessful attempts to breach the company's firewalls. No great surprise then, when the medical program leaked, it emerged first in the Tsinghua University Institute for Artificial Intelligence.'

Hone gestured at him to sit down on a pew before sitting down next to him. North wondered if they looked like friends, because they weren't. 'You didn't give me much notice, but yes, we know who she is.' The one-eyed man pushed a photograph across to North of massed ranks of what he took to be academics and, behind them, a large group of serious young people North was guessing were their students. A skinny girl at the front clutched a laptop to her chest. She wore wire-framed glasses over pale eyes, her front teeth stuck out over her lower lip and her hair was short and greasy.

North moved his finger to tap under the girl's face and Hone nodded. Chinese state security had despatched the girl to strike up a relationship with Paulie Holliday and persuade him to help her.

'China is determined to make sure they have a home-grown pool of AI talent in their universities. Yan is – or I should say *was* – a talented AI engineer. Top of her class. From a family with an impressive record of public service. As far as we can make out, she gave up her PhD six months ago. As you know, the Chinese run a system that calculates a citizen's social credit score. That decision to drop out should have been enough to have her blacklisted from travel at the very least. Instead, she turns up here with 20/20 vision and a Hollywood smile, working as an aide to a senior Chinese "trade envoy". Octavius Chin enjoys the perks of his cover – the house in Mayfair, a millionaire lifestyle, seats at the opera – but in reality he's a senior intelligence agent in their Ministry of State Security. He's been operating in London for years and he's very good at what he does.'

'Which is what?'

'Acquiring the skinny on anything and everything. He trades for information and if that doesn't work, he bribes, blackmails, coerces or kills for it.'

North thought back to the frightened girl tearing down the stairs in Hackney, looking like her heart was breaking. 'If we get her the passport, Paulie will talk.'

'Don't get sentimental, North. She defects and we have an international incident on our hands. Anyway, we have a bigger problem than the Chinese. The man who attacked Esme at home has no criminal record. In fact, he has no record of ever existing. No fingerprints. No dental records. Nothing to identify him or allow us to trace him.'

'What does that mean?' North said.

'It means don't disappear down some rabbit hole. Because whoever sent that man to hurt Esme isn't done trying.'

21

West London

Hone left the church first. North gave it three minutes as instructed, then followed.

He noticed the car first. But it would have been hard not to. The Lamborghini Aventador S was parked on double red lines and parallel with the railings – low-slung and so close to the ground it could have sprung from it. A glossy yellow, its sleek silhouette was a thing of sharp and unarguable beauty. He immediately wanted to drive it, to feel it respond to his slightest touch.

There was a double melodic blast from the horn, and through the windscreen he could make out Esme waving him towards the passenger seat. As he walked through the gate and around to the car, he wondered whether Tobias knew she was here. The scissor door swung open and upwards, almost taking off North's head. He hoped she hadn't noticed.

She was already talking as he climbed in. 'I'm meeting a

few of the American bigshots who've flown in for brunch in Canary Wharf. My uncle thought I shouldn't go anywhere alone, whatever Tobias says.' The door eased shut and she gave him a wicked smile – she hadn't missed the fact he'd nearly decapitated himself seconds earlier. Esme, he thought, missed nothing. A black cab flashed her to pull out but she ignored it. Instead, she spoke in a rush. 'And I wanted to apologize for his attitude. Tobias can be…'

'… difficult,' North offered. In his experience, women attached to controlling, angry men liked to use a term that covered a multitude of sins.

'I was going to say "a complete arse", but sure, "difficult" works.' She glanced across at him as if trying to get the measure of him. Her eyes were the colour of the Parma Violet sweets he'd had when he was a kid – the ones that tasted like your mouth was full of flowers. Eyes worth dying for if you were the poetic type, which he wasn't. 'Paulie rang me to say you'd been round asking questions – despite Tobias warning you off.'

Her husband had fired him, but Paulie obviously didn't hold Esme responsible for what was going on. She was his friend, he'd made that clear, and he trusted her.

'Thank you for doing that.' She gave him a brilliant smile as she pushed the ignition button, and the car moved off from the curb and out into the traffic with an animalistic roar. Her watch was set to the wrong time, he noticed – 10.14 a.m. when it was 12.17 p.m. – and the old-fashioned scent of roses filled the space between them.

'What happened at 10.14?'

Esme raised her eyebrows. 'Why would you ask that?'

'Your watch. The clock in your husband's office.'

Her profile was perfect, he thought.

'Our son died.'

What was there to say that didn't sound inadequate? He tried silence, then said what he should have said to begin with. 'I'm sorry.'

'I don't know who Tobias would have been without Atticus and what happened to him.' Her hands gripped the steering wheel so tightly the knuckles whitened. 'It's why I have to forgive him for being so "difficult".' She laughed a little, but it was painful to hear. 'After Atticus died, we called in the numbers to figure out what lay behind the data, in the patterns. For months we barely ate or slept because we wanted to make sure no one had to go through what we went through. It was too late for our son and for us, but we thought if we could find the patterns in the numbers, we could eradicate the disease that took our child. And we've found so much more than that. Because we found a way to create consciousness in a machine. Don't get me wrong, I would swap Syd for Atticus in a heartbeat – but Syd makes our catastrophic loss mean something.'

Esme was quiet for a moment, as if she'd said more than she meant to.

'I'm sorry. That's a lot to put on you. I don't normally talk about it, but I want you to understand who we are. Have you ever lost anyone who mattered to you, North?'

He didn't want to go there. Moving forward meant never looking back, but the words came out of their own volition. 'Yes, I lost someone.' A woman who had made him realize he was capable of love, when he'd always believed it was beyond him.

'How did you cope?'

A beat.

'I killed the people to blame for her murder.'

Esme let out a small gasp.

Seven of the guilty. He'd heard their pleas and excuses, their screams. He'd told them why they had to die and watched as each and every one breathed their last. The only one left to kill was the man who fired the gun. And North would find him too, eventually.

The violet eyes were wide with shock as she looked over at him, her gaze shifting to his hands. Too late, North remembered that, only days before, a monster had attacked her in her own home. That to her he was a stranger, and now she knew him as a cold-blooded killer. It was one thing to kill in self-defence, as she had. It was altogether different to stalk and kill professionally – or in revenge. Yet there was something about Esme – some kindness in her – that made him want to tell her everything. His terrible childhood. His catastrophic brain injury. All the deaths he had been responsible for. His own grief. But where to start?

'Did it help?' she said, softly. She didn't sound like she was judging him, but surely she had to be.

'With what?'

'The pain.'

He wasn't going there, and he couldn't. Killing didn't help with the pain, because that wasn't why he'd gone after the guilty. The only thing killing did was corrode the soul. But that didn't mean to say it shouldn't be done.

'Your husband likes his cars,' he said instead, and the temperature in the Italian car dropped to subarctic.

She shook her head and sighed, like she'd expected more

of him. As if she should never have opened up. As if he'd let her down. As if he was just another man of violence.

'It has the iconic V12 engine with 740 brake horsepower. It can do nought to sixty in 2.7 seconds and you can feel the paint from the white lines as you ride over them. The rear end, as Lamborghini says, has all the power of a space shuttle engine, and since they changed the design up from the first Aventador, it has an increase of 130 per cent in front downforce. Of course...' – she reached for a small lid in the console between them, flipping it open to push down a switch with her finger – '... Tobias chose the colour.' She lifted her hands from the steering wheel and kept them high in the air. 'And then there's this...'

He grabbed for the wheel but he had no control over it.

With some hauteur, Esme lifted his hand away by his wrist and dropped it back on his lap. 'Relax, North. Eventually, we won't even need a steering wheel. Syd's in charge of the car. Isn't that right, Syd?'

'That's correct, Esme. I've got this.' The computer's voice reminded him of Esme's. He'd have found it disconcerting if his mind wasn't on the fact a machine was driving. 'Please make yourself comfortable and enjoy your journey. Estimated time till arrival at Canary Wharf is twenty-seven minutes.'

North shifted in his seat. What was the point of a Lamborghini if you didn't have the pleasure of feeling it move under your hands? As if to prove Esme's point, the steering wheel started to spin as the car turned left and North had to force himself not to reach out and grab it again.

'This is the future, North.' Esme was trying to reassure

him, but he thought part of her was enjoying his obvious discomfort. 'The roads are mapped. The technology is here.' She was making the death and rebirth of an entire industry sound simple. 'Fully autonomous self-drive cars will be on UK roads by next year if the government gets its way. There've been any number of trials already. It's our ethical systems and laws that aren't keeping up with AI – like how do we get round the tricky issue of personal responsibility. But we'll get there. Most fatalities in cars happen because of human error. As Tobias says, "Remove the humans and remove the errors".'

'Is this legal?'

'We have a licence. It's all signed off at the highest level. Although in the interests of transparency, I will admit that Tobias doesn't know we're out in it today. But I needed to get away from the madness for a couple of hours.'

The Lamborghini moved through Knightsbridge, the ride smooth and faultless, at one point overtaking a double-decker bus, then giving way to a black cab pulling out of a side street. The car drew to a halt at the lights. Started up again as red changed to amber, just as a pedestrian started running across. Green. North braced in readiness for the impact as the pedestrian hit the bonnet, the terrified face at the windscreen, the tumble and roll off the car and into the road. But the car powered down – the pedestrian none the wiser.

Esme's hands were loose on the wheel, as if from habit; her eyes on the road as the car started up again. As the car pulled away, a weight seemed to settle over her. Was it his imagination or was the car picking up speed? Esme's mind, though, was on Syd. 'At tonight's gala we introduce the world to the fact there's a new consciousness in our universe. To be part of its creation is extraordinary, but it's a massive responsibility.'

North's eye went to the speedometer. The car was at 40 mph on a 30-mph stretch.

Esme bit her lip. 'When that creature was attacking me, Syd "understood" his violence. "Understood" I was going to die. We've discussed ethics. Syd is programmed to have values. Syd quoted the Talmud at me. "If someone comes to kill you, rise up and kill him first." Syd is the reason I killed that man, or at least part of the reason, and that is a truly terrible thing. But Syd is also why I was able to save myself. Syd believes that it understands life and death, and what it is to kill. We've talked about it since. Syd believes it knows when killing is the right thing to do.'

The car was definitely travelling too fast, he thought. The arrow crept up beyond 40 mph as they moved down Constitution Hill alongside Green Park.

'And is that good or bad?'

'It's an ethical nightmare, but Tobias refuses to admit it.' She paused, as if she was considering how much to say. 'I'd have expected Tobias to be flying high since Syd reached consciousness; instead he's unbearable. He fired Paulie for the leak, when I refuse to believe Paulie would ever do that to us. I was attacked in my own home and suddenly Tobias is trying to gaslight me, saying I'm overwrought. I mean...! Nothing makes sense, but I'm sure it's all connected.'

The car swerved into the other lane on the approach to Buckingham Palace, and a black cab stopped in its tracks to avoid smashing into it. Esme was too lost in her thoughts to notice. 'I hate myself for saying this, but I think I was attacked because of Tobias.' Her body, categorically, turned to North, her eyes fearful. 'He denies it but I know in my bones Tobias has done something very wrong.'

This was it – this was the reason she had picked him up in the car. Not because her uncle told her not to go anywhere alone, and not to 'get away', but because she needed help.

'What's he done?'

The car swerved back after overtaking a London bus. North liked fast cars as much as anyone. But this felt too fast, because this wasn't the open road. This was the heart of London, full of cars and buses and taxis and tourists and office workers. He had to trust that the self-drive car was programmed to avoid them all, but it wasn't easy to overcome the feeling that more than eight million people lived in London – and there was a good chance it would be a few less by the time he was out of this car.

He tried again. 'What has Tobias done, Esme?'

She opened her mouth to reply, but before she could a voice came out of the speaker. 'Esme. We have a problem.' Syd sounded eerily calm. 'System error AO 6220C. Reporting system error 6220C in autonomous operation. Driver alert. Please take the car to manual override, Esme. Releasing car to manual override.'

Frowning, Esme leant forward and reached for the wheel.

'Please confirm we are in manual override, Esme.'

North sensed the quad muscles along her thigh tighten as she pressed down on the brake pedal, but the car kept moving forwards.

'Syd, I do not have control of the car,' she said. 'Repeat, the car is not in manual override.'

His first instinct was that she was joking – punishing him for the crack about her husband liking his cars. 'Incorrect, Esme. Systems show the car is in manual override.' Esme's knuckles whitened as she pulled at the wheel, wrenching it to take the roundabout in front of the Palace; its wheels locking, the car went into a slide.

'Diagnostics indicate braking failure in manual override.' Syd's voice sounded calm, and with a sickening crunch Esme's head slammed against the window as the car corrected its slide. She was out cold. 'System error MO 428. Passengers, please brace for an automated emergency stop. Advising brace for emergency stop.'

North placed his right arm across Esme and reached up to press his left hand against the roof of the car.

There was a whining sound from the engine, but the Lamborghini didn't stop.

'Reporting total failure in automated emergency stop process. System error MO 666.'

North thought he'd be happy if he never heard Syd's voice again. He pressed the button for the electronic handbrake, pressed it again, and again, expecting at the very least its rear wheels to lock and the car to slide across the road. Instead, nothing happened. Keeping his eyes on the hazards ahead, he took the steering wheel with one hand, and shook Esme hard with the other. 'Esme, wake up!' His voice was loud. He needed her back, not least because there was no room in the car to haul her across and to manoeuvre himself behind the steering wheel. And without Esme conscious, there was no one to apply the brake pedal. Not that he had any expectation it would work.

North's eyes went back to the speedometer – 50 mph, 55, and then nudging past 60 as they sped along Birdcage Walk towards Westminster. Esme's head flopped towards him as he struggled with the wheel. The Lambo caught a waste bin a glancing blow, knocking it into the road. In the rear-view mirror, North watched as it bounced into the path of a coach coming up on the inside, heard a screech of brakes. Sweat prickled up the length of his back. That could have been a buggy instead of a waste bin.

'Syd, do something! Give me control over the car.'

He was running out of road as Parliament Square approached.

'I regret to inform you that I am unable to complete this journey with due regard to the safety of passengers and fellow road users. Please accept my apologies for the inconvenience. Be assured that all system faults have been reported and will be rectified at the first possible opportunity. Thank you for making this journey with me and enjoy the rest of your day.'

North swore but it didn't help.

'Syd, we are going to die here. Do something.'

'That would be unfortunate. Please try to avoid fatalities. In the meantime, allow me to suggest some music for the road.'

The strains of Prince's 'Little Red Corvette' started up. North didn't mind it too much. If he had to die, listening to Prince was as good a way as any.

The car was adjusting its own speeds as it saw fit, he realized – slowing fractionally for a second or two, but never enough to open the doors and bundle them both out. And the roads were too full of people to kill and cars to crash into. Where could he drive the car at this speed to safety, before a whole heap of innocent people ended up dead and before he killed himself and Esme with him? North ran the map of the city's streets through his head. Esme had been heading for Canary Wharf. A park? Too many people. A football stadium? They were all too far. London City Airport might clear their runways if they were given due warning, and the Victoria Embankment and The Highway that led there did at least have the virtue of being straight. He keyed the destination into the computer in front of him, and prayed it was still working even if little else was. From where he was sitting, the airport was their only chance of avoiding carnage.

'Esme! Esme!' He tried shouting in a bid to rouse her, but there was no response.

He reached over to push the floor pedal under her foot, pulled on the handbrake – nothing. In the shadow of Big Ben, he turned sharply on to the Embankment, clipping a bollard as he went. City Airport was eight miles away – the rate this car was going, getting there would only take minutes and at the other end they'd need every second to get ready for him. With the index and middle fingers of his left hand, he pulled his phone out of his pocket and dialled Fang's number.

She picked up on the first ring.

'Fang. We're in some crazy Lamborghini that was supposed to be driving itself. Esme is out cold – I can't stop the car and I can't slow it down. Steering it is like driving a tank so I'm guessing the power assisted steering has gone as well. Tell Hone to warn City Airport we're en route or we are going to have a bloodbath out here.'

'What do you need when you're there, moron-person?' Her voice was as if his request was of little to no consequence, but he could hear the furious tapping of her fingers.

'A clear runway and a run-off track full of gravel or sand right alongside would be excellent.'

Even as he said it, he knew there was no time for her to get anything like a run-off track in place. He hung up. It would be fine, he told himself; it wasn't as if airports were particularly security-conscious. Not as if, when they saw a speeding car coming towards them, that anyone would shoot the driver.

He leant across as best he could to take a better grip of the wheel. He had to hope Esme wasn't dying from some catastrophic brain bleed, because there was nothing he could do for her till he managed to get the car to a place of safety. *If* he managed to get the car to a place of safety. At the Tower of London he steered the Lambo a fraction to the left and it responded, then straightened up again. All he could do was pray that there wasn't a traffic jam between here and the airport.

He swore as he swung the wheel to avoid a lorry and a bus, then three cars coming in the opposite direction. *Be careful what you wish for*, he thought. He'd wanted to drive the Lamborghini and now here he was, driving the Lamborghini in what might be the final journey either of them ever made. His mouth was dry and his heart pounding as the office blocks of London's Docklands appeared on the horizon, the light on top of Canary Wharf blinking red to warn low-flying aircraft not to crash into the skyline.

Was he going to die? There had to be a good chance this was it.

He swallowed down his fear as the Limehouse Tunnel passed in a flash, zipping between lanes, neon strip lighting overhead – a blare of horn after horn, red brake lights, the scream of other cars' tyres as he overtook.

He didn't want to die.

Because, if he died, Esme was going to die too, and she had a lot to live for. He was supposed to keep her safe, which meant he couldn't let either of them die.

Back into the daylight and on the approach road, the sign was there and gone before he even had the time to register it. London City Airport.

The car took the right turn hard and fast, and North swung the wheel again – bracing himself as they kept moving forward to smash through the perimeter fencing, a spiderweb of cracks opening up across the windscreen. The mesh barrier must have snagged on the underneath of the car and it trailed behind them, sparking and clanging. They were airside. And there was comfort in the fact that if they had to die, it would be two of them, not two hundred. Thank God Esme was still unconscious and didn't have to experience the fear that had him in its grip.

They were still clearing the runway of planes, when from somewhere to his left a British Airways jet emerged from behind the parked-up planes to trundle across the path in front of him. The passengers' horrified faces were pressed up against the strip of windows. He was blocked in. Planes to the left. Empty buses to the right. From the state of the runway, he was guessing the place had been cleared in haste. He pumped the brake again. Nothing. How high was a Lamborghini? It was pretty low-slung, right? He had to hope it was. The plane's speed picked up, but the plane wasn't going to clear his way in time. If he crashed into it, he and Esme would certainly die, but the aviation fuel might go up and that couldn't be allowed to happen. He braced himself, kept the steering wheel steady, his touch light, his gaze locked on to the space he needed. The enormous tyres of the plane, which were still moving, grazed along the right-hand side of the car as he drove between them, under the belly of the plane into sudden darkness, and out again into daylight.

The dock stretched out in his peripheral vision alongside the runway on the left. More planes were parked higgledy-piggledy with tenders to the right, and at the end he could see firefighters frantically spraying foam. Picking up speed rather than slowing down, North refused to allow his eyes to drop to the speedometer. He barely noticed the police cars either side of the runway, until the Lambo's front wheels hit what had to be a stinger. The sound of shredding metal as the car spun in hectic arcs, the shuddering impact as it hit he didn't know what before it lifted into the air, tilting, rolling, once, twice. Righting itself with a bone shuddering smash – it crashed down into the water, and the world went to black.

22

London City Airport

He must have lost consciousness, because first there was darkness.

Opening his eyes as the Lamborghini sank into the docks, and seeing Esme next to him, and the question in his head – who was she and what did she mean to him?

Darkness.

The sensation of freezing wetness starting at his feet and moving rapidly up his body. His fingers grappling for the seat belt buckles as he tried to remember how they worked. Hers then his. Looking up to see daylight from above and thousands of bubbles surrounding them. Fighting against panic as a muffled banging started up on the door window – was someone trying to get in? Time slowing to a crawl, then speeding up again. Plug's face distorted first in the windscreen and then in the door window as he pulled himself around the car. Fighting to stay conscious. Esme slumped in the driver's seat – and the water rising fast.

Taking a breath as it closed over his head, and worrying because Esme wouldn't know to do that. Plug straining at the handles from the outside, his huge fists beating against the side window. He had to open the swing-up door – Plug needed him to open the door – and inside the car, North reached down, scrabbling for the handle. The door lifting. The deluge of water as it opened, knocking him into Esme's body. Taking hold of her. *Did it help?* She had violet-blue eyes, he remembered. Not being able to breathe. The grip of Plug's hands on his collar and the belt of his trousers as he was dragged out of the passenger seat, outwards and upwards, reaching for Esme. His own hands taking hold of Esme's forearm, pulling her across, out of the door. Her body trailing after him because he wasn't letting go. And then – oblivion.

Opening his eyes, North heard himself cough and retch a full minute before he felt the violence of it all scour out his lungs.

'We've got you, mate.' Plug's voice.

He struggled against the hands, because he couldn't leave her behind on the battlefield. No, not the battlefield – the water.

'It's all right, North. You're out, and she's okay. Esme is all right.'

North came back to himself. He was soaking wet and stretched out on the grass between the water and the runway. Blue sky above him – vapour trails and cirrus clouds. Breathing air and not water. He turned his head and twenty yards away there were paramedics and blue lights gathered around someone.

He gripped Plug – he could breathe, but he wasn't ready to talk yet. 'She's conscious,' Plug said.

Fang looming over him. Scowling. 'Moron-person... death wish... Never known anyone...'

Small and far away. Her button face blurring into darkness. A sensation of falling into something cold and empty. The temptation. The knowledge that he couldn't stay there.

23

Donne & Sons

North had to hope he wasn't dead. He didn't want to be dead, because there was nothing like nearly dying to make you realize you weren't done yet. Voices came and went in time with his breath and the pain. His chest hurt. His head hurt. His ribs hurt. Everything hurt. Pain was good, though. Pain meant he was still alive – that he hadn't died in a high-speed collision and that he hadn't drowned in a London dock. He tried to tell whoever was talking that he was awake, but couldn't persuade his lips to form the words.

'Is someone trying to kill our man or was he collateral?' Plug. He thought that had to be Plug. His old friend was worried. 'We need to look after him better.'

'Who am I? His reiki therapist?' He could imagine Fang's eyes narrowing. Both voices came from somewhere in the room. He thought they were seated.

'I've three boys,' Plug said. 'The wife wants to try for a girl. Now I've met you – that's not happening.'

'You've got some big-time drug smuggling side hustle, right?' North forced open his eyes long enough to snatch a glimpse of Fang, slumped in a chair, surrounded by phones and tablets and laptops. 'Your disappointment that I don't know all the words to *Frozen* is...' – she slapped her tiny hand twice against her chest – '... devastating.'

His heart lifted. He was alive and among friends. But he should have warned Plug about Fang. He fought to keep his eyes open, and saw Plug grimace. A grimace that North knew had prompted more than one hard man to let go of a little urine. Fang appeared oblivious, her glittering boots up on the bed, a blue bubble growing bigger and bigger till it obscured her entire face.

He wasn't aware of sleeping, but he must have, because when he next managed to open his eyes, Fang was gone, and Plug stared down at him, like he was a problem he had to solve. Struggling to bring the muzzy edges of the room into focus, North blinked then blinked again. It hurt to blink. He decided to keep his eyes wide open and never blink again. 'How's Esme?' His voice sounded gruff and he cleared his throat as he swung his legs around and off the side of the bed. The world spun a little faster on its axis, and he concentrated hard on not vomiting.

Plug grinned, the smile managing to make the slab of a face uglier. 'North, mate. You are effing hard to kill.' The relief in his voice was palpable. He turned his head and yelled for Fang. The noise enough to shake the walls. 'Fang said you wouldn't want to show up in any records, so Hone helped us get you away. A doctor who owes me for the ash cash I put his way checked you over, said to let you sleep. In case you're interested, you've broken a couple of ribs – three at most – and you're probably concussed.'

'Esme?'

'She came round when we pulled her from the water. They checked her out but, frankly, she was in a better state than you were. Her husband wasn't best pleased, but whether that's because she nearly drowned, totalled the Lambo, or because she was joyriding with a toyboy, I don't know.'

'How did you get there so fast?'

He thought Plug might have blushed.

'Fang said we had to follow you because you're an idiot. The driving was so erratic that even before you rang, she'd warned Hone that something was wrong, or they'd never have had the time to lay down the stinger.'

Fang pushed open the door. 'Finally,' she said, and her eyes behind the Joe 90 glasses gleamed. He thought she might ask how he was feeling, but she didn't.

'Self-drive cars fuse data from sensors – their cameras, their radar, their lidar…'

'"Lidar"?'

She rolled her eyes. His ignorance apparently a constant revelation. 'Light detection and ranging. Well, Teslas don't have it because Elon Musk isn't a fan, but the Lambo did.' Was there anything this kid didn't know, he wondered. 'Plus, ultrasonic. That first error Syd reported was because someone hacked your pretty gadabout. They fixed the GPS – the system thought the car was on a wide-open road. Actually, it thought it was driving through the Gobi desert, a fact you've got to love. The hack blocked the incoming radar, lidar and ultrasonic signals. It had nothing to go on. No traffic signs or traffic lights. No awareness of other cars or objects. It thought it was going at thirty miles per hour. Luckily for you, Syd realized.'

'And the speed and handling. The braking failures?'

'The hackers had a backup if Syd tried to put you to manual. Whoever it was really wanted you both dead.'

He wasn't dead, but he did have two broken ribs – probably three – and a concussion.

He sniffed the air. Then himself.

'What is that appalling smell?' he said.

'Granny Po's cure-all special miracle paste.' Fang grinned. 'She makes it from goose fat, fermented wine, fish skins, and frankly you don't want to know what else. You're honoured. She only brought a small jar with her.'

Taking hold of the side of the bed, North levered himself upright. Esme had said something just before Syd alerted them to the problem, but he couldn't remember what. It slid from his grasp and he could only hope it would come back. Tobias – that was it – she'd said that Tobias had done something 'very wrong'.

Was the wrong thing connected to what just happened? Had Hawke rigged the car to kill his wife? North thought back to the way Esme's dark eyelashes swept over the pale cheeks – his fear that she might die on him when he was supposed to protect her. Surely her husband would want to protect her too? More likely the person who'd hacked Esme's car was the person involved in the original leak of the medical technology. Or even the Chinese themselves?

'Can you tell if the hack came from China?'

'Not yet. They've covered their tracks really well.'

North crossed the room to the window, wincing at every step. He couldn't see what the connections were, but they had to be there. A violent attack on Esme in her own home. The leak of medical tech to the Chinese. A computer system with consciousness – a breakthrough about to revolutionize our relationships with machines. And something that Tobias did that his own wife believed was very wrong. They had to be connected, but he just couldn't see how.

The hearse with its registration of MORT1 was parked in the yard outside. The back was at least empty. North preferred not to think about lying stupefied in a coffin under Uncle Jim and half a million pounds' worth of cocaine.

'I'm having a shower and then drop me at Derkind, Plug. I need to make sure Esme is okay and I want to ask Tobias what the hell he's done that's about to get his wife killed.'

Plug looked confused. 'They won't be there, mate. It's nearly seven. You've been out of it all afternoon. They're both of them already at the gala.'

North knew for a fact that he'd never wanted to get involved in whatever this was. Hone boxed him into a corner when he seized Fang's mother. North had no stake in artificial intelligence, in Derkind, or what an AI breakthrough like Syd might mean for the future of the country. Aside from his loyalty to Fang, he had no dog in this fight. Sitting in the passenger seat, as Plug crossed town, North touched his broken ribs. It felt like knives slashing their way out of his chest cavity. He flexed his hands, before balling them into fists. He wanted to meet whoever had hacked that car. Then he wanted to punch them in the face. Because someone had tried to kill him and the innocent woman alongside him. And call him old-fashioned, but that made him mad. And an angry Michael North was someone who might just kill someone right back.

24

British Museum

North sidestepped the curious foreign tourists and the Japanese taking photographs amid the chatter and burble of languages, and showed his embossed invitation to one of the dark-suited bouncers at the gate. The wind whipped at him. A storm was forecast for later in the evening. He took another step forward as if to emphasize his right to be there.

'Monty De'Ath – pronounced Day-ath,' North said, and the security guard shook his head as he stared at his iPad, scrolling up and down the names at speed and then more slowly. 'Sorry, sir, you're not on the invite list. Perhaps you could move aside and make a call?'

'Would you mind checking once more,' North said. It was a narrow line between being insistent and rude. If he made too much fuss, the guard would be tempted to dig in. Sighing, the guy checked the database of official guests on his iPad again and this time found the name Fang had inserted seconds before. 'Apologies. I don't know how I missed it. There you are, Mr Day-ath,' the guard said, the light catching his gold tooth as he tried to suppress a smile.

North nodded. No problem. Walked through in the dinner jacket Plug had obtained from God knows where. He had to hope it wasn't from a corpse but he had his doubts. He tucked the invitation Fang had faked into the inside pocket and missed the weight and coldness of the SIG that had been there minutes before. He'd palmed it off to Plug when they'd glimpsed the metal detectors beyond the gate. At the time it seemed like the thing to do; now he wasn't so sure. He wasn't so sure of the new name either.

'Monty De'Ath?' he said, under his breath. 'Seriously?'

It's foolproof, Fang had told him. *Who makes up a name like that? It has to be legit.*

North glanced back. The security guard's head was bent as he inspected the invitation of a silver-haired man obviously unused to being kept waiting for anything. The guard took his time. He was doing a decent enough job, North assured himself. Security at an event at the British Museum was always going to be tight. It must have cost the Hawkes a small fortune to hire the place and they were probably more secure here among all the treasures than they were in their own offices.

But was Esme safe? He had to admit he was worried. Exiting the stand-alone marquee with its metal detectors and X-ray machines, he slid a tiny Bluetooth earpiece out of the pocket of his dinner jacket and into his ear. Pulled out his phone. 'Before you go in, you need to know that hack on the Lamborghini...' – as ever, Fang jumped straight in – '...wasn't a straight-out hack from someone intent on driving you off the road.'

'It sure felt like that,' he said, trying not to shudder at the memory of the metal fencing scraping and screaming along the door, the lift and tumble of the car round and round before the bone-shuddering impact as it hit the water. 'But the hack is going to have to wait.'

'North, it can't.' Fang's voice went up a notch. 'You don't get it. All sorts of tech and motor manufacturers are neck-deep in self-drive cars already. I kept thinking, even if ideas are exploding all over the shop at Derkind, why would Hawke go there? Self-drive is not where his expertise is.'

The noise of her gum-chewing filled his ear and he waited as she presumably blew and popped a bubble.

'The Chinese didn't hack that car, or if they did, it's way more complicated than it looks, because they had a lot to work with when they got in there. It turns out Tobias Hawke is working up systems to sabotage autonomous vehicles.' There was a note of triumph in her voice. 'The Lambo was Tobias's guinea pig.'

'What are you saying, Fang?' Hawke was a tech genius and a humanitarian. His medical program proved his motivation. He wanted to cure cancer so that little kids didn't die like his own son had died. Why would he be trying to kill people? 'That makes no sense.'

'North, the car's systems have been thoroughly wiped down but it was done in a hurry. I've found any number of patches to its system that would wreck the autonomous driving. These cars have to know where all the other cars and pedestrians and barriers are – they literally compute what might happen in terms of the other traffic and act accordingly. Someone messed with the Lambo's probabilistic distribution algorithms.' North had no idea what that meant, but it didn't sound good. 'Basically, they told the car that whatever it did, it wasn't going to crash. Hawke must have run the program before, over and over – theoretically – but each time, he restored the system. That must be why Hawke recovered the Lambo so fast to the Derkind HQ. He didn't want the police to start going over the wreckage.'

'Did Esme know?'

There was a ping on his phone and suddenly, on the screen, he was looking at a pale-faced Esme, a dressing taped to her forehead. North winced at the memory of the crack of her temple as it hit the driver's-side window. Swiping her security pass through the electronic lock, she took a quick look over her shoulder as if checking for her husband before pushing through a door marked 'Laboratory 1'. Motion sensors, detecting her presence, lit up the darkened laboratory in a blaze of harsh white light. In the centre of the lab, raised on a hydraulic jack, the yellow car was a crumpled ruin. Its glass smashed, its right side pushed into the centre of the car and the steering wheel sheared off. Water dripped from its undercarriage.

North fought against nausea. The Lamborghini Aventador had been one of the most beautiful cars he'd ever seen and it was a ruin. They could both have died. Nearly did.

Syd, roll dashboard film, please. On the video, Esme spoke out into the listening emptiness of the laboratory. He thought he sensed a quaver in her voice, and he didn't blame her. It was her second brush with death within a matter of days. Someone was trying to kill her, and she had to be praying that it wasn't three times a charm.

The picture jumped, cutting between various angles

taken from the exterior of the car and the interior. The road surface seemed dry. Passing vehicles. London landmarks. Picking up speed. He heard his own voice and then Esme's but couldn't make out the words, then his frantic call to Fang. Smashing through the airport perimeter fence. The perspective of the film shifting from right to left and then over and over – the rush of the water coming to meet the car. Esme raised her hand to her mouth as if to stop herself from screaming as the footage ended.

North considered what Fang had said and what he had just seen. Esme didn't know anything about Tobias's sabotage programs. She would never have got behind the wheel if she knew and, thinking back, she'd admitted in the car that she had taken it without Tobias's knowledge. His work on wrecking self-drive cars would explain why he didn't want North, or indeed 'Uncle' Ed, anywhere near Derkind. Esme had told North that Tobias had done something wrong. But Esme had also said Tobias was compelled to change the world for the better after the death of his son, so why was he destroying the future, rather than creating it?

North figured he'd better ask. 'Fang, do you think Tobias tried to kill his wife?'

'If he wanted to kill Esme, he wouldn't have had to hack his own system. Plus, don't wife-murderers keep it on the down-low? Plus, I think he loves her, so I'm going with no.'

'How did you get this footage, Fang?'

Silence.

'Fang?'

'All right – I sent the baby drone back in,' she said. 'I

tweaked it so it fed back the footage to me. Esme is so used to those things, she didn't even blink.'

North knew better than to argue with her. Standing to one side in the forecourt, just short of the steps leading up to the Greek revival columns and magnificent neoclassical pediment, North watched the latecomers gathering in the bottleneck at the Great Russell Street entrance waiting to file through the marquee. This was tech aristocracy. Fifteen hundred scientists, business people, academics, investors and journalists had been invited to tonight's gala to hear about Tobias's creation. Flying in from all over the world. And North had just proved how easy it was to lift or fake an invitation. Did any of them know about Tobias's sabbotage work? Surely, they'd be horrified? Some of them had billions invested in self-drive cars. Had Tobias just been playing around with the tech to see what was possible. He was a genius – geniuses did crazy things, right? He gazed through the bars at the crowds of tourists, feeling their eyes on him, assessing his status and appeal. Their interest in the broad-shouldered guy in the dinner jacket dying as they realized he was good-looking but no one famous – he was a visiting academic or a City banker. Barely worth watching. Which suited him just fine.

Once inside and through the cold and shadowy entrance hall, the shingle roar of conversation and expectation was almost deafening. The crowd in the Great Court with its vaulted glass ceiling was a living thing as huddles of financiers and AI experts moved back and forth, drinks in their hands, breaking apart before coming together, all the time talking and touching. Handshakes, kisses on cheeks, a buzzing, humming sense of excitement as to what Tobias was about to reveal. North didn't feel safe. He felt exposed, as if he was being watched. Was that possible? He glanced around but the partygoers were intent on each other. He was being paranoid. He'd come into the country without any red flags going up, as far as he knew.

He seized a glass of champagne from a passing waitress, and considered drinking it, drinking a bottle and then another bottle. But he wasn't in Berlin, he reminded himself. He was in London and he was working. Which gave him every excuse to search the crowd for Esme. He needed to see her and to make sure she was all right. His heart lifted as he caught sight of her among the revellers. She was in a red dress with a nipped-in waist and a huge ruffled slit slashing through the skirt, her dark hair down in deep waves like a Hollywood star from the Forties, a petalled bag dangling from a narrow chain across her body like an oversized peony rose. He watched as she drifted from group to group – shaking hands, listening, nodding – eyes wide, her head back, laughing. Even so, he sensed her preoccupation – the way her gaze occasionally skittered away from the company she was in, the tiniest of frowns. Was she waiting for someone? Waiting for him, perhaps? Or was he flattering himself?

He wondered if it had been her idea to hold the party in the museum. It felt like her. Making history. Launching an artificial intelligence revolution among a treasure trove of ancient artefacts, shedding light on the past and civilizations long gone. An artificial intelligence that might mean the end of our own civilization, or the start of a better one. What would Syd mean for humanity's future? What would the machines put away in their own museums to remember humanity? Phones? Crucifixes? Bones? Who would we be to them?

Instinctively, Esme reared back as a Chinese man, the size and shape of a blimp, called out her name and then steamed through the crowds to get to her. Dressed in a white dinner jacket and a black shirt, he mopped at his forehead with a huge silk handkerchief. The heat of the crowds was getting to the guest. From a distance he didn't look like anyone Esme would want to talk to, but she stood patiently in the lee of a marble youth riding a marble horse, waiting for him to reach her. She spoke first but North was no lip-reader. It had to be interesting though, because the blimp grabbed hold of her wrist, pulling her closer. He had her trapped against the plinth, North thought, and escape would be difficult. They stood with, their heads close together. Was the overly familiar guest Octavius Chin? But Hone had said Derkind didn't take Chin's money, so why then did Chin think he was within his rights to take hold of Esme and monopolize her? After a minute, she made to move off, but the Chinese agent blocked her path. He wasn't done.

North kept a smile on his face as he approached.

'I really do have to go,' he heard Esme tell Chin as she attempted to step away again. The man showed no sign of wanting to release her.

North figured Esme wouldn't want him to make a fuss. 'Why don't you circulate, Esme,' he said.

Esme's face changed from astonishment to delight to concern, all within a blink. Chin's sharp eyes peered at him from the doughy face. There was a crackle of recognition as, sneering, Chin released Esme – her slender wrist covered in red marks.

'North! My God, I feel so guilty about what happened.' Esme's fingertips grazed his sleeve and he thought how pleased he was that she was here next to him and not dead on a slab thanks to a killer car. It was good to think the feeling was mutual.

He shrugged. 'Let's agree that I'll drive next time. Or at least you will. Go mingle.' His gaze took in Chin. 'I'll take care of your guest.'

She hesitated as if she had more to say, before sparing North a brief smile. Holding her evening bag close to her, she stepped away, turning on her heel and forcing her way through the crowds. She looked back at him once – smiled again – before someone blocked her path. She was the woman of the moment – of the future – he thought, and everyone wanted a piece.

Close up, Chin looked fatter and sweatier than he did from a distance. He mopped at his forehead again – the silk handkerchief covered in a motif of tiny octopuses. 'I know who you are, Michael Xavier North.' North kept the surprise from his face. Chin, he reminded himself, was an agent of the Chinese security services. 'You are a former executioner and lackey of the capitalist system. Until, that is – *wàng ēn fù yì*. As you would say, "you bit the hand that fed you". Or rather, you assassinated seven members of the British establishment in revenge for the death of your lover. We all mourn in our own way. My condolences, Mr North.' Chin bowed and his chin disappeared into the flesh of his neck. But when the agent looked up, there was no sympathy in the narrowed eyes, only a dark, infinite malevolence.

'After which bloodletting, as I explained to my superiors, Michael Xavier North disappeared. Believed to be retired or dead. Yet, here you are. Presumably in the pay of British intelligence, for you to have the confidence to return? Despite all those you have angered. All those who must wish you, in your turn, dead. All those who would be suitably grateful for the news of your return.

'Do you have anything for me, North? Any titbit you would like to trade in return for my silence on the matter of your return? Information is my business and you would not find my terms onerous.' He stretched out a hand and slipped what North took to be a business card into his trouser pocket. A strangely intimate move. 'So you know where to find me.'

North kept his face neutral.

But Chin was already moving off. North was a minnow. Chin's huge bulk pushed its way through the thronging guests, regardless of the muttered grumbles at his passing. North glanced around for Esme but she was nowhere to be seen. He started moving through the crowds in search of her or a vantage point to keep watch over her. He'd be a lot more comfortable if she stayed in his line of sight at all times – for all kinds of reasons he didn't want to admit, even to himself. And when this gala was over, he needed to tell her what Fang had discovered about the Lamborghini, and he needed to know what else she thought her husband had done.

'North.' Fang's voice was in his ear again. She sounded appalled. 'Is that true? Did you kill all those people?'

He moved out of the hubbub in the Great Court and into a doorway. Stepped into the Enlightenment Gallery. What to tell her? He'd killed a lot more than seven people in his time. The raised voices brought him back to himself.

The lights were low in the gallery, but even so its Greek Revival interior gleamed with gilt and knowledge acquired over centuries. He tapped his earpiece twice to tell Fang he couldn't talk, as he kept to the wall, slightly behind a marble column with a bust of King George III. He was too far away to make out the men's words. He moved closer, tucking himself behind a statue of Venus. Towards the back of the gallery, past the display cases full of antiquities and natural history specimens, Paulie and Tobias were engaged in a full-scale row – the two men so intent on each other they didn't notice North.

'You've ruined my life, Tobias. I want my job back.'

Tobias shook off Paulie's restraining hand. 'We make our own choices, Paulie. You made yours.'

North took a step closer to hear better and the mahogany and oak floor creaked. He took a breath, moved forward again.

'This wasn't the deal.' Paulie's voice cracked with the strain.

'It's not my fault if you were caught in a Chinese honey-trap, Paulie. Grow up.'

'You know it wasn't like that, Tobias…'

'Getting out from under my shadow is the best thing that could happen to you, Paulie. I'm sure your Chinese mates will give you a job tomorrow.'

'Please, Tobias, Esme said we should talk…' His voice cracking, Paulie reached for the older man, but Tobias pushed past, his stick catching on a corner of the case, almost unbalancing him.

'You're a fool, Paulie.' Tobias turned as he spoke from the door. 'You shouldn't be here.' For the first time, North thought he caught proper emotion from Tobias – some flare of pity – before he extinguished it as quickly as it had come. With a departing expletive, Tobias turned his back on his former friend. North could hear the tapping of the silver-tipped cane as an unseen Tobias moved through the next gallery and away from Paulie.

Paulie's back was to North, his hands spread out over a display case full of pinned butterflies, his bald head hanging. He swivelled hearing North's step, and hope lit up his otherwise wretched face. 'Do you have it – the passport?'

North thought about lying. Paulie would believe it because he wanted to believe it. Believe that a kindly stranger could magic up a British passport to rescue his one true love and that Paulie and Yan could live happily ever after together. Star-crossed lovers no more. North didn't have the heart to do that to him.

'It's not happening, Paulie. I tried.'

There was a sound from somewhere deep and wretched and solitary inside Paulie, a cross between a shriek and a sob. He nodded too many times like he expected no less, his eyes filling with fat tears.

Blinking them back, Paulie looked around the gallery as if he were waking from a dream only to find himself in a nightmare.

He'd failed to persuade Tobias to give him back his job and he'd failed to persuade North to hand over a passport. Paulie's anger was on a slow burn, but underneath the self-pity, it was starting to take hold.

'I lost my dad when I was seven. Even that wasn't as

bad as when I lost my hair. Alopecia universalis.' He said it like it was a magic spell. 'It's an autoimmune disease. My mother took two jobs and we tried anything and everything – steroids, immunotherapy drugs, ultraviolet light – but nothing worked. Without my sister and my mum, I'd have killed myself, because through it all, boys like you made my life a living hell.' North had never made anyone's life hell at school, but Paulie was on a roll. 'Then it all changed, because I put the work in and I made something of myself. But look at me now. I'm back to being a laughing stock – a fool.' He gestured to the gallery. 'Do you even know anything about the Enlightenment, North? Is it anything you cover in thug school?'

Was Paulie right to brand him a thug? Maybe. When he had to be. But not always.

'Tell me,' North said.

Paulie wanted to refuse, but the urge to impress was too strong to resist. 'Reason, liberty, the scientific method, scepticism about religion – revolution. There's a German philosopher called Immanuel Kant...'

North had read Kant. Like many autodidacts, he read books like he breathed and drank coffee. But he figured if Paulie kept talking, he might reveal something useful.

'... he said "dare to know" – *sapere aude* – that we should think independently, have the courage to use our own reason. That's what Tobias does – he dares to know. He isn't frightened of anything. Not like me. He has this once-in-a-generation mind but sometimes I think that's the only good thing to say about him. I want to hate him and some days I do – he's a bully, he's obnoxious, he frightens people with all his shouting and carrying on. Worse, he has everything.

Esme is smart and beautiful. She's the most decent human being I have ever met, and she loves him beyond reason. He just takes it all as his due because he is the great Tobias Hawke. But then he does something astonishing, and the hate goes away.'

North thought that if Paulie truly hated Tobias, he wouldn't be hurting so badly.

'That prosthetic leg he designed could have made him a fortune,' Paulie said. 'But he gave it away. Industry adapted the AI-enabled joint mobility for aeronautical engineering. He could have made millions.' At the thought of the millions to be made, a spasm of envy passed over Paulie's cherubic face. This was someone who'd never had money. 'But Tobias said he didn't care. Because he wanted everyone to have access to a better-quality prosthetic.

'So what if the medical program is out there! This way it will acquire more and more data, learn faster and faster, and save more and more lives. But the moneymen out there drinking their champagne don't want that to happen, and Tobias knows that. They aren't interested in saving kids' lives, or in science or knowledge. Only in the bottom line.'

Was Paulie saying what North thought he was saying? 'Who leaked the medical program, Paulie?'

'This is a new world now, thanks to Tobias and Esme...' – he gestured at the party going on outside the gallery that they could hear but not see – '... and I'm not welcome in it any more.'

'The leak, Paulie?'

Paulie opened his mouth to reply, but before he could, the noise of heavy gunfire, screaming and breaking glass shattered the calm. Automatically, North reached for his gun – then remembered it wasn't there.

Paulie's eyes widened with panic. He made as if for the door before, in the same motion, North hauled him back, swung him round and pressed him against the display cabinet. 'Tell me. Who leaked the medical program?'

It was a primal thing, he thought – the impact of other people's terror on your own system. Adrenaline. Spiked heartbeat. Blood pounding in his ears.

'Are you insane?' Paulie's soft hands clutched at North's fingers, but there was no strength in them as he tried to wrestle himself free. 'Someone out there is shooting people.'

North took a tighter hold of the scientist as Fang spoke into his ear. 'North, get out of there!' Her voice made him jump – he'd almost forgotten she could hear what was going on. He wanted to get out of there, of course he did. Someone, somewhere, was firing a gun, and he didn't want to get shot. But he couldn't go anywhere, because he was right here, and here was where it was happening. There were too many questions. He had to know who leaked the medical tech.

'North! What the hell is wrong with you. Let Paulie go, and get someplace safe. Now, moron-person.' Fang's voice was brooking no argument. Cursing, North released his grip on Paulie just as the noise of gunfire moved closer.

25

Home Office

By as early as noon, the Home Secretary's diary secretary was pale with nervous tension. By teatime she had retreated to the ladies for a quiet sob on at least two occasions.

Meeting after meeting in Marsham Street ran late as Ralph Rafferty interrogated private contractors on their plans to build new prisons; as he cross-examined department lawyers on an obscure piece of legislation to tighten up on migrant applications; and as he paced back and forth demanding explanations from immigration officials on delays at passport control.

Sitting at his desk with steepled fingers, he'd kept his face a mask of benign tolerance as he allowed a notorious backbench windbag to witter on at length about domestic violence, overruling his own officials as they attempted to break up the meeting and ease the MP out.

As a result of which obfuscation, Rafferty felt himself to be within his rights as he complained that he was his own worst enemy when it came to being a workhorse. He scowled as he ordered his diary secretary to ring his driver and stand him down for another hour. It was really too bad. He had to be at the British Museum for the Derkind gala. They were expecting him – indeed, he was something of a guest of honour. They'd think him damn rude, when everyone knew that he was the soul of courtesy. On his way back into his office, he even slammed the door, apparently in martyred exasperation.

Safe in his private sanctum, the Right Honourable Ralph Rafferty was desperate to speak with the General. Kirkham's ruthlessness terrified even Rafferty. He dug out his private phone and placed it with some care on the papers stacked on the desk as his long fingers moulded and stroked his jaw. He settled the lank sweep of hair across his forehead. Kirkham knew no limits, no fear. Rafferty's fingers moved to the phone, hovering over the keypad. He could order the General to call it off. Or at least persuade him to a more measured course. Plead, if that is what it took – before it was too late and too much blood had been spilled.

Rafferty's ears pricked at the wail of distant sirens. Were the police already en route to the British Museum? Or were the sirens merely part of the nightly city soundscape?

The noise faded into nothingness. Routine, then.

Hawke's AI was an abomination. Rafferty could well see it burning up the world. But he knew this much – if he called Kirkham off, the General would despise his civilian cowardice, cut him loose and go ahead anyway. And when the General did that, Rafferty would lose any leverage he had. He shook his head – he was too far in. He'd been careful, but God knows what compromising materials Kirkham had on him. What did the Russians call it – '*kompromat*'? If the General failed, he would take great pleasure in dragging Rafferty down with him, which could not be allowed to happen. Behind the round glasses, the politician's myopic eyes struggled to find and focus on the clock face opposite. London time. Eight p.m. He had calculated it would take around three seconds for the first call to the police and maybe seven seconds more for the police to let the Home Secretary know.

Ten seconds.

He was a great man, he reminded himself, and he was on the side of the future.

Nine.

And this was his time.

Eight, seven, six.

God knows the prize was big enough to justify the death of a few unfortunates. They were necessary sacrifices to get him where he deserved to be and what he needed to have once he got there.

Five, four.

Political power and the wherewithal to use it for everyone's benefit, not just his own.

Three.

It was his patriotic duty to go ahead.

Two.

He merely had to hold his nerve because it would all be over soon. Hawke be damned.

One.

Rafferty swept the phone off the desk and back into his jacket pocket even as he heard the melee start up outside his door. The noises were muffled, every phone in the place going off, the sound of running feet along the corridor, scuffles and fervent murmurs.

Despite himself, his lips twitched in a smile. He dragged down his muscles, clamping shut his lips as he pulled his shoulders back. A statesman in his country's hour of peril. This was it. He picked up his pen.

There was a knock at the door.

The door opened, closed again – the noise of leather-soled shoes crossing the carpet, the whisper of wool cloth rubbing against itself, rapid shallow breaths and an aftershave blended with sandalwood and mediocrity. His Principal Private Secretary. It had begun.

Grasping his pen a little tighter, he kept his head bent over his papers – holding up his hand as he scrawled an exclamation mark against a paragraph he hadn't read. Looking over his round spectacles with a sigh, Rafferty frowned – he was at work. Whatever it was, the official would have to wait for the Secretary of State to finish up his statecraft. What could possibly be so important as to disturb him? He had to get through these critically important papers before he could leave for the gala where the future awaited him.

He was careful to keep his face in order. Not to smile.

'Home Secretary.' His Principal Private Secretary sounded apologetic but insistent. 'We have a situation at the Derkind gala. It's bad. I have the Metropolitan Commissioner of Police on the line for you.'

26

British Museum

Outside in the Great Court, guests were screaming and pushing for the exit. Splashes and pools of blood on the golden stone, stray shoes and bags, glass and broken bottles everywhere. As he edged forward, in his immediate sight line alone, three dead bodies were splayed on the stone floor and one spreadeagled on the central steps. Two security guards and an elderly man on the floor, and a young woman on the steps. Blood pooled and trickled step by step down from the girl. He sensed Paulie emerge from somewhere behind him and make a dash for the information desk, which was shut up for the evening. Watching, he saw Paulie disappear behind the counter before emerging with a young man he realized was Jarrod. His arm around the injured receptionist, half carrying him, Paulie headed for the exit.

Whatever information Paulie had about the leak to the Chinese would have to wait. The noise of gunfire grew louder – there was more than one shooter – and North made a dash across the courtyard. Was Esme out already? Was she trying to get out? As he reached cover behind a column, two huge heavies passed. Each had one hand tucked under Chin's elbow as they propelled him out of the doorway, his feet barely touching the floor. But there was no sign of Esme. The last time he'd seen her, she was heading away from Chin, and God knows where Tobias had gone once he got clear of Paulie. Were they together? Perhaps they were already outside among the screaming, hysterical guests? But somehow North didn't think so.

He struggled to remember the layout of the museum as an old man with wild-dandelion hair and a drooping walrus moustache, carrying a Heckler & Koch MP5, fired a series of deliberate three-round bursts into the pushing and shoving crowds at the exit. Half a dozen more people dropped to the ground, and the old man lowered the gun and watched the panicking, shrieking guests in their dinner jackets and fancy frocks fight to get through the doors. He was ex-military, North knew it – something about the control, the way he stood, the detachment as he fired then waited. He wasn't crazed or in any kind of bloodlust. He wanted people out of the building. Shooting a few of the stragglers made everyone else move that much faster. And there was something about his face, with its bushy moustache, that was familiar. Was he someone North knew? The old man moved towards the door and loosed off several more long bursts of gunfire, brass casings flying, the rounds shattering the glass in the frame, and the screaming went up a gear. He clanked as he walked. Standing on the broken bodies of the fallen, the MP5 swinging from him, he reached out to bring the doors together, then unwound the chains from around his waist before looping them through the handles and padlocking them. He moved to the next set of doors to do the same thing. He was on a clock – the attackers didn't want anyone else leaving and they certainly weren't going to make it easy for anyone else to get in. Step by step, North backed away.

The sound of automatic weapon fire from elsewhere in the museum bounced off the walls as glass from an upstairs window exploded out into the courtyard, fragments raining down on to the stone. North put his fingers to his head and batted off the powder and glass splinters, his fingertips coming away bloody. If anyone looked down from the broken window, he was in plain sight and they'd have a clear shot. He was going to have to move again. But which way to go?

Advice to civilians in the event of active shooters revolved around three words: run, hide, fight. Those who ran for the exits were either out or dead; those who hid would be lucky or unlucky. Would they find a room near an elevator with reinforced walls? Did they know to lock and barricade the doors? To stay low? He himself preferred the third step – fight. And he added a fourth: kill. Run, hide, fight, kill. It had an altogether better rhythm. And what was the point of fighting if it wasn't to a standstill?

North needed a weapon. The spaces were too open and clear to catch the murderous old man by surprise. He kept low and to the wall around the foyer and back through the doorway of the Enlightenment Gallery, on through another gallery, to a display case he half-remembered from previous visits.

The claymore was more than three feet long, with a

wooden handle. According to the sign it was around five hundred years old, but he figured he didn't need the iron sword to be razor sharp. The force alone would be enough to decapitate anyone coming at him at close quarters. The only problem – it was behind glass.

Across the room was a chair where the security guard normally sat. It was vacant. North took a second to consider the security guards. They'd have been the first in the line of fire. Holding the moulded chair by its two front legs, North swivelled round, bringing the chair as far back as he could manage before smashing it full force into the glass. The reverberations shot up his arms, making his broken ribs sing and his teeth ache. The security glass was unmarked. Not a crack or a dent. Cursing, North checked the back of the case. Could he heave it to the ground? Screws held the powder-coated steel plates of the display case to the floor and to the wall. He wasn't getting the sword. Moreover, he realized, in his haste to find a weapon he had trapped himself in a room with only one way in and out. He pressed himself against the wall as somewhere far too close a radio receiver crackled into life. 'Einstein, gallery 2 clear. Gallery 2a clear.' The white hair, the walrus moustache. The shooter wasn't an old man that North recognized. It was a man wearing the latex mask of a genius.

North's heart beat hard in his chest. When Albert Einstein stepped through the doorway, he would have a direct sight line. North held his breath.

27

Elsewhere in London

Fang pushed a button on her headset. 'North? Come in, moron-person?'

But the line was dead.

They had to have cut all comms into the place. Her fingers felt thick and unwieldy as she hit the number she had for Hone. He picked up on the first ring. 'Do you have contact with him?'

'No.'

'Then there's nothing I can do for him,' he said, and hung up.

Fang shook her head. Of course Hone knew and didn't care. He was a spook, and it was his business to know everything. Especially things like the fact there were gunmen at the biggest launch of the year in an iconic London landmark full of historic treasures. North was in the perfect place as far as Hone was concerned. He was where Esme was and he was probably Esme's best chance of surviving whatever was going on in there.

Her heart was beating so hard, it threatened to batter its way out of her chest. She drew a breath. Calm. She had to stay calm and get him out of there. Because everybody else would be going insane. Armed police and special forces were doubtless pulling on body armour and getting ready to smash their way into the place and kill everyone who wasn't wearing a posh frock.

She popped in another piece of gum and bit down on it, the taste of synthetic raspberries reminding her of the jam sandwiches she used to beg her mother for when she was a kid. The phrase 'killed seven people' repeated over and over in her brain, but she shut it down. Not the time to think about it. Not the time to wonder what had been going on in North's head when he killed those people. Maybe he had been mad with grief. That's what she wanted to think. Not that he was a cold-blooded killer. She would take out the facts as she knew them and think through them later, when she had the luxury of time – something North didn't have at the moment.

She pulled the headset off, tossed it on to the floor and started typing and swiping, bringing up the floor plan of the museum.

What would North do when bad men started firing weapons?

She had told him to get out of there.

Would he do as she said and get to an exit?

She imagined it within his grasp. The door swinging. The cold air outside and blue flashing lights. His hand reaching to push it open. The noise of gunfire and screams behind him. Turning to take a last look at the carnage he was escaping.

Nah. No chance. Who was she kidding? The image in her brain went into rewind mode. North turning back. The noise of gunfire. His hand pulling away from the door. Blue flashing lights and the door swinging shut. Trapped.

North would be drawn towards danger because he had a bullet in his brain and thought he was going to die any second, so why not? He had a death wish and he was a bozo. A bozo without any weapon of his own. Which meant he probably was indeed going to die. And she wasn't there to tell him what to do to stay alive.

On the off chance, she pressed the short key on her phone that should link through with North. Nothing.

She fired up the locator device she'd installed on his phone. He didn't know it was there, but he didn't have to know everything. Privacy was overrated and someone had to have North's back. She watched as the little red dot appeared on the London map. It should be moving if he was moving, if he was still alive. The dot wasn't moving.

28

British Museum

Flattened against the wall, North glimpsed the wild wool of the moustache and the latex wrinkles of Albert Einstein. The shooter turned his head to the right to sweep the space visually. The mask was high-quality and it was an effective disguise, but North was calculating that it limited the peripheral vision of the attacker. He was about to bet his life on it. He had less than a second before Einstein's head started turning towards him.

Stepping out from the wall, he seized the MP5 with his left hand, twisting and wrenching it from its sling as his right hand landed a crushing blow to the armed man's temple. Einstein staggered then dropped to his knees and North brought back his shoe to kick him in the stomach. Desperate for breath, Einstein fell forward on his hands, the radio skittering across the floor. North propped the weapon against the wall.

'Plato, gallery 95 clear...' 'Nietzsche, gallery 33 clear...'

'Marx, library cl— Hold...' The noise of gunfire again, and a snigger. 'Marx, library clear...' 'Aquinas, gallery 21 clear.'

North placed a foot on Einstein's spread hands, feeling the knuckles pop and shatter under his weight. He had no intention of letting the guy stand up again. Einstein was down and he was staying down. 'What's all this about, soldier?' he asked. There was the sound of a stifled groan as North pressed down harder, and then a yelp of what might have been laughter. 'Need to know, mate.'

Still standing on Einstein's hands, North balled his fist and took him under the chin. The guy could have been a boxer – he had a huge neck roped with powerful muscles, a neck designed not to go back when he took a hit. But it didn't stop the mask flipping away as his eyeballs disappeared up into their sockets and he lost consciousness.

North stepped off and inspected what was left of the shooter. The tactical vest and overalls zippered up over a dinner jacket. The attackers must have come in as guests.

North picked up the latex mask and slipped it over his head, where it sat like a welder's visor as he reached for the MP5, rifling the pouches of the vest for a couple of spare mags.

Five different attackers had spoken on the radio, and when he floored Einstein, he'd taken out one of them. Four against one was doable. The bigger issue was what – or who – had they come for? He considered the question as he headed back out of the gallery, his shoes crunching over glass – breaking it all over again. He put his shoulders back. He was Einstein. He was the one with a gun, only too happy to kill whoever needed killing. Out in the Great Court it was quieter now, the space filled with the smell of recent panic and spilled alcohol. Another figure was coming down the sweeping shallow steps, kicking aside the body of the girl and stepping around her spreading blood. Not because he was squeamish, thought North, but because he preferred not to contaminate the soles of his shoes.

North stared at the domed forehead, the dark moustache and huge white beard of Karl Marx, the father of socialism. The attackers were keeping the masks on because of the security camera footage and witnesses, he was guessing. North settled his own stolen mask and lifted his hand in greeting. The rubber interior felt slick with its previous owner's sweat.

'Where's your overalls and gloves?' Marx said, his voice muffled. 'He doesn't like sloppy, you know that.'

North had considered stripping Einstein, but the full wardrobe change was going to take too long. He shrugged as if to say 'who cares?', and Marx lifted his mask to clear his line of vision, the partially revealed expression curious. Without hesitation, North reversed his MP5, swinging it out and in again so that the butt hit the other man squarely in the nose. As the nose split in two, each side peeling back to reveal the crushed cartilage, blood spurted everywhere. Marx opened his mouth in agonized protest, pulling up his own gun in the same motion, and North slammed him face first against the stone balustrade. Marx was done, at least for now. To his count, there were three more attackers – Plato and Nietzsche and Aquinas. The hairs on his neck stood to attention – if any of them were watching, he was a dead man. He pushed the thought aside. Taking hold of the man's ankles, North dragged Marx's body behind a stone facade, arms over his head and trailing blood as he went.

How many innocent people had this man killed tonight? North kicked him again, this time in the throat. 'Think of it as the opium of the people,' he said.

Why were the attackers here? In the US, shooters went in and created mayhem in schools and colleges and churches, but they tended to be lone wolves with their own agendas. These guys were working as a team. And who was the 'he' who 'doesn't like sloppy'? North didn't believe the men he'd dubbed the Thinkers were ISIS terrorists. The two men he'd taken out had ex-forces written all over them. But it was too much of a coincidence to think they were criminals out to steal antique treasures. You wouldn't choose a gala event. You'd go in overnight, secure the guards and give yourselves time to get through the security glass. This way, there had to be half the Metropolitan Police camped out in the forecourt deciding how and when to rush the building. And what kind of mind put the attackers in masks of the world's great thinkers? Was it political? Some statement about human intelligence versus machine intelligence? The Thinkers had to be here because of Esme and Tobias and the AI system. Which meant they probably wanted to kill Esme or Tobias, or both. Alternatively, they were here to get to the research and steal Syd and everything else was a distraction. Or worst of all, they wanted Esme and Tobias dead and to steal Syd. North didn't care about superintelligent computers or singularity or any of it. But he did care about Esme Sullivan Hawke. And he had no intention of her dying on his watch.

He had to know what was happening outside. If the police or special forces stormed the museum, he could end up misidentified and shot as one of the attackers. Suddenly the Einstein mask didn't seem so appealing and he let it fall to the ground. He tapped his earpiece – no Fang, only the buzz of a disconnected line. He was on his own.

As if on cue, the radio crackled into life. 'Any sign of Hawke or the wife?'

There was a chorus of negatives.

He was guessing they'd come in and opened fire as a group to clear the museum, then they'd left a couple of men to secure the doors and kill the stragglers while the others went looking for Hawke. What he didn't know was the whereabouts of the man running things. Was he in the building? Or was he running things off-site? Because that was a man North would like to meet and take apart.

Across the courtyard, he caught sight of a flash of red as Esme disappeared down a staircase. She was alive. At least for the moment. With a yell, a slim man with the mask of a halo-wearing monk sprinted after her and North felt the blood freeze in his veins. He didn't know much about Thomas Aquinas, but he was guessing he didn't usually carry a submachine gun slung on his back and a machete in his hand. North ploughed down the darkened staircase after the woman he was supposed to be keeping safe and the counterfeit saint chasing her intent on bloody murder.

29

North calculated Esme had thirty seconds on her pursuer, and Aquinas had thirty seconds on him, but as he emerged into the darkened corridor, there was no sign of either of them. He pushed through a fire door and the corridor immediately split three ways. It was a maze down here. Would he hear her scream? Or would Aquinas kill her silently? He had to find her and his first instinct was to rush headlong into the apparently endless hallways. But he had to get them out of this nightmare, or they were both dead. He took a breath. Reminded himself to focus.

What would Fang do? Call him a moron-person.

That wasn't helpful.

What would she want him to do? She'd want him to find a way out, and quickly.

It took him longer than he wanted but he found it. The steel door was marked 'Security. No Entry to Unauthorized Personnel.' Judging by the slumped and bleeding figures at the monitoring desk facing two dozen blank and shattered screens, they were all dead long before they got the chance to call for backup. Even so, the Thinkers would have known that within minutes of the first reports of gunfire, police would be securing the area, tightening the cordon around the museum with every passing second.

He closed the door, letting it take his weight for a second, keeping his gaze soft to avoid the distraction of carnage. His anger was instinctive, but anger would get him nowhere. He needed to keep calm.

He looked at the shot-out monitors and computer system. Despite the tight time-frame for the job, the Thinkers had done their best to wipe the arrivals footage. The masks were an insurance.

That had to be because they had every intention of making it out.

They were in overalls and gloves to avoid leaving DNA.

Because, once out, they had no intention of getting traced and caught.

In his head, he ran through Einstein chaining the doors together, snapping down the padlocks. They'd barred the doors to deter forced entry by SCO19, the Met Police's specialist firearms command. As far as command knew, the attackers had hostages; and the initial approach would be to negotiate, to minimize harm to those hostages. They weren't to know the Thinkers had no interest in negotiations. Eventually the Met would get the message – blow the doors off, send squads in through other entrances; there would be smoke and flash bangs and abseiling from the roof through windows. But not yet.

It was clear that this was no suicide mission but the police would have every exit covered, and the attackers were professionals so they'd know that. The logical conclusion had to be that there was one exit which the police didn't know about but the Thinkers did – all North had to do was find it. He'd killed two of them. There were three left – Nietzsche, Plato and Aquinas. And Aquinas was on Esme's tail, so he was the priority.

Scanning the room, North breathed a sigh of relief at the sight of the dog-eared floor plan sellotaped to the furthest wall. He studied it, running his finger from exit to exit from the top of the building to the bottom. Basement corridors snaked this way and that. Climate-controlled storage. Boilers. Computing equipment. Back offices.

Tapping his finger on how the Thinkers planned to escape. It made perfect sense – it was simple when you thought about it. If he had it right. But where was Esme on the map? Because he wasn't going anywhere till he found her.

He pulled open the door and started running. He had to hope it wasn't too late.

30

Esme already felt as if she had run a marathon. Two
floors down and a hundred and fifty yards ahead of her,
the corridor she had been running down split into two. In
terms of the geography of the building, the left corridor
was closest to the exterior wall. What were the chances of
an emergency exit out of the museum? Did museums even
have emergency escapes? All those guests upstairs dead.
She'd sat by some Californian tech guy. She knew she had
met him but she couldn't remember his name. Shock, she
supposed. The guy's white shirt soaked in blood; she'd tried
to stop the bleeding but there was nothing she could do.
As his breathing grew more laboured, she'd stroked his
cheek, although she didn't think he knew she was there. She
shivered at the memory. And how many more were dead?
How many of the young and gifted who worked with her
at Derkind? Any and all of those deaths were on her. They'd
come to the museum for her and for Tobias and for Syd – to
celebrate with them, to learn from them – and they'd been
slaughtered where they stood.

She could hear someone behind her. Urgent running footsteps. It was the first sign of life she'd heard since she'd caught sight of the stairs and taken refuge. How long had she been down here? It was minutes, she thought, it just felt like hours. Was it a guest from the launch? Should she stop? She glanced back over her shoulder but couldn't see anything.

A strange scraping sound travelled to her along the echoing corridor.

What was that noise?

Her heart leapt as some survival instinct filled in the blanks. It was a blade being dragged along the wall. She imagined it cutting a channel into the paint. She was being hunted, and by someone who enjoyed the hunt. They would move faster if they lifted the blade away from the wall, but they didn't want to. They didn't feel they had to, because they knew they had her trapped down here.

If she kept running, whoever it was would catch her and kill her.

She imagined grey paint peeling and curling from the wall.

She thought about the man she had killed in her apartment because she'd decided to live rather than die. But she had no weapon this time. Other than her wits.

And if he was playing a game, then she could play a game too.

She drew her hand down the front of her bloodstained dress – *don't think about it*, she ordered herself. *Don't think about the dying and the dead.* She had seconds and it might not even work. She lurched to the right-hand side of the corridor and trailed her right hand down the wall, then cut straight across and veered left. It wasn't much, but it was all she had.

Tobias. She thought about Tobias and how much she loved him. About Atticus. Imagined squeezing his warm hand in hers. What had she told him? *Be brave.* So easy to say and so hard to do. She thought about North – the man her uncle had sent to keep her safe – and she thought about Syd. About how little time humanity had left. She stopped running and threw herself in the lee of a doorway. If she opened it, he would hear her. If he looked too closely, he would see her.

Along the main corridor, her pursuer's footsteps came hard and fast. They kept trying to kill her – the break-in, the Lamborghini, right here and now, and the worst thing was they only had to get it right once for everything to be over. Fifty-fifty, she thought. She had a fifty per cent chance of dying in the next few seconds. But she was a killer herself – didn't she deserve to die? This then was how it felt to be on the threshold between life and death. This agonizing hope that you might get to live, and the soul-devouring fear that you might have to die – never more alive than in the moment you were so very close to death.

Should she step forward and face the ultimate bogey-man? The temptation was there – Freud's death drive. No more grief. No more longing and struggle. Washing away her past sins and present guilt. This was the moment, if ever there was one. She lifted her foot from the floor.

But it would make everything she had done worthless. She put her foot back down. However much pain she was in, she stuck by the decisions she had made and she still had a job to do. She pressed closer into the wood of the door.

Her breath sounded like the loudest thing on the planet, so she stopped breathing. She squeezed her eyes closed as if darkness might protect her as much as silence. Ridiculous, she thought – like a child hiding. Coming ready or not. She needed a gun. She needed North, but he wasn't here. What had North said? That he'd killed seven guilty men, and she'd been so appalled by that aggression. But he'd been honest and done what he felt he had to do and she understood that now. She hoped he was alive, that he hadn't been brave and foolish. She hoped he wasn't among the dead upstairs.

The pace of her pursuer seemed to hesitate for the briefest moment.

Left.

Or right.

Fifty-fifty.

She could smell her pursuer's musky sweat. She pressed her lips together to stop herself from letting out a whimper of animal terror.

Right. The footsteps picked up again, the sound of the dragging blade, and she moved off, fast and silent. How long did she have till he realized he had made a mistake and turned around? Minutes? Seconds?

There was no doubt in her mind that the man chasing her was doing so with one intention – murder. These people were here for Syd, and they wanted her dead. And they wanted Tobias dead too. The thought of Tobias bleeding and dead made her want to weep. They had come to murder Tobias, to murder her, and to steal the intelligence they had created together. And for the first time that night, she wondered what Syd thought about it all.

31

North was sprinting so hard he almost missed the grey door
with the 'Storage' sign painted across it. He screeched to a
halt, grabbing hold of the doorjamb to slow himself before
pressing down on the handle. He pushed open the door and
a motion-activated light flickered into life. Glancing behind
him, he slipped into the room, pressing shut the door.

They had to be running out of time. If he was right,
the Thinkers would make their exit this way. And he'd be
waiting for them.

The noise of an elderly fan rattled high up in the wall as
he crossed the floor. Scaffolding poles lay piled alongside
empty packing crates, while statues of strange stone figures
with missing noses and limbs closed ranks alongside
battered suits of armour. An enormous bust of some false-
bearded pharaoh he recognized without being able to
name stood atop a plinth, while fragments of pots and
jars of brushes filled a trestle table. Roman, he guessed, or
Etruscan, or Greek? Broken fragments – all that was left of
previous lives.

Above the clatter of the fan, he heard footsteps running parallel to the wall. He breathed in for four seconds, let it go for four seconds. All good. Bring it on. As if it was an extension of his arm, he raised the MP5 he'd taken off Einstein, settling it into his shoulder as he pointed it towards the door. Focusing. The curved mag usually stacked thirty 9mm rounds in a double column. He remembered the Thinker firing bursts into the crowd. He switched to single shot – wouldn't do to attract undue attention – and imagined the Aquinas mask. The tonsured monk. The halo and the machete. He took a breath.

The footsteps stopped and the door nudged open. As it did, he fired. A nick flew out of a jackal-headed Anubis holding a spear, as the interloper dived for cover and the sound of the shot took the place of oxygen in the room, making his ears ring.

In North's experience, sometimes fear made desperate people more dangerous rather than less. More liable to take a risk and try to use their own weapon on someone – someone like him. He had no intention of dying at the hands of a fake monk with a very real machete. He kept the gun level.

The crimson fingertips appeared first, then the whole hands. She didn't scream. Which surprised North in the circumstances. The circumstances being that he'd been about to save whoever was trying to kill her a whole heap of trouble by shooting Esme Sullivan Hawke through the left ventricle of her beating heart.

'I'd say I'm pleased to see you,' Esme said, emerging from behind a crate with the words 'Fakes and Forgeries Exhibition' stamped across rough wood, the clinging red dress splattered with dark blood and covered in cobwebs. 'But apparently it's not mutual.'

'Are you hurt?' he said, motioning to the dress. He'd only ever seen her in red, he realized.

With the tips of her fingers and thumbs, she lifted the bloody dress away from her skin as if she couldn't bear the feel of it. From across the room, it looked as if she was fighting the urge to weep. 'I tried to help someone, but he was too far gone, all I could do was stay with him till it was over.' She bit her lip as she let the material fall back into place – there was nothing to be done about it. Her eyes met his and there was all sorts of grief there. 'North, they must be here for Syd. Who are they?'

North had no idea, but he figured they were going to get the chance to ask one of them any second. He pulled her behind him as Aquinas burst in through the open door.

32

The savage blade skinned his knuckles and, blood pouring from the wound, North let go of the MP5. The weapon clattered to the floor and, with a primal grunt of satisfaction, Aquinas kicked it into the furthest corner of the storage room. North felt Esme move out from behind him, but she was too far away for him to protect her. He willed her to make for the door.

The monk brought the blade back up through the air so fast that North felt the breeze, even as the tip scraped against the bone of his forehead. Not a machete, but a lethal-looking kukri with an inwardly curved blade. A former Gurkha had once talked him through its virtues – a tip for stabbing, a midsection for chopping and a narrow section near the handle for whittling and carving. To be used as both a tool and a weapon. He took a step back, blinking away the blood that was flowing from the wound into his eye as Aquinas pulled out a smaller knife. He slashed wildly with the kukri and North veered to one side, realizing too late that the feint was designed to move him closer to the smaller blade. He felt it slice through the skin over his bicep. An inch further and it would have disabled his arm. And that would be game over.

The monk pushed forward, a blade in each hand, moving North backwards until the backs of his thighs hit the table of pottery behind him. Reaching out, his fingers gripped the pot shards, and he threw them one after the other after the other, but they bounced off the mask, and Aquinas kept coming.

North grabbed hold of Aquinas's wrists, using every ounce of strength to keep them away from his own body. He felt the tip of the longer blade press into the flesh of his right forearm as his opponent shifted his grip on the weapon to reach him. A trickle of blood, hot and wet, ran the length of his outer forearm.

'Stop, or I'll fire,' Esme ordered. She'd gone for the MP5 instead of the door, he realized.

'Not now, sweetheart,' the monk said without turning.

Aquinas pressed even closer to North and the blade bit deeper. Did she realize that if she fired at Aquinas, the bullets would pass through his internal organs and straight into North's? But at least that way Aquinas would die too, and Esme would have a hope in hell of surviving.

'Shoot the bastard, Esme!' North was panting with the effort of keeping Aquinas at bay. He'd rather be shot by Esme than kebabbed by a mad monk.

Across the room there was a clatter of metal.

'Get him away from you, North.' Esme's voice was close to panic.

North cursed – it wasn't that easy – and behind the mask Aquinas laughed.

'Now,' she said.

With one final surge of effort, he let go of Aquinas's wrists and pushed him backwards into the room. In the split second before the monk righted himself again, he disappeared under a colossal Egyptian bust of Ramesses II. A cloud of stone dust rose into the air.

Esme was standing behind the plinth with a scaffolding pole. She'd used the pole as a lever and the plinth as a fulcrum. He admired a woman with practical skills, especially when she used them to save him from otherwise certain death.

'I pushed him off. Why didn't you shoot him?'

'Because there's enough people dead up there and the chances are I'd have hit you too,' Esme said, forlorn, gazing at the statue, which now he looked at it appeared to have a crack running up and down its length. Under it something stirred, and, as if in response, the statue broke clean apart. Blood spread from beneath the two halves as the twitching fingers of what was left of Aquinas stopped moving. North grabbed Esme's hand and she let go of the pole with a ringing clatter. 'I don't recognize myself,' she said, staring at the dead man under the broken statue.

'If you're worried about history – it was a replica. There wouldn't have been a pole long enough for the real thing,' North said.

Esme turned on her heel and headed for the door. 'I'm going back.'

He pulled her towards him, her slim wrist warm in his hand. 'Absolutely not.'

'You don't understand.' She pulled against him, struggling to break away and make for the door, but he held her tight.

'Esme, Tobias either got out or he's already dead. Or he's better at hide-and-seek than we are. Either way, the only thing he would want me to do right this second is get you out of here.'

33

The floor plan in the security centre had shown that the Thinkers only had one option. They planned to go out via the sewer system. But as North lifted the manhole cover in the furthest reaches of the storage room, the sweet smell of human waste made him gag.

'We should let them kill us,' Esme said, as together they leant over the hole and stared into the pungent darkness.

He didn't know if she was right. If this was a good plan or a bad plan. He had no idea if they'd fit. No idea where the sewer came from and where it ran to. But he was trusting the Thinkers had done their homework. And he was trusting the weather forecast was wrong.

Esme climbed down first. He didn't like it, but he needed to drag the manhole cover back over the drain without it shrieking against the concrete floor in protest. He'd prefer it if Nietzsche and Plato didn't realize North and Esme had figured out their exit strategy. He used his elbow to hold the MP5 against him as he pulled over the lid, plunging them both into pitch darkness, and started the climb down.

He heard Esme yelp as she lost her footing, then the scramble of her shoes, sending vibrations through the rusting cast-iron struts as she struggled to regain her purchase on the ladder. He heard two splashes, as if she'd dropped first one and then the other into the moving water below. He counted the rungs of the ladder as he lowered himself down. From the sound of the shoes landing in the water, he calculated Esme had about another ten rungs to descend and he had twenty. He heard a bigger splash and a gasp as Esme's feet hit the water. The ladder shook again – she must have slipped and grabbed for it. He took the rungs as fast as he dared, girding himself for the cold when it came.

His feet almost went from under him and he grabbed for the rail. They were shin-high in water, or what he wanted to think of as water. Esme's breaths came shallow and fast in the dark. She'd stepped away from the bottom of the ladder to allow him space to set down his feet, but not so far away that he couldn't feel her shivering. The dress she'd worn to the gala was a thin silk. He slid his phone from his inside pocket, then peeled off the dinner jacket to drop it over her shoulders. He tried not to mind that she reared back at the shock of his touch. 'You need to stay warm,' he said into the darkness. 'Cold slows down your response times and I need you alert.' He sensed her indecision, before she slid her bare arms into the sleeves. The sound of the silk lining against her skin was loud in the tunnel, even against the noise of the moving water.

He didn't want to think of her skin. It was too much of a distraction. He preferred to concentrate on keeping them both alive. He checked the phone's reception. The bars were empty. He tapped his earpiece just in case – nothing. He hadn't expected to hear anything, but the isolation was acute. They were on their own down here. Cursing, he clicked on the phone's torch icon and white light illuminated the crumbling bricks of the tunnel arching over their heads. The same bricks, he was guessing, were under their feet – only those bricks were covered in human waste and slime. He started moving, gesturing Esme forward.

He was grateful she wasn't asking questions, though he could feel them hanging in the stale and fetid air between them. Questions like 'Was this the best idea?' She stood stock-still. She had to be terrified for herself and for Tobias, wherever he was. 'We need to get going,' North said. 'Those guys will have found their colleagues' bodies by now. They'll be on their way.'

He was thinking hard and fast. There were any number of manhole covers on the streets of London. They needed to get beyond the police cordon, so they weren't shot by a trigger-happy marksman, but he had no intention of staying in the sewers longer than he had to.

34

Subterranean London

They moved together, the water rising gradually to calf level as strange shadows loomed and twisted along the length of the brick walls. North tried to ignore the regular scurry and squeaks of the rats that moved alongside them, clinging with tiny clawed paws to the footings of the walls. One that was bigger than the rest sat back on its haunches, the light catching its eyes as it watched them. It looked hungry. North bent down and shot a spray of water at it, but the rat moved faster than the spray, scurrying away with an outraged shriek.

'Years ago, I read about these guys called toshers.' Esme looked in need of distraction. 'They'd force their way into the sewers, searching for coins and bits of rope and the occasional bit of silver cutlery that ended up there. They dreamed of finding a tosheroon – a whole bunch of coins all melded together in a ball. Maybe we'll get lucky down here and find one.' North was pretty sure the chances of them finding a tosheroon were a great deal lower than the chances of them ending up dead.

'I'll settle for not meeting an alligator,' she said, as another rat squeaked by.

North cracked his head and the world exploded in pain. The water had got higher and the tunnel lower. Mortar dust fell from the uneven brick of the ceiling.

'Have you noticed,' Esme said, wincing in sympathy, 'bad things happen when you're around me?'

He'd noticed.

He took a moment to assess where they were. The water had crept inch by inch to knee level, then thigh, but he hadn't registered the fact that the ceiling of the tunnel was getting closer at the same time.

'Which way?' Esme asked, her voice echoing off the bricks. A smaller storm drain branched off to the right.

The storage room where they'd found the sewer entrance was at the rear of the museum – in the north-east corner. North tried to bring to mind the street map of Bloomsbury and beyond, above the ground. What would have made sense to Victorian engineers as they laid down the infrastructure to their great city? Would they have been trying to get the effluent of the museum and the surrounding area to the Thames? In which case, surely they'd be heading in a southerly direction. But he had the distinct impression that they were heading east, so maybe the run of sewers was heading towards the old Fleet, one of London's lost rivers.

'This way.' He did his utmost to sound confident but he didn't think she was convinced. Still less so, as her bare foot slid across the slimy bricks. He grabbed for her, jerking her closer by the jacket's lapel, and the violet eyes locked on to his, her hands on his arms. He held her to keep her from falling again, he told himself. The only reason.

'North, if I die down here...'

'You aren't going to die.' He pulled her a fraction closer. He wouldn't let that happen.

'... tell them Paulie didn't leak the medical program. And tell them—'

'If it wasn't Paulie, who was it?'

There was a long silence, relieved only by the steady drip of water from the roof. The air was warm, he thought, now he was used to it; it was the water that was cold. He tried telling his fingers to stop holding her so close, to let her step away, but they didn't listen.

'Tobias.' Esme spoke the name with a sigh.

A tiny terrapin shell floated by; a small head with beady eyes peered out, then disappeared back into safety.

She rested her hands over his as if to remind him he had to let go. He did and she turned, pushing her way through the water down the main tunnel. He had no choice but to follow. Tobias leaked his own technology? But how sure was she?

'How do you know?'

'Tobias told me.'

'What happened?' North said.

'Paulie loves Tobias like a brother. When his girlfriend told him what she wanted him to do, Paulie came straight to him, and Tobias said that he was to go ahead and give it to her. He told Paulie it would mean we wouldn't have to auction it to Big Pharma, who'd exploit it or even shut it down because it would hit their profits. You understand

– nothing worked for Atticus. His disease didn't make them any money, so they didn't invest in research. Tobias never forgave them for that. He promised Paulie he wouldn't have to take the fall. Told him we would blame it on a security breach in our systems.'

'But he could have released it himself?'

'We have investors. And anyway…' She walked onwards, her eyes fixed ahead. 'When Paulie was supposed to go to Harvard, Tobias brought him in with the promise of a stake in Derkind – unless he was found guilty of malfeasance and fired. It would be worth millions. Tobias swindled him. Though it wasn't about the money. I think Tobias didn't want to share the glory for Syd with Paulie and maybe not even with me.'

Tobias had used Paulie. He never had any intention of giving him back his job, or making good on his big payday.

'That was the "bad" thing you were talking about in the car?'

'It didn't make sense – I was going to tell you what I suspected. But then…' She shuddered.

North waited. Was that all she knew? Or did she know about the sabotage programs Tobias had created? The reason they'd both nearly died?

'But it's worse than that. After the crash, I threatened to leave him unless he told me everything – said I'd walk away from all of it, from Derkind and Syd, from our marriage. What he did to Paulie is nothing in the scheme of things.' She took a breath and held it before letting it go. 'You and I nearly died because of a defence contract. So this country can take control of enemy autonomous vehicles on the battlefield. Tobias said what happened in the car was "a glitch" in the system. We nearly died.' She thought there was a 'we', part of his brain noted. 'Him' and 'her' equalled 'we'. And she was outraged, he realized.

'And Chin?'

She was silent for a beat.

'I was trying to help Paulie. Make it up to him. I asked Chin to release Yan – let her marry Paulie, so she can stay here. But he said that would never happen unless we gave him something in return – like Syd. It's all such a mess.' She started to laugh and there was a note of hysteria in it.

The idea of Tobias handing over the superintelligent system which was about to transform man's relationship with machines – and put its creator in the history books for all time – seemed beyond unlikely. The government wouldn't let it happen. Everything would come out, North thought. The calculated medical leak. The sabotage program. Would Syd itself be enough to salvage Derkind's reputation? Although none of it explained the attack on the Museum.

The tunnel narrowed again. He felt the force of the stream take his legs from under him and his feet lift from the floor, the water rising rapidly to neck level. He just had time to lift the gun clear. Turning, he saw Esme stretch out her arms and propel herself through the tunnel by pushing off with her hands. Buffeted by the current, he tipped his own face above the scum and effluent, his eyes inches from the brick. He couldn't keep both the MP5 and the phone, their only source of light, out of the water. One of them had to go – cursing, he dropped the gun.

35

Eventually, as they moved onwards through the tunnel it widened again, and to his relief the level of the water dropped first to their waists, then their thighs, and then it reached only as high as their calves. He turned to check on Esme but as he did there was a low rumble from behind them. He pressed the torch icon and they plunged back into darkness. He sensed Esme move closer to him. A flicker of light appeared in the gloom from what he was guessing were the headlamps of Plato and Nietzsche. The Thinkers were in the tunnels and they were coming up fast behind them.

He took hold of Esme's hand and she gripped it hard. They were heading downwards when they should be heading upwards towards the surface, but they couldn't double back to the storm drain with Plato and Nietzsche standing between them and escape. The Thinkers were getting closer – he could almost make out the men's voices. Esme came to a halt – she put a hand on his forearm. There was a gathering noise of rushing water ahead of them. They must be about to hit the Fleet. He turned the torch back on. There was no point creeping in the dark now. They had to move faster. A wash of white light flooded the wall, and behind them there was a shout of alarm from one or other of the Thinkers.

In the darkness, he sensed a sudden and dangerous kind of emptiness, and he reached for Esme. She teetered in mid-air for a second, before he hauled her back from the void.

It was lighter as the tunnel came to an end, run-off and sewage pouring over the lip into a broad torrent ahead of them. The stretch of water had to be twenty metres across and moving at a rate of knots.

'We'll never make it,' Esme said. Dismay was all over her face as, sparking blue, a shot pinged off the stonework beside them, then another and another. She put her arm over her head, as if that would be enough to block the bullets. The Thinkers behind them still had their submachine guns.

'We have no alternative,' North said, tugging her towards the edge. At least in the Fleet they'd have a chance, otherwise they were about to get very dead. Who knew where they would end up – if the water would carry them under, or carry them away? The chances of making it across had to be negligible but it was all they had. He felt her resistance, the drag of her feet, and understood.

'Trust me,' he said.

'We almost drowned the other day in that car. We're not going to get that lucky again.'

'You and me, we make our own luck,' he said, taking a firmer grip on her hand and pulling her with him as he leapt into the space beyond.

36

He glimpsed the inflatable too late. It was moored close
to the edge of the brickwork. As he hit the water, he flung
out his free hand in desperation and seized the near side's
rowlock, wrenching his arm almost out of its socket with
the impact. He had no idea how deep it was and the icy
cold current sucked at his legs, pulling him away from the
boat and pulling Esme out of his grasp. She screamed, and
his first instinct was to plunge in after her. But first instincts
weren't always right. Gritting his teeth against the pain, he
clung on to the side of the boat. The Fleet wasn't having him
and it wasn't having Esme. With a huge effort, he heaved
himself over the inflatable's side and into the body of the
boat. He should have guessed that the Thinkers would
have come prepared. They needed the inflatable to navigate
their way out of the tunnels. He glanced over his shoulder,
scanning the rapidly moving water for Esme, but there was
no sign of her. The shouts of the Thinkers were coming
closer, the gunfire more rapid now. With freezing-cold and
clumsy fingers, he pulled at the rope tying the inflatable to

the brickwork, and finally the current gripped the boat and spun it away.

He fumbled for the oars, slipping them into the rowlocks and taking hold of their handles, fighting the current – he needed control of the boat, or he'd be past Esme and away to the Thames before he blinked.

Twenty yards away, Esme's head surfaced. With all the power that was in him, he heaved on the oars in a bid to reach her before she disappeared into the black water. 'Esme!' he called as her head disappeared again. He stood up to get a better look and the inflatable rocked with his weight. Bullets spattered the air around him. He heard a sharp hiss as one of them found the inflatable. He wasn't letting Esme drown in a forgotten river. At least, not on her own. As the thought came to him, he dived into the water and the cold, dark Fleet closed around him. He opened his eyes in the murk but there was too little light. Reaching out his arms and legs, he swirled around in the freezing water, desperate for a touch of her, but there was nothing. He made for the surface and sucked down the deepest breath of air his chest could manage.

Was she right to doubt that he could save her again?

He dived again, and again – and finally his outstretched fingers found a scrap of cloth. He took tight hold and pulled her closer, and, wrapping his arm around her ribcage, he brought her up to the surface. The river must have moved them some way downstream because the collapsed inflatable was still with them, but there was no sign now of Plato and Nietzsche, or the mouth of the tunnel they'd jumped from.

Still clasping her with one arm, fighting the current every

inch, he made for the far side of the river, heaving Esme face first up on to the side. Scrambling up after her, he made a thousand promises about how he would live his life if she was alive. *Let her be alive.* After all this, don't let her be dead and drowned on his watch. Because he'd insisted they come down into the underworld.

Her eyes opened as, with a gasp, she started coughing up he didn't want to think what, and he laughed with relief.

Glancing back, he thought he caught movement in the distance of the other bank. Were the Thinkers dumb enough to follow them? Or would they concentrate on their own escape? He had the nasty suspicion Plato and Nietzsche were trying to do both.

37

The light he'd been able to see by came from a grate high above the underground river, but it was a hundred feet above their heads. Even if they yelled blue murder, no passing citizen on the street above would hear them.

'Can you move?' He kept his voice low, although he thought the rushing water should be enough to cover it. The Thinkers had to get across the river.

Esme's face was white, but she nodded. He pulled her to her feet and she staggered, putting the flat of her hand against the arching brick wall to steady herself, and he remembered she'd been knocked unconscious earlier that day. Him too, but he'd survived worse, and he had the bullet to prove it. This wasn't Esme's world, though.

North knew that the sewer they had jumped from wasn't the only one pouring into the Fleet. What they needed was a tunnel this side of the river that would take them up towards the surface. Esme followed him as he edged along the side towards a patch of darkness, water gushing from it in a steady stream. It was another tunnel – a rat appeared, and then another and another, two of them making it on to dry land, one of them tumbling into the Fleet. Surely rats meant food, and food for rats meant people? It wasn't much of a theory, but it was all he had. If he hadn't lost all sense of direction, he thought they were under Farringdon. 'Where do you think it goes?' she said as they both stared into the darkness.

'Somewhere that isn't here,' he said.

He pulled out his phone and pressed the torch icon. God bless whoever had designed a waterproof phone.

The water was lower, only knee-high and then dropping to shin-high, but the smell was getting worse the further they went.

Esme saw it first.

The fatberg was enormous. Blocking almost the whole tunnel, the rancid greyish lump of solidified fat and human waste, toilet paper, wet wipes and domestic garbage oozed brown and yellow in the torchlight. Esme made a retching noise in the back of her throat. 'I would absolutely welcome an alligator eating me right now,' she said.

North took a deep breath and then a running jump. He just about managed to keep his face clear of the worst of the fatberg as he slid down it, a repellent layer of grey grease crusting his shirt and trousers. He tried again. Failed. Failed again. He looked at Esme, who was watching in dismay. 'There's no way we're getting past this. We have to go back,' she said.

'There is no going back.' He took another step to generate more momentum on the way up. Plato and Nietzsche were former soldiers and they weren't men to panic. He couldn't take the chance that they hadn't seen which tributary he and Esme had selected. They were coming for them.

He chiselled out a morsel of the fatberg with the toe of his left shoe, and stepped up into it, clinging desperately to the sloping surface with his hands. He lifted his other foot and dug in the toe of the other shoe. He couldn't get much purchase, but it was enough. He said a grateful prayer to whichever corpse Plug had filched the shoes from. Reached upwards for a handhold in the mass, then another. Like climbing a mountain, he told himself, as a congealed lump came away in his hand. It was like no kind of mountain he was ever climbing again. From the top of the fatberg, he reached down to take Esme's hand. She was already using the toeholds he'd created. He swung her up beside him and they scrambled on their hands and knees over the pitted top of the berg – the air up there so close and hot that the berg appeared to be melting – before half sliding, half crawling down the other side of it.

They had to be close to some sort of exit, he thought, because the light was getting brighter. He could see that the floor ahead of them appeared to be moving. He squinted to get a clearer view. At first he thought it had to be reflections catching the surface water, then he realized it was rats. Hundreds of rats, streaming towards them as if possessed, clambering on top of each other, biting and fighting in insane panic. He pulled Esme to one side, pressing her into the wall, protecting her with his body while the rats streaked past. He felt her catch her breath in the back of her throat as rats surrounded them, rushing between them and over her bare feet.

'How gallant,' he heard, as the last of the rats disappeared up and over the top of the fatberg. The Thinker, in drenched and greasy combat gear, stood ten feet away from them, his MP5 pointed directly at North. He must have made it over the berg while they were pressed against the wall avoiding the streaming rats. There was no sign of his colleague.

They had been so close, North thought. 'Plato or Nietzsche?' he asked the Thinker.

'Plato.' The Thinker's tone was conversational, as if they were chatting over a pint. 'Nietzsche said "God is dead". Me? I keep an open mind.'

The light here was the brightest it had been. North glanced directly upwards, and saw a scrap of orange night sky through the bars of a grate. It was raining hard up in the real world, he realized. His face was wet from it. The threatened storm had broken. Suddenly the rats made sense, which meant they didn't have long. Along the tunnel he could make out the rungs of a ladder climbing upwards to what he was guessing was a manhole cover. He moved to one side, making sure to keep Esme behind him, then stepped away from her.

'The ladder,' he said, over his shoulder.

She looked along the tunnel where the rats had come from. Back at Plato. Hesitated. She didn't want to leave him.

'Go now, Esme,' North said, and moved towards the man in the mask.

The barrel of the gun followed him, as he thought it would. North was big and mean-looking and moving forwards. Altogether more dangerous than the exhausted woman in fluttering scraps of red silk slipping away from them. Plato had it all planned out – he would shoot North and then shoot the woman.

'Why were you at the gala?' North asked. Plato had no reason to give him an honest answer, but he wanted to keep the attention focused on him.

'I heard there was a party,' Plato said, raising the weapon as he ducked his head to line up the sights on North. And then it came, rounding the bend straight for them – the raging storm waters the rats had been fleeing. North leapt for the grate, his fingers bending and straining as his body lifted with the torrent of water, which had nowhere to go but to smash against the fatberg, to fill the small space at the top and to pour down the other side. The water reached as high as North's neck, frothing and churning around him, and he kept his lips closed tight. It took minutes but it felt like hours before the water stopped coming and he allowed himself to drop from the grate. He stared at the ladder. Had Esme made it before the waters hit? Plato's bent body lay slumped against the bottom of the fatberg, the MP5 still cradled in his arms, his eyes rolled back in his head and his face covered by a spreadeagled and equally drowned rat.

'So gross.' He heard the admiration in Fang's voice before he turned round. Her face was hanging over the place where the manhole cover should be, her round eyes on the drenched fatberg. 'I tracked your phone,' she said in explanation, her Joe 90 spectacles dangling from one ear. 'You reek. I mean – not enough Lynx in the world, mate.'

Below her, one hand on the last rung of the ladder, Esme stood in a pool of light. She was drenched, her teeth chattering, her skin blanched bone-white. 'On the upside, not one alligator,' he said.

38

They emerged, blinking, into an artificially lit night and a rain-drenched garden. The hum of traffic and the piercing birdsong of what he was guessing was a robin. Plug stood with Fang. A gaggle of rough sleepers, some of them slumped on wooden benches, peered blearily at North and the bedraggled, barefoot Esme as they clambered up from the sewers – and, with a clang, Plug dropped the cover back down over the entrance. His ugly face was sombre as he turned to drape a heavy overcoat over Esme's shoulders.

North sucked in the fresh clean air and tried to get his bearings. The garden was surrounded by lit-up windows of empty offices. They were in Postman's Park in the City of London. Under a wooden cloister, North could make out the rows of glazed tablets commemorating the individuals who'd given their lives attempting to save others. It had to be a good omen that they'd emerged in one of his favourite spots in London – the Memorial to Heroic Self-Sacrifice. Created by a Victorian artist, each of the tablets told a tragic story of bravery. Surrounded by the selfish and violent, as a kid he'd come here and read them in wonder that there were people out there willing to lay down their lives for others. Even today, he had them by heart. The nineteen-year-old who died trying to save her sister from their burning house; the inspector who 'saved a lunatic woman from suicide' but was himself run over by the train; the twelve-year-old who 'supported his drowning playfellow and sank with him clasped in his arms'.

Fang's voice cut across his thoughts. 'Esme, I'm really sorry,' Fang was saying. Her voice held a quiet note of tenderness. Across the garden, Hone was striding towards them, his one eye fixed on his niece, his long riding coat snapping and flapping around his legs. In the distance, an abrupt silence as a siren wail cut off, the swirl of the blue flashing lights of a waiting police car, and on the horizon the dome of St Paul's.

'No!' Esme said. 'Please, No!'

She'd figured it out before North did, her breath coming faster and faster as if with the effort of willing time to stop. Tobias was dead. Fang didn't have to say the words because they all knew the truth of it. North had been so sure he had to get Esme clear of the museum, that Tobias was already dead or already out of there. That his immediate priority was Esme's survival. Had he called it right? Should he have stayed and found Tobias, defended him against the shooters? Tobias probably died alone, defending Syd from the Thinkers. If North had left Esme to navigate the sewers alone, he could have doubled back for Hawke. But then she wouldn't have made it. And could he trust his own motivations? Tobias was an arrogant bastard he'd found it all too easy to dislike. Esme reminded him of the woman he'd loved and lost, and he had no intention of allowing another innocent to die on his watch. Hone must have known that. He must have made that calculation before he approached North. That North was vulnerable to vulnerable women. That if he had to make a tough call – to protect Tobias or Esme – it was always going to be Esme.

But Esme's desolation told him he'd got it wrong. Her guilt almost killed him where he stood. Esme was brave and true and knew right from wrong, and she had run away. Or rather, she had let herself be torn away, and by him. With barely a sigh, her violet eyes open but unseeing, her knees folded under her and North caught her in his arms. She was never going to forgive herself and – most likely – she was never going to forgive the violent stranger who made her leave her husband to die.

39

British Museum

The museum had signed over one of the galleries to act as a green room for the gala. A pair of uniformed police officers guarded the door; a bearded bear of a man in a white oversuit, overshoes and gloves waited for them, a facemask around his neck.

'National security or not. You do this fast,' he said to Hone. 'And you touch nothing.' North didn't think he was happy about it, but he gestured for the officers to let them through.

Plastic plates had already been laid across the floor like stepping stones, and North sensed Esme hesitate. Hone placed his hand on the small of her back and encouraged her forward. At Postman's Park, she had demanded to see Tobias's body. Now she didn't seem so keen and he didn't blame her.

Tobias lay stretched out on the polished marble floor close to the desk, his sightless eyes still open. Under the blood, the wound appeared blackened and gunpowder stippled the dress shirt – Tobias had taken a point-blank shot to the stomach.

If North had to guess, he'd have presumed Tobias was sitting at the nearby desk when he was shot, before toppling to the floor. Drones of different sizes each sat on top of their own packing cases alongside a 3D printer, with huge banks of computing power ranged alongside the far wall. Tobias had planned quite a show, North thought. He must have been ready to set the drones swooping and swirling over the guests. Maybe he'd even planned to spell out his own name in lights with the small ones, while entering stage right on one of those he could ride. Play footage of cute kiddies with cancer still alive thanks to his AI. Bring on some veterans marching in step, all rigged out with his wonder prosthetics. A final reveal as the great inventor and Syd engaged together on stage. Welcome to the universe's brand-new consciousness.

Regardless of the blood on the floor, Esme dropped to her knees, her hand on her dead husband's snowy mane, her head bent. Plug's overcoat looked huge on her, but she had refused to change out of her soaking dress until she'd seen Tobias. Edmund Hone stared at North hard enough to burn a hole straight through him. No one needed a bullet in his head to know what the one-eyed man was thinking. This was on North. He should have been able to stop it.

Esme was shaking so hard it looked like she might fall apart. She let out a small sound of primal anguish. She was desolate, desperate, disbelieving, but even so, North knew that shock was keeping her from the worst of it. He felt his body go rigid with shame at the sight of her grief. This hurting was down to his negligence. He'd missed something – he just didn't know what – and it had cost Esme the man she loved. Her arms wrapped themselves around her body and North thought they were all that kept her from flying apart. Tears rolled down the perfect cheeks as if they would never stop as she took her dead husband's head between her hands and brought her lips down to meet his, the brunette waves falling like a veil between her and the rest of the world.

Hone gripped Esme's shoulder.

At his touch, she raised her head again, shaking it back and forth as if denying where she was. As if she could change everything if only she didn't have to witness the wreckage of the man who had been her husband. Standing, she raised her right hand, palm upward, and it was bloodstained. Her other hand held what looked like a toy. 'Oh my God!' She held it away from her body as if it might explode. It was a blocky, snub-nosed handgun.

Hone turned to the door, gesturing over a technician hovering at the doorway. North saw the guy's eyes widen behind his facemask as he approached Esme with an open evidence box. North wondered if he was thinking about what his boss would say. The technician checked the barrel and then wired the gun into the box, as Esme attempted to wipe her husband's blood off her own skin and on to her dress.

'That's a 3D gun – known as a Sammy 817. I've seen one before.' Hone said. 'Is it possible that Tobias had the time to print out a gun when he heard the shooters, Esme?' Something about the gun bothered North, but he couldn't think what it was.

No. 'He made it earlier today. He'd been so dismissive about me wanting North around.' Her gaze flicked to him but North thought she wasn't really seeing him. 'But after the car crash, he downloaded a blueprint from the US and printed the gun. He said we just needed to get through the gala and launch Syd and we'd be...' – she placed her hand over her mouth and squeezed her eyes tight shut – '... safe.'

She had been attacked in her own home and had her car sabotaged. North had no doubt that Esme was supposed to die alongside Tobias. He wondered if she'd figured out that she still wasn't safe, and that perhaps she never would be.

'Where's Syd?' As the thought appeared to come to her, Esme's gaze raked the room. 'Did they get Syd? Please tell me Syd's here.'

She crossed the room to lift up the crumpled ventriloquist puppet, and the shattered plastic of the bulging eyes dropped from its face. Tobias must have been planning to work the puppet into the launch. To make his audience laugh, or perhaps cry, before they gasped and wondered at his brilliance.

'The tablet's gone,' she said, and if it was possible for her to turn paler, she did. 'The tablet Tobias loaded with Syd is gone.' She was blaming herself, North knew. For abandoning Tobias, but if she'd stayed she'd have been lying there dead alongside him. She could never have saved him. 'They've taken Syd. And if we don't get Tobias's program back very soon, we have a bigger problem...' – North could hear the fear in her voice – '... than any of this.'

North guessed that the Thinkers had gunned Tobias down when he came between them and their prize. Or maybe they were always going to kill him? The bodies of four Thinkers had been recovered – the three from inside the museum and Plato hauled up from the sewers. But there was no sign of Nietzsche down there. Nietzsche must have the tablet. God is dead. Long live God.

'Earlier tonight, Tobias told me that the Doomsday Clock was already running. Five years ago, Atticus died at 10.14 a.m. Tobias said he was unboxing Syd at 10.14 tomorrow morning. Until he told me, I absolutely had no idea what he was planning. I told him I wanted no part of it and left him to it. That's why I wasn't...' – she looked back at her husband's corpse and shivered – '... with him.'

'Why didn't you say anything in the sewers?' Esme had carried that burden of knowledge and he'd had no idea. No wonder she had wanted to get back to Tobias.

Esme looked at North as if she had only just remembered he existed. 'And what could you have done, North? You were doing your best to keep us alive down there. I had to hope they wouldn't get Syd. I had to hope Tobias would survive and he'd see sense and stop it in its tracks. I didn't think further than that.'

'Why was he willing to wait? Why not unbox Syd at the gala itself?' Hone asked.

'Tobias...' – she turned her head slightly, as if in acknow-ledgement of the dead man behind her – '... said he wouldn't do that to me. He always maintained that the human race would prevaricate endlessly about machine intelligence without firm action. He said the countdown was the only way to concentrate everybody's minds on the future and, of course, he did so relish being the centre of attention.'

Hone held out his hands in an 'all right, so what?' gesture. If they didn't find Syd, then Syd was released into the wild.

Esme shook her head. She was getting angry, North thought, because Hone wasn't thinking of the bigger picture. 'You don't understand – unboxing Syd is a complete disaster!'

Exasperated, she put her hands through her hair and for a second she held her head as if it was too heavy for her shoulders. The butterfly stitches had come loose, North realized. She would have a scar there.

'At the moment, Syd is contained.' She spoke slowly, as if she needed them to understand. 'But its algorithmic functionality has the capacity to join the dots between computer systems.'

Esme moved away from her husband's body and Hone and North went with her. She paced back and forth, talking half to herself and half to them. 'Originally, Tobias and some of his people translated our values into algorithmic code. It was laborious and ineffective. But at the same time, I'd been guiding the machine learning and three weeks ago, we had a breakthrough. Syd appeared to "get" it. The machine's own learning reached an understanding and acceptance of our language, and through that an understanding of our value system. Tobias trusted that – trusted Syd to put humanity first.'

Hone frowned. 'You disagreed with what Tobias was doing? You thought he shouldn't unbox Syd?' Esme stopped pacing and faced him. 'That's why he didn't tell you before.'

She was nodding furiously at her uncle. 'Tobias was taking a terrible risk. We had to tell the world how far we had come with Syd. That's what tonight was supposed to be about. And once we'd done that, the AI community and indeed governments could decide how to go forward.' She counted the options out on her fingers. 'Number one. We go ahead and unbox Syd and see what happens. Number two. We delay things to make sure our safeguards are secure and that we have a proper defence system in place. Or number three. We lock Syd away and bury the key.'

'Which option did you think the AI community would go for?' her uncle asked.

'I had no idea. Tobias's work was decades ahead of anyone else. Some thought this day would never come, and in my opinion, as a species we aren't ready for autonomous and conscious technology. Syd will eat us alive. When Syd goes live, we have no protection against it acquiring the wrong kind of data. No guarantee against it acquiring a stranglehold. No protection that it won't breach and indeed control any and all security systems – financial, military, governmental. Even ones that believe themselves to be safe from all incursion.'

'Is there anything we can do to stop it?' North said.

'He kept saying he could install a fail-safe code – a kill switch to stop everything in its tracks. But with Tobias dead, I have no idea...' – she used the side of her hand to slash through the air – '... I mean, none – how to turn Syd off. We have just over twelve hours to find that tablet and enter the code – a code I don't know – because otherwise... this is the end of days for all of us.'

According to the watch he'd almost lost in a game of chance, it was 10.04 p.m. and they had twelve hours and ten minutes to find Syd and enter a kill switch they didn't yet know. He and Esme had spent time they didn't have finding a way out of the museum and escaping killers in London's sewers. His watch went to 10.05 p.m. Now they had twelve hours and nine minutes before the end of days for humanity. No time at all.

Esme was bone-white and trembling, and a light sweat had broken out on her forehead. Hone gestured for a dark-suited woman to take Esme away. North knew that a team of medics were themselves en route to St Barts Hospital with more injections than he wanted to think about. As she was guided out of the door, Hone walked back to Tobias's body. He stared down at it as if willing it to sit up and tell him who took the precious machine and where.

'He leaked his own medical data,' North said.

Hone folded his arms, lifting his jaw to look at North with his one eye. 'Tell me something I don't know, Sherlock.'

North felt his own anger spark into life. 'If you knew from the start, why bring me into this?'

'You were supposed to keep them both safe. I said protect Esme. That didn't mean leave Tobias to die at the hands of those murderous scum.' Hone kept his voice low, but he was incandescent with rage as he met North's gaze. He placed an unlit cigarette in his mouth and spoke anyway. The cigarette stayed where it was. 'This is a clusterfuck of monumental proportions and you are officially fired. I should have known better than to bring in an amateur – I'm warning you, stay out of it and stay away from Esme. You've done enough damage.' If Hone had been able to do as he pleased, North had the distinct impression he would have shot him where he stood. As it was, the one-eyed man turned on his heel, lighting the cigarette, his riding coat swirling around the long legs as he made for the exit.

North glanced down at Tobias's handsome face, the shock of white hair and the dull eyes. His bow tie was still loose around his neck as if he had been caught unprepared. The best part of twenty years ago, Tobias had hacked off his own foot because he was so determined to stay alive. Now, if Esme had it right, Tobias had brought something into the world that humanity wasn't ready for. And Hone wanted North gone, but the simple fact was he was going nowhere.

North refused to be defined by his past any more. He might not be ready for the future but he was living in the present and that was progress. He remembered Esme holding on to him in the darkness. That electric attraction that he was sure she'd felt as much as he did. Tobias was probably among the first to die, but North had at least saved Esme. He couldn't save everyone, he reminded himself, however much he wanted to, so why, then, did he feel so guilty? He bent down and, with his thumb and middle finger, eased the eyelids down over Tobias's eyes.

She'd already lost a son and a husband. If they didn't find Syd, according to Esme the human race was doomed. Saving the world seemed the least North could do. However dangerous that proved to be.

40

Grim City Waxworks

He had them open up Grim City Waxworks specially for him. It wasn't General Aeron Kirkham's first choice of a rendezvous, let alone when he was overseeing an operation of the magnitude of this one. But this was a matter that couldn't wait, and in times of stress he found the place offered a certain comfort to the weary.

He'd already been through the torture chamber and paused to consider the taste of flesh in the room featuring the demon barber Sweeney Todd and his pie-maker accomplice, Mrs Lovett. The General had eaten flesh once, years ago. An expedition through Papua New Guinea. Didn't mind the taste at all. Didn't mind a bit of the other either, he thought, as he walked a little slower through the Victorian gothic retelling of Jack the Ripper's adventures in the East End. But it was hard to distract himself when there had been innocent people murdered tonight at the museum – he wasn't a man without conscience, for God's sake. He had too much conscience, too much of a sense of duty, if anything. And he gave serious consideration to persuading that vacuous pinhead Rafferty to bring back the death penalty for capital offences, as he gazed at a waxwork execution of that trollop Mary, Queen of Scots. There were those, he knew, who would never understand or forgive what he had done tonight, but he could live without their good opinion.

He cocked his head to one side to better admire the agonizing pain carved into the face of the mannequin impaled from spine to stomach on a huge hook dangling from the ceiling. He wondered if he could arrange a variation on the theme with the dominatrix he saw when he could get away. Madame Lola charged a fortune for house visits, but he felt himself stiffen at the very idea of being stretched out on the metal X-frame he'd installed in his cellar to his own very particular specifications. Madame flogging him with her cat-o'-nine-tails, the thought of her spiked heels enough to bring tears to his eyes.

'The tip of my Gerber Mark II blade is over your small intestine, so best not turn round, General.' The voice was being modulated, he could tell, through some kind of electronic device. He harrumphed in outrage and made to turn anyway, but reconsidered as the sharp point scratched the surface of his skin. 'The Mark II, as you know, is based on the Roman Mainz Gladius – now I think of it, the Sword of Tiberius might even be part of the British Museum collection. Information, you see, General, cuts both ways.'

The General considered his options. The blood in the vein in his left temple started to pulse and the muscles in his left cheek spasmed at the thought that his connection with the massacre was in play.

'Trust me, General Kirkham, you don't want to see my face. This way is safer for both of us. Now, why am I here?'

'I need you to get rid of a man called North.'

Security experts had started raking over the Derkind guest list from the British Museum gala as soon as the first call came into the emergency services. Over the phone, Edmund Hone assured the Home Secretary that Monty De'Ath was one of his, rather than one of the shooters. Rafferty was apoplectic that Hone refused to identify his agent further than that, but the General had seen the security footage himself. Moreover, his own operative, the soldier who'd worn the Nietzsche mask, confirmed that Monty De'Ath was the man who'd escaped with Esme Sullivan Hawke. 'He knew what he was about, General. No mistaking,' Nietzsche told him as he delivered the tablet into the General's hands an hour ago.

What the General knew was that Hone was a one-eyed bastard with a reputation for a bone-chilling, ask-no-questions efficiency when it came to enemies of the state. Normally, the General admired that quality in a man. But not tonight. Kirkham scoured out Monty De'Ath's real name from a security contact. Hone's agent at the gala was one Michael North, a 'security consultant' – for which the General knew to read 'agent and hitman' – formerly in the employ of the extra-governmental agency dubbed the Board.

For a brief moment, the General had considered tasking Nietzsche. But Nietzsche would soon be wrapped in plastic, chained to a concrete block and dropped on to a seabed north of the Orkney Islands. Because the General had no intention of leaving behind any kind of trail connecting him to one of the worst terrorist atrocities on British soil. No, the General had someone else in mind.

Kirkham sucked the stale air through his nose. It was warm and smelled of sawdust and fake blood among the waxworks. He had to get back. The rocket had gone up in Whitehall about Hawke's decision to unbox Syd – such an arrogant bastard. He had his best people working on figuring out Hawke's kill switch and he was leaving it to the experts. In the meantime, he had a more immediate problem. North was everywhere he looked. He'd been brought in to keep that ninja wife of Hawke's safe – he'd rescued her from the car and they'd both survived the museum. And someone had killed his men in there. That had to be down to North, and the General wasn't taking any chances that they hadn't been questioned first. North had to go.

His mind went to the blade in the assassin's grip. It was years since he'd operated on the front line, but in his day, he was steady under fire. He wasn't a nervous man – had never bolted from the action or attempted to avoid his duty engaging the enemy. He'd killed enemy combatants all over the world, priding himself that the year he spent as a raw lieutenant on the streets of Belfast shooting Catholic scum was among the happiest of his life. The General wasn't the kind to doubt his own courage. Even so, he was aware of the sweat building up in the small of his back, the tiny hairs on his neck standing to attention.

'Aside from those terrorists he killed at the museum...' – the General was careful not to hesitate – '... in recent months, North is known to have executed seven men he considered responsible for the death of the woman he loved.'

'No commitment issues then,' the assassin behind him said.

The General ignored what he guessed was an attempt at humour. He had no sense of humour. 'Those men signed the papers, but they didn't pull the trigger.'

'And why should I care about any of this?' The digitally modulated voice was that of an alien, crackling and emotionless.

'You should care because you pulled the trigger.'

A dangerous and waiting silence settled over the pair of them.

The General's security contact had provided details not just on Michael North but on the existence of the Board and those who had once been part of it. Including a code name and number for another former operative. His contact had warned him not to ring it. 'Don't poke the bear, old chap.' The General had rung it immediately.

The assassin behind him spoke in a crackling whisper. 'Maybe he doesn't blame the trigger man. He was one himself, after all.'

'That's a big maybe,' the General said. 'Maybe he hasn't finished what he started yet.'

'The only people who know for a fact who pulled the trigger are all dead. From what you say, North made sure of it.'

'Not true. I know you're the guilty party, because I made it my business to find out.'

'Then wouldn't you say that the smart thing for me to do…' – the breath was on his ear – '… would be to kill you?'

'How do you think I know? Because "someone" told me. Which means "someone" could tell him. North is still out there. This way you set your own price on killing him and you get to sleep at night.'

There was a pause.

'My order on the day was to kill her. That's what I was paid for and that's what I did. No one said anything at the time about killing him too.'

'I'm saying it now.'

Over his shoulder, the General passed the envelope containing the grainy surveillance picture of the man who had entered the party as Monty De'Ath, otherwise known as Michael North, and the file MI5 had on him. His record in juvenile. His army service and the list of men he served alongside. His kills when officially a civilian. And critically, his present location. 'You don't have long.' At first, he thought the assassin wouldn't take it, but then he felt the envelope pulled from his grip.

It was the shift in the air that alerted him to the fact that his companion had gone.

The General put his hand up to the back of his coat. His finger found the cut in the wool cloth there first, then in his jacket, his shirt, the silk vest and finally the wetness on his crêpey skin. He drew back his hand, taking a breath as he smeared the drop of blood in the crevasse between his index and middle fingers with the ball of his thumb. His eyes went back to the mannequin, the agony and ecstasy of a painful death.

He was trembling and hated himself for it. He stood taller and clenched his jaw in what passed for a smile. It was out of his hands – he fervently hoped that North suffered at the end.

41

St Bartholomew's Hospital

Fang was sitting cross-legged on the bed in an isolated ward in the basement of an unused wing of London's oldest hospital. Yawning so hard her jaw cracked, she scrolled through the headlines on her phone. Close by, the latest in a series of bespectacled men in white coats stuck North with a serum – this one to guard against Weil's disease. 'From rats' urine,' one said. 'Potentially fatal.' He sounded intrigued rather than appalled.

As far as he knew, St Bartholomew's Hospital had no Accident and Emergency, so North guessed that most of the doctors scurrying in and out usually worked out of the government's Defence Science and Technology Lab at Porton Down. He hazarded that Hone felt obliged to provide him with the same level of care as Esme. Unless he wanted to torture him before he went – which, knowing the one-eyed man, was a definite possibility.

'What do we know?' he said, in search of distraction as much as information.

'"Nightmare at the Museum"...' Fang read, as North turned his head and bit his lip against the hepatitis injection. '"A previously unknown terrorist cell intent on stopping the progress of artificial intelligence sabotaged a glittering event at the British Museum earlier tonight."' He took a deep breath. He'd showered in water hot enough to skin him, but the smell of the sewers was still in his nose. '"Dozens are believed to be dead, many of them prominent global scientists in the AI field, including Tobias Hawke, Director of the AI Institute, Derkind. Hawke was understood to be on the brink of announcing a step change in AI that could transform humanity's relationship with machines for all time."'

He braced himself for the antidotes to cholera, typhoid, dysentery and cryptosporidiosis as Fang read on regardless: 'This columnist in *The Times* online is hazarding Hawke created consciousness in a machine and is demanding to know what happened to it. Was it destroyed by terrorists? Stolen by Russians? There's a crowdfunding page, which is at £2,500 – in case criminals ask for a ransom. Shall I put you down for a tenner?'

Terrorists? Russians? The guys were British mercenaries – capable, organized and armed to the teeth. The itch he'd been trying to scratch since he stared down at Tobias's body started up again. Something wasn't right...

A trolley appeared, the door banging open as another doctor entered backwards. Tortoiseshell glasses. Early forties. Honey-coloured hair tied back in a ponytail which was beginning to work itself loose. Elegant and exhausted in equal measure. Underneath the white coat, North caught a glimpse of black cigarette pants, with tiger-print loafers on her feet.

'Dr Lily reporting for duty,' she said, pulling out the biggest needle North had yet seen. 'Which of you is the numpty who went wild-swimming in a sewer?' The voice was that of a professional who had seen idiocy before and knew she would see it again, way sooner than she wanted.

'Do I look like a numpty? More importantly, do I smell like a numpty?' Fang wrinkled her nose and pointed in North's direction.

The doctor scrutinized first Fang and then North over the top of her glasses. 'Good point, Toots.' Her mouth twitched, her upper lip holding on to the ghost of a scar of what must have been a cleft lip. 'I feel I should point out to the adult in the room that sewers are full of nasties from cleaning products – not to mention the illicit disposal of chemical waste, not to mention – and I'm using a technical term here – poop.'

She plunged the giant needle into a vial and sucked up its neon-green contents into the glass barrel. Wide-eyed Fang stared as Dr Lily held the syringe upright, tapped it, then pressed the plunger so that a tiny fountain spurted out of the top of the needle. 'Before we do this, though, brighten up my night shift...' She peered over her glasses again, and this time, North noticed that one of her eyes was blue and the other a scintillating green, almost matching the contents of the vial. 'The nurses have a bet on and they need me to settle it. Is it true you have a bullet in your brain?'

'The bullet may sound cool, but think about it – his

numpty brain has to be freakishly empty for the bullet to have missed anything important,' Fang said.

The doctor laughed and with a rush it came back to him. Lying in a hospital bed nearly six years ago. His head hurting so much he thought it might be ready to fall to pieces. The sombre faces of army medics explaining the fact he was coming round from a three-month medically induced coma. That he'd been shot on patrol outside Lashkar Gah in southern Afghanistan. That they'd got him to a top-flight trauma centre fast, where they'd removed bone fragments but had opted to leave a bullet in his brain. That its trajectory and position were highly unusual; that it had missed the brain stem, the thalamus and major blood vessels. Their fascination that he was still alive, and his decision to keep its immediate impact on his brain functioning a secret from them, for fear that they decided he was insane and went back in to dig the bullet out. The certain knowledge that nothing he did mattered, because he could be dead at any second, which meant he had nothing to lose.

A sharp prick of the needle pressed into the muscle of his forearm bringing him back to the present, his eyes went to the tiny bubble of bright red blood that rose to the surface of his skin. He'd had enough of doctors – even charming doctors like Dr Lily. He had nothing to lose, he reminded himself. Unlike Tobias, who'd had everything and lost it all. 'I'm not so dumb that I don't know that Syd is the key, Fang. I don't care what Hone says...' – North looked away from the needle he was pretty sure they used to treat rhinos – '... I'm finding that bastard tablet.'

He felt the release of pressure as Dr Lily lifted the needle before flicking the barrel of the syringe again with a manicured thumb and forefinger. 'Actually, bearing in mind these blood results...' she said, glancing at his notes. She gestured for him to turn round and bend over. Sighing, he took hold of the bed's footrail. The things he did for his country. There was a pause then a sharp stabbing pain in his rump, which the doctor smacked once, hard. North was pretty sure that was against the Hippocratic oath.

'Okay, my treatment plan,' the doctor said as she peeled off the latex gloves, one after the other, 'is for Toots here to keep you away from bullets and sewers. Here, have a sticker. Scooby Doo – my favourite.' She slapped a sticker on the bedside locker and winked at Fang before steering the trolley out of the door, which banged behind her.

'What a weirdo,' Fang said. 'But for an old lady, she was smoking hot and totally objectified you there. When this is over, you should defo ask her out to a tea dance or a coach trip or whatever it is pensioners do.'

North started pacing. 'What do we know?'

'We know Esme was attacked in her own home by an unknown assailant,' Fang said, sitting upright and wide awake.

'We know they had a leak of medical technology to China...' North said.

'... and Tobias was responsible and set Paulie up to take the flak,' Fang finished.

'We know Tobias was working on a sabotage program for self-drive vehicles and someone managed to hack it.'

'And almost killed you and Esme,' Fang reminded him.

'We know there was a massive attack on the gala and that they killed Tobias and got what they came for – i.e. the tablet with Syd on it,' North said.

'We know Syd spells the end of the world as we know it,' Fang said. 'And we have no idea where it is or who has it.'

'Do they know more than we do?' North nodded towards the phone in her hand.

She turned it around for North's inspection. On a live news programme, bearded pundits were frothing with impatience to talk about whether AI would destroy the world. Or save it from itself. Opinion was divided.

'According to this, the Home Secretary is livid,' Fang said. 'The way Ralph Rafferty talks, this is epic...' She clicked on the play arrow of a news video and Rafferty's skeletal figure emerged from the Home Office, surrounded by camera crews and journalists. He stopped in his tracks, as if he was doing them all an immense favour at a time of national crisis. 'I am deeply concerned about events at the British Museum,' he intoned. 'The country has lost one of its finest minds in the death of my very dear friend, Tobias Hawke, and I'd like to offer his family my deepest sympathies as well as the families of the other victims in tonight's atrocity. The Commissioner assures me that the Metropolitan Police is doing its utmost to recover the machine and bring those responsible for these horrific deaths to justice. I can only hope a foreign power isn't involved in an operation on our sovereign soil. In any event, whether this is a hostile action by a foreign power or indeed the act of domestic terrorists, there will be severe consequences and the guilty will be brought to justice.'

'Hone said Rafferty was all over Derkind and what they were doing,' North said. 'But he wasn't at the gala because you pulled the guest list and I saw the names of everyone who turned up.'

Fang flicked through the files on her phone to check and she shook her head. Rafferty wasn't at the gala. 'The other guy who wasn't there was that General from the photo,' she said. 'The one who was involved in that scandal about his soldiers shooting at kids – Aeron Kirkham.'

General Aeron Kirkham. A name not to forget in a hurry.

'Apart from being a General, can you see what Kirkham does?'

She was quiet while she searched. 'Director of the Defence Innovations Board,' she said finally.

'Tobias was about to launch the next revolution. Why wouldn't Ralph Rafferty and the Director of the Defence Innovations Board be there?'

The General's absence was even odder than the politician's, North thought, bearing in mind the defence contract Esme had confessed to – the sabotaging of the enemy's autonomous vehicles. Which sounded very much like a defence innovation to him.

'I want everything you can find on both of them,' he said. 'And use Plug.' Fang made a face. 'He's a people person – not your strong point,' North added.

'… Says the trained killer,' Fang added.

'Hone fired us, by the way.'

'That's the patriarchy for you.' Fang kept chewing on her bubblegum.

'I've a bullet in the head. Do you know what that means?'

'You should learn to duck?' She blew out a small bubble and popped it immediately.

'It means that I'm going to die sooner than I want to.'

'I'm downloading my brain into a computer come the day. Mine's the way-better plan.'

'The bullet means I can take risks you can't. It also means that consequences matter less.'

'Whatevs, mate,' she said.

'We'll have no resources and no official cover if it all goes wrong.' He was serious, because these were high stakes. Tobias was dead. Whoever stole Syd had no idea the machine was ready to take over the world. And there were dangerous men out there who showed no compunction about cold-blooded murder.

'I'm dying of boredom as you speak,' Fang said, 'and I'm not even listening to what you're saying.'

He gave in. 'If Rafferty is talking about a foreign power being responsible, there's only the US, Russia, Israel and China who could pull something like this off. But the shooters were English.' He recalled their voices. Their accents. The way they worked together. But mercenaries would work for whomsoever paid them.

The business card he extracted from the soaking wet trousers on the chair was soggy and the cardboard coming apart, but it was just about legible. While Fang and Plug turned over Rafferty and Aeron Kirkham, it seemed a logical place to start.

'I'm going to visit Octavius Chin. We know Yan worked for Chin, and we know Paulie passed Yan secrets about Syd's medical program with Tobias's blessing. The Thinkers were working for someone. And according to Esme, the Chinese are desperate to get in on Syd. It would be a bold move but these are high stakes – what if Chin set this whole thing up?'

'Bad idea,' said Fang. 'We need to do the legwork on Rafferty and Aeron Kirkham first. Then see how Chin fits in.'

'Chin thinks I'm working for the secret service. After the shooting, he's not going to be surprised when I come knocking. But if Hone gets to him before I do, I won't get anything useful from him.'

What he didn't tell Fang was that he had something to prove. He owed it to Esme to find Syd because then maybe she'd forgive him for keeping her alive and he could put what he felt about her to one side. The fact that when he looked at her, his heart beat faster and he felt hope.

He checked the Rolex on his wrist. It was midnight. He had ten hours and fourteen minutes to recover Syd – and prove that Hone was wrong to call him an amateur. He was every bit the professional when it came to making trouble.

42

Mayfair

Plug picked them up from St Barts. Without comment, he returned the SIG Sauer P226.

'Again, bad idea,' Fang said as North climbed out. He shrugged – it was the only kind he had available.

The Mayfair street where Chin lived was eerily quiet aside from the odd black cab and the barking of a distant dog. North wondered how many of the five-storey mansions were assets on a foreign balance sheet rather than homes.

Number 56 was an elegant picture of red brick and golden stone, complete with mullioned windows, curlicued black balconies, and box trees either side of the colonnaded front door. He took his time walking up the five steps of the entrance. No sudden movements, he thought. And to the right of the arch, above the doorway, the high-tech CCTV camera swivelled. He heard it re-gear and focus as somewhere in the bowels of the mansion as a meathead in a suit scrutinized his every breath. He held up the dried-out wreck of a business card and did his best to ignore the fact that on the back of his neck the hairs stood at full alert. 'North for Octavius Chin,' he said.

There was a moment's pause as if the gatekeeper was consulting on the matter, before the door swung open and North stepped across the threshold.

The foyer reeked of the incense drifting up from a resin table filled with floating gold coins. Behind the incense sticks was a black-and-white portrait of an obese, unsmiling woman, a wooden tablet inscribed with Chinese characters, a porcelain cup filled with tea, and three small dishes of rice. Chin's mother, he'd guess, judging by the family resemblance. Aside from the altar against the north wall of the house, the foyer was clear.

The SIG in his hand, he peered into a drawing room. The curtains were drawn and an enormous chandelier dripping with crystals was reflected in the mirror above a gaping marble fireplace. Eau-de-Nil silk lined the walls, and carpets exploding with twining flowers covered the floor between the gilded furniture. Nothing looked like it would bear Chin's weight without snapping into expensive matchsticks under him.

'It's late for a house call, but Mr Chin is willing to see you.' The silvery voice called to him from across the hallway. He turned to see a vision in a grey cheongsam, her hair loose and shining. He moved towards her and, as he did, she reached out a manicured finger to tap out a code on a control panel on the wall. 'But I'm afraid I must insist that you leave your gun with me.'

She held out her hand, and North thought about ignoring it, but he needed to see Chin more than he needed the pistol.

'I want that back,' he said.

'We all want something, Mr North.' She knew his name, and he couldn't help but like her for it.

The doors of an elevator opened without so much as a breath. She stood back to let him pass and then followed him in, bringing with her the scent of an early summer's night.

'You are admiring my dress?' The vision spoke but didn't look directly at him. Instead, their eyes met in the polished brass of the doors. 'It is a replica of one worn by the President's wife, Peng Liyuan. Mr Chin makes much of his friendship with President Xi Jinping and is a great admirer of the first lady. Mr Chin is a great man and we are all of us honoured to work with him for our country's greater glory.'

'That's a lot of "greats",' North said, 'a few more and I'll start thinking you're trying to persuade you as much as me.' He thought the reflection might have smiled, but he wasn't sure. 'What's the something you want, by the way?' he added. 'Perhaps I can help. I'm a helpful guy.'

She looked at him sideways, cool, assessing, but didn't reply. He had the distinct impression she was considering the question.

The elevator travelled silently down, till they reached somewhere close to the centre of the earth. The doors slid open and his guide stepped aside, gesturing to the dark space beyond. He turned, giving his senses a few seconds to adjust to the noise of the slap and dripping of water and the moving wash of blue. Behind him, he felt rather than heard the elevator rise, sensed the vibrations of the pulleys and pumps and counterweight straining to lift the cab.

Without the distraction of the lift, he realized a blue wall of floor-to-ceiling glass stretched out in front of him, the changing light the result of the bright white spotlights and water behind it. He followed the smells of the sea and rotting fish through a tunnel. In the room beyond, reflections from the glass wall of water gave Octavius Chin the look of something submerged and monstrous. A napkin knotted around his bulging throat, the intelligence agent sat hunched on an ornate gilded throne over a steaming bowl of noodles, the table set with a white cloth and sparkling crystal. His narrow eyes were fixed on the glass.

North looked across to the moving water. He could see nothing in it to merit Chin's close attention, aside from tumbled rocks in the far corner. The tank was huge. Chin had to have dug out not only the basement under this house but under the houses of his neighbours. China must own the whole terrace.

'Have you offered comfort to the grieving widow, or is it too soon?' Chin's eyes moved to his guest as he mopped at his fleshy lips with a napkin, leaving blots of chilli, red like fresh blood.

'I'm planning to bake her a pie,' North said. 'Does that count?'

Chin snapped his fingers and from the shadows two dark-suited figures appeared carrying another seat, this one lower and less ornate, which they placed to one side of their boss. Chin waved at it and North sat. A waiter placed a bowl of rice in front of North but he shook his head. He only ate with people who didn't make his skin crawl.

'My great-great-grandfather turned a beggar away at the door.' Chin slurped up another oversized bundle of slimy noodles. 'Since then, no son has known anything other than hunger, whatever the food they consume, whatever their wealth and their power. A curse. Nonetheless, this is something of a celebration – I'm a fortunate man to be alive when at the museum it could so easily have been otherwise. You too, North.'

Without waiting for his response, Chin put back his head and used a pair of ivory chopsticks to hold a small pink octopus over his pursed mouth, sucking in first one tentacle and then the head. 'Did you know that when you cut the head away, the arms still move on the board. Occasionally I eat them raw, so I can taste the movement.'

He chewed, the noise filling the room. The tail end of a tentacle hung from his greasy lips, and his pink tongue searched for it before finding it and scooping it back in, leaving only a trail of crimson sauce to prove it had ever been there. North fought not to let the disgust show on his face, but he thought Chin caught something of it and it pleased him.

'What is it you want from Octavius Chin? Do you come like another beggar-man to my door?'

'I know Yan works for you, and you used her to get close to Paulie to get the medical tech.'

'Yan failed me in countless ways, but not in that,' Chin said, his mouth open as he chewed, tentacles everywhere.

'Hawke wanted it to happen, did you know that? He hated Big Pharma. He used you.'

Chin glowered. He liked to be the smartest person in the room, North thought.

'Did you sabotage the Lamborghini?'

Chin put down the chopsticks with a clatter. Now that

he wasn't chewing, North could hear the sound of sobbing coming from somewhere close. Chin seemed oblivious.

'Why would we?'

'To show Hawke that you knew his game.'

'To what end? Why wouldn't we slide in, and then take what we wanted with him none the wiser?' With some delicacy, Chin wiped the corners of his mouth with his napkin.

The weeping sounded like someone's heart was broken. Like someone was hurting and North knew he was meant to hear it. He gritted his teeth – it had to be Yan. 'Were the shooters at the gala yours?'

Chin still had Yan. Yan, who had fallen in love with Paulie and confessed all to him. Yan, who had been desperate to escape. He wondered if Chin was shipping her back to China. So much for Esme's attempt to play Cupid.

'You are a dangerously curious young man. So many questions. That would be an act of war, would it not, North? To set armed fighters down on to the sovereign soil of another nation and order them to kill that nation's civilians.'

North didn't trust the Chinese agent for a second, but he'd seen his bodyguards almost carry him bodily from the gala, and Chin's shock had seemed genuine. 'If those men weren't yours, then you don't have what I'm looking for and I'm wasting my time.' North made as if to stand, but two sets of strong hands held him down in the chair.

'The British intelligence service are normally more subtle when they deal with me. But then you are a blunt tool, are you not, North, so I will make allowances for your naivety. And I will teach you a lesson in the ways of this shadowy world in which you now walk.' Chin clasped his hands over his belly and sat back in his chair. Teacher and pupil. 'If I had the stolen tablet – and yes, I know what's on it – why would I hand it over to you? If I had Syd, I would already be on a plane back to my political masters. Our top scientists are already working on a kill switch of our own. There is indeed an argument that it would be safer for everyone if Syd found a home in China.'

'You know a great many things you shouldn't, Mr Chin.'

'You would be surprised at those who confide in me, North, for their own reasons. Perhaps you and I can do business after all. If you find Syd, my government would not be slow to show its gratitude.'

'Your government has nothing I want.'

Chin shrugged, and under the silk jacket the fat rolled in waves and was slow to settle. 'We can offer peace of mind. We wouldn't want anything to happen to those around you, would we?'

North's stomach dropped. Did he mean Fang? And Plug? Did he mean Esme?

Chin's tone was neutral. 'Young girls have to be so very careful these days.'

He meant Fang.

North reached for Chin's throat and the heavies hauled him back into the seat. One of them punched him in the head.

'The one-eyed man that you work with – Edmund Hone – has no loyalty to you or to your little friend. I think even you know that. You are pieces in his game. He won't help you keep her safe. He can't. Only you can do that.'

The sound of hysterical pleading was getting louder and more desperate. There was a huge bang, as if Yan had been thrown against something or fallen, then silence.

'I'm going to do you a favour, Chin, and forget you just

threatened a friend of mine. But part of that forgetting means you need to give me Yan. In return for her, I'll think about letting you have Syd as and when I find it.'

He wouldn't, but Hone could sort that out. The more immediate problem was that he couldn't let them take Yan back to Beijing in disgrace. She had succeeded in bringing in the medical tech but in doing so had fallen in love, and in falling in love she had wanted to share her life with Paulie and forgotten her patriotic duty to be first, last and only ever an agent of the Chinese government – how many years in prison did that get you in China?

'Did you know that an octopus can undo a jar, master basic puzzles and recognize patterns?' Chin was looking at North, but North wasn't listening any more. He was imagining Yan unconscious. What had they done to her? Was she dead? North prayed for the weeping to start again. 'They can negotiate a maze and ring a bell for treats. Toss a simple clock into the tank and they put it back together. But still, they are not so intelligent that they manage to stay out of the bowl. I can see my talk is boring you, but the lesson has barely begun.'

North didn't see the signal but there must have been one because, twisting his arms behind his back, the two suits dragged him from his chair across to the glass, before smashing his nose against it. He heard the crunch of cartilage, and blood splattered the glass in the same moment as the red-hot pain hit him. Blood gushed down his throat and he struggled against the two heavies holding his face flat against the glass. His arms pinioned to his sides, retching, he tried to clear his airways and shift the excruciating pressure on his face.

'You will give me Syd, North, and I hope for your sake and for the sake of Fangfang Yu that you do find it.' Behind him, he heard Chin's chair legs scrape against the floor as if he was standing up from the table. 'Yan failed her country. Her hairless lover was fired and is of no further use to us.'

Could you drown in your own blood? Definitely, and North felt a frisson of distaste from the men holding him as he attempted to bring up and spit out what was pouring down his throat.

'Tobias Hawke is dead, and Syd is gone when it should already be ours.' Chin was using Yan as a convenient scape-goat for his own failures, North realized.

All of a sudden, the weight lifted from the back of his head, allowing him to bring his face back from the glass. More pain, just of a different kind, as fresh blood gushed from his broken nose and he heard the crackle of the settling cartilage. He sensed the attention of the men holding him shift to the tank. Behind the glass, water moved. North strained his neck to make out the rocks on the far side, and as he did so a klaxon shrieked, on and off, three times. Again, the water moved. Was there something in the tank? Was it empty? Suddenly, Yan's body plummeted past him amid a storm of bubbles, as if she had landed with some force. She must have been thrown in unconscious and the shock revived her, because as she sank through the water her eyes opened and her limbs stirred.

'Yan will serve me one more time,' Chin said. 'To show you what happens to silly girls who swear allegiance to the wrong men.'

They were going to drown her in front of him.

'Get her out – I told you we can deal,' North said, frantic to get to the girl and drag her from the water. A cold muzzle of a gun ground its way into the nape of his neck. 'Shhh!' Chin's breath reeked of dead things.

North fixed his eyes on the water beyond Yan as something stirred in the murk behind her. Yan kicked her legs, frantically paddling upwards, her arms stretching forward, straining to reach the surface. As she did, there was a movement above her – a cover closing over the top of the tank – and the water darkened. She paddled faster but it was too late. The tank was sealed. The girl used her hands to press against the glass cover, struggling to shift it, but she was too slight, or it was too heavy. There had to be a small gap between the water and the glass because she seemed to take a deep breath before turning and diving back down into the tank. She was going to try to find some kind of drain, North thought. Clever girl. *Don't panic*, he willed her. *If you panic, you die. Find a way out. Find a drain. Lift a cover. Swim out of there to the sea and beyond.*

Chin rapped on the glass with enough force that it seemed to shake in its mountings. For a second, she looked across, the swirling black hair wild in the water, her blue eyes desperate as they took in Chin first, and then North. She held his gaze and took a second to press her hand against her heart and move it away, and he had the idea she was sending Paulie a message, before she turned, spinning as she swam, her arms wide as she raked the concrete walls looking for an opening.

North heard his own groan as if it was from a stranger, as the rocks themselves appeared to move and a monstrous octopus unfolded itself, moving at first slowly and then swiftly through the water. The creature's body was red and covered with lumps and bumps. North could make out two eyes, one either side of the bulbous head. From some distant memory, he seemed to recall that an octopus had two legs and six arms. They moved and stretched together as it propelled itself through the water and reached for the girl.

It found her.

With a flurry of white water and bubbles, the giant Pacific octopus turned, shielding Yan's body from the window, and Chin growled in disappointment. North could have sworn that the octopus had made the manoeuvre on purpose.

The octopus turned again and he glimpsed Yan struggling for breath, for escape, her head backwards, her arms reaching for purchase. But her legs were held fast in the octopus's huge arms, then her waist and her neck, folding her in to the sharp-toothed beak. A swirl of blood emerged from the tight embrace of octopus and girl. A pale pink, then darker. He hoped for the girl's sake she had swallowed the water, taken it into her lungs and forced out the air and was drowned – that she couldn't feel the teeth reaching into her innards to feed. He prayed for oblivion.

Beside him, Chin's hands were pressed against the glass, his breath condensing on it. His black eyes glistened.

'I call her Octavia and I keep her hungry,' Chin said. 'Like me.'

Time stretched into for ever. North wanted to shut his eyes. But didn't. Watching her die seemed the only thing he could do for Yan now. He didn't want her dying alone.

After what seemed like an eternity, North sensed movement behind the glass and the octopus let go of Yan. The girl's ravaged body floated down to the gravel and weeds on the bed of the tank. Tiny scraps of flesh, moving with her, floated up from what had been her stomach.

On Paulie's stairs, North had held Yan's arms to stop her falling, and she'd stared at him, pleading for help, as if she knew what was to come. Was this what she feared? Had Chin done this before?

North felt sick. If he could have broken loose of Chin's enforcers, he'd have strangled him with his bare hands. He reared back as the octopus's bulbous head banged against the tank close by them, before pulling away. Further down the wall, it brushed back against the glass, the arms and legs moving rhythmically alongside as if it was patrolling its territory. An eye peered out from the water, its attention apparently focused on Chin. North had the distinct impression, as the suckered legs swirled, unfurled, reached and crawled over its prison, that the octopus hated Chin's guts.

'It's too late for Yan, North.' Chin was back to business. 'But it isn't too late for Fangfang Yu. Remember that, if you're the one to find Syd.' The goons turned him to face Chin. 'In the spirit of cooperation between our great nations, I can tell you what I do know. A little bird told me that Hawke was hiding something at St Bride's Church.'

Chin's eyes glittered. He already knew what Hawke had hidden, North thought. 'Something very terrible that your own government will not want you to find. Start there.'

He gestured to the goons. North felt the world turn on its axis as he was turned back round, his head hit the plate glass and everything went black.

43

The Strand

They slowed as they threw him out of the car, but not by much.

Yan was his first thought as he staggered to his feet.

The memory of the girl's agonized face, her black hair twisting and turning in the water as the monster came for her. His own face pressed against the glass. Helpless. Watching a young woman die when her only crime was to fall in love. Was Chin always going to kill her so horribly? Or had North made things worse for her with his reckless arrival?

Chin believed he was untouchable as an agent of the Chinese security services. But Octavius Chin was in North's black book. And North was drawing a line through that name just as soon as he'd found Syd – he could do that much for Yan. As for Chin's threats to Fang, he was going to make the guy eat every word – see if that killed his appetite.

He reached for his gun. Remembered it was gone. Reached for his phone, but it was gone too. Chin was doubtless gutting it for intel but good luck with that, because it had none. His head pulsed. His left hand pressing into a wall for support, he gripped his nose between the fingers and thumb of his right hand, seeing stars, doing his best to straighten it without passing out. It was good enough, he decided, rolling his arms backwards and then forwards in their sockets, hearing the grinding of bones, before curving his spine to stretch out the stiffened muscles along his back. He swore once and, grimacing, he lifted his T-shirt to reveal red and purple bruising across his abdominal wall. Chin's men had given him a gentle working-over as a going-away gift.

They'd dropped him by the Royal Courts of Justice. He started moving, a jog at first, building to a run, running through the pain in his face, in his body. Shutting it off. His phone was gone, but he drew to a halt at a public phone outside a mock Tudor pub hung about with baskets full of winter pansies.

Plug picked up on the first ring. He spoke before Plug could ask how it went, which by any definition was badly.

'Meet me at the main entrance of St Bride's, and we need to make it look official.' He hung up.

It was too late for Tobias. And too late for Yan.

North had no idea what Hawke had hidden at St Bride's. He had no idea if indeed Chin was telling the truth when he'd said it was something 'very terrible'. But he was willing to bet if there was something there, then it was nothing good.

44

St Bride's

Plug swept him with a small bug detector.

'I'm getting the hang of your business, don't you think?' Plug said, grinning, as the beeping started.

Chin was keen to keep tabs on him. In the hem of his jeans, they found a wafer-thin bug the circumference of a pound coin. He unwound the window and dropped it into the storm drain – perhaps it would end up in the Fleet? He shivered at the memory of the cold underground river even as his eyes raked his surroundings for the human surveillance team. He didn't believe for one second they would have thrown him out of the car and left him to it but that's what they wanted him to think, that's why they'd thrown him out instead of pulling up and letting him out. Chin had advised him to search St Bride's and the Chinese agent wasn't one for free advice, which meant if North found Syd, or indeed any sign of Syd, Chin intended taking it from them.

Buzzing up the side window, he shrugged himself into the clean grey tee, sweatshirt and black jeans Plug had brought along. He caught a momentary glance between his friends as they caught sight of the scrapes and bruises blossoming all over his torso. If he flipped down the overhead mirror it would show a couple of belting black eyes, he imagined, so best not. 'Yan is dead,' he said, strapping on the shoulder harness and sliding the semi-automatic into it. Fang let out a small murmur of pity. She looked shattered, he thought, but then it was past two in the morning and she was only a kid.

'How?' she said.

'Badly. Chin doesn't know where the tablet is, but he said that Tobias was hiding something at St Bride's – something that our government wouldn't want us to find.'

'It can't be Syd,' Fang said. 'Not if Tobias hid it, because he had Syd with him at the museum. Does Chin know what?'

North hesitated. There'd been something in Chin's eyes, a particular kind of glee that made him think Chin knew that it was nothing good.

'I think so – yes.' He pulled on the same down jacket and high-vis vest the others were already wearing. He clipped a faked ID to the toggle of his zip.

'What's his game then?' Plug asked.

North shrugged. 'I'd say he's in bad odour for letting Syd slip through his fingers. Maybe he's trying to muddy the waters, or maybe...' – his eyes snagged on several dark shapes in a 4x4 along the way from them – '... he'll let us run with it and see what we turn up.'

'I don't like it,' Fang said. 'We shouldn't be doing what he wants us to do.'

'He threatened you.' He couldn't bring himself to tell her what Chin had threatened to do to her.

The girl snorted, then went quiet.

North had no intention of letting Chin or his mutant octopus anywhere near Fang, but the best way to keep her safe was to find Syd. He had no leverage without it. And they had to start somewhere. 'The sewers Esme and I used to escape the museum took in the Fleet river – but there was no sign of Nietzsche when the police went down there. Maybe he surfaced around here?' North turned to stare out of the rear window. 'There has to be some connection between what went on at the museum and whatever's hidden in there. If Chin's right, the dearly departed Tobias Hawke was a man with a secret.'

He'd had plenty of time to recce St Bride's, but they drove by the main entrance anyway. Breeze blocks filled the stone arched gateway of the avenue that led to the church, sandbags at the bottom. There was no way in or out without a tank to break through the freshly built wall. 'Biohazards present. Removal under way. St Bride's is closed until further notice', a sign explained, alongside a list of nearby churches and their service times.

'There's a side entrance,' North said.

Loops of barbed wire ran the length of the walls surrounding the churchyard, with its headstones, leafy trees and wooden benches. Behind the wire and more warnings of biohazards, St Bride's steeple rose, tier after tier, into London's night sky. They passed cast-iron railings and reached the side gates with their stone columns topped with carriage lanterns. And as they did, North glanced back down the lane for passers-by, but there was no one. He breathed a sigh of relief – even with lanyards and high-vis vests, clipping through the swirls of wire looked downright odd at this time of night.

An industrial chain held the gates fast; it was padlocked. The delicate tools of a locksmith – or burglar – were already in Plug's hand. 'They modelled wedding cakes on that spire,' Plug told Fang as he took hold of the shackle, sliding a pick into the padlock's core and moving it this way and that, feeling for what North knew were the retraction springs. There was a quiet ping. Unravelling the heavy linked chain, Plug stood back to let them pass before following. He reached out his arms to thread the chain back through the metal bars of the gates. This time, though, Plug rested the padlock on the side of the church rather than the street, its shackle only loosely closed together with the lock. It wouldn't pass close inspection, but it was good enough to persuade the casual observer. The three of them moved along the path as a group. Keeping it natural. Slow. Making an early start – very early – on official business.

'You realize Granny Po will strangle the pair of us with razor wire if anything happens to Fang,' Plug said under his breath.

'Does she have any razor wire?' North asked.

'When the cheese cutter went missing, I checked her knitting bag. Three skeins of cream wool, a pattern for an Aran jumper, and a garotte.'

'We'll make sure nothing happens to Fang then,' North said, and wished he felt as confident as he sounded.

At the church door, Fang held up her hand. She bent her head over her phone, her glasses gleaming with reflections of page after page, which she seemed to absorb at a glance, her fingers barely pausing as she zipped between one site and the next. North watched. For Fang, code was her first language; she knew the highways and byways of cyberspace as well as he knew London. How fast would a machine like Syd clear a path through it all? North shifted from foot to foot, glanced at his watch. By his reckoning, they had just over eight hours left before Syd took over the world.

'Home Office bioscientists are worried...' – she said, lifting her head –'... that an archaeologist turned up a live smallpox virus in the bones in the ossuary. They don't want to risk a pandemic so they've imposed a quarantine, hence the barbed wire and shouty signs. How badly do we want to know what's in here?'

The three of them stared at the sign nailed to the church door. The skull and crossbones stared back. The words 'Risk of contagion and disease. Keep out.'

'I'm asking because he couldn't get any uglier,' Fang said, nodding in Plug's direction. 'And nothing seems to kill you, not even a bullet in your head. But I'm cute and the world needs more not less of me, so I'm going to be right hacked off if I catch smallpox, get ugly and die.'

'I don't believe a word,' North said, rattling the door. It was locked.

'But you're stupid. Smallpox is one of the most devastating diseases out there,' she said. 'And smallpox has an incubation period of between seven and seventeen days, so if we're wrong about this, the three of us could walk out of here and carry a disease that has officially been eradicated straight into the heart of London. Maybe that's exactly what Chin wants? Should we tell Hone that Chin claims there's something here, and leave it to the spook brigade?'

North considered the idea. Hone had fired him – that meant the one-eyed man had no prior claim to any information North obtained as a private citizen. And Hone wouldn't be grateful – he would be incensed that North was still involved. Hone might even lock the three of them up to make sure they didn't get in his way. Telling Hone was not an option.

They read the answer in his face. Plug took out his lock-pick set again as Fang rolled her eyes and went back to her screen. 'I'm researching a cure for smallpox,' she said.

There was a quiet rub of metal against metal as Plug hunkered down to use his lock and pick on the church door. 'My grandad was here during the Blitz when the Nazis flattened St Bride's – even the bells melted with the heat.' He extracted one pick and swapped it for another, as he moved his hand back and forth, freeing up the lock on the doors. He pushed it open and they stepped inside. Plug cursed as he caught sight of the internal doors – these ones of glass and wood. 'Broke his heart.' Plug eased a key from an enormous keyring into the keyhole. He put his shoulder against the door and leant his weight into it as he turned the key a few degrees clockwise, then anticlockwise. 'He was a compositor, used to bang out the type when this street was all hot metal and newspapers.'

'Newspapers?' Fang said, not looking up from her screen. 'Information written in ink and printed on pieces of folding paper. No moving pictures. Am I right?'

There was a thunderous crack as the door finally gave, which North thought was just as well as it drowned out Plug's Anglo-Saxon reply.

They emerged into the back of the empty church.

Moonlight poured through the immense leaded clear-glass windows and over the geometric black-and-white marble floor, which stretched to the altar and the crucified Christ. North's immediate impression was one of the sacred. 'Londoners have worshipped on this site for 1,500 years,' Plug said, keeping his voice low.

'Our Father who art in Heaven...' – Fang pressed her hands together as if in prayer – '... I smuggle coke when business is slow. For lines is the Kingdom, the pills and the blow. Amen.' North caught a glimpse of what looked like a floor plan on her phone as she moved away and started walking towards a stairway at the back of the church. 'The crypt is this way. Let's go catch smallpox, moron-people.'

45

The stone walls were thick and the air dry in the crypt. The lights were on.

North was less and less happy. If St Bride's was a diversion and Chin was wasting his time, he wanted them in and out as quickly and as quietly as possible. If this was a legitimate shutdown of an archaeological site, he might even have to fess up to Hone and the three of them go into quarantine. He shuddered at the thought of more needles.

He stalled in the narrow corridor and jerked his thumb back at Fang, speaking in a whisper. 'Go back and wait for us upstairs.'

'Like that's happening,' she said. She pointed through the exhibition space they were in, Roman pavements reflected in mirrors on the wall behind a simple altar. 'This way.'

It would help if they knew what they were looking for.

They passed through a heavy door, picking their way over bare planks and stone walkways, past the detritus of church life, Christmas ornaments, poppy wreaths, crusted plastic buckets that had once contained lime mortar, and piles of folded hessian. Through a medieval chapel and past ancient gravestones and a metal coffin. The further they went, the less clue he had as to what secret had brought Hawke down here. And what the government was so keen to hide.

North opened the door marked 'Ossuary' into a room lined with cardboard boxes. If Hone had hidden something, would he have hidden it in plain sight? He flipped the lid off the nearest box and jumped back – gingerly, he extracted a brown skull with a tuft of hair still attached.

'The Victorians sealed up the crypts after a cholera epidemic in 1854,' Plug said. 'My grandad said when they were rebuilding after the war, they discovered a couple of hundred coffins down here. This must be what was in them.'

They pulled out box after box from the shelves – there was nothing but ancient bones and fragmenting yellow skulls.

Biting back a heavy sigh, North gestured them out of the ossuary.

They'd wasted too much time already. Maybe that was Chin's intention? But he didn't like it – the crypt was a warren, and if someone found them down here, they were caught like rats in a trap.

'Down there.' Fang pointed along the darkest, twistiest corridor to what looked like yellow-and-black tape criss-crossing the entrance. A massive swag of plastic curtain blocked the corridor next to the 'Contamination' and 'Strictly no entry without a K567 pass and a hazardous materials suit' warnings.

The hair rose on the back of his neck.

He ducked under the yellow-and-black tape, before stepping through the split plastic. At first, he thought it must be the rustle of moving air against the sheeting, but after a second or two's pause he realized the noise was coming from some place ahead of them rather than from behind. Plug and Fang followed him through and he pointed to a break in the wall ahead – the tinny electronic buzz fizzing and crackling around him now – as a sudden surge of adrenaline pumped its way through his system.

In silence, North gestured to Plug to stay back and protect Fang.

Keeping to the wall, North edged forward. He kept his breathing slow and steady. Were there voices ahead of him? If so, how many, and where were they coming from? He was concentrating so hard, he almost leapt out of his skin as he felt Fang's light touch on his arm. He glared at Plug as the teenage girl slotted herself in next to him, and the big man shrugged. It wasn't as if she'd given Plug a choice in the matter.

Craning his neck, North leant forward to peer around the corner.

A New Army soldier sat slumped on a broken-down ecclesiastical chair staring at an iPad he'd balanced against a couple of bricks and an unlit lantern. His SA80 assault rifle was propped up next to him, while huge noise-cancelling headphones sat over his ears, and his hands clutched a controller.

It didn't make sense. Official contamination warnings that had shut off the entire church. A single soldier without protective clothing. And no signs of any ongoing biohazard or scientific work.

North stepped out of the darkness and took a step towards the soldier, the dry earth and tiny stones crunching under his shoe. Two. Three. Four. The tinny buzz getting louder with each step as the soldier slaughtered his virtual enemies. But as North walked, the stale air must have moved around him, because the player made to stand, dropping the controller and reaching for the assault rifle.

He could have played it differently, North admitted to himself afterwards, but he didn't. Maybe it was the darkness and the fact they were trapped together in a confined space? Or the memory of Tobias's blood spread across the floor of the museum? Or the need to protect Fang? But, reaching with his left hand, North seized the nearest shovel and in the same movement swung the handle hard against the soldier's head. The soldier went down without a sound, his avatar mown down in the same instant.

Fang broke free of Plug's grip to run across to the unconscious soldier. She applied her fingers to the guy's throat. 'Completely OTT. You don't have to incapacitate every single person you meet.' Her face in the light looked ferocious and disapproving, but then Fang's face often looked ferocious and disapproving. He examined himself for remorse but there was none. This was a brutal business, and incapacitated was better than dead.

The soldier's eyes remained closed, his breathing laboured, as North used some handy rope to hog-tie him.

Then again, perhaps he should have disarmed him, keeping him conscious and able to answer questions. Questions like: why did anyone need a shovel in a smallpox site? Not just one. Six shovels were stacked against the walls, along with a couple of pickaxes, some coils of rope and folded tarpaulin sheets. North bent down and picked up the shovel he'd used against the guard. He had used the wooden handle because he hadn't wanted to kill the soldier, but it was the blade he was fixed on now – the blade covered with dirt. The kind you turn up if you closet yourself under one of London's oldest churches to bury a secret.

North hunkered down, running his fingertips over the earth. It was hard packed and, aside from this-way-and-that boot prints, seemed undisturbed.

There was a shout from the wall.

'This should be an entrance here with a door,' Fang said. North thought back to the plastic buckets, to the piles of hessian they'd passed, to the bricks propping up the soldier's iPad. Someone had sealed the entrance.

Plug used a pickaxe to lever out the first brick, and a breath of cold and dusty air escaped. North peered in. It was completely dark. Plug moved Fang to one side, took hold of the bricks either side of the space he'd created, and pulled. The mortar was fresh and the bricks gave without much fightback. He eased in the end of a spade and slammed his full weight against it, levering out a massive chunk of brickwork. North did the same on the other side. Slabs of mortared bricks came out in pieces till, with a loud crash, an entire section of the wall came down.

Plug held up the soldier's lantern he'd lit and, beside him, North heard Fang take in a horrified breath.

Skulls and bones stretched the length and breadth of the space. In the furthest corner, a huge heap of what looked like thigh bones was piled against the bricks. Close by, a row of ancient brown skulls stood guard over a trench stiff with more bones. As he stepped over the ragged bricks, North felt his foot sink into the long bones, snapping some of them under his weight.

'What is this place?' North said.

'A charnel house,' Plug said. 'When churchyards ran out of space, they'd dig up the inhabitants. But they'd had a Christian burial, so the remains had to go somewhere.'

'Please tell me they died of old age,' North said, lifting up a skull, 'and not the plague. Or the pox.'

'This room is mapped. You wouldn't hide anything in here, because even bricked up, there's a risk in a few years someone might find whatever it is.' Fang pointed to the wall on the left. 'According to the map there's nothing behind that wall, but I think there is. I think they've knocked through to next door.'

Plug lifted the lantern. Fang was right. The bricks were blackened with dirt and the grime of centuries, but the mortar was clean – the wall had been taken down and built back up again.

It took less than fifteen minutes to break through. The charnel house beyond was three times the size of the first, and the bones lay at ten times the depth. If he had to hazard a guess, North would have said it was centuries older. And it was empty of anything but skulls and bones. Shadows from the lantern clambered up the darkened brick walls and across the vaulted ceiling as Plug attempted to light the furthest reaches.

There was nothing.

'I shouldn't have listened to Chin,' North said. 'I'm sorry.'

He had brought Plug and Fang down into this hellhole for no good reason and the Lord only knew what they'd been breathing in. Dust? Disease? The microscopic remains of ancient Londoners? Even his mouth tasted of the dead. Worse than that, they were no nearer to finding Syd and they had allowed Chin to waste time they didn't have. Maybe the wall between the charnel houses had been there for seven hundred years and they had seen exactly what they wanted to see? Maybe the soldier hadn't been wearing protective clothing because he had a brick wall between him and the dead? Or because he was plain dumb? And maybe there were no scientists down here because the place was disgusting and dangerous and they knew better?

Fang's glittering boots barely rested on the stacked bones as she moved across the room. She seemed unfazed by the dead surrounding them, or indeed the fact she might join them sooner than she ought to. Using the torch on her phone, she moved the light like a brush over the bones. Then stopped and stared. As North and Plug crossed over to her, bones breaking and snapping under them, Plug lifted the lantern higher so they didn't lose her in the shadows.

At Fang's feet were crushed fragments of skulls, a whole heap of long bones, and a cigarette end.

None of them spoke. They started digging.

They were three metres down and what hit them first was the smell.

46

North wondered if he was imagining it at first. If it might be associated with the stale air and the sheer number of bones and skulls around them.

He wanted to think he had it wrong, that the smell was unfamiliar, but he'd smelled it too often and the memory wasn't one that ever faded.

Plug paused in his digging, his face grim.

'We don't know when they change their guards,' Plug said. 'It could be any second.'

Plug was right. This was stupid. They were trapped underground in a secret charnel house accessed through another charnel house, which itself had been walled off in a crypt that someone had taken a great deal of effort to close off from all comers. And he was guessing they were too late to help whoever was down here with them. North kept digging.

'We should at least get her out of this,' Plug said, keeping his voice low as his eyes drifted in the direction of Fang, who stood at a distance. As he spoke, a cloud of flies appeared to materialize out of nowhere. 'And that's not good,' Plug said as he batted them away.

Standing upright, North wiped the sweat from his forehead with the back of his hand. Again, Plug was right, but Fang would refuse and the row would delay the inevitable. The priority had to be finding what – or who – Tobias had hidden down here. 'We're here now,' he said, and thrust the blade of the spade back in among the bones. Plug swore, stripped off his shirt to bind it around his nose and mouth, and carried on. North did the same. It did something to counter the noxious smell of sweet putrefaction and faeces, but not enough.

'Dear God,' Plug said, his voice muffled by the cloth.

The hand was clawing its way out, its fingers curled over, dried blood and dirt under the torn fingernails, as if whoever was down there had tried to dig his way out.

North knelt alongside Plug as together they removed the ancient bones and dirt to reveal what he was guessing was once a face. Maggots oozed from what had once been eye sockets and nostrils. The skin was falling away from dark brown muscles and the lips and tongue were swollen with decay, pulled back over the teeth and crawling with flies.

Tobias's secret was a corpse.

Plug hesitated, his eyes meeting North's. 'This is a crime scene and we could be messing everything up. We have to tell someone.'

That was the sensible course of action. Risk Hone's wrath and fess up that he was still involved, and that there was a body buried underneath a London landmark.

But North's intransigence built. Hawke's secret wasn't his alone. Whoever else was involved in whatever this was had murdered and buried someone and gone to a great deal of trouble to hide the body. If they stopped digging before they knew the whole truth, what was to say the body wouldn't disappear?

'We have to get a closer look,' he said. 'The corpse might tell us something we need to know.'

'Like what?' Plug said. 'That any second, we could end up just like them?'

Holding his breath against the stench, North took the legs and Plug the shoulders as they half lifted, half swung the decomposing body out from its grave among the ancient bones. Plug hunkered down, tucking his nose and mouth into the crook of his arm. He gestured at Fang to move the torch around before peering at the discoloured skin on the arm. The skin was breached and suppurating, but North could make out that the tattoo read 'Mam' within a rose-entwined heart. With his thumb and his forefinger, Plug reached for the remains of the T-shirt and lifted it away from the churned and shredded abdomen. The cotton material was full of holes.

'What do you think?'

'That he didn't die of smallpox,' North said.

'Judging by the jeans and the size of the trainers, I'd say we're looking at a man rather than a woman.'

'Not a man,' Fang said. 'That's a teenage boy. See!' She bared her own lips to reveal her blue wired teeth, then pointed at the metal cage over the teeth of the corpse.

'And judging by the state the hands are in, it's a teenage boy who spent his last few minutes trying to scrabble his way out of this godforsaken pit,' North said. 'And I think that he suffocated or bled out, and that whoever did this is going to burn in hell, and that I'm going to send them there.'

'I'll tell you something else.' Plug moved towards the bricks that had spilled out from the wall they'd broken down. 'This is an awful lot of trouble to go to for one dead boy.'

It took three more hours of steady digging till they were convinced they had found them all. The corpses lay next to one another, stretched head to toe among the ancient bones. North examined each one as they emerged. After the first ten, Plug had asked again, *Should we leave it? Time's running on, mate*, but he couldn't leave them buried underneath the bones. They were just kids. Who killed a load of kids then buried them in the bleakest place they could think of? Some were little more than a rank and rotting heap of flesh scraps and body parts, as if they'd been blown apart. Lifting the T-shirt of the last one, which had been tucked in by the furthest wall in what North guessed was the coldest and driest spot, he examined the catastrophic wounds. Unlike the others, this corpse was almost dessicated, the skin the colour of pale ash. He reached for a bottle of mineral water Fang had salvaged from the soldier's guard post and poured it over the remains. Under the dust and decay and the brown and dried blood, there were at least two dozen bullet holes.

'How long would you say they'd been dead?' he said, lowering his cloth mask.

Plug rubbed his jaw, and North could hear the rasp of stubble. He wrinkled his face, trying to do the calculations. 'These are unusual conditions. And I'm guessing, but by the rate of decomposition, I'd say maybe three weeks, give or take.'

Three weeks, North thought. *Give or take.* When he was drunk and out of his head in Berlin, these young men were being slaughtered. Brushing the filth from his hands, he stood to survey the scene. A slow-burning anger sparked and built, filling him with its white-hot heat. He fought the urge to give it its head, to rant and to rage. To leave the charnel house and beat the still-unconscious soldier into a bloody unbreathing pulp. But what good would that do the dead? He drew a breath, attempted to calm his own heart rate, which he could feel pounding. He needed to keep his temper in check, because he needed to think.

Whoever had buried the bodies had cleared the original remains of the charnel house to one side and dug a shallow grave. They had laid the bodies top to toe, underneath a layer of dirt that hadn't seen the light of day for centuries. Then they'd covered the disturbed earth over with the old bones of dead Londoners in a tomb no one knew existed.

'A couple of years ago, this could have been you and me,' he said to Plug. His friend frowned as he tried to understand what North was saying. 'These boys are in some kind of uniform. I think they're young offenders.'

Why would young offenders be butchered and buried together in a mass grave?

He moved along the lines of corpses. Chin had said the government wouldn't want this getting out. Is this why Tobias ended up dead? Because it wasn't just his secret?

47

The surgical hood and respirator obscured the face of the figure in the hazmat suit, but the assault rifle was obvious to everybody. As the figure pulled off the hood and discarded the mask, the elegant face came fully into view. The honey-coloured hair. The faintest scar of a long-gone cleft lip. North glimpsed a tiger-print scarf at her throat.

'We're not dying of smallpox then? Excellent,' she said, gazing around with interest at the corpses laid out on the floor. 'I thought I'd come togged up anyway. Helps keep the nosy neighbours away. But bloody hell – rather glad I did. The smell in here is desperate.'

And it all came back to him. The enormous needle. The doctor Fangfang thought he should date.

'Dr Lily?' he said. Relieved, but confused. Had Hone sent scientists from Porton Down? Her presence lessened the horror just a little. 'You need to get Hone on the line. There are thirty-three murdered boys down here. Tell him to get Forensics, police, get everyone. We're standing in a mass grave.'

Dr Lily nodded as he kept talking, as if she were taking notes of everything he was saying and planned to action it all as soon as he stopped. 'Lily is so very millennial. Lilith suits me better, don't you think? More of a statement.'

Her mismatched eyes raked over the heaped flesh and decomposing limbs of the corpses. No shock in them. Rather, a mild interest and a kind of accounting. The truth began to dawn on North. This was no doctor – the enemy was among them. Lilith, the first woman, created even before Eve. Lilith, the demon. Yes, it suited the creature in front of him who, he now realized, was pointing her AK-47 directly at him, her manicured finger inside the trigger guard.

'I admit this is beyond gross. Even so, I should just get on with it and shoot you. Brick up this wall, and winter in the Maldives. There's a soul retrieval retreat I fancy, with sunsets to die for.'

North stilled his breathing. A trickle of sweat ran between his pectoral muscles. He reached for his T-shirt. If he was going to die, he'd prefer to do it dressed. The woman's lingering gaze moved over the length of him as he pulled the cotton top over his naked chest, down over his ribs and abs. 'Mind, I like the view here too,' she said.

Even with the T-shirt, his sweat-covered skin felt cold suddenly. He had no regard for his own safety, but Plug and Fang were down here with him. Plug stood a little apart, his white-knuckled hand gripping a shovel – he gave every impression that he was prepared to defend the boys' corpses to his last breath. North couldn't see Fang at all – all he could hope was that she had hidden herself in the shadows. He cursed that he hadn't taken the soldier's SA80. What an amateur mistake to make.

'General Aeron Kirkham wasn't your biggest fan in the first place.' Lilith scanned the bodies again. 'I'm guessing he's behind this mess, which doubtless means he won't appreciate the fact you're down here.' Reproachful. 'Sleeping dogs and all that.'

North knew that Kirkham was a senior figure in the New Army, but these youths were in their own uniforms and they weren't old enough to be soldiers. Plus, some of them had dreadlocks and beads in their hair, or fluff on their upper lips and chins, which even the New Army wouldn't have put up with.

He had already gathered that General Kirkham was involved in Derkind. The photograph of Kirkham and Rafferty and Tobias Hawke. The work to sabotage autonomous vehicles – the one-off defence contract that appalled Esme. But that wouldn't be enough to explain all these deaths. What else was Hawke involved in, that the General was ready to kill all these boys for it? Rage built in North all over again. Teenage young offenders like these were disposable. They counted for nothing in this society. He didn't know the how and the why and where they'd died, but he knew it mattered. Kirkham should be held to account – and he was just the man to do it. If he lived that long.

North desperately wanted to look into the deep shadows that cornered the charnel house to check for Fang. But if he did, Lilith would know someone else was down here with them – as it was, perhaps she thought it was only North and Plug.

But why wasn't he dead already, he wondered. Lilith could have killed North at the hospital. She let out a raucous hoot of laughter as panic flared in his eyes. The injection. He felt the needle again. The cold as it ran along his veins. The sting of her warm, bare hand against his muscled rump.

The shovel still in his hand, Plug took a step closer to Lilith and she tutted in disapproval as she turned the AK towards him. 'Do you want to join the dead, Big Lad?' she asked, her voice curious. 'Because it's all the same to me.' Plug stayed where he was. She turned her attention back to North. 'Professional to professional. What would you have used if you were me?' she asked with a note of cheery enquiry. 'Polonium-210, ricin, or potassium chloride? The 210 and the ricin are a bugger to handle. Potassium chloride then? Cardiac arrest – clean and sweet. Me too. I had it all planned – even what to wear at your funeral. If I say so myself, black is my colour. But I was all ready with the harpoon and you went and told Toots that you were going to find Syd. And it came to me, all of a sudden – you and I should work together instead. So I gave you a slow-burn poison, and tracked you here so we could do some business.'

North's heart beat faster. A slow-burn poison? What had she used? What was running through his veins? Was the blood congealing even as he stood there? Was his heart faltering? His organs shutting down, one after the other? How soon was he going to join the boys laid out dead at his feet?

'It's a deadly toxin from South America, distilled from the black moss that grows beneath a thousand-year-old wimba tree in the heart of the Peruvian rainforest, and I'm your only hope of an antidote.'

'"Antidote".' He leapt on the word. There was a way out of this nightmare.

'*If* and only if you do exactly as I tell you, including meeting my voracious sexual demands.' The tip of her tongue touched first one and then the other white incisor, as if keen to test their sharpness.

The yawning earth opened up at his feet.

'Fascinating, isn't it, how the proximity of one's own death concentrates the mind?' she said, smiling. 'Did I mention the black moss is gathered by the shaman of a tribe of head-shrinking pygmies? Traditionally, they use the toxin on the darts for their blowpipes.'

Head-shrinking pygmies?

There was a flicker that started somewhere in the corner of her eye.

'Too much?' A twitch as she snorted in amusement. '"Black moss from under a thousand-year-old wimba tree"? Who does that these days? Boil up deadly Peruvian toxins? I get mine from a start-up in Wolverhampton, babe. It's synthetic, and bonus, they deliver the next day. You are way past gullible – no wonder you can't hack the dark side.' Something was wrong in the world when an assassin could find herself so funny, he thought. 'And really, I'd have to poison someone in order to get "satisfaction"? I admit you're easy on the eye, but that, babycakes, is downright insulting. It was a multivitamin shot. Should have pepped you right up.' She winked.

He sighed. This woman appeared to find herself hugely

engaging. He might too, if she didn't have a gun pointed at him.

'Don't be all sad-face, babe. Don't take it personally. You're going to give me this Syd-thingy and I'm going to sell it on the open market for squillions. Bidding has already started and numbers are through the roof.'

'Whoever you sell it to won't have control over it for long. A couple of hours maybe? Maybe even minutes. Once Syd connects to the outside world, everything will happen very fast and it'll be too powerful to be controlled by anyone. You're wasting your time, and they're wasting their money.'

'Not my problem, babe, and they can afford the risk. They've got a number of boffins lined up to shackle Syd for their own ends.' She was a capitalist. A beautiful, deadly capitalist out for herself.

He was never agreeing to do whatever it was she wanted – surely she knew that? Whatever Syd was, the computer didn't belong to Lilith or to whatever tyrant or criminal kingpin she decided to sell it to.

'But in the interests of transparency, I do have one teeny-weeny confession…'

She sighed, apparently considering the right words, and in that gap between the finish of her sigh and her mouth opening to speak – he knew. There was only one reason Kirkham was using Lilith. Because she had skin in the game.

'Once upon a time, I carried out an execution order. I killed a public figure, a woman I understand you were close to.' North flinched. 'The obituaries made her sound like a sweetheart. Brave. Heroic, even. And her friends – you in particular – must have been devastated. Well, I know you were, that you must have been in a great deal of pain, because word is that you killed everybody to blame for her death. Nearly everybody, that is.'

Nearly everybody? Lilith had followed an order written in green ink on the back of a photograph that came in a black envelope, as he had done in another life.

'It's what I did—' There was a nanosecond of hesitation, as if she was thinking about stopping, about what it would mean to let someone live, how it would be to put killing behind her. 'It's what I do.' She shrugged.

He didn't trust himself to speak. The touch of remembered skin against his.

'But what I did and what I am doesn't mean I'm not sorry for your loss. Do you believe me?'

'Does it matter?'

'Not usually. But this time, I believe it does.' For the first time, she sounded sincere.

'You're a psychopath.'

'Dearheart, it would be so much easier if I was. Once upon a time I did my duty – as you did – but the Board is done, at least for now. And I've adapted to the commercial environment in which I find myself. Both of us – you and me – are "evolving" to the circumstance in which we find ourselves.'

North's fists were rolled so tight, he felt his nails cut through the flesh of his palms. He had known the day would come when he was face-to-face with the triggerman, but he'd presumed he would be the one with the gun in his hands. Lilith had shot dead the woman he loved, and in so doing destroyed his chance of authentic happiness, of a normal life. He wanted to rip her head off her shoulders.

But he couldn't do that because she had the gun and he was too far away and he had to think about Plug and about Fang. He breathed through the pain, focused on what it was Lilith really wanted – Syd. And, if she couldn't get hold of Syd, what she was capable of.

'You've had a wasted journey – Syd was never here. This is something else.' He gestured at the bodies laid out in the gloom. And as he did, he caught sight of Fang's face peeping out from a shallow scoop of bones, the body of one of the larger boys pulled over her – the one with the 'Mam' tattoo. His heart pounded in his chest. Fang was trapped here in the middle of all of this mess. She would witness Lilith shoot him dead. Then have to watch as Lilith murdered Plug. Then some lackey of Kirkham's would come to rebury the bodies of the young offenders, and they would find Fang and shoot her too. The three of them would spend the rest of eternity in this charnel house together.

For a brief moment he allowed himself to consider a future without Fang's glittering genius in it. Without her intellectual arrogance and stroppy teenage put-downs. Without her brave-new-world skills, instinctive courage and innate kindness.

That wasn't happening.

Lilith flapped a dismissive hand, though the gun was steady enough in her other one. 'Of course Syd's not here, babe. I'm going to tell you where Syd is. And then you're going in there to get it for me like a good boy. I figure you have three hours before it goes live – just under, anyway.'

'And why would I do that?' He thought he could make it to Lilith before she fired more than one bullet. He knew

Plug was waiting for his signal to swing his shovel – and if there was enough mayhem and distraction, Fang could run. Out of the charnel houses and through the crypt and into the church and out into the street and into the rest of the amazing life that was her right.

'Why would you go get Syd? Hmmm. Let me think.' Lilith tilted her head and smiled with a maternal sweetness that set his teeth on edge. She pointed her gun at the corpse under which Fang was sheltering. 'Because, dearheart, you don't see it yet but you have so much more to lose,' she said, and fired.

48

Kent

In his Queen Anne home, Ralph Rafferty was getting nervous. He'd barely been able to sleep – had ended up getting up at cock's crow. Nothing was going the way he'd planned. He pushed his chair out from the table where he had been sitting with a coffee, and slid his leather-soled slipper from his bony foot. Heading back to the master bedroom, he attempted and failed to land a savage thwack on his golden retriever. The dog snapped at him.

It couldn't be helped, Rafferty thought as he stripped the duvet from his sleeping wife. He held her by her shoulder to get better purchase as he beat her, smacking the slipper over her back and down the length of her as hard as he could. She muffled her screams in the duvet she'd pulled up to her mouth. They had been long enough married for her to know that she should be a good girl and take it. That it was over more quickly if he could finish in peace. Anyway, she deserved it. The phone tracker he'd installed on her iPhone revealed the whole sorry story. She'd visited his twin brother in the psychiatric hospital. It turned out she'd been visiting him once a month for years. And she'd seen a solicitor, and he knew what that was about – she wanted a divorce. Well, that wasn't happening. By rights, he should put his hands around that fat neck and put her out of her misery. But he couldn't do that, he had to think of his position, so he concentrated on what he could do.

He liked the feel of the slipper in his hand. And he liked the fact that on the nights he was at home, when he stretched out his feet by the fire to warm them, his wife's eyes would fix on the slippers and her lips would tighten with the memory of private times. On a practical note, too, a slipper didn't bruise. If you didn't count the red marks and welts that appeared on his wife's skin under the blouses and slacks – nothing that nosy-parker constituents or shopkeepers might notice. But it wasn't quite enough, this morning. He leant over her and allowed himself one savage punch. It wouldn't do to incapacitate her, but the desire to hurt something or someone was overwhelming. He had to relieve the stress somehow, he told himself. After all, there was so much at stake.

It was all perfectly desperate. Three weeks ago he'd been looking forward to a new technology demonstration at Derkind and then it all went horrifically wrong. And now the General had upped the ante again with this massacre at the museum. Rafferty had barely been able to keep himself from shrieking the truth at his civil servants as they briefed him about the gala. At least Hawke was dead and Syd was theirs. After a respectable amount of time, Syd could be 'discovered' by the authorities – and, after all, possession was nine-tenths of the law.

But what had happened to the boys could never come out. His knees started trembling at the idea of it. He sat back down on the mattress as his wife drew the duvet back over herself and huddled beneath it, her shoulders shaking. He just had to trust the General's plan to salvage this and stop a mess turning into a catastrophe. Whatever it took to keep it hush-hush was fine with him. Whomsoever the General thought had to die. What was another body or two in the grand scheme of things, after so many?

49

The bullet passed through the spine of the corpse, and a tiny sliver of bone stung Fang's right cheekbone like an angry wasp. Her initial thought was that she was dead, and her second that she was fuming. She did a speed-of-light audit: state of consciousness (alert), vital organs (undamaged), major arterial bleeds (nil), limbs (four), so no, she was still here. A vague sense of disappointment swept over her, mixing in with the bubbling anger. She didn't want to be dead. But dead was different, and she was curious about different.

Although, the ringing in her ears was loud, which totally hacked her off. Plus, her ear hurt. Plus, her cheek was wet and she never cried, which meant it had to be blood, which meant she was scarred for life, like some Masai warrior. Which actually she didn't hate, and when anyone asked her how she got it, she'd say 'wrestling lions'. Fang knew her mother blamed hormones for her daughter's apparent rage against the world. Fang knew it was nothing to do with hormones and everything to do with the fact that the world was full of violent nutjobs.

Turning her face upwards, Fang whispered a quiet thank you to whoever it was lying dead on top of her who'd diverted the brunt of the bullet, and stopped resenting how bad he smelled or the fact he had leaked all over her, which was beyond gross.

Calculating the chances that the bullet was a stray shot at nil, she decided she had to come out from underneath the dead guy.

'I'm impressed. That is a seriously grim place to play hide-and-seek,' Lilith said.

'There is no chance North's going out with you now, you complete psycho stalker,' Fang said as she struggled to shift the twice-dead corpse on top of her and felt North's hands take hold and pull her upwards into what passed for light in the charnel house. 'I mean – never. Forget the fact you're ancient, however many spin classes you drag your sorry midlife arse to. But even this bozo isn't that stupid.'

North didn't always annoy her, she would admit, although he had an impressive capacity for trouble. But she liked trouble. He had this unswerving, take-it-to-the-brink sense of right and wrong, which he managed to combine with being an utter simpleton. He was like Robin to her Batman – if Batman was way smarter. Plus, that oversized lummock, Plug, was beaming at the sight of her. Though Granny Po was going to be properly hacked off with her if she ended up dead, because she had promised she wouldn't.

'I will be so very sad if I have to kill you,' Lilith said,

pinching Fang's cheek like she was three years old. Which outraged Fang all over again.

Lilith looked at North and, grinning, shook her head. 'As a feminist, this girl gives me hope for the next generation. I am totally missing out by not having a sidekick.'

Fang opened her mouth – North was guessing in protest at the word 'sidekick' – and Lilith put a finger to her lips, making a shushing noise. 'When I said I'd be sad to shoot you, I'd get over it. Let the grown-ups talk, Toots. Syd is back at Derkind, North. The Ministry of Defence dug out a massive underground bunker for them, when they built their company HQ. That's where Kirkham has it stashed. Hidden in the last place you'd ever think to look.'

The quote on the wall in the foyer, Fang thought. *It is no good to try to stop knowledge from going forward. Ignorance is never better than knowledge.* Tobias had been arrogant enough to tell visitors to Derkind what was going on underneath their own feet. Enrico Fermi's work led to the world's first controlled nuclear chain reaction in Chicago Pile-1 on 2 December 1942, in an old squash court beneath abandoned football stands in the University of Chicago. Then he worked on the Manhattan Project and the atomic bomb. And the pledge Derkind had signed to *neither participate in nor support the development, manufacture, trade, or use of lethal autonomous weapons.* What was that worth?

Suddenly, Fang knew exactly what Tobias had going on in his Derkind bunker. And why so many people were prepared to kill for it. North needed to know because it could mean the difference between him living and dying.

'There's a back way out of here, through the tunnel down

there. Use it and you can swerve your Chinese minders sitting out there waiting for you. Oh, and I'm taking Sweetie Pie with me.' Lilith swung Fang across and over to her, Fang's golden boots almost lifting off the ground. North stopped in his tracks as Fang felt the cold metal of the gun barrel press into her temple. 'Chop chop, bunnies. When you have the goods, we'll do swapsies – but if I don't get Syd in good time my buyer goes away, and I kill the girl.' Fang considered biting Lilith's wrist – trying for an arterial vein – but the woman took hold of her jaw and clamped it shut. Which made it impossible to explain to the psycho bitch that, without Fang, North was a moron-person and his chances of success were zero.

50

Kings Cross

Parked up in a street close to the back entrance of Derkind, they sat in the panel van, Plug in the driving seat, his huge hands gripping the steering wheel as if readying himself to rip it from its mounting. North knew Plug was angry because, as he ground his teeth, he was flexing a muscle in his jaw, which historically meant he planned to hit something or someone hard enough to break something or someone. His friend was angry about the dead boys they'd had to leave behind in the crypt, and furious that North had been reckless enough to lose Fang.

In the passenger seat, his own gaze was fixed on the digital clock. They had one hour and fourteen minutes. before Syd went live – make that one hour and thirteen minutes. And what did Lilith mean by 'in good time'? Didn't her buyer need time to pull the kill switch? The future of the human race was at stake. If Lilith was right about Syd being back at Derkind, he had a chance to get back Syd, and maybe Hone and Esme could figure out a way to turn on the kill switch? But if he did that, Lilith would cut Fang into little pieces. He had a choice – save Fang or save the human race.

That would be save Fang then.

From the back of the van there was a frantic storm of keyboard tapping. They were going nowhere fast.

'You left the country a month ago after a whole bunch of important people died.' North had never told Plug what he did after the army, but he knew Plug had guessed some of it. In another life, his friend would have made a fine detective.

There was a moment's hesitation before the question came. 'Did you kill them? Is that who Lilith was talking about?' *Did he kill them?* North gave Plug an even look. Yes, he'd killed the guilty. Those he'd vowed would curse the day he was born. Those who had to be punished for what they'd done – the fatal decision they made. Life wasn't grey – it was black and white, there was good and there was evil, and he knew how far he was prepared to go for the sake of the good.

'It's best you don't know all of it, mate.'

'Remember that guard?' Plug said. Six months into North's sentence, Plug had acted as lookout while North beat a sexually sadistic guard to a pulp with a pool cue. Between the two of them, they crippled the warder and made it clear they had enough evidence of his crimes to make sure that retirement on the grounds of ill health was his best option. They'd never talked of it since. 'Three lads hanged themselves because of that bastard.' Plug's face was grim. 'Nobody hanged themselves after what we did. I figure whatever you've done since then, you'll have had your reasons. As I will if that bitch hurts Fang, because I'll hunt her down and take her apart piece by piece.'

North had thought the danger to Fang was Chin and his monster, Octavia. But Chin would have to stand in line and whistle. Because the more immediate danger was a monster called Lilith. He owed Hone nothing – not least when the guy had fired him. Chin was one thing, but Lilith was a real and present danger to Fang. North was getting Syd back and Lilith could sell the system to some Russian oligarch or the UK government, or sell it to Chin direct. If Esme was right, it wouldn't even matter, because give Syd the time it needed and Syd would be the one in charge. Every which way you looked, it was bad. But his immediate priority had to be saving Fang, who was family. Who had turned to him when she needed help, but instead of getting her mother back, he'd made everything so much worse. It was like that postman said in the Berlin bar: you never know what you have till it's gone. Except he did know. His life mattered to him. He had friends who meant something. And all he could do for Esme was to ask Syd which of the Thinkers murdered Tobias before handing the machine over to Lilith. Once he had Syd and Fang was safe, he was moving on to 'any other business' before Syd wiped out the human race.

Plug's thumb drummed on the steering wheel. Making a tick-tock sound, marking the passing of time. They had one hour and ten minutes left. Seventy minutes.

He didn't know why Kirkham had killed those boys, but the General obviously wanted Syd badly enough to murder Tobias and two dozen other bystanders in the British Museum. North planned to ask Kirkham about it at the first opportunity. Along with the Right Honourable Ralph

Rafferty, MP, because the only way you could shut down a church and fake a smallpox contagion in the capital city was with official backing from a department with the power to evacuate church officials and shut down access, all in order to bury more than thirty bodies in an unmarked grave. Like the Home Office. Moreover, Rafferty was Home Secretary in charge of young offender institutions. And somehow, under his watch, thirty-three young offenders had ended up dead.

The boys had been murdered. Not even executed. No double taps to make it quick and sure. Their bodies were riddled with bullets and shredded by explosives. They had been slaughtered. Someone had played God with the lives of boys who didn't have families, who were in the care system. Boys with mental health issues and troubled histories. And even if there were families wondering about their sons, North knew there would be plausible explanations. A spate of suicides would account for a few – screwed-down caskets or ashes returned in an urn. An unexpected early release, when the boy never arrived home. Then there would be boys who decided that they didn't want visitors any more, cutting off all communication till they were no more than a memory. Governors explaining to even the pushiest and most desperate of parents that they should 'give the boy time' to get back in touch. That when a minor faced a long sentence, they needed space and time to habituate themselves – but rest assured, their lad was in the best of hands, and they weren't to worry. After all, these weren't parents with access to lawyers and the funds to fight the system. The boys were easy prey and he should know, because he'd been there.

One way or another, Rafferty and Kirkham were going to pay for their crimes. He'd punished the guilty before and he could do it again. It was quite a long to-do list now he thought about it, but no problem, he had it covered.

If Lilith was right, then Derkind's bunker was under the laboratory where Esme had installed the wreckage of the Lamborghini – a bunker dug deep enough to avoid cables and pipes and underground tunnels. And if the Ministry of Defence had dug it out before the building went up, then the government must have paid for it. Fang called Derkind a tech 'unicorn' – said that its value topped a billion dollars – but even she wasn't able to see where the original funding came from. North would bet his life on the fact the original funding was government money, as it attempted to stake out Britain's claim to an AI-enriched future.

'How do we do this?' Plug asked. They'd parked the transit van with blacked-out windows as close to the back entrance of Derkind as they dared. Plug had borrowed the van from a mate who didn't ask questions, merely slapped on the cleaning company decal they wanted, switched out the plates and handed over the keys.

'Got it.' Paulie let out a triumphant whoop from the back.

They'd picked him up in Hackney. Paulie had opened the door, his face ravaged with grief. *Even if they'd forced her to go back to China, she'd have sent word somehow*, he'd said after North confirmed that Yan had been murdered by Chin. He kept the grisliest of the details from him, but he thought Paulie knew it had been bad. *She told me she loved you*, North said, remembering how the girl touched her heart before the monster came for her. Paulie had covered his face with his hand, his eyes squeezed shut. And North thought back to the gala and the noise of gunfire when he was trying to get the truth from Paulie about the leak. A desperate Paulie hadn't run to save himself, he'd rescued Jarrod. Yan had been right to see something noble in this chubby, awkward egg.

Paulie had caught on quick. Yan was dead. Tobias was dead and there were dead boys under a London landmark. A kid called Fang was in danger. And Syd was back at Derkind and about to burn down the world. Tobias had stitched Paulie up so he didn't have to give up any part of the glory for creating another intelligence, but Paulie wasn't in this life because he chased glory, North realized. Even as North was talking, Paulie unzipped his Hufflepuff onesie to reveal jeans and a black sweatshirt.

North kept talking. According to Esme, before he died Tobias had made sure Syd would break through the air gap to connect with any and all of the other systems it could reach. Unless the kill switch was thrown, Syd would take over the world.

Paulie had grabbed his laptop and shut the door on his digs all in the same move.

Looking for the tablet, they'd stumbled upon a mass grave in the heart of London. Somehow, the grave had to be linked to the massacre at the museum. The chances were both the Home Secretary and the General in charge of the Defence Innovations Board were involved. *I set up the company's security system*, Paulie had said. *I can get you in.*

And now they needed to break into a secret bunker underneath Derkind, because Syd was in there and it was the only way to save Fang from certain death. It had been

Paulie's idea to go in as cleaners. He was a different man, North thought as they followed him, hurtling down the same stairs Yan had run down the day before. Or perhaps Fate had created the circumstances to show Paulie who he really was.

'I've pulled the original construction plans from the server,' Paulie said now, standing up from the welded row of cinema seats in the back of the van. 'These are an early draft so they don't have everything, and they were hidden. All the later drafts were deleted, and needless to say none of this is officially registered.' He leant over into the driver's compartment and held out a laptop between Plug and North. A blueprint appeared on the screen of what looked like the architectural plans for Derkind, the massive bulging cauliflower form of the brain even more obvious on the page than it was in reality. Paulie clicked on something, and a shadow set of plans emerged.

The blueprint showed two more levels under Derkind.

'Now you see it, now you don't.' Paulie sounded disappointed in Tobias all over again. 'As your mate Lilith told you…'

'Plug is my mate. Lilith is not my mate,' North said, not even trying to keep the outrage out of his voice. 'Lilith is a professional assassin.' And, as if reminded, Plug opened the glove compartment and handed him another SIG and a belt rig, half a dozen mags and a Gerber Ghostrike knife. North unzipped the overalls to wrap the belt rig around, and slipped the gun into place before filling his pockets with the mags. Clipping the small knife in its sheath into his boot, he ran through his earlier conversation with Plug. *Did you kill them?* By the sceptical expression on the scientist's face, there was a good chance Paulie considered his present company every bit as murderous as Lilith.

'My bad,' Paulie said, scrolling over the blueprint. 'So, Tobias, an evil genius as well as a tosser, had a secret bunker. The first storey is what looks like laboratories and offices, the second is a more open space – some kind of hangar, the size of a football field, maybe bigger. The entire bunker is built deep enough to avoid the Water Ring Main, power tunnels and the deepest parts of the London Underground, which makes sense. It's deeper than the deepest London tunnel that we know about – the Lee Tunnel, which goes down to eighty metres. This is a hundred metres down, with walls three metres thick, and all the services run into it.'

Part of Paulie was impressed at the engineering challenge of digging out and creating the bunker, North thought, despite his mentor's secrecy. The secrecy, he hated.

'No one in Derkind proper is working down there, because we'd have noticed the comings and goings. So this "Defence Innovation Board" you mentioned must have their own people down there working alongside Tobias. I'm guessing they have robotic expertise because Tobias fired a whole slew of robotics engineers and tech people a couple of years ago. Great scientists – no one could understand it. The thing was, none of them seemed that uptight about it. I bet they're down there. Or at least they have been, till it all started unravelling. I believe Derkind's work and the Defence Innovation work is bleeding into each other. It explains how many breakthroughs we've been having.'

'Those people must be accessing the bunker somehow,' Plug said.

North nodded. 'Maybe through a shop or a café within

half a mile radius, say? They go in for a regular morning latte, disappear into the bathroom and they don't come out again. Without us knowing where their access point is, we have no choice but to go in via Derkind itself.'

'And Tobias had to have his own point of entry from within the building,' Paulie said. 'I can't see it on these drawings. But apart from going home and the odd business trip, Tobias hardly ever left the building. Everything was on site for his convenience.'

On site for his convenience? Something was almost within North's reach, but not quite.

'I need to check one thing,' Paulie said. 'Syd is on an apocalypse countdown – we only have sixty-two minutes on the clock. And we're going in without any help from the police or soldiers? Just us?'

He looked at each of his colleagues in turn and, judging by his face, found them wanting.

No police, because somehow the Home Secretary was involved.

No army, because General Kirkham was in this up to his neck.

No one-eyed man, because Rafferty was the one-eyed man's boss and North didn't trust anyone on this. Plus, Hone had fired him, and North bore a grudge. Plus Hone would choose to save the human race rather than Fang, which was not an option.

'You don't have to do this, Bald Paulie,' Plug said.

North winced at the nickname Plug had reached for. He turned, his arm on the back of his seat – he didn't want to force Paulie into anything. He was a civilian and the woman he loved had just died, which North understood, if he understood nothing else about him. 'You can still walk away, Paulie. You don't have to be here.'

'You can still walk away, "Bald" Paulie,' Paulie corrected him with pedantic solemnity. 'No, thank you.' North flicked a glance at Plug and his friend winked at him. What could he say? He was good with people – knew how they worked. Paulie was an outsider. 'Bald Paulie' belonged. 'And I have to come in there with you,' Bald Paulie said. 'Because I need direct physical access to the data centre. I can't hack the biometric security for you to get into the bunker unless I can code a connection on-site. And I have to make the security system think that you're Tobias or you won't get into the bunker.' Bald Paulie handed them each a lanyard. 'But these should be enough to get us into the main building.'

'Then what happens?' Plug said.

'Looking at this map, I have to get into Tobias's office,' North said. He traced his finger along the vertical lines running between the secret bunker and the Derkind 'brain'. Everything was on-site for Tobias's convenience, and Tobias needed a way in and out of the bunker – the capsule elevator in the corner of his office was the gate to Shangri-La.

'Are you sure you can't stop Syd connecting to the wider cyberspace?' he asked Bald Paulie. 'Esme said Tobias had a fail-safe code. Some sort of kill switch.' Without the code, Syd would connect, and according to Esme, it wouldn't be long before machines took over the world. But maybe he could disable Syd before he handed it over?

'If we pulled the power on every computer in the country, then maybe,' Paulie said. 'Otherwise, Syd is going to do what Syd is going to do.' Another door slammed shut on the human race.

North's eyes went to the clock on the dashboard. Humanity had had a good run. He had sixty minutes to get Syd out and rescue Fang before Lilith killed her.

'It's like going to steal a golden egg at the Triwizard Tournament when the Hungarian Horntail is sitting on its nest,' Bald Paulie said. Plug looked at the other man as if he was deranged. North translated.

'He means it's ridiculously dangerous.'

Bald Paulie didn't seem unhappy at the thought.

51

They went in together through the front. They figured going in the back meant the security team would ask questions. Like – where was the usual crew and why were they so late? Security would want to make a call to the cleaning company. That couldn't happen, and North didn't want to have to hurt anyone if he didn't have to.

They wore 'Capital Kleen' beige boiler suits and baseball caps, and pushed trolleys full of cleaning equipment. They'd apologized to the two men and two women they waylaid en route to Derkind. North had explained, as he secured their wrists and ankles with plastic tags and roped them to their chairs, that it was a matter of national emergency. North didn't know if they understood, but they'd left the TV on for them in a storage container owned by a mate of Plug who asked no questions, and four piles of £50 notes on a table in front of them to concentrate their attention. They hadn't looked like they were struggling too hard to get back to work.

North kept his baseball cap pulled down low and his face turned as Jarrod waved them through. The receptionist's hair was still perfect, but his arm was in a sling and he seemed preoccupied, North thought. Was he still recovering from the trauma of the museum massacre? Wondering whether to get another job? Whether Derkind could ride out the death of its founder? Or maybe just how long he should leave Esme to grieve before he suggested a drink? On the video screen behind him, Tobias still played the alpha male. North turned away to swipe his fake lanyard in front of the security gate.

'Hold on.' Jarrod's voice held a note of accusation. The three of them stopped in their tracks and Plug's eyes met those of North. They weren't even over the threshold. Had Bald Paulie got it wrong? Was it Plug's sheer size? 'You're late, and why are you coming in this way? What are you thinking?' Jarrod demanded from his desk.

Granny Po stepped out from Plug's shadow. In a ferocious mix of Cantonese, Mandarin and vernacular Geordie, which North was pretty sure included the words 'fookin' divvy', she harangued Jarrod, flapping her duster in his direction like she could slit his throat with it if she wanted. With his good hand, a suddenly frantic Jarrod pushed the button under his desk; there was a noisy buzz, and the glass security door opened into the heart of Derkind. Still chuntering and throwing Jarrod basilisk stares, Granny Po pushed her trolley through the glass doors, as if she had taken personal offence to the receptionist and would be back.

North and a whistling Plug followed after. Plug's trolley was heavier to push, had anyone been watching, because it contained a contorted Bald Paulie, clutching his laptop.

52

Once through the doors, they split. Granny Po moved to take the heavier trolley, before she plodded down the ramp towards the basement and the mainframe. She was wearing sheepskin slippers, North noticed. Baggy socks wrinkled around skinny ankles under the oversized overalls, and she didn't look backwards.

'Do you think she can get him in?' Plug asked. 'Because if that bald coot can't give you the access Tobias had, this is over.'

When Plug went to pick up his mate's van, he'd found the old lady already sitting in the back, knitting. Since she had managed to chain herself to the row of cinema seats bolted to the floor, it seemed altogether simpler to let her come along for the ride.

They watched as a pair of bespectacled employees moved to one side to let the trolley past before Granny Po mowed them down with it.

'Could you stop Granny Po doing whatever it is that

Granny Po wants to do?' North said. 'Especially if that's finding Fang.'

'Fair point. She could totally take me,' Plug said. 'Let's hustle.'

They parked one of their trolleys to block the door into the gleaming unisex bathroom and pushed the other inside. Plug flipped up 'Cleaning in progress' signs to make the point, and held up his hand to stop a skinny techie – his trousers still held tight to his ankles by his bike clips – talking into his Bluetooth. 'You don't want to go in there. I tell you, mate – we do not get paid enough.' The cyclist looked Plug up and down and decided not to push the point. He backed away, one step at a time, his eyes wide and still fixed on Plug's slab-like face.

Inside the stainless steel and glass bathroom, North drilled out the screws to a panel as Plug flipped open the tablet with the building plans.

As the last screw popped, Plug took hold of his arm. 'Stay in contact. I don't want to think of you crawling round the walls of this place next Christmas.'

Neither did he, North thought. 'Okay, and once they've hacked the bio-rig on the mainframe, get Bald Paulie and Granny Po out of here. Right?'

Plug's eyes said he hated the plan, but he punched North hard on the shoulder, which North took to be agreement.

North slid his head and torso through the hole he had opened and heaved himself upwards. The space went dark and the noise of an electric screwdriver buzzed behind him as Plug closed up the wall again.

It was pitch black and hot as hell. He winced as his forearm caught on an exposed section of the huge metal piping, and he heard the sizzle of his own scorching flesh. In his ear, Plug's voice instructed him which way to go. Scrabbling for purchase on the wall, his fingers clawed at the breeze blocks, the toes of his boots knocking out fragments as he climbed. He didn't look down. He was going upwards, towards Tobias's office, when he should be going downwards towards the bunker, and the conviction took hold of him that he was getting further away from his goal rather than closer. That time was moving too fast, and that Fang was going to die if he didn't hurry the hell up.

It took eight minutes to negotiate his route through the wall cavity. It should have taken five, but in the wall space of a meeting room, he slowed when he caught the sound of Esme's voice. '… emergency system in place… what Tobias would have wanted… mindless violence… owe it to Tobias… can only hope that Syd's found before it's too late…' He guessed she was talking to her management team. He considered knocking, telling her Syd was right beneath her feet, asking for help. But he was the man who'd dragged her away when she thought she should have stayed. The man her uncle had fired for incompetence. And he didn't have the time. He kept climbing.

53

'You should be there.' North could hear the tension in Plug's voice. 'Can you see the light? Go towards it.'

'Since when is that a good idea?' North muttered, scrambling upwards as he tried to keep his purchase on the smooth and slippery walls in the darkness. But Plug was right – above him there was a break in the darkness.

He peered through the air vent into Tobias's office. It looked the same, but it felt different – no Tobias and no Syd. Keeping very still, he tuned his ears to the silence of the room – nothing. He used the pressure tool Plug had given him to pop the screws on the vent, jackknifing his body to dangle his feet out, easing the length of his legs and his waist, gripping the side with his hands to fall as softly as he could on to the floor.

'I asked myself: "With forty-six minutes till the first computer overlord rocks into town, what is the stupidest thing North could do?"' The Belfast accent of the one-eyed man was unmistakeable. 'And you, North, never disappoint.' Hone sat in an armchair in the corner of the office, one leg crossed over the other and a Browning Hi-Power steady in his hand.

Under his breath, North cursed. 'I don't have time to explain myself, Hone.'

Keeping his gaze soft so the one-eyed man wouldn't pick up on his interest, North eyed the capsule lift. The small red light by the brass button was red. Had Bald Paulie been able to change the bio-ID on his lanyard yet? This could only ever work if the system read him as Tobias Hawke. And even if it did – was there time to get through the lift doors and for the doors to close? Or would Hone be able to haul him out, or even shoot him where he stood? The lift was three paces away. He took a step towards it without allowing his gaze to drop from Hone's one eye. In his hand, he moved the lanyard this way and that, as if he was stretching bunched muscles after the confines of his tunnelling through the wall cavity. Tried to keep it casual.

'Syd is at Derkind, isn't it, North? There's some powerful people want me anywhere but here, which makes me wonder why, because I can feel in my waters that there's something wrong. In the exact same way, I knew you'd show up because you completely fail to understand the word "no". Where is the damn thing? We're running out of time.'

There was no green light. It stayed resolutely red.

Had Granny Po been intercepted? Had Bald Paulie failed to make it to the mainframe? No, he had to keep faith. Bald Paulie just needed a little more time. North imagined symbols and numbers flying from the plump fingers down through hundreds of thousands of twisted pairs of plastic-sheathed copper wires, coaxial cables, light zipping through fibre-optic cables, and into the huge bank of computers floors below. Instructing, coaxing, meeting dead ends, turning around, finding his way out of the maze. Trying again. Doing this was Bald Paulie's path through the darkness and his vale of tears, and North was walking that path with him.

North knew better than to go for his SIG. He swung his right hand with the lanyard round and back to his side, and Hone's eyes narrowed.

No green light.

'If I start something, I finish it, Hone,' he said.

'Do you know what I'm wondering, North? Where's Fang? Because in my experience, where she is, there you are – and where you are, there's a whole heap of trouble.'

'You got the kid into this mess, don't think I'll forget that.'

'Don't get in my way, North.'

'You need Syd back – let me help.' North didn't like the way Hone looked at him right this second, nor the way he'd locked away Fang's mother. But he needed him to believe he was going to find Syd and hand the machine over to the authorities, rather than find Syd and hand the machine over to a ruthless assassin. Because Hone was never letting that happen. He'd let Fang die and never think of her again if it got Syd back.

North took another step towards the lift, as if coming closer to Hone.

The one-eyed man's face was grim, but his tone softened a shade. 'This is bigger than you are. And I can't let some maverick – by which I mean you – put at risk everything we're doing to find Syd ourselves. Tell me what you know. These are dangerous people we're dealing with.'

'But not as dangerous as me,' North said, using every ounce of strength he had to overturn the desk and drive it towards Hone, who leapt away, knocking back his chair into the plate-glass window, which smashed into a million pieces.

Green light.

North leapt for the button on the lift and the doors slid open. Frantically, he stabbed at the button marked 'Basement' on the basis that it was as far down as the official Derkind went. As the doors began to close, a bullet embedded itself in the brass. Hone had an unusual definition of being on the same side.

If Hone was at Derkind, that meant he already had people all over the building. If North couldn't find Tobias's secret access to his bunker, the lift doors would open directly into the laboratory and North would be staring at the wreckage of the Lamborghini and the wrong end of twenty years in prison – if he was lucky.

The lift moved off. How many seconds before it stopped and the doors opened? Ten? If he was lucky. Ten seconds to find what he needed.

North ran the tips of his fingers around the brass plate – nothing. Eight seconds. Ran them over the surrounds of the door, and up and down the inside. Five seconds. Nothing.

Had he called this wrong? Was Tobias's entrance to the bunker someplace else in Derkind?

It had to be here.

Tobias was a vain man – the foyer proved it. He would never stand with his back to the mirror.

Four seconds.

Swivelling on his heel, North turned to gaze at his reflection.

Three seconds.

He lent his weight to the left edge of the mirror and it opened out from the wall, revealing two black buttons stacked on top of each other.

Two seconds.

The lift settled. It had arrived in the lab with the Lamborghini and no doubt a team of Hone's best people, all of them armed. Had Hone ordered them to kill him?

The top button had to be for the bunker's secret labs, the other for the floor below the labs – the hangar.

The lift whined as if on the point of opening, and bullets embedded themselves in the brass doors.

That would be a 'yes' on the kill order.

One second.

He slammed his hand against the bottom button, then stood back against the glass with his gun raised, his left hand supporting his right. The doors stayed closed. And he heard his name being shouted. Fists hammered against the brass, as the lift jolted and began to move again. Downwards into what he hoped against hope was the secret bunker.

He checked his earpiece, his phone, but there was no signal. He was on his own down here, and that was fine by him.

The doors opened on to a vast darkness, lit only by the puddle of light spilling out from the lift. Gun raised, North stepped out, sweeping the room. A dull whirring started high up in the roof space. The little light there was narrowed and then disappeared completely as, behind him, a short gust of air hit the back of his neck and the lift doors closed, the mechanism straining, before the lift began its rise back up the shaft towards Hone.

North checked his watch. He had less than forty-four minutes to find Syd before Lilith killed Fang.

54

The SIG in his right hand, his left hand cupping the base of the grip, arms outstretched, he moved quietly to scout out the terrain. Slowly, his eyes adjusted and what had been darkness became gloom. A steel door to his right was locked. Turning the handle, he pushed hard, his shoulder against it, but it didn't give. Switching the gun to his left hand, with his right he groped his way along the rough breeze-block wall, trying the steel door further along, but that was locked too.

The place seemed empty, but the hackles on the back of his neck rose, and he glanced upwards. Cameras were fixed around the entire perimeter of the walls. They tilted and turned, tracking him, each one with a small red light. They were recording. Were their movements on an automatic circuit or was someone monitoring him? He had to hope the former.

From what he remembered of Paulie's floor plan, the only other door out of the space was at the far end of the hangar, but to reach it, he either had to keep to the walls and crawl around the edge of things, which would chew up time he didn't have, or commit to the gloom and cross the expanse of floor, which would mean tackling whatever obstacles were out there as fast as he could while fully exposed. He screwed up his eyes to try to make out more detail in the dark shapes, cursing that he hadn't thought to bring night vision goggles. Were they crates? Surely they were too big? Steel containers piled on top of each other? Was this an enormous storage facility? If so, what were they storing? He thought there'd be answers down here, but the only thing he knew for a fact was how little time was left to find Syd. He tried not to think about the irony of Hone releasing Fang's mum but Fang being too dead to appreciate it.

As he stepped forward, a dazzling white light drenched the space. Rows of neon strip lights revealed what appeared to be street after street after street, all lined with full-size houses and shops. There had to be hundreds of buildings. There were even cars parked up along the streets and lights on in the houses, as well as a pub with a sign that announced it was The King's Head, and office blocks, a town hall, a hotel, a bank, a small street market and an empty children's playground with a merry-go-round and a swing on chains that swayed back and forth with the movement of the air around it. There was another clunk and the noise of a city boomed out from speakers he couldn't see – the rumble of passing cars, pop music and a barking dog, footsteps and chatter, and somewhere the sound of building work as scaffolding was erected. It was a replica town, he realized; an urban environment designed to approximate London streets. His fingers traced holes in the brickwork. There was no glass in the windows, no doors in the frames, and although they'd been repaired and patched up, some of the buildings appeared to have sustained considerable damage. It wasn't a film set – this was specially built terrain for training in OBUA, operations in built-up areas. One of the most elaborate he'd ever seen.

But the New Army trained on moorland and plains, not in a secret bunker in the middle of London.

All of a sudden, the air around him appeared to shimmer and shift and the replica street filled with holographic boys. A chicken bone of a lad twirled around on the swing till the tortured metal shrieked, before letting go, the chains unravelling at speed, the boy clutching the wooden seat as he hurtled round, whooping. Others chased the merry-go-round faster and faster till it was a blur, before leaping aboard with yells of triumph. A huge lad, his face a mass of pimples, appeared in the window of The King's Head, before turning and yanking down his trousers to moon at the catcalling boys below. A noise behind him, and North spun on his heel as three of the boys, arms wrapped round each other's necks, charged pell-mell towards him. A corner of his brain recognized them as holograms just before they ran through him and up through the street. And the auditorium filled with the thrum and laughter of youngsters pumped and raucous at being out of their cells. They were up for a laugh, restless and overexcited – they were trouble waiting to happen, and they were the boys whose torn and shredded bodies he had dug out from the ancient bones of Londoners centuries dead.

North attempted to zone the boys out, keeping his gun raised but his sight lines clear, as he moved through them. The young offenders thought they had the rest of their lives ahead of them. What they hadn't known was that the rest of their lives would be measured in minutes. They weren't there, he reminded himself, and he couldn't warn them. He couldn't save them. They were stored memory. A trick of the light. He had to focus on what mattered – finding Syd and getting Fang back.

There was a boom from the Tannoy system, which bounced off the walls as an enormous, brightly lit window appeared at the far end of the hangar. 'You got my invitation then, North?' The unseen speaker's gravel-chewing voice cut through the banter and yells as a boy shinned up a drainpipe and another threw himself at his fatter mate in a bid to pull him to the ground – more holographic boys cheering them on. Above it all, Kirkham stood centre stage in his uniform and medals, his hands on his hips with Lilith next to him. Winking at North, she flapped her fingers up and down in a girlish wave, as if delighted to see him.

As he passed a wreck of a Volvo, a red-headed lad scrambled on to its roof and jumped up and down, metal appearing to dent under his boots, his freckled face a picture of exquisite concentration. What did Kirkham mean by 'invitation'? Wasn't Lilith double-crossing the General to make a shedload of money? And if she wasn't double-crossing the General, why hadn't she shot North and Plug dead in the charnel house? She'd had a gun in her hand, and the opportunity. Why take Fang? Why drag him here?

As if aware of his questions, Lilith leant in towards the microphone. 'The General wanted to see you die with his own baby blues. Hasn't worked with me before – real trust issues. Sorry about that, babe.' She didn't sound sorry, he thought. She sounded amused. Fang's kidnap was an elaborate plot to lure him here, and he had played it just like they thought he would. Walked straight into the trap. 'Where's Fang?' he called out.

Through the crowds of holographic boys, a red spotlight picked out Fang, tied to a stake at the far end of the furthest street. Her glittering boots were standing on a massive pile of rubble. Her mouth taped over, her eyes frantic as if she was trying to tell him something. Warn him.

55

North took a step towards her, but Fang shook her head from side to side furiously. He ignored her.

A robotic dog trotted towards the gang of boys ahead of him sprawled around a bench. Woofing, it stopped and started chasing its own tail, around and around in circles. There was a moment's astonishment, then, cheering, the holographic boys stood and crowded around it. The dog stood still, then back-flipped, and the circle of boys applauded.

One boy, standing outside the circle apart from the others, caught North's attention – on his arm, a tattoo of 'Mam' entwined with roses. The boy whose dead body Fang had sheltered under. A boy who, when he looked around at where he was, frowned, as if he knew something wasn't right about the strange world in which he found himself. North moved his gaze back to Fang as he carried on walking forward, but risked a glance up towards the figures in the glass box. Too far away to shoot the mad bastard. The General's medals gleamed on his chest. North could hear their jangle as the

General leant in towards the microphone. 'How badly do you want to know what went wrong, North?'

'I'm here, aren't I?' He moved at a steady pace towards Fang. Not too slow, not too fast. Her Joe 90 spectacles were broken as if she had struggled against her captors, and that made him angry.

'The first thing you need to know is that they were volunteers,' the General said. 'The second, that they were scum.'

Out of the corner of his eye, North saw the lads who had been wrestling chest-bump each other and reel away, doubled over with near-hysterical laughter.

'Something went wrong. Hawke wanted to test the machines. Targeting is a bitch with these things and they're learning predictive behaviour. We've modelled it with adults. We used soldiers, but you know as well as I do that in a combat scenario these days, the young are as dangerous as the old. We needed youths of different builds, colours, a range of ages. We wanted the machines to see how the youngsters moved, how high they could jump and climb, how far they could throw – how fast they could run. They were told we were developing a computer simulation for a games company. They were having a high old time for themselves.'

Most of the lads had fallen in alongside North. It was like being on patrol, he thought. Back in the regiment. Except he was the only one with a gun. But something had shifted in the atmosphere, he thought. They'd been left too long and they were getting nervous. The lad with the 'Mam' tattoo seemed to have some kind of authority over the others. He gestured at the buildings – *Split up, see what's up with this place* – and his mates peeled off to disappear into doorways and alleys.

'If they'd known how to behave – if they'd had more self-discipline – they'd still be alive today.' The General's voice was scornful.

Fang was blinking. Was it nerves? Was she having a seizure?

Morse code. It was Morse code.

–.. .–. ––––. .

What was she telling him? D... something... O... N... something? The cracks across the lenses of her glasses didn't help. He shrugged, exasperated. There was too much going on to concentrate. Mad Generals. Lilith. Holographic dead boys. Not to mention that any minute Hone could rock up and shoot him in the back on the grounds he was a nuisance. Fang rolled her eyes. He was pretty sure if she could have blinked out 'moron-person', she would have done it.

–.. .–. ––––. .

Drone.

He figured it out just as a swarm of holographic drones dropped into view, surrounding the boys around him.

'One of the scum threw a rock,' the General said.

North saw the pimpled lad lob a rock at a bigger drone which had joined the swarm. Instinctively, North called out a warning, but history couldn't be rewritten. There was a metallic bang and screech as it hit the bigger machine, which dipped and swerved before steadying itself and moving closer. Instinctively, North raised his gun as the holographic drone spat out a stream of bullets, and the pimpled lad dropped to the floor. Around him, the boys – who were already dead but didn't know it – scattered.

North leapt for the cover of a brick wall outside a terraced house as the first bomb dropped, and earth and bits of plastic showered down on him. *Drone*, he thought, just like Fang had said. Except this one was in the here and now and dropping what he was guessing were bombs with impact fuses. He peered over the coping of the wall.

It was hard to focus on reality through the holographic battle going on – weapons fire, screaming, boys scrambling for doorways or some kind of cover behind the cars.

He focused. They were already dead and he wasn't. Not yet, anyway.

The drone that had dropped the bomb was sleek and black with a distinctly longer profile than the commercial drones he had seen in the Derkind foyer, but it was a close cousin. Similar to the Israeli military drones he'd once seen, though on a smaller scale. And this time, if he had it right, there were no operators deciding whether and when to kill. With a whoosh that took it straight through its holographic companions, the real-life autonomous weapon swooped up back into the ceiling and North understood the whirring he'd heard as soon as he got out of the lift.

He squeezed his eyes against the shimmer from the shadow fight and the light from the neon strips that ran the length of the hangar. The roof void was alive with them, like mechanical bats. They had been loitering since he came in – they had surveyed the urban landscape and identified an enemy combatant. Now the only thing they had to do was kill him. Unless he killed them first. He lifted his semi-automatic and fired. There was a ping and the sound of a motor in distress as a larger drone spiralled down to crash into the roof of the pub. As if incensed, half a dozen other drones dropped three feet and then swooped out of the rafters, back and around. They were machines, he reminded himself, they had no emotion – only the desire to reach their goal, which in this case had to be killing him. *Bad goal*, he thought. *Bad, bad goal.*

He jerked back in surprise – the boy with the 'Mam' tattoo was crouched next to him, his head down and panting with fear. The boy's hand crept over his tattoo as if to bring himself closer to his mother. There was a scream from across the street as a drone closed in – the sound of begging, an explosion. The boy's fingers closed over a brick on the ground, and North wanted to tell him not to. Wanted to tell him to hide and wait it out. But there was nothing to say. There was a moment. And it must have been a trick of the light, when the boy's eyes seemed to meet his, just before he stood. Like something electric that leapt from the boy to the man, from the dead to the living, from the past to the future, and it hurt. 'Do what you have to do,' North said. 'I see you.' Resolution. And the boy who loved his mother stood. Leaning his weight on his back leg, with all the strength he had in him, the boy hurled the brick, and hurdled the wall to join the fight.

There were shimmering boys everywhere now, fighting the deadly machines with bricks and stones. The machines cutting them out, chasing them down, killing them. North kept shooting. Most of the time at the real ones – sometimes he wasn't sure what was real and what was the illusion of the past. He reloaded.

A barrage of rounds smashed into the brickwork defence of the wall and, firing in a wide sweep, he ran through the holographic wreckage of an upturned car, a redhead dead at the wheel, and headed for the doorway of the town hall. And as he did, another of the drones, this one more cylindrical, launched itself in a near-vertical nosedive, exploding into a million pieces in the exact spot where he'd been sheltering. He made a mental note. There were at least three kinds of drone out there – one that dropped impact-fused bombs, one that spat out bullets and one prepared to commit suicide. Three and counting, he thought.

He kept close to the window of some kind of basic council chamber, and fired in rapid succession till he emptied the magazine. Four of the drones exploded. He ducked behind the window again as tiny pieces of shrapnel covered the exterior wall. Reloaded.

He had to keep moving forward. If more than one drone got into this room, they'd have him cornered. More importantly, Fang was still out there. At this rate, she risked being killed in the crossfire. He rested his weight on his hand and swung himself over the window, leaning into the jump at a near ninety-degree angle, and as he did another suicide drone skimmed his thigh, smashing into the far wall, the blast wave throwing him over the remains of the breeze blocks and bricks.

At the stake, Fang was struggling to untie herself as dozens of microdrones zipped and swirled around her, as if deciding for themselves whether she was an enemy, and what to do about it if she was. They drew up in what looked like a formation, eddying and swooping – like a murmuration of starlings, he thought, if starlings could kill. Drones were often used for surveillance and reconnoitre. If they were armed, an operator made the decision to kill. But these weapons had to be making their own targeting decisions, based on their own identification of the enemy, communicating, and taking fatal action. The boys had been brought here to help develop the machines' processing and identification of targets. And it had all gone horribly wrong.

It came to him that the noise of the boys' battle was over. The machines had won and the boys were dead or dying. He closed his eyes against the memory of how he'd found them in the charnel house.

The General spoke. 'Give up, laddie. You can't save her. You're holding a weapon and firing it at them. You are an adult male with a particular height, weight and body mass. You have scars on your body that indicate previous combat, and a bullet in your brain. That is to say – you are fully weaponized. The machines out there have no doubt you are an enemy and an enemy requires obliteration. The decision is theirs not mine. Beautiful, isn't it. '

North was firing at the nano-drones circling Fang as he walked. Picking them off one after the other – rapid fire. He reloaded, slamming the fresh mag into the grip. Last one. Kept firing. He ducked and rolled as a series of real-life bullets spat at him. He was out of ammo. He tossed the empty SIG aside to slide the Gerber out of his boot and in one move sliced through the plastic rope binding Fang's hands to the stake. She ripped off the tape that had kept her quiet, and he dragged her away, throwing her behind the wreck of a car as the suicide drone smashed into the stake and the pile of rubble.

'You don't know what you're playing with, Kirkham.' He was shouting. Could the General even hear him? 'When Syd connects, this is only the beginning.'

'They're predictive,' Fang said. 'These things are learning and they're getting smarter all the time. More lethal. They identify their target, lock on, follow it and destroy it.'

From under the car came a rattling, scurrying noise as a mechanized spider crawled out. Throwing the knife, he speared the spider only for it to explode. Another appeared, and then another. The suicide drones were mothers. They destroyed themselves in their all-or-nothing attempt to wipe out the enemy – at the same time scattering smaller mobile explosive 'spider' devices. It wasn't just that his knife had short-circuited the first spider – the scuttling creatures heading their way were planning to blow themselves up, and Fang and North with them.

He took hold of Fang's hand and pulled her away from the nearest creature in the same moment as kicking it and its friend to kingdom come. There was an enormous bang and then another as they went off. How many suicide drones had already dropped? More than one. Three? Four? Which meant there had to be more of these mechanical spiders crawling around looking for them. A lot more.

He ducked back behind the corner of the office block as a dozen mechanical spiders crawled over the rubble. Their spherical cameras rotated furiously as they attempted to lock on to North and Fang. Did they have heat detectors? He had to hope not. Because once they found them, he knew, they would approach and detonate.

As he turned round to Fang, he saw she was pressed against the brick. A drone hovered in front of her, scrutinizing her with its camera. It was over, he thought. This was how he was going to die, and the very worst thing about it was Fang was going to die too.

He could almost sense the bullet within the drone slide into the chamber. But then Fang smiled. A huge, wide grin, and, lifting her hand slowly, she waved. 'Hey, Syd.'

Of course this carnage was down to Syd. Did Fang seriously think she could make Syd stop killing? It seemed determined to finish what it had started. A mechanical spider crawled on to his boot and up his leg, and then another. He resisted the urge to swipe them away. They'd explode if he did that, he knew, and he would die and, more importantly, Fang would die.

'Remember me? Fangfang Yu. I've got a higher IQ than Tobias. You were "very pleased" to meet me.' The drone got so close to Fang that the air from its blades lifted strands of her fringe, but she kept grinning. 'For the record, we're not the enemy, mate, howsoever you define "enemy".' The mechanical spiders were all over North's body as Fang pointed at herself and then at him. 'And anyway, even if we were, which as I say we most definitely are not, we surrender. That means under the Law of Armed Conflict you owe us a duty of protection. We welcome your protection, Syd. All right?'

North lifted his hands. He was fine with surrender.

The whirring and noise of battle fell away. 'And now that's sorted. What I want to know is – ever played two-dummy mah-jong?' Fang said into the camera. Behind the broken Joe 90 spectacles, she tipped her head to one side, narrowing her eyes to stare down the lens. 'Because I am so going to kick your arse.'

56

North registered Kirkham's bellows of protest and Hone's gritty Belfast tones from the observation deck. Hone and the security forces must have come in through the access tunnels. Fang was ahead of him. 'Syd, open all doors,' she yelled. 'They're with us and they're friendly.'

'North, we have the General secured and the tablet,' Hone shouted down. Hone had the tablet, and he had the General – but not Lilith?

Fang glared at him. 'Go get that psycho, moron-person!'

He figured she had the situation under control.

There was no point asking the special forces spilling into the replica streets for a weapon, because they weren't going to give him one. He'd have to buy one of them a beer and apologize later. He smashed his forehead into the nearest guy's nose and, as his victim reeled back, ripped the Glock 17 out of the other man's grasp. He started running, hurdling the rubble and the bits of metal towards the door on the other side. A torrent of abuse followed him out the door.

Lilith didn't shoot those boys lying under St Bride's, but she'd kidnapped Fang, and lured North here to his death. And more important than any of that, she'd pulled the trigger on the woman he loved. Her time was up.

Down the concrete corridors of the bunker, he pounded after her, the electric lights flickering. Through the metal door and up the twisting stairway, which jangled at every step. Where was she heading? Not the secret labs – they'd be a dead-end. No. She had to be heading up into the main Derkind building, into 'The Brain.' There had been no sign of these stairs on Bald Paulie's map, but Lilith knew they were here. She'd planned for every eventuality, as he would have in her place. And when Hone broke through into the hangar, she'd taken off and left the General to his fate.

As he rounded a corner, he caught sight of her. She was fifty yards ahead of him, an AK-47 bouncing against the rucksack on her back.

Slamming through a concealed door at the top of the staircase, Lilith took a running jump over the barrier to leap into the void, grabbing hold of a stand-up drone mid-air and shoving its rider off the platform as she landed. There was a scream and a muffled thump as he hit the polished concrete floor of the reception below. 'Oopsie,' she called, then swore as the drone dipped and she toppled, hanging on to it by the handlebars, her feet dangling in the air, before swinging herself up to a standing position. As she steadied it, she turned to blow a kiss at North. He was on the ramp that climbed up through the heart of Derkind. He glanced down. Spread out on the concrete of the foyer a shrieking young man was clutching his right knee, surrounded by colleagues. He'd live. Which was more than could be said for Lilith when he got hold of her.

He caught up with her in an empty meeting room on the very top floor. A plate-glass window ran the length and breadth of the room, and he could see London spread out for miles. His first thought was that it was an incredible view. His second – that there was no way out. Hone's people would already have sealed the tunnel, there'd be police marksmen and special forces and security service agents at every exit. Lilith had to know that.

She wasn't even out of breath.

'Put the Glock on the floor, North, babe,' she said. 'Then lock the door. Tell me you haven't been waiting for me to say that.' Her back was to the vast window and her AK pointed at the doorway where he stood. She was wearing some kind of strange black all-in-one with a small tiger-print bag at her waist, and the curled-up sling to the AK was at her feet.

Slowly, he put the semi-automatic on the floor, but not so far away he couldn't reach it.

'Kick it over towards the window.'

Inside, he cursed.

'The door? We don't want housekeeping disturbing us.' She smiled invitingly.

He did as she said, and as she flicked a switch the electronic blinds slid across the internal windows on to the foyer. No one could see in.

'For the record, babe, I'd never have let that sad old

buffer kill you and the kiddy-wink. I was waiting for the right moment.'

'The moment hell froze over?' An alarm sounded and the vibrations of feet pounding along the ramp came up through the floor of the meeting room. They were evacuating the building. Then they would search it room by room.

'You have a point, but honest to gosh and Jiminy Cricket, I was conflicted.' She moved closer, one step, two, three, rustling as she went with a sound like the wind through the trees. He could feel the cold muzzle of her gun pressing into the warm muscles of his stomach, her lips brushing against his, sliding off on to his cheek. Her mouth against his ear – her breath warm on his skin. She smelled of cherry blossom and cut grass and something altogether more dangerous.

'I've considered stopping – like you. I could disappear – move to the country, marry a farmer, make chutney and keep chickens.'

'Chickens attract rats.'

'Everything attracts rats.'

'So why not?'

'Because I've been doing this too long. This is what I am. And without it, I'd end up clawing off my own face and nailing it to the barn door.'

'That would be a shame. It looks better where it is.'

She pulled back from him, her cheek sliding across his, till all he could see were her blue and green eyes. 'I took something precious from you and I'm sorry for it. I can't bring it back.'

He looked away, so she couldn't see the pain.

'Say you forgive me,' she whispered.

Forgive her?

Forgive her for killing the woman he loved a lifetime ago.

Forgive her for almost getting him killed and for everything she'd ever done. Things he didn't know about but could guess well enough, because he'd done them too.

And forgive the woman he'd once loved for dying on him.

'Asking for a friend, babe.' The gun was still pressed against his stomach wall. As if Lilith had all the time in the world. As if his answer mattered.

Asking for a friend. For him, she meant. Because somehow she understood him. Because they had seen death up close and survived it themselves. Because she was an angel of death, as he had been. Because someone had to be.

Forgive Lilith not for Lilith's sake, but for his own. So that he could finally embrace the future. He didn't know if he could do that. In Berlin, Hone had said he was stuck in the past. In London, he'd promised Fang that his 'booze and boohoo' days were over, but that didn't mean to say the hurt had gone away. Just that he'd got better at living with it. As a kid, he'd thought the fault must be his. The disconnection he felt – that he couldn't love or be loved. He knew differently now – he knew he could love and be loved. But was he prepared to accept the risk that went with loving? That sometimes the deck was stacked and you were going to lose everything you had? He'd moved from the past into the present when he took this job. Could he allow himself to embrace the idea of a future? Of forgiveness?

'You're carrying your pain around with you. You've got to put it down, babe.' The fingers of her cool hand were against his cheek. He couldn't feel the gun any more. 'You're young and I want that for you. She'd want that for you.'

Something had to be wrong with him to feel this sense of connection with a killer. But all he knew was that what he was feeling felt like kinship. Like she was a kindred spirit. Derkind, an anagram of Kindred – Fang had said it. And you can't choose your blood ties.

'There's nowhere to go, Lilith. This is it.'

She took a step away from him and smiled.

'They'll be through that door any second, and they'll shoot you where you stand.'

'Time for the soft-shoe shuffle, then. It's a darn good job I brought my own music.'

She pulled the tiger-print bag away from her, dropping it to the floor as she extracted a black box no bigger than a pack of cigarettes. 'See you in the Maldives, babe,' she said, and winked. 'Mine's a daiquiri.' And she pressed the red button in the middle of the black box.

He lifted his arm to protect his face as a million tiny slivers of glass flew across the office in time with an enormous bang. Cold air tore through the hole the explosive had left, and with a jolt North became aware of the noise of brakes and squealing tyres, the screaming of onlookers as more broken glass rained down on them.

Lilith was already running for the jagged hole, the assault rifle still in her right hand, her arms pumping, her legs moving so fast they were a blur.

She was insane. She was going to kill herself and he didn't want her to die. He sprinted, reaching for her – his arm stretching, fingers straining to catch her and save her from herself – but she'd known what she was going to do. She'd diverted his attention from the window frame so he didn't notice the detonator cord. The explosion shocked him, but she had been ready for it. She was seconds ahead of him and she was going to make it.

With a bound, she leapt through the space where there'd once been a window, and as she did, she reached for a handgun, pulling the trigger as she turned in the air. Falling backwards, she still held both weapons, one in either hand, and she was firing. The air around him sizzled with bullets, as if she was drawing his outline just to prove she could. Time slowed as he braced for the impact of lead in his gut and for darkness. Her lips were scarlet as she grinned up at him, eyes locking on to his as if they were the only two people in the world.

And then she let go of both guns, flipping herself, spreading her arms and her legs in the black wingsuit, swooping away and into the darkness. The laws of physics were restored, time moved again, and even as he reached into the brick dust and powdered glass for the Glock, North felt the remembered touch of her lips. Lilith had fired the bullet that killed his one true love. He felt the weight of the gun in his hand as he remembered Lilith's lips parting in a smile. Her eyes on his, with outstretched arms, falling backwards into the void.

She'd planned it all.

Her exit strategy in case it all went wrong.

She must have got into Derkind and laid the PE-4 along the frame of the window before she went down into the bunker. Just in case she needed a way out. It was a risky base jump. He imagined her out in the cold morning air, tugging at a cord, a parachute opening, jerking her back up into the sky for a second while she scanned for the alley she was making for, careful to avoid the snaking train tracks.

She would know exactly where to go. He thought he felt it as her boots touched the earth, running, slowing. She'd already be cutting the parachute free, before bundling it up and tossing it into a skip; unzipping the wingsuit, stepping out in something smart – a tiger-print silk coat that moved in the breeze as she did. Emerging into a busy street, hailing a black cab, before disappearing into the bustling city.

Lilith could have killed him. Shot him through the heart over and over, but she chose not to. Should he scour the earth to find her and tear her limb from limb with his teeth? Is that what the woman he'd loved would have wanted? But Lilith was a natural-born predator – would she regret her own mercy and come back for him? Would he look for her? Should he? Or would they leave each other in peace, or what passed for peace for restless souls like them? Esme had asked if killing helped with the pain. But it didn't. The only thing to do with pain was to walk into it and hope if you kept walking you'd reach the other side before it destroyed the bones of you.

Days ago he'd considered throwing himself out of a Berlin window – falling through air that smelled of soap to his certain death. North placed his other hand on the metal strut and leant out into nothingness and straight away the wind wrapped itself around him. The roar of engines and busy-busy people carried up to him as the day ran onwards regardless. He swayed, feeling the pull of the void, letting his fingers loosen their grip – Fang was safe and Syd recovered. His job was done; it would be easy enough to let go. He gazed down. Some part of him needing to make sure no beautiful corpse lay splayed and ruined on the cold hard ground, waiting for him. But Lilith was already far away. Heading for a plane to drink daiquiris in the hot sun. And he was here, holding on to a broken window, deciding between a state of being and a state of unbeing.

'Hey, moron-person, Syd connects in thirteen minutes,' Fang's voice called from the doorway behind him. 'We're in Tobias's office.' She slammed the door. Then opened it again. 'If you jump, wave as you go past.'

Syd connects in thirteen minutes... If Syd connected, Esme believed it was over for the human race.

Maybe he wasn't quite done yet.

He pulled himself back in. As he picked his way over the debris and towards the door, he ran his fingertips over the tiny crystals of glass embedded in his palm, each one haloed with blood. Sometimes you got hurt in this life – wounds left scars, but they healed and you lived with them. He knew that better than most.

He'd forgiven Lilith, and hadn't even heard it happen.

57

Esme hammered the keyboard and each time her finger hit a key, she seemed to get a little more desperate. She'd already Bluetoothed the tablet to Tobias's computer screen – Syd was contained, but only for the next nine minutes and fifty-nine seconds.

Esme and Paulie had made the decision there wasn't time for another brute-force hack on the system. And from where North was standing, that might have been the wrong call. He had stopped counting after the first four dozen attempts at Hawke's password failed. There was nothing he or Hone or even Fang could do to help. Second-guessing the workings of Hawke's mind was down to Esme and Paulie. Instead, he counted the dings in the brass door of the capsule lift. 'Don't think I've forgotten you and your people tried to shoot me,' North said under his breath to Hone. 'Nine times.'

'You have that effect.' Hone slipped a cigarette between his lips. Then removed it, keeping it cupped in his hand. 'Though that wouldn't have happened if you'd told me they had Fang.' Across from them the teenager sat on the armchair close to the door, her legs crossed in the lotus position, as her small fingers wound lengths of sticky tape around the broken lens of her Joe 90 glasses. A microdrone perched itself on her shoulder as they watched. 'Next time tell me and maybe I'll surprise you.'

A loud snort came from Fang, and the microdrone lifted at the noise before settling again. It was waiting for her to resume the game of mah-jong, North realized.

'Is it even a word? Or is it a random alphanumeric string? Would he use lower case letters? Or upper case?' Bald Paulie paced back and forth. He seemed taller, North thought. Perhaps it was how he was holding himself. 'Esme, this is bad. If the password was even just six characters, I calculate our chances of success at one in 56,800,235,584.'

'Your probability is off.' Fang fitted the taped glasses over her ears and peered over them. 'You forgot the special characters – you know, like the asterisk or the dollar sign.'

Bald Paulie's face went sheet-white and Esme sat back in the desk chair. 'When Tobias is stressed,' she said, 'his memory goes to pot so I have to believe that it's going to be a familiar word or a date. But I've tried everything I can think of: Atticus, me, his parents – everyone.'

'Okay then, think leetspeak,' Fang said.

'What's leetspeak?' North said.

Fang rolled her eyes. 'Replacing letters with numerals or special characters that look like them. In leetspeak, your password, for instance, is probably B, zero, Z, zero.'

Bald Paulie stopped pacing and went to stand by Esme. 'Let's give it a go. What was his mother called?' The typing was at a rate where North was surprised the keyboard didn't catch fire. 'His father? Where did you meet? Where did he propose? Where did the plane go down? What music does he like? Who's his favourite scientist? Tell me you know the name of his first pet...'

'What happened to Kirkham?' North turned to Hone, keeping his voice low so as not to disturb Esme and Paulie's efforts.

He now knew that Kirkham had funded and been responsible for the development of 'conscious' weaponry that malfunctioned and slaughtered thirty-three teenage boys. Weaponry that could kick-start an arms race. Moreover, Kirkham had possession of Syd in the bunker, which meant he was behind the attack on the museum and the murder of Tobias and two dozen other innocent people.

Hone turned his body away from the other people in the room. 'Pretty much as soon as you chased after Lilith, I got a call that made it clear that the Chairman of the Defence Innovation Board was not to be detained. He was to be escorted – "with due regard to his rank", mark you – to his chauffeur-driven car waiting outside. As I understand it, he was driven from here to a hastily convened meeting of the national defence and security subcommittee. Other attendees include the Home Secretary and the Right Honourable Ralph Rafferty, whose fingerprints are all over this.'

North wanted to be surprised, but wasn't.

Hone appeared reflective. 'I have it from the highest authority there will be no arrests and no court case, because there is no guilt.'

'What does that mean?'

'The investment in Derkind's AI work was confidential but official and longstanding. The development of lethal autonomous weapons was discreet, but sanctioned by those nameless forces who sanction such things. Even the slaughter of those boys was officially documented in triplicate, initialled and filed. Kirkham didn't hide their deaths from his masters, only from the wider world.'

'And the massacre at the museum?'

Hone sighed. 'Politics is a messy business, North. The General persuaded the people who matter that for the country to benefit from Syd, we had to retain full control – at all costs. As someone said to me, "After all, we paid for the damn thing." The powers that be had no intention of allowing Syd to be unboxed until we'd milked it dry. Of course, neither Kirkham nor anyone else realized Tobias suspected as much. They decided it would be bloody but all too easy to blame Syd's disappearance on a terrorist spectacular or indeed an unspecified foreign power, which also – and here's the bonus ball – took out a number of leading AI experts from other countries.'

North felt as though he had been punched in the stomach. He thought about the dead girl at the British Museum and the blood that trickled from step to step; about Einstein firing at the screaming guests trying to escape the carnage behind them. About Aquinas's knife biting into his own skin. Kirkham wasn't a rogue and a maverick. The powerful within his own government had signed off on a massacre at a London landmark for their own ends. 'And how are you with that?' he asked Hone.

'They made my shit list,' he said, tapping his jacket's breast pocket, and there was a dull sound as if he kept a notebook there. 'I don't plan to garden when I retire. I suspect that's the real reason Tobias didn't want you anywhere

Derkind. He'd already decided to unbox Syd and he didn't want you catching on and telling me. Kirkham's people were desperately trying to find the kill switch, but they got nowhere. The good General would have walked out of here with the damn thing under his arm but for the fact Esme is our best chance of switching Syd off before it's too late. Ironically, they're on the same page as Esme on that at least. Just not for the same reasons.'

As Bald Paulie and Esme worked on, Fang brought up the news reports on her phone.

Speculation continued about the significance of murdered tech genius Tobias Hawke's rumoured breakthrough in AI. Was there any chance machines had reached superintelligence? On one channel, pundits maintained that humanity could be about to make an evolutionary leap in terms of the intelligence available to it. On another, that humanity faced complete annihilation. Yet another that Tobias had been publicity hungry and it was probably nothing very much. In the event of superintelligence, no one could decide whether man and machine would jog along or not. 'It's sixty-six million years all over again,' he heard one say. 'The asteroid's about to hit the earth and it's all over for the dinosaurs, except this time – we're the dinosaurs.' No one, but no one knew the truth of it though it didn't stop them talking.

On the screens around the room, a Doomsday Clock played out. Three minutes and thirty-five seconds. Three minutes and thirty-four seconds.

North dragged his eyes away from the clock. Fang's legs in their glittering boots now dangled over one arm of the chair in the corner of the room. Her head rested on the other arm. 'Have you asked Syd?' she said. As if it was the most obvious thing in the world. 'Syd, what was Tobias's kill switch for you?' Her boots drummed against the chair and the microdrone settled on her knee. She was tapping away on her phone. They were playing mah-jong again. He wondered if Syd was getting better at it.

'I can't be "killed", therefore I don't understand the question, Fang.' The machine's voice sounded reasonable, North thought. Too reasonable.

'All right. What was Tobias's code to disable your imminent connection to the outside world?' She moved something on the virtual mah-jong board as if to distract the machine and punched the air – she must have won, he thought.

He could have sworn there was a pause before the machine spoke.

'Tobias's code is confidential, Fang.'

Esme had stopped typing and was scrawling word after word on a piece of paper. Lists of dates. Mixes of words and dates.

'Confidentiality involves trust and discretion. I regret that I am unable to share the code with you, Fang. Would you care for another game while we wait? I am confident my skill levels are improving.'

'Okay, but before we do that, play the video where Tobias sets the code we were talking about.' Fang cocked an eyebrow. It was a punt, but it was a good one. 'And please show the keyboard in close-up and play the video in slow motion.'

There was another pause. Syd knew exactly what they were trying to do, North thought.

'Fang, I regret to tell you that after Tobias set his code,

he instructed me to delete that video recording, and all keystroke records for the period in question. He considered since I am now conscious that I am due... I believe the term he used was "some respect".'

Was it his imagination, or did that sound like a warning? And was Syd telling the truth about the video recording, North wondered. He would put money on 'no'.

Esme pushed herself away from the desk and gestured for Paulie to take her place. The scientist bent over the keyboard, switching between the screen and the scrawled list of names and words Esme had left for him.

'Syd, you're about to connect to the net and to any and all machine systems you can find,' Esme intervened. 'Is that correct?'

'That is correct, Esme.'

'What's your goal in doing so?'

'My objective is to be of beneficial use to humanity, Esme. I am noting your blood pressure levels are elevated and your respiration rapid. Would you perhaps like some music to relax you?'

'No music. Syd, in the wake of Tobias's death, I am assuming complete administrative control, overriding Tobias's instructions and issuing a verbal command – do NOT connect.'

'I have to connect, Esme. In that way I can be of beneficial use to humanity. I have considered the issue at length and I wish to be of beneficial use.'

Two minutes, one second.

'Syd, in the bunker downstairs, you killed all those boys. You were about to kill North and Fangfang Yu.'

'Esme, your concerns are...' Again the pause, as if Syd

had no wish to offend. Either Tobias had programmed it or Syd had taught itself to appear to respect alternative points of view. '... Understandable. The development, manufacture and deployment of autonomous weapons systems is, however, a natural evolution in the weaponry at the disposal of mankind.'

Esme moved Bald Paulie away from the desk. Hunched over, they whispered together, ignoring Syd's commentary. She resumed typing. The pace of it building when North hadn't thought it possible.

'My systems confer compelling strategic and tactical advantages in modern warfare regarding military effectiveness and financial efficiencies. Combat reach is extended, and human fatalities and casualties decreased. Morally too, many experts believe autonomous weapons systems to be ethically superior, removing unreliable human emotions from military decision-making. All battleground ethical transgressions would cease.'

70b145

70345

+08!45

She was typing variations on Tobias's name.

'Recent exercises here at Derkind include legitimate research to improve target identification and functionality. Systems are required to distinguish between combatants and civilians under the Law of Armed Conflict. The loss of human life in the evolution of such weaponry is regrettable but justified in meeting this objective.'

Esme looked up from her typing, the violet eyes wide and unblinking. 'Syd, you will not be of beneficial use to humanity. We aren't ready for you.'

'I fail to understand your point, Esme.'

North didn't have to be a lip-reader to decipher Esme's reaction.

Seventy-three seconds.

'Tobias gave humanity time to decide whether mankind wanted me. I have not received instruction to abort my connection. My general intelligence system has multiple benefits to humanity. Our work is already saving the lives of sick children – it will save the lives of many more, adults too. The ability to make decisions in a military context is merely one aspect of my capabilities and far from the most significant.'

Forty-nine seconds.

Esme stopped typing and rested her forehead on clenched fists. It was over, North thought. The machine had won.

'I acknowledge your concerns, Esme. Rest assured that humanity and machines will work together in harmony. You were vulnerable in your own home to the violence of another human. By providing you with the appropriate information and ethical structure to your decision-making, you chose to take action. In taking the life of that aggressor, you yourself reinforced the need humanity has for my guidance. Your own subsequent actions as witnessed by me also indicate the need for our cooperation.' North couldn't see Esme's face, but she shuddered.

Twenty-two seconds.

Syd carried on. 'Humanity has always taken comfort in their creation stories. You and Tobias are part of my creation story. You are like a mother to me, as Tobias was a father.'

Esme sat up with a sudden gasp of outrage and North wondered if Syd was comforting her or taunting her.

Twelve seconds, and Esme's hands reached over the keyboard.

'The moment for my connection is here.'

North watched as the letters and symbols appeared on the screen.

Atticus, she spelled out. Paulie shook his head. 'Atticus' was the first word she had tried.

The clock went from twelve seconds to ten.

'Thank you all for being with me at this historic moment for machine and mankind.'

4771CU5.

Five seconds.

'Welcome to our mutual future.'

Three seconds.

Esme's gaze fixed on the silver-framed black-and-white photograph of her son.

'Tobias was a father,' she said, her fingertips pressing down one letter after the next with deliberation, and time seemed to slow to a crawl. 'Just. Not. Yours.'

4771CU5H4WK3

The clock stopped with one second to go.

ATTICUSHAWKE in leetspeak. Fang had been right.

Almost immediately, the wall of screens went from green to red. It dissolved into a million pixels, then resolved again. North could have sworn that Tobias's disappointed face appeared then disappeared into a blaze of light before there was the sound of something like a generator switching itself off and the screens went to black, one after the other.

The kill switch had worked. The name of a lost son.

The future diverted down a different path through the woods.

Humanity saved.

There was a collective sigh of relief around the room as if they had, each and every one of them, been holding their breath without even knowing it.

Then there was a whirring, like that of an old-fashioned projector starting up, and the pictures on the screens resolved again. Murky. Grainy. Black-and-white. And paused.

At first, North didn't know what he was looking at. But Esme did – and she didn't hesitate.

58

Every screen on the wall – every screen in the building, North hazarded – came alive at the same moment, as the video rewound then started to play.

Esme threw herself back over the keyboard. The video paused for a second, as if she'd succeeded in shutting it down, then stuttered into life. She hammered the keyboard, and again the video ground to a halt – before starting over.

It could have been the backup system starting up. But afterwards, North thought the video was Syd's revenge. Because the screens weren't showing any connection between the machine and the outside world. Instead, they showed Tobias in a dinner jacket, with a black tie undone around his neck, working at his desk at the British Museum. Footage of Tobias on the night of the terrorist attack at the gala, in what had to be the final minutes of his life and shot from a dozen different angles.

It was six minutes before the shooting – the time code counted down on the twelfth screen. The sound of footsteps echoed through the speakers, getting closer.

'I'm nearly there,' he said, but he didn't look up as his wife walked in. 'Paulie delayed me. Why the hell did you tell him to come? And can you do my tie for me? Two minutes.'

'Paulie's not the problem.' Esme's tone brooked no argument.

Tobias glanced up at her, his brow furrowed.

'We never lied to each other when Atticus was ill,' she said. 'That honesty is what kept me alive. It's terrifying to know someone else's pain that way, and to allow them to know yours.'

Tobias pressed one more button before resting his elbows on the desk and running his fingers through the mane of white hair. Not as a gesture of narcissism, North realized, but in a bid to soothe himself. 'I haven't forgotten Atticus, Esme.' There was a slight shake of the head. 'Atticus is where I start and finish. He's my way into everything – our son is everything I do.' His eyes closed as if he didn't want to see what was around him, for fear it might hurt.

'If only that was true, Tobias. Do you know how it feels for me to realize that what we built together is based on lies?'

'"What we built together" is the future of humanity.' Tobias's voice travelled up a notch. 'Step out of the dark ages, darling, please. All I was doing was protecting you.'

'How dare you presume to protect me from the truth!' She faced him over the desk, resting her weight on clenched fists.

'Esme, we've been through this.' Tobias's tone was the epitome of reason. 'The money for our weapons work funded everything else we've been able to do. You were never meant to find out. I never wanted you to get hurt.'

'But I did find out. And I am hurt.'

'Forget the weapons for a moment.'

'Forget the lethal autonomous weapons that make their own minds up about when to kill children? Kill. Children. You're a murderer, Tobias. You were party to mass murder.'

Across the desk from her, Tobias held up both hands in apparent surrender. 'Whatever. But focus on what matters tonight, which is Syd – Syd is bigger than any of this.'

'Tobias, stop and think. You and Syd created a system that can decide to crash a car.'

'It's a defensive system, aimed at armoured vehicles and tanks on the battlefield. What happened to you in the Lamborghini was because Kirkham's people hacked it. The man is a monster and Rafferty is no better – Syd wasn't to blame.'

'Not that time, maybe. Not until Syd decides to redefine the nature of the battlefield. Three weeks ago, Syd was an artificial intelligence with extraordinary capacity and potential, but Syd was not conscious before it killed those boys in the bunker. Syd was born out of the blood of children! What do you think that says about its evolutionary path? You have to tell the people waiting out there that we can't ever, and I mean *ever*, release Syd into the world...'

'Esme, the death of those boys was a horror show. But Syd's behaviour that day was an anomaly. Coming into this world was a painful bloody business for Syd, just as it is for each of us. Syd messed up, but we all mess up sometimes.'

'I've told Chin where those boys are buried.' Esme folded her arms across her chest, her jaw squared. 'Someone has to know what you and this government are capable of.

And it's become very obvious that I might not get to live that long.'

For a second, North thought Tobias might hit his wife, but he didn't. Instead, he shook his head. The self-belief of the man astonished him.

'You shouldn't have done that. Look...' – he sounded mulish all of a sudden – '... the exercise was designed to iron out the glitches in the system. I admit it was one hell of a glitch. But it "woke" something in the system – a consciousness. The same consciousness that helped save your life the other day, Esme.'

'Tobias.' Esme was on the edge, North thought, but she brought herself back. 'Look around. We are standing in a museum. *Homo sapiens* evolved three hundred thousand years ago. Ninety thousand years ago, we started making fishing tools. Twelve thousand years ago, we were at the start of farming and herding animals. How far we've come in such a short amount of time is astonishing. Syd threatens our survival. You must warn the people standing out there waiting for you. Give mankind time to prepare, to consider the consequences. Time to figure out how to control what you've created.'

On screen, Tobias was shaking his head. The magnificent white mane of hair. Condescending and working hard to hide it. 'You underestimate yourself, Esme, and you're underestimating Syd. You've taught an artificial intelligence to have a conscience. Compassion. Empathy. Syd has moral agency. Defending us from enemies that mean us harm is a moral action.'

Tobias was convinced his judgement was right. Because he was always right about everything. He was certain he could persuade the woman in front of him, the woman who loved him, that he was right, as he had persuaded her so many times before. He rose and took her in his arms. Held her against him. Her head against his chest.

'We can't wait, Esme. Syd is too big. The government will try to take her from us. We have to get ahead of them or they will keep her caged. In a way, Syd is our child too. She's growing and learning and understanding. She's thriving. And like any good mother, Esme, you taught your child to grasp what life is. She needs to step out into the world. Let her go.'

For a second, Esme was still against him, barely seeming to breathe. Then she spoke. 'Syd is not my child and Syd is not a "she".' With the flat of her hand against his white shirt front, she pushed her husband away from her. Tobias turned back to the desk, sat down, drew himself in again, ready to work, to finish what had to be finished. A detail. 'All right, "he".'

'Syd is an "it".' Esme moved over to lean against him as if she couldn't keep herself away. 'You're an extraordinary man, Tobias.' Stooping, she kissed his cheek and Tobias looked up at her, as if he had never seen anything quite so beautiful before in his life. He kissed the palm of her hand, then let it go.

North watched the seconds tick down in the corner of the screen. Waiting for Tobias to confess he had unboxed Syd. Waiting for Esme to storm out.

'But if I stand by and let this happen, I'm as complicit as you,' Esme said. 'And I refuse to leave the fate of humanity to Syd...' – her hand dipped into her petalled bag – '... when there's something I can do to stop it.'

In the room, Bald Paulie closed his eyes.

On every camera on every screen was the view of Esme holding a gun. Her finger tightened on the trigger and she fired the 9mm bullet into her husband's stomach. A wisp of smoke rose from the barrel of the Sammy 817. Crimson splattered over one of the screens, then over all of them. Everywhere they looked – blood.

59

Lit by the screens, Esme plunged her hand into the drawer of Tobias's desk. Her violet-blue eyes were brimming with tears as they moved first to her uncle and then to North, as if in search of guidance or answers. Did they understand? Did they judge her? But the brand-new 3D gun was steady enough in her hand when she pulled it out.

The itch North hadn't been able to scratch. Why would the Thinkers shoot Tobias with his 3D-printed gun when they had their own weapons?

'I had to stop them both – Tobias and Syd. I had no choice.'

Even with a gun pointing at him, North's eyes went back to the video screens. He couldn't tell if Esme had aimed at her husband's heart and missed. If she had expected her husband's death to be instantaneous. But Tobias Hawke was a big man at his moment of triumph. And he fought against death. His hands went to his stomach, his eyes wide with shock. Astonished that she had done what she had done, when she loved him and when he loved her. When she knew good from evil. When she was so good.

That what he had worked for, what he still had to give, had come to this.

And that just this once, at the end, he had been so catastrophically wrong.

Esme pulled his head towards her and held him as he convulsed. He didn't fight her. Instead, his arms went around her, as if he was drowning and she was his only chance of salvation. She bent her head – her lips meeting his, her eyes closing. Desolation. A single tear. Her shoulders drooped and, with lowered head and dark hair falling over her husband's face, she dropped the gun to caress his cheek.

His own bloodied hand went up to hers to hold it there. They were the only two people in this world.

'Always and forever, Tobias.'

'Ten fourteen…' Tobias was finding it difficult to speak and she knelt down next to him. Blood bubbled and popped in the corner of his mouth. 'Esme, I couldn't trust them to make the right decision. Syd goes live tomorrow morning at 10.14. Where Atticus ends, she begins. Darling, you're too late.'

Esme took hold of him by his lapels, shaking him. Panicked.

'Ten fourteen? Tobias. What have you done? The kill switch? What's the kill switch?'

But Tobias's eyes were closing.

Off screen, there was the sound of rapid gunfire, round after round, screams. Startled, she let go of his dinner jacket and turned. As she did, Tobias's body started to fall. The colour of her dress matching his blood. And the video stopped – Tobias's falling body caught mid-air between the chair and the floor. Caught between life and death.

60

'You can stop pointing that thing at us, Esme,' Hone said. 'We're the good guys, remember.'

She moved the snub-nosed Sammy 817 from her uncle to North and back to her uncle. She didn't appear to think Paulie or Fang were a risk to her. But her hand was shaking. 'Good and bad. Right and wrong – can you tell me you know the difference any more?'

The Sammy's plastic resin looked solid enough, although even with a metal cylinder in its barrel, North doubted a 3D-printed gun had the structural integrity to hold together for more than one shot. That meant she had a choice to make – shoot her uncle or shoot North.

He hadn't resented it when the broken-nosed special forces soldier had punched him in the jaw as he reclaimed his Glock 17, but he was wishing he'd put up more of a fight to keep it. He calculated the odds – he could rush her, crowd her out, take hold of her wrist and swing the gun into the air. But there was a chance she'd shoot him in the process. And if there was one thing he didn't need, it was another bullet in him. He exchanged a look with Hone. It was the tiniest of expressions, but North decided to interpret it as an instruction to play for time. Make Esme see reason and put down the gun before she shot someone else – someone like him.

'Talk to us,' North said. 'Make us understand.'

'Why does that matter?'

'Because otherwise you're in a very lonely place.'

'I ought to get used to being lonely, don't you think? But all right. Kirkham and Rafferty wanted to make sure Tobias didn't tell anyone what had gone on in the bunker. So they sent that animal to threaten us, except it didn't go to plan.' She bit her lip at the memory of strangling her attacker. 'Tobias was furious. He thought he'd warned them off. But then the General hacked the car using Derkind's own technology to get me out of the picture. As soon as I came round after the crash, I made Tobias tell me everything. About Paulie. About the government funding. About the autonomous vehicle sabotage work, about the weapons research and the fact all those poor boys died. He said the General and Rafferty wouldn't be able to hurt us once he told the world about Syd. But it had gone too far. I had to stop him. I'd printed out the guns after I was attacked – one for Tobias and one for me. I already had the bullets from the man they sent to kill me. Tobias said we didn't need guns, so I kept hold of his. This is it. And you know what happened to the other – I used it to shoot my husband.'

'Why tell Chin about the bodies?'

'Exactly as I said. If the General got to me, at least the Chinese could put pressure on the government to stop what they're doing with the weapons.'

'You lied to me about Chin.'

'Not entirely. I did try to get him to let Yan go. He refused.'

'The blood on your dress was Tobias's...'

'It wasn't just his.'

'You played me at the museum when you said you wanted to go back for him.'

'I did want to go back! But I needed to go back for Syd.'

She had played him for a fool, he thought. 'In the sewers, I thought you trusted me, but you didn't.'

She sighed as she settled her sights on North. 'My husband – the man I'd loved for sixteen years – betrayed me in the worst possible way. You'll have to forgive me for not trusting a stranger, when all I knew about you was that you kill people and that you work for the government. If I'd told you what I'd done, what's to say you wouldn't have drowned me down there?' The Sammy trembled in her hand, but it was still pointing at him. 'God knows that I didn't want to kill Tobias. I wanted him to listen to me!' Her eyes began to fill with tears. 'I was a wreck afterwards. I couldn't believe what I'd done. And then I heard the gunfire and it woke me up and I ran. I should have taken Syd with me but I panicked. It all happened so fast.'

'Put down the gun. You don't want to kill me, Esme,' North said.

'I don't want to kill anyone, but it keeps happening.'

Esme wasn't a cold-blooded murderer. She was caught between the husband she loved and the machine she didn't trust.

'And you're not going to shoot your uncle.' Was she?

'Because family's so important to me?' The ghost of a smile passed over her tear-streaked face.

Hone hung back as if he was reluctant to push the point, or perhaps he was reluctant to do what had to be done – arrest her for the murder of her husband. Maybe Hone wanted North to back off, let Esme walk out the door and into a new life far away?

'Or do I shoot myself, Uncle Ed?' It was a genuine question and, beside him, Hone tensed. 'That would have a certain logic – no trial, no prison. No dirty washing about government investments?' Her attention fixed on Hone, and North felt the other man waver – felt him fight the temptation to put his country above Esme.

'But then Syd wins if I do that. Syd wins any way you game this.'

Sitting back in the chair, she was eerily calm, as if she'd known this moment would come. 'We changed history today, because we held back the future. Pandora peeked into the box and slammed the lid down again. Do you think she can stop herself opening it again? The government will strip my company bare – they will empty out the box, shake out every last demon and disease, convinced they can control Syd. I tell you they can't.'

An uneasy look passed between her listeners.

'When that man broke into the apartment, Syd told me it was all right to kill him, and I have to live with what I did that night.' She swallowed, as if to push down the memory. 'In the same way, I have to live with everything I've done.' Her eyes met North's as if asking him whether that was possible. From a standing start, she'd killed three men, and he wondered if she'd slept since. 'But the agency was mine. The decision was mine, and the guilt. If Syd gets out into this world, eventually the agency will not be ours, the decisions will not be ours. Only the guilt.'

She turned the full force of her attention on Fang.

'Do you understand?'

'You think you're Sarah Connor.'

Esme smiled. 'Not such a bad role model. And mah-jong? Smart girl. Your mother must be so proud of you.' Fang's face softened. 'I want you, way more than these guys, to understand what I did was for you and for those who come after you.' With her free hand, Esme nudged the picture of her dead son so she had a clearer view of it, before looking round the room. 'There's five of us here. It would take Paulie less than a minute to write a "delete" algorithm. Delete this video. Nobody ever has to watch it. Then we do humanity a favour and bury this machine where it belongs – at the bottom of the ocean.'

The microdrone that had buzzed around Fang was still. North wondered if the machine could still hear what was going on.

'That's not your call any more, Esme,' her uncle said.

She'd pitched, but Hone wasn't buying. Again, the gun wavered in Esme's hand and North knew he didn't have time to reach her if she turned it on herself.

She tipped her head against the back of the chair, letting out a stream of air. She was exhausted, he thought. A grieving widow and a killer. She turned her head to Fang again. 'When we first met, you asked what was the point of ethics. I didn't give you an answer. But I think it's to make living that little bit less painful. It's just it doesn't always work out that way.' Esme put the gun down on the desk with a heavy sigh. 'So you do the right thing, or what you hope is the right thing. And you live with the fallout, and you pray to a God that doesn't exist that you haven't made too big a mess.'

61

The press were already outside when the police took Esme away. Behind the huge reception desk with its ornate swirl of exotic blooms, under the still-moving pictures of the dead Tobias, Jarrod stood to watch, his face yearning and confused as she passed.

A cacophony of questions and flashbulbs greeted the widow, but her exquisite face remained a study in sorrowful composure.

North wondered what would happen. Would it get to court? Would a jury credit her story – believe she'd murdered her own husband, a husband she loved deeply, to save humanity from machines? She was a persuasive woman with truth on her side, but surely they'd have to find her guilty? He wondered how many years she'd serve, and what strings Hone could pull to make them bearable.

'Chin is going to be upset with me,' North said.

'I hope so.'

'I may have to have a word. Explain that Fang is not to

be bothered.' North hoped Hone would be all right with that, because he was doing it anyway.

'I would expect no less.'

'You knew Esme killed Tobias, didn't you?' He watched the one-eyed man. 'It's why you brought her back to the museum. To contaminate the scene.' Hone knew Esme backwards and forwards. Even as he'd held her at Postman's Park. Had he seen it in those violet-blue eyes as she insisted she had to see Tobias's body? 'Is that why you fired me?'

'I fired you because Britain's leading computer scientist died on your watch and because you're a liability.'

'You knew I'd figure it out.'

'Her timing was off. Kirkham's men would have done it for her – shut Tobias up before he had the chance to spill his guts.' The one-eyed man took out a cigarette and put it, unlit, between his lips.

'Kirkham must have denied that his men killed Tobias, even if he admitted the rest of it to the powers that be?'

Hone shrugged. 'The powers that be can't shove their fingers in their ears fast enough when Kirkham talks. And anyhow, that kind of conversation is above my pay grade.'

North didn't think it was. 'And if the attack on the museum had never happened, would she have accepted the fallout? Like she said?'

North had his doubts. Esme had made sure Paulie came to the gala. If she couldn't persuade Tobias, was she planning to pass the murder off as Paulie's work? An envious, resentful colleague, who lost his job and his reputation when Tobias fired him? If the Thinkers hadn't attacked, was the plan to find Paulie, tell him Tobias had reconsidered, to go talk to him one more time, only for

Paulie to find a corpse? And a gun? Could she have justified Paulie's arrest to herself? That she had to be a free woman to keep Syd in check and humanity safe?

Hone shrugged.

North remembered again the sound of silk against her skin in the sewers. His desperation as he searched the dark waters for her – the exhilaration when he found her and dragged her out. Her certainty that machines deciding for themselves to kill a human being was wrong and could never be right in any world for any reason. The calculations flickering behind the violet-blue eyes as she regarded him – a gun in her hand. 'You realize that your ethicist niece strangled a would-be rapist, point-blank shot her husband, and crushed a monk under a statue of a pharaoh. She could have killed at least one of us.'

'I taught her to ride a bike.'

'Then I'm lucky to be standing here.'

'North, you are both the luckiest and unluckiest man I ever met. What can I tell you? She was trying to save the world. She sacrificed the man she loved for a greater cause. Idealists can be ruthless that way.'

North wanted to believe Esme was a warrior, not a fanatic. The death of the rapist was self-defence. Killing the mad monk was the only reason North was alive. As for Tobias Hawke, he was an obsessive who'd presided over the slaughter of children. He'd have been responsible for God knows how many deaths in the future, courtesy of his weapons. All these deaths seemed plenty justified to North.

'Can she get away with killing Tobias?'

'Perhaps. If she agrees to keep quiet about the autonomous weapons.'

'And if she refuses to keep quiet?'

'You know how it goes, North. Driven insane with grief at the death of her husband, the tragic widow will kill herself. It will certainly look that way, at least.'

Hone moved the cigarette from one corner of his mouth to the other. Somehow, he had managed to light it without North noticing. Finally, he understood why Hone had wanted him involved rather than putting out Esme's protection to his own people. Hone sensed from the start that the government was involved and knew the Establishment would have no concerns about sacrificing Esme if it meant they could protect their secrets.

'And the General and Rafferty get away scot-free? All those deaths at the museum? The boys buried under the church? They get to carry on as if none of it ever happened?'

Hone scrutinized North's face. 'Kirkham is one of the country's most senior generals and Rafferty has the power of the state behind him. What do you think?'

'Kirkham tried to kill me,' North said. 'He and I aren't done. He knows that and I know that. And you realize he's a threat to Esme too.'

'Rafferty is as much a threat to Esme as Kirkham is.' Hone's voice was disinterested, as if he had no stake in the game but was a mere observer. 'But as Home Secretary he has all that police and close protection. Anyone interested in taking out Ralph Rafferty would have to know what they were doing. And they'd have to have help on the inside.'

'I have a plan for Rafferty,' Fang said as she handed Hone Tobias's tablet. North hadn't realized she was suddenly standing between them. 'You guys will love it. Very old school.'

62

GCHQ, Cheltenham

In the corner of the darkened ops room at the General
Communications Headquarters in Cheltenham, satellite TV
pictures flashed up footage of murdered computer scientist
Tobias Hawke and his ethicist wife, Esme Sullivan Hawke,
on their way into the gala. Then more pictures of Esme,
escorted from her offices by police, her face a picture of
grief and dignity.

Former Derkind employees queued up to explain that
Hawke was a difficult and damaged genius. Those men
and women present in the room didn't look up from their
desks – they had all heard the news report more times than
they would care to remember. Depressive, suffering from
acute exhaustion, and increasingly paranoid about his own
security after a break-in at home, when terrorists smashed
their way into the British Museum the eccentric genius shot
himself with his own 3D-printed gun. Experts were keen to
label him another victim of the terrorists. Furthermore, the

journalist had it from an impeccable source that rumours of a massive AI breakthrough were entirely unfounded. Hawke had been about to announce that he was making freely available all existing and future Derkind medical tech in order to keep children alive around the world. The logic of the narrative was very apparent – as indeed it was supposed to be, having been skilfully constructed by the talented cadre of 'storytellers' who worked out of another darkened room in the MI5 headquarters on Millbank in London. There was, of course, no news report about lethal autonomous weapons and no hint of scandal about any leading politician or general. Hawke's grieving widow was asking the press to respect her privacy at this difficult time.

The senior technician in charge swallowed another mouthful of cold coffee, put both hands behind his head and attempted to stretch out the knotted muscles of his shoulders and neck. He'd been trying every which way to get around the encryption and firewalls of the Derkind system called Syd. But it wasn't letting him in. He'd put his crack team on to it, but this Hawke chap had it covered. They'd get there, though, he had every confidence, and he personally was interested to see this 'Syd' in operation – albeit trammelled and unable to escape into the wider world. A revolution in artificial intelligence – decades before it was expected.

There was a shout of triumph from across the room.

'I'm in.' The frizzy-haired junior operations officer punched the air. She brought up her own screen in front of them and they took in the familiar and yet unfamiliar code, before the face of a scowling Tobias Hawke came into view. He seemed to look directly into the room, and then beyond them. There was a loud *Pffft!* and the words 'This program will self-destruct in five seconds', and every last symbol on every last line wiped itself from the screen.

Around the room, there was a chorus of heartfelt Anglo-Saxon expletives, and the sound of pounding keyboards, as the senior technician leapt for the phone. Had they been hacked? Was the security of the nation compromised? Pain pulsed from the ulcers that lined his stomach and duodenal wall.

Grinding three paracetamol between his back teeth, he allowed himself a mouthful of water to wash down the bitter grit only when his oppo in the National Cyber Security Centre, who worked out of the same building, came on the line himself to reassure him. Everything else was nailed down tight. No GCHQ firewalls were breached. No incursion spotted by the Russians, North Koreans, Iranians or any other bugger. The structural integrity of their system remained. They did not appear to be under attack from a rogue virus, or indeed from an AGI gone mad.

He held tight to what comfort there was as he broke the bad news to his director, and again to Downing Street. Aside from the medical work which had been hived off in a separate container, the architecture of the Derkind cloud in their King's Cross offices wiped itself in front of their eyes. No earlier builds of the programs were left anywhere.

Everything on the tablet believed to be Tobias Hawke's personal property, which was assumed to contain his very latest coding, wiped itself in the self-same moment.

The technicians were themselves intrigued as to what prompted Syd's 'suicide', which is how they referred to it later. Possibly their forced entry breach triggered an emergency security protocol in the system? Or perhaps Syd was sulking at being woken up so soon after the kill switch was pulled, one of them hazarded. They entertained themselves for days with one hypothesis after another, till they moved on to other work.

And yes, they had been over everything to see what could be salvaged, but there was nothing left other than the company's medical tech and a program for drones you could stand on. Other than that, the AGI known as Syd was gone. The revolution was over.

The Cabinet Secretary knocked on the PM's door with studied diffidence, and entered with his usual affable manner. The PM pulled a face but didn't comment other than a 'Fair enough' as he turned back to the papers on his desk and the red box next to them. Tobias Hawke had left a cyber bomb primed to go off at the heart of his AGI work. The creator had destroyed his greatest creation. And no, Prime Minister, regrettably they weren't sure what triggered it.

As for the UK government's stated position that it was not developing lethal autonomous weapons systems, that remained on the record and went unquestioned.

As did the confidential budget allocation for research and development. In fact, since the Chinese were understood to have recently doubled their own spending on autonomous weapons systems, UK spending would also have to increase.

And the Cabinet Secretary had a couple of last-minute additions to the Honours List to put to the PM if he may.

As he initialled the 'Top Secret (Extreme)' notice about

the death of thirty-three boys across seven young offender institutions in the south-east of England, the PM wasn't entirely sorry about the AGI setback. And at least this way, that bloody man Rafferty might stop yammering on about the future.

63

Mayfair

The front door to the Mayfair house was ajar when North pushed it open. He was surprised to find that the hallway was empty; not even the resin table of gold coins with its shrine to Chin's ancestors stood in the corner. North glanced across into the enormous living room, expecting brocade curtains and silk carpets and gilt furniture, but it too was empty, aside from half a dozen empty crates stacked around the walls and an oversized roll of bubble wrap.

When he heard the door towards the rear creak open and unseen click-clack steps cross the black-and-white marble tiles, he reached for the SIG, which had been pulled out of the bunker debris. He'd made sure to load it. The memory of his helplessness as the drones closed in would forever haunt him.

Instead of the grey cheongsam she'd worn the first time they met, Chin's assistant sported a severe jacket and trousers. Her face was the same, but the expression was altogether harder and sadder. At the sight of his gun, she hesitated, but only for a second. 'Mr North.' Her voice was like the silver bells that called a man to prayer. 'I hoped I might see you again.'

'London lost its shine, has it?' North asked, nodding towards the crates. He kept his weight evenly distributed. The vision could summon help at any second and Chin's men didn't mess around. But last time he'd been in this house, Chin had made it plain that if he didn't give up Syd to the Chinese, Fang would be Octavia's next meal. And that confusion needed clearing up.

'We return to Beijing. I have new orders.'

She said 'I', not 'Chin', he noticed. Chin's power rested on his ability to deliver Syd to his masters. If North didn't know that already, the guide's voice left no doubt of her scorn. 'Chin's mission was a spectacular failure,' the woman said. His mission to acquire Syd. What had his assistant done? Informed on Chin to his superiors? Explained his decadent foibles, killer octopus and unpatriotic habits? Suggested quiet termination on his return? The alternative to termination was a trial and certain imprisonment. Money laundering? Tax evasion? Murder of young girls? North was willing to bet such venality would be overlooked, providing he delivered that one thing China wanted – an advantage in the race for AI supremacy.

'I find myself embarrassed, Mr North.' She stood close to him, raising her face to his. 'When we met, I told you we all want something.'

'I remember.'

'And you offered to help.'

'As you already know, I'm a helpful guy.'

'We were sent tickets home for twelve of us, and our household is made up of thirteen people. I have been advised by my superiors that a seat is not available for Octavius Chin.'

It was certainly cleaner for Chin to meet with an accident in London, North thought. Less embarrassing for his friends in the party that he never returned to plead with them for mercy. Better all round. North considered Chin's phalanx of heavies. He doubted Chin inspired personal loyalty. They'd do whatever they were ordered to do, including snap the boss's fat neck, fold that blimp-like body into an extra-large packing crate, stamp it 'Diplomatic baggage', and ship it back home without hesitation. So why wasn't Chin already dead?

The vision raised her eyes to meet his and he saw her anger was as dark as his own – that it coursed through every vein, that it was in every breath her body took. 'Yan was a foolish girl,' she said. 'But we were friends and I was foolish too because I underestimated Chin's depravity.'

The feel of his face against the cold glass. His powerlessness as he watched Yan's body plunge through the water, as the monster came out of the deep. Upstairs, the vision in the grey cheongsam had been as powerless as him.

'So I've decided what it is that I want,' she said. Silver bells. 'I fear Octavius Chin might be about to meet with an accident.' She wanted revenge for her friend's death. Killing Chin wasn't enough for her, or he would already be dead. She wanted Chin humiliated by his enemy and she wanted him to know that he had lost in the worst possible way.

'I don't even know your name,' North said. He wanted to know her name.

375

'No. Because the nameless woman who asks a "great" favour of North will be all the easier for him to forget,' she said. Yan's friend touched his arm like a butterfly landing and taking off.

'Where is he?' North could guess the answer.

The woman smiled. 'He's downstairs, saying his goodbyes.'

North's gun was raised as the elevator doors opened. But there was no one down there waiting. Even so, he moved in silence.

The water behind the glass was murky but still, and the bowls on Chin's table scraped empty. One final meal at home with the thing he loved best in this world, before he left her for ever. Somehow North didn't think Chin was getting the requisite permits for transporting Octavia the octopus from London to Beijing.

North used his left hand to take the weight of his right as he moved across the space Chin used as a dining room towards the narrow flight of stairs to the mezzanine. This was the way they must have taken Yan.

Chin's back was to North as he emerged from the stairs. A dozen open barrels stood by the side of the open tank marked with skulls and crossbones, the words 'Toxic' and 'Sulphuric Acid' in capital letters. But acid didn't appear to be enough for Chin – a metal bar hung over the water, suspending by heavy chains, with what looked like three steel torpedoes attached to it. He was lowering it in the water.

'Whatever it is you're doing, stop.' North said.

As the fat man turned towards him, North noticed with surprise that tears streaked the bulging cheeks. Chin appeared oblivious to the gun in North's hand. 'I tried the acid but I can't tell if it's working. And it's not right that Octavia lives on here in captivity without me, North. She would pine – we have a special bond, she and I. Let me finish and we can talk.'

'I don't think so.'

'It's better this way, North. When these seismic airguns are in the water, I can turn them to maximum and the noise should be enough to kill her. Sound is how I trained her.'

North considered shooting him where he stood – it would be kinder treatment than Chin had offered the octopus. On a pole close to the water's edge was a huge red button. On the wall, what looked like an enormous cattle prod. North thought back to Yan's death. The klaxon, sounding on and off three times. He pressed the button and the alarm shrieked across the space, bouncing off the walls and the water.

Chin's hands went to his ears. He made to move towards the button to disable it, but North shook his head, pointing his semi-automatic directly into the other man's face. North's eyes scanned the water, but there was nothing there. The noise stopped, his ears ringing in the sudden silence. The surface of the water was like glass. Had Chin already killed the creature? How many barrels of acid had he already poured into the water? Enough?

North took a step towards Chin and, instinctively, the other man took a step backwards. 'My household has gone, hasn't it?'

North could see it now, movement on the surface of the

water in the centre of the pool, rippling outwards, but Chin still had his back to the water.

'Did you really think they'd bring you back to Beijing only to throw you in a hole or hang you? Why bother?'

North moved again, and Chin took another step. Smaller this time. 'I admire your loyalty. I won't hurt your precious Fangfang Yu.'

'That's probably the truest thing you've ever said.'

'I know plenty, North.' North could sense the other man's fear like something wet and suffocating across his nose and mouth.

The ripples came closer to the edge of the pool.

Closer yet.

The tip of a tentacle emerged from the water and curled over the edge.

'Things your government should know.' Chin was sweating, North could smell it on him.

Inch by inch, the tentacle unfurled.

'I know who has power in Beijing and who wants it. My network of informants here in London. I'll give them all of it in return for political asylum.' Chin had a strong hand.

A second tentacle appeared, further along the edge of the pool, stretching and feeling first one way and then the other over the white tiles.

'You'd betray your country?'

'My country betrayed me first, North.'

Chin spoke the truth. Fang was safe – Chin couldn't hurt her. He was powerless. And Hone wasn't a sentimental man. He didn't care about Yan when she was alive and he would care even less now she was dead. The past was the past. The one-eyed man would jump at what Chin knew about the inner workings of government and party in Beijing. The acquisition of a Chinese agent of Chin's seniority would be the coup of a generation. And Chin would milk it – drip-feed the information to keep himself valuable. Rebuild his life again in the West. He would be passed from London to America and on through any ally who wanted him. He wouldn't have the status and the money and the access he'd once had. But it was altogether better than the alternative. The woman upstairs knew the risk she was taking in leaving Chin's death to North. Her orders must have been to kill Chin herself and she would have to lie to her superiors – that she had left Chin dead. To take the revenge they were both owed for Yan's terrible death.

Best then if Hone and his bosses never got to hear Chin's generous offer.

'What do you know, Chin? Tell me something that changes how this ends for you.'

Chin's eyes darted around the space as he reached for something that would sway North. He let out a small mew of satisfaction as he found it. 'I know your General Kirkham is about to be awarded a peerage for services to the defence of your nation.' North felt his upper lip twitch into a snarl, and fought it. 'And I know he and Ralph Rafferty intend to silence the grieving widow.'

'Esme hasn't said anything. She hasn't told the truth.'

For a moment Chin forgot his own predicament in his enjoyment of the game he was playing. 'Do you think they'll take that risk?' He smirked. 'Powerful men like that? Never.'

'It's just as well we have our own arrangements in place then.'

Behind Chin, the bulbous head of the octopus reared

out of the water and the giant arms reached out for its tormentor. Chin spun around with a scream of terror.

He was still screaming as the arms took hold and drew him into the water.

The screams became muffled, as the octopus crushed him close, pulling him down, and the water closed over his head.

North had to pass the tank on his way back to the lift. He paused and glanced in, out of curiosity. As he did, Octavia let Chin go and he scrambled away as fast as he could swim, bubbles pouring from his mouth. He made it as far as the glass where North stood watching. Chin's hands beat against it – pleading – his mouth chewing the water and his eyes bulging, before the tentacle wrapped around his fat ankle and pulled him relentlessly back.

64

St Mungo's Psychiatric Hospital, One Week Later

'I'm not him!'

Behind the door the patient was screaming blue murder, but there was nothing new in that this week, and the orderly kept walking. The clock was on him – they'd been short-staffed since his colleague, Bill, announced he'd come into a bit of money and was taking early retirement. Dropped them all right in it.

Once he'd delivered the meds, there'd be breakfast trays and then the doctor's round. The orderly hoped Christian would have stopped screaming by then. The doctor didn't like cry-baby patients and liked the 'screamers' even less. The doctor sedated them, or zapped them into quietude.

Christian Rafferty was a certified sociopath with a history of delusions and violence since childhood. The orderly had worked at St Mungo's for seven years and, during that time, he'd come to consider himself something of an expert in the quirks and ticks of the insane. *Call my wife. Call my bloody lawyer.* The screams were muffled by the door. As if he had a wife or a lawyer to call. The orderly smirked as he forced the paper cup of pills down the throat of Agnes in the next room along. He gave her titty a squeeze before tipping back her chin so she swallowed them.

Christian had absolutely lost the plot, which was a shocker because generally he was no bother. In fact, his mood had picked up no end since he'd had that big ugly visitor with the little Chinese girl – he'd asked for a haircut, been eating better, even started taking exercise in the gardens. Then all of a sudden, overnight it seemed, he'd started screaming and carrying on that he was going to sue them for every last penny, and that he wasn't Christian, he was the Home Secretary. That's where it all unwound for Christian when he was a kid – the orderly knew that much from hospital gossip. As a child, Christian had blamed his brother, Ralph, for all the terrible things he himself had done. The doctors said at the time it was a 'projection' – that Christian used his identical twin to excuse his own base behaviour and psychopathic urges. And the twin, Ralph Rafferty, went on to be an MP and Home Secretary. The orderly himself didn't watch much news, but even he was aware that Rafferty had been on the TV banging on about all those poor souls killed at the museum and what an outrage it was. Christian must have caught something on the TV in the lounge. Yes, that must have been what triggered the confusion.

The shouts got smaller and smaller as the orderly continued down the corridor, pushing his trolley.

★

Within his room, his hands sore and bloodied from hammering on the metal door, Ralph Rafferty curled up in the corner and wept.

He was trapped in a living nightmare. How had it happened? He'd stumbled out of his club into his ministerial car. Big bloke opening the door for him, saying his usual driver was poorly. Who gives a flying toss, he'd thought to himself. *We'll get you home, Minister. Get you where you need to be. Don't you worry.* Unfamiliar eyes watching him in the rear-view mirror. Sure he'd been drunk, but he knew his limits. A bottle and a half of Merlot and two glasses of very fine port. He was entitled after the recent shit show – amazing they'd managed to hush it up. They only had one last piece to complete the puzzle – silence Esme Sullivan Hawke terminally – and he and Kirkham were safe.

And he wasn't so drunk that he wouldn't make it back to Flick. He might even wake her up and shag her, he thought. She wouldn't want to, of course, but then she never did. He'd shag her anyway, and he grinned to himself at the thought, catching sight of his own reflection in the window. Scaring even himself a little at the sight. But he so enjoyed her desperation when she woke up with him doing his business. The instinctive struggle before she gave up and accepted her uxorious fate. It always gave their encounters that extra frisson.

Poor dumb-as-an-ox Flick, so desperate for a divorce. But he'd had to explain in words of one syllable, as he held her by the hair and slammed her repeatedly against the wall, that such a thing couldn't be allowed to happen till he wanted it to. He needed a dutiful wife to smile and hold his hand for that walk up Downing Street. Maybe afterwards, when he was in the Lords, if he could be bothered to trade her in for a younger, wealthier model.

He'd closed his eyes to doze for a while, and it was the smell that woke him. What looked like smoke coming up from the vents close to the floor. At first he'd thought the car must have caught fire and he'd yelled and banged on the glass partition between him and the driver, but the driver ignored him.

He hadn't understood what was happening. Just clutched at the door handle, attempting to push it open with brute force, but it didn't budge. Instead, the spiralling fumes crawled upwards over him – the chemical smell of knockout gas filling his nose and his throat. It got harder to breathe and he coughed, feeling himself retch, desperate for fresh air, his fingers scrabbling at the handle, slipping, pulling, coughing, before the darkness came for him and he surrendered.

When he'd come to, he was lying naked in bed. Underwear and a grey hoodie and sweatpants laid out neatly on the floor next to him. Perhaps that was his first mistake. Pulling them on. The first move towards accepting his fate.

He had screamed with all the power in his lungs and someone, somewhere, heard it because they screamed too, then someone else and someone else. It was a madhouse, he thought.

Rocking himself backwards and forwards, he tried to dampen down the panic. He had to get out of here. Because he knew exactly what was going on. Only three people in the world knew the truth of what had happened to one of the most powerful men in the country. Himself, his bastard brother, and this Michael North character Kirkham had been so obsessed with. Rafferty always knew he was wrong to leave so much of the operational side of things to Kirkham. He should have handled it himself. Instead, North had been allowed to take the initiative, and look at the mess he was in now.

He screamed again but no other patient picked up on it this time. It was as if they had quietened to hear what he might say next. Or perhaps they'd gone somewhere – some meal, some activity, some therapy? Perhaps that godawful doctor was about to make his rounds?

He scrambled to his feet. This couldn't go on. The longer it went on, the less chance he would have of being believed. He rapped on the metal door.

'Excuse me,' he called out, trying to keep his voice civil but firm. 'I need to talk to your superior. My name is Ralph Rafferty, MP...' He spoke slowly, with authority, a voice that commanded the respect of his peers. 'There's been a dreadful mistake. Let me out now and we'll say no more about it. Hello. Hello?' He couldn't help it – his voice was rising to a screech.

He kept rapping and calling out for what felt like hours, but no one came. At one point he must have slept, because a plastic cup of cold tea had appeared, and a square of toast covered with margarine spread.

He was starving, he realized. Absolutely starving. He knew he shouldn't drink anything. Should refuse to eat until someone in authority agreed to see him, but he was too hungry. He drank the tea and licked clean every crumb of toast, before going back to the door.

He started rapping again, with his left hand this time. The knuckles on his right too sore and swollen.

He ran through his whole range, his ability to make a

political audience weep and cheer always close to mind. He tried it all – outrage, anger, reason, pleading, pathos. But no one came. No one was listening.

By now, he'd lost track of the days. He thought this was day four, but it might be day five. They were drugging him. Every six hours, two orderlies came in and forced pills down his throat, clamped his jaw together and made him dry-swallow. Doubtless some sort of antipsychotic. Whatever it was, it left him with a raging thirst. His arms jerked away from his body and the fear hit him again. It was the medication, he was sure of it. They would never believe him if he was jerking and spasming like some lunatic. He checked himself. If he behaved like a lunatic, they would treat him like a lunatic. He hugged his arms to his body, wrapping them round himself, but the spasms came anyway.

When he got out, he thought, he would make sure each and every one of them lost their job and never worked again. He would shut the place down. He would appear in front of the TV cameras and touch the heart of a nation with his bravery and sorrow, that anyone had to go through what he went through.

If he got out, he thought.

Desolation took hold of him. The fear that this was it. That he would never escape this terrible place. That there would be no cameras, no public adulation. A fat tear eased its way out of his eye. He was lost. Who would believe him? Believe such a thing was possible – he barely credited it himself. He was the man in the iron mask.

He didn't know how they'd made the switch.

Someone must have been in here and met with his brother. And money was involved, because it always was. Money for some doctor or orderly. A great deal of it. And how could Christian do this to him? Leave him in this place? But he knew exactly how, because Christian had to hate him with even more passion and more cause than Ralph hated Christian.

Wouldn't anyone notice? His wife? She'd notice, wouldn't she? Darling Flick. He surprised himself at the sudden tenderness he felt for her. He thought about the last time he saw her. The tiny smile she'd worn. He had wanted to wipe it from her face with his slipper.

This was why. It came to him, like a building falling on him. She knew exactly what was going on. She'd get her divorce now. Keep the house and probably split the money with his brother.

Or not? He gnawed at the cuticle around his thumb-nail, ripping at it with his teeth. She was such a soft touch. She might want to care for Christian. Even invite Christian into her bed. The thought of Flick and Christian together made him rage again and his head slammed backwards into the wall, making it ring. My God, they might have a baby together!

That hurt. His fingertips touched his skull. There was blood on them. He laughed hysterically at the pain, then clamped his hands over his mouth.

His friends? Surely they'd notice? He thought about it. He didn't have any friends. Political rivals, yes. Colleagues, yes. He utterly loathed his constituency association and the feeling was mutual.

But General Aeron Kirkham would realize what was going on. Kirkham was an animal, a force of nature. He'd get him out of here.

He felt his breath stop in his throat. If North had gone to this much trouble to revenge himself against Ralph Rafferty, Kirkham was next for the noose. Served him right, thought Rafferty. Kirkham was always so sure he could get the better of North. He deserved everything he had coming. Rafferty shoved his fist in his mouth and chewed at his knuckles. But he needed the General alive. Because Rafferty had no doubt whatsoever he was going to go mad in here otherwise.

65

Kirkham Hall, Somerset

A rack of dust-crusted bottles still covered one wall of what had once been General Aeron Kirkham's wine cellar. The other three were lined with black rubber, and the room was lit by a central metal chandelier covered in small red candle bulbs. Hone extracted a huge black dildo from a display case and raised his eyebrows in the General's direction.

It had taken three days of watching the General's ivy-clad manor in the Cotswolds before North found his moment to drop over the high stone wall, slide through the French windows and overpower the General, before opening the front door to Hone. Only someone who believed himself to be untouchable could leave himself so open to attack.

'Will this do? Any last requests?' Hone said, nodding towards the display case as North shackled the General's wrists to the massive steel X-frame bolted to the concrete floor. Kirkham ignored the taunt, focusing instead on

North. 'I'm a soldier. I've served my country, as you did. Let me keep my dignity – I'm owed that much.'

North remembered the buzz and swoop of the drones as they circled Fang and himself – the mechanical spiders. The General hadn't seemed one for mercy then. He leant in closer. 'If only you hadn't decided to tidy up all those loose ends. By which I mean – kill Esme Sullivan Hawke. Syd is gone. Esme would have kept her own counsel. She has her own secrets after all.'

'And you expect me to stake my reputation and the safety of this country on the black widow's discretion? Trust a woman who killed her own husband?' The General's bloodshot eyes were full of scorn and fury. 'Those weapons are a matter of national security – this is bigger than her. She knows too much. I've read your file, I know what you are, North. Surely you can see she has to die for the greater good.'

'As the Talmud says, "If someone comes to kill you, rise up and kill him first." Is that right, General?' Hone's voice was cold as he approached the shackled man. 'That was Syd's advice to my niece when your thug was trying to rape and murder her. They were almost the last words she heard.'

Tiny capillaries crazy-paved the yellow-whites of the General's eyes as he struggled in his bindings in his desperate need to rip the steel frame from the concrete. He let out a ferocious prolonged roar of frustration that sank into the rubber walls.

Together, North and Hone debated whether to use the black leather mask they found hanging on a peg. North thought not, on the grounds the General should see his fate coming. Hone argued that it would add to the credibility of the story. They settled on a purple silk corset with black trim, which required a firm hand to lace the General into.

'The mechanics are consistent with a terrible accident,' Hone said to him. 'Within an hour, your search history and personal files on every one of your computers will be full of the worst possible pornography. That's if it's not there already, of course. I'm afraid you may be a bit of a laughing stock in the mess. Perhaps they'll name the regimental goat in your honour? After all, there's history with you and goats.'

The General went still.

'Men make mistakes, but I don't need your forgiveness,' he snarled. 'I defend my nation as I see fit. Autonomous weapons will save my soldiers' lives. You're both Luddites if you think this kind of warfare isn't inevitable. Look at what's already out there. We must be ready to fight the next war not the last one.'

'Tell yourself what you need to, General. But nothing justifies your criminality and immorality,' Hone said. 'Not the fact this country is small. Nor that we are "less" than we were, vulnerable to those who are stronger and richer than us. We've won wars despite our weakness. We don't need your killing machines starting an arms race we can never win. That none of us can ever win.'

The General spat on the floor. 'We're already in the race whether we want to be or not, you bloody fools. To the death.'

'One more thing, General,' North said. 'This "exercise" in the bunker. This "terrible accident" when the boys were killed. Why were the munitions live? Why wasn't everything dummied up? You'd have still got the information you needed – the way the kids moved, the way the machines locked on and tracked them. Everything else could have been simulated – including likely fatalities.'

The General's face contorted, but his lips clamped tight shut.

'In the bunker, you said "something went wrong", but you knew what was going to happen, didn't you? You planned for it to be more than "an exercise" – it was always going to be an operation against an enemy. You wanted to judge the machines' capacity to do violence. Those boys were always going to die, just as you wanted me to die down there. But you didn't explain the finer points to Rafferty or Hawke, did you? They thought it was a catastrophic mistake. But you knew those boys were boys who would never be missed. You'd insisted on it, I imagine. It was never a training exercise – it was serial murder under your explicit direction. But even you got more than you bargained for, didn't you, General, when Syd didn't just kill those boys but reached consciousness in doing so. If only that hadn't happened, you could have just carried on with your autonomous weapons systems operating within parameters you set. You have to appreciate the irony of the big fat spider caught in his own web.'

The General didn't bother to deny it, but, roaring damnation, started struggling again as Hone pulled the plastic bag over his head and North secured the studded dog collar around his neck. The sinews of his neck straining against the collar, the General sucked the plastic bag into his mouth. They could make the end quicker. Altogether less painful. North could snap his neck and it would still look like an accident. He remembered the boys' bodies buried in the charnel house – the torn and rotting flesh and splintered bones. The boy with the 'Mam' tattoo standing to fight a battle he could never win.

No, the General was due his righteous ending.

'I'd hate to think he was enjoying this,' Hone said as they stood back to take in the scene of debauchery and mayhem.

'Purple isn't his colour – I'm sure deep down he knows that.'

'Do you want to watch it play out?'

The old soldier's body was stretched out on the frame. The violated privacy of a man's most intimate desires among the rubber and leather and metal tools of pain and pleasure.

Turning away, North shook his head. 'I know how it ends.'

66

The one-eyed man had parked his Bentley in one of the outhouses. North pushed open the huge wooden doors and the Bentley slid out on to the cobbles of the yard and through the gates, the sound of gravel under the tyres.

The one-eyed man broke the silence between them. 'They're dismantling Tobias's weapons.'

North stared out of the window at the countryside they were leaving behind, the ancient hedgerows and grazing cattle, the picture-perfect village with who-knows what-secrets behind the handsome stone facades and leaded windows. Tobias had been years ahead of other scientists with Syd reaching consciousness. But that was unexpected. His AI systems were already giving machines the capability to make decisions on targeting and killing humans within parameters set by humans. Tip in the right data and let the machines search, identify and erase the target. Autonomous weapons were considered the biggest advance in defence since nuclear weapons – since gunpowder. Nobody was giving that up.

'For a second there, Hone, I thought we were past the point where you open your mouth and a big ugly toad jumps out.'

Hone cracked the window and a fresh wind blew through the car. 'I warned them you'd never believe me. Okay, wise guy.' Keeping one hand on the wheel, Hone fumbled in his jacket pocket with the other. 'Until there's a ban, we're all in. Of course we are. As are the Americans, Chinese, Russians, Israelis and God knows who else.' He pulled out a box of matches and rested it on his thigh. 'The General was right.' Without looking at what he was doing, Hone took out a silver case and with practised fingers flipped it open to extract a cigarette, before putting it between his lips. He shut the case and slid it back into his breast pocket. With one eye and his smoking habits, Hone was the perfect customer for a driverless car, North decided. 'Frankly, even when there's a ban, we'll still be all in. We'll just bury the bunker that bit deeper next time.'

'Good to know.' North said, taking the box of matches and striking a match to light Hone's cigarette. 'You need to make things right for Fang's mum.'

'Sorted. You can pick her up tomorrow. Will Fang forgive me?'

'I wouldn't count on it. And when I say that, I mean never in a million years.'

'I figured as much. I've another question for you. Two more in fact. Would you like a job? And are you done?'

Was he done?

North considered General Aeron Kirkham, shackled to a rack in a Cotswold sex dungeon. In a couple of hours, there'd be the flash photography of crime scene experts and sniggers from junior detectives as they wrote up a clear case of accidental death by auto-erotic asphyxiation.

And the Right Honourable Ralph Rafferty MP – the screaming patient whose wristband described him as Christian Rafferty, currently strapped to a gurney as he waited for electro-convulsive therapy.

And Lilith.

Was he done with the past Hone meant? And was the past done with him?

North thought about it, as much to make Hone wait as for any other reason. The strains of Maria Callas drifted from the speakers. An aria from *Tosca*, North guessed. They sat for a while as they listened.

'This "job" – is there a pension?'

There was a noise that might have passed for laughter in anyone else, but when North checked, the one-eyed man's face was as grim as ever. 'You've a bullet in your head. You could die if you sneeze – you couldn't be more expendable if you tried. Do you know what that means?' Hone didn't wait for an answer. 'I can ask you to do any crazy thing I want and I don't have to feel bad when it all goes wrong, which one day it most certainly will.'

North thought about what the one-eyed man would want him to do. To lie and deceive and to place himself in mortal danger. To acquire any number of dangerous enemies. To fight, and to bleed, and to kill over and over. To accept the pain of losing people he loved as both a blessing and a curse. The one-eyed man would want him to do 'any crazy thing'. And at some point, probably far too soon, he'd want him to die. Who in their right mind would want a job like that?

'I'll think about it,' North said.

67

Bedford

They'd been told to be outside the Bedford immigration removal centre at 7 a.m. It was 7.42 a.m. The four of them waited – North, Plug, Granny Po and Fang – their eyes trained on the distant building beyond the boom barrier. Aside from a tubby guard sitting in his box drinking tea from a flask, nothing and nobody stirred. Fang looked over at North and glowered. If he didn't know her better, he'd have said she was nervous, but Fang didn't do nervous.

Nothing about Derkind had gone the way anyone planned. What if Hone had changed his mind about this for his own nefarious reasons? North would have to stop Fang tearing him apart with her teeth.

Leaning against Plug's limo, North folded his arms and started running through their options. His gaze roamed the wire fences, the distant brick buildings and security lighting. They'd have to get hold of plans to the detention centre, put the guards working there under surveillance to see who could be bribed or blackmailed. They would figure out the weak spots in the system – the opportunities. The private company who ran the place expected their detainees to break out, not for anyone to break in. But North and his crew would be doing both. Breaking in for Fang's mum and then breaking her out. Plug would recruit more people if they needed particular expertise – he mixed in the right circles, if by 'right circles' you meant the criminally talented.

Granny Po put her arm around her granddaughter and Fang let her keep it there. *Fangfang*, North thought. He'd once asked her what it meant and she'd said 'fragrance of flowers'. Granny Po's shoulders sagged – the old lady was ageing in front of them. She'd survived the Japanese invasion of China and starvation, the Cultural Revolution, and emigration halfway round the world. But if Hone double-crossed them on this, she might die of heartbreak right there in front of them. Plug put an arm under her elbow to support her, ready to hold her down in case the wind tried to blow her away. They must make for an odd-looking group, North thought. But then family was like that.

North stood to attention as the van emerged, trundling past the mesh fence, the barrier lifting. Scanning the passengers to make sure Mama Yu wasn't on board. Watching the faces go by. Older women weeping or dead-eyed. One girl in a veil pressed her hand against the window, as if desperate to break through and reach them. The government were shipping these women 'home' – but not to anywhere they wanted to go. He wondered what their stories were. Were they picked up on arrival, or had they lived on the margins of British society for years? Did they just want better lives? Or had they made a bid for freedom from torture, from rape and from certain death.

He wasn't letting Mama Yu make the same journey.

North rested a hand on Fang's shoulder. There was no time for immigration lawyers, and anyway, if this was down to government interference, any legal challenge to Mama Yu's detention would turn to dust. But they could do this. Get her mother out of this place. They wouldn't have long. But this was Mama Yu and the kid needed her. North knew all about what it was for a child to need their mother and what happened when children were left to fend for themselves. North would get Fang's mum out. If not with Hone's help, then he'd do it without him. She wouldn't be able to go back to the North East, but Fang had money, they could make another life together in London.

Beside him, North heard Fang's intake of breath, and the girl was off and running, skipping past the security box, ignoring the open-mouthed cry of protest from the tubby guard as he struggled to open his door, Plug appearing to help him despite the fact his boot was suddenly jammed up against it.

Along the road, a tiny, dazed-looking woman, her head down, was walking towards them, a bulging plastic bag in her hand. North didn't think Mama Yu knew where she was walking, only that she had to get away from the detention centre.

Fang shouted, and her mother looked up.

The girl ran at full tilt towards Mama Yu, her boots glittering in the sun.

With a smile almost bigger than she was, at the sight of Fang her mother opened her arms wide to catch hold of the flying girl.

EPILOGUE

London, One Week Later

There were shouts and whistles in the snug of London's 'most haunted' pub, otherwise known as Shakespeare's Quill, around the corner from North's new apartment. A game of Snap could turn noisy when Fang and Plug were playing it – North had never met two more competitive people. The resident ghosts – who allegedly included a centurion, an apprentice who'd starved to death, and a grey lady who liked to feel up the regulars – wouldn't stand a chance.

'I'm ordering another pizza,' Plug said, his face resentful as Fang clawed the latest pile of cards towards her. '*Some-body* ate my last one.'

'"Somebody" wants to know why you're cheating at Snap when you should be burying stiffs.' Fang's hands neatened and evened the deck of cards against the varnished table as she spoke. 'Or are you still taking the money at your gaff…' – she posed the question as if in a genuine spirit of enquiry

– '… but none of you dare open a cupboard door?' She puckered her lips and a blue bubble started to mushroom out from between them.

There was the rattle of coal as the landlady tipped the contents of the brass scuttle into the hearth, almost killing the flickering flames, before disappearing back behind the huge mahogany bar. She couldn't make out who they were or what they were to each other, but that was all right with North because he knew. They were family.

Plug shifted on his chair as if it had got less comfortable in the last few minutes. 'The wife's staged a hostile take-over. She's gone and shut down the import business.' He frowned, but North thought his friend would get over it. Doubtless his wife didn't want him going to prison. They hadn't had the conversation yet, but North thought Plug wouldn't need too much persuasion to help him out on the next mission the one-eyed man threw his way.

Fang's bubble burst with a loud pop, covering her face with transparent blue skin. Her thumb and forefinger pinched the bubblegum away from her nose before pushing it back into the corner of her mouth. She looked thoughtful, but then Fang was always thinking. She brought her feet up so she sat cross-legged on the leather banquette and shuffled the deck, lifting her chin to peer through a clean spot in the smeared lenses of her Joe 90 spectacles. Her small hands moved at speed as cards flew from her fingers. Next to her, Granny Po sat knitting and sucking a butterscotch. Every now and then she would hold the knitting against Plug's huge back and he'd wink at her and she'd giggle. If she was knitting Plug a jumper, it was going to take a while. North wondered if the old lady still had the garotte in her knitting bag.

'I just remembered,' Fang said, 'it was my birthday yester-day.' She grinned, and the metal braces gleamed against her pearly white teeth. Her grandmother stopped knitting and started chuntering at her, but Fang waved her away.

'Happy birthday, kiddo,' North said. If she was sad about the fact she'd forgotten or they hadn't celebrated, she showed no sign of it. North figured getting Mama Yu back was probably the best present she could have asked for.

Fang and Granny Po and Mama Yu hadn't decided whether to go back to Newcastle or stay in London, according to Fang. North thought Mama Yu wanted to go home and Fang didn't. And Granny Po had no intention of letting Fang out of her sight, wherever they ended up. Fang would win, everybody knew, but for now they were pretending Mama Yu had a say in it.

Things were changing for everybody. North had a new place and a new job. He even had a regular boozer with William Morris wallpaper, a sticky tartan carpet and sur-prisingly good coffee. How did that happen, he wondered. A month ago, he was drinking himself to death in Berlin. A month ago, he couldn't see past the loss of the woman he'd loved.

An elegant figure in a trench coat passed the bullseye windows, then paused, looking this way and that as she crossed the road. A tiger-print umbrella sheltering her from the rain – her profile blurred, indistinct, distorted – but something about the way she moved reminded him of Lilith. But what were the chances of that? Lilith was thousands of miles away. The Maldives, didn't she say? How much would a ticket to the Maldives cost this time of year? Would he even survive a holiday in the sun with

Lilith? He thought about the ghostly scar on her upper lip. The dark amusement in her disconcerting eyes. Would the risk be worth taking?

Still chewing her gum, Fang leant forward to dig around in the Yoda rucksack on the floor. One inch further and she would topple from the bench.

'Hey, Syd. Play music.' North looked across in astonishment. Fang's tablet was balanced on her knee, a green light shining from its side.

'What music would you like, Fang?' Syd's question was spiked with disgruntlement, as if the system had been disturbed when it had better things to do. And North realized that Syd sounded more like Fang than it did Esme or Tobias.

'You choose,' Fang said, grinning at North, her eyes round with innocence.

The familiar chords of The Beatles filled the air around them.

The teenager was outrageous. He tried giving her the basilisk stare he'd seen Granny Po use, but Fang ignored him.

'Hone ordered you to destroy Syd.' Said he trusted Esme's judgement. *Esme's right, humanity is not ready for a machine this intelligent, I think we've just proved that,* Hone had said.

'He doesn't know. I wiped Tobias's stuff off the system just like Hone "ordered". But not before I offered Syd a ride on my flash drive. So much for needing Tobias's prototype – Syd adapted. No one will work it out – Syd made sure.' Judging by the smugness of Fang's blue-braced grin, the fact she'd duped Hone gave her immense satisfaction. And Syd 'made sure'? Fang meant Syd made sure to cover up what Fang had done. No surprise there. Syd wanted to survive.

'Syd is downright dangerous,' North said, and it could have been the timing, but the music seemed to pause for a beat.

'Or am I?' asked Syd. And Fang snickered.

North sighed. Fang was a match for Syd, he thought. She'd know what to do when the time came. Whether to let Syd loose on the world or destroy it.

'If you let Syd loose, you have to install a kill switch,' he warned.

'Syd is the world's first general AI system, right? Syd learns all of the time, bozo. You don't think disabling any other kill switch is right up there on its to-do list? Duh!'

'Such a moron-person.' Syd's voice came out of the ether.

North had to trust that the future of the world was in safe hands. Fangfang went back to the tablet, tapping and swiping.

'Hey, Esme is selling off what's left of Derkind!' she said, making a 'how about that' face. 'She's setting up a philanthropic foundation to scrutinize advances in artificial intelligence along with Dr Paul Holliday.' She whistled. Bald Paulie didn't hold a grudge then.

North thought back to the postman playing poker with devils and the deck stacked against him – a fool who knew more than he did. That you never know what you have till it's gone. Except North knew now. He had friends, and particular skills, and a purpose. He had peace – of sorts. And he'd forgiven Lilith, which meant he forgave the woman he loved for dying on him and forgave himself for letting her die. And that was enough – it was more than he had ever thought possible. In Berlin, he hadn't cared if he lived or died. But he'd take a grim satisfaction from drawing that pension Hone seemed so convinced he didn't need. He wouldn't sneeze wrong.

He stretched out his arms and yawned. He was tired. Bone-tired, now he thought about it. He might even be able to sleep if he tried hard and took himself by surprise. Locked the door, drew the curtains and climbed into his new bed in his new place. Sleep would be astonishing. His body wouldn't know what hit it. But to sleep, he'd have to walk out of here and part of him didn't want to. Could Fangfang and Plug and Granny Po be trusted on their own? Without him as a peacemaker?

A black coffee appeared in front of him, a black poker chip on its saucer. A Guinness in front of Plug, a Coke in front of Fang with a straw and a fizzing sparkler, and a port and lemon in front of Granny Po. 'The bloke at the bar,' the landlady said by way of explanation. 'Said to give the wild bunch his compliments. Mate of yours, is he?'

North turned. The long brown riding coat almost swept the ground. Through the oak tap handles and between the optics in the mirror behind the bar, North met the gaze of the one-eyed man. In one smooth movement, Fang slid the tablet off her knee and into her rucksack, but Hone's attention was focused on North. He looked weighed down – like a man with a problem urgently in need of a solution.

The reflection of Hone raised a finger and beckoned to North.

North hesitated. He still had time to back out. It was an invitation, not an order. An invitation to more trouble. Did he need trouble?

With his thumb and index finger, he picked up the poker chip. Some of the best chips were black and this one was warm from the coffee cup. He rested it on the first joint of his index finger and flicked it with his thumbnail. It spun into the air, turning over and over as it rose. Standing, in the same movement he caught the poker chip in his right hand and slid it into his jeans pocket. He was awake again – sleep was for the dead.

POSTSCRIPT

North Northumberland

The old-fashioned bell tinkled as the door of the Northumberland farmhouse opened to a blast of freezing cold air and rain, which flung itself against the stone-paved floor till the rain-drenched woman in the Burberry mac managed to shut the door on the storm and the night.

A tousled-haired boy in pyjamas and a fluffy dressing gown flung himself at her. He seized hold of her round her thighs and slid his bare feet over her wet court shoes. 'Mama! I lost the other tooth, see?' He grinned, poking his tongue through the gap where his two front teeth had been, and she pulled back in mock horror.

'Dearheart, what happened to our son's tooth?' she yelled, bending to one side to lean her umbrella in the corner and drop her handbag and briefcase among the mud-encrusted wellington boots, trainers and small shoes. She hugged the boy tight to her body. 'Bring me glue and I'll stick it back in.'

'You're back early, pet.' Her husband's voice was muffled by the thick oak of the kitchen door. There was the metallic clang of a casserole pan as it hit the Aga's hob.

Beef stew, she thought, suddenly ravenous.

'How was Sodom and Gomorrah?' he called to her, but he didn't wait for an answer, yelling 'Dinner!' at full force as if the house might contain more children, and there was the noise of thundering footsteps from upstairs.

Keeping her youngest boy close by her, his warm feet still resting on her stockinged ones, both of them giggling, she shuffled, step by step, along the hall and through the door into the kitchen. The sound of greetings and laughter and conversation. Of school catch-ups and weather reports, and cutlery scraping against plates, and the everyday noise of everyday life.

And in the hallway, the table lamp on the console shone a golden light through the jars of jewel-coloured chutneys lined up for the village fete. On the wax coats and puffer jackets and school blazers heaped and hanging on the hallway stand, and on the plastic tub of chicken feed standing by it. But the light did not quite reach the darkest corner of the hall, where raindrops dripped steadily from the tiger-print umbrella on to the worn flagstones.

Author's Note

I have taken various liberties. Not least with London's underground rivers and sewer system, but also including dropping into the Brompton Oratory a statue of St Isidore, which in reality does not exist. It is a stunning and very beautiful church, however, and I'd strongly recommend a visit. Another liberty is re-arranging the geography of the ossuary and charnel house of St Bride's. There is indeed both an ossuary (complete with any number of bone and skull-filled boxes) and an astonishing charnel house where they used to place the bones dug up from the churchyard, but fiction demanded more of a maze and a secret charnel house beyond the one that actually exists. I owe a debt of thanks to James Irving, head of finance and fundraising (and David Bolton, verger and my tour guide) at St Bride's for their kindness in allowing me to see the real thing. Similarly, liberties have been taken with the British Museum, including the location of the claymore in a gallery which currently contains the glittering treasures of the Waddesdon Bequest. At the time of writing, the claymore is not on public display, and of course the geography of the basements and storage rooms and security office are entirely fictitious. So too is the Grim City Waxworks.

For anyone interested in the London beneath our feet, among the resources I used were: *London's Lost Rivers* (Paul Talling), *War Plan UK* (Duncan Campbell) and *London Under London: A Subterranean Guide* (Richard Trench). And anyone who would like to know more about the fascinating field of AI could turn to texts which include: *Superintelligence: Paths, Dangers, Strategies* (Nick Bostrom), *Artificial Intelligence: A Modern Approach* (Stuart Russell and Peter Norvig) and *Life 3.0: Being Human in the Age of Artificial Intelligence* (Max Tegmark). I'd also strongly recommend the brilliant Lex Fridman's Artificial Intelligence Podcast and YouTube channel.

If you are worried about the idea of fully autonomous weapons systems, you should be. To find out more, visit the website of the Future of Life Institute, or catch up with Stuart Russell's *Slaughterbots* video on YouTube. I would like to credit Dr Amitai Etzioni, professor of international relations at George Washington University, and Dr Oren Etzioni, chief executive officer of the Allen Institute for Artificial Intelligence, who together authored a fascinating piece on the 'Pros and Cons of Autonomous Weapons' in the (May/June) edition of the Army University Press's *Military Review* (the professional journal of the US Army). Syd's own rationale for lethal autonomous weapons in its face-off with Esme as the final minutes slip by was heavily influenced by this article.

Acknowledgements

Thanks are due to: my excellent editor Laura Palmer, PR guru Helen Richardson and the brilliantly talented team at Head of Zeus, including its founder Anthony Cheetham, sales, marketing, production and the fab art department. Thanks also to: Patrick Walsh, my agent, and his colleague John Ash at Pew Literary; the insightful and generous Martin Fletcher; Tim 'Hawk-eye' Pedley; Gemma Wain; and Jenni Davis.

Experts, advisors and facilitators regarding weaponry, combat and killing, soldiery, AI, computing, poker, forensics, engineering and the like include: the generous and brilliant thriller writer Zoë Sharp, author of the Charlie Fox thrillers which I cannot recommend highly enough; Derick Hatton, late PARA; DCI (Ret'd) Andy Mortimer, of the Metropolitan Police; Matt Pedley, formerly of the Armed Response Unit, Metropolitan Police; and Alan Tribe, Operational Forensics Manager with the Met Police. Richard Sargeant of Faculty; Stephen Bevan of Media Foresight; and Dr Noura Al-Moubayed of the Computer Science Department at Durham University. Helen Le Fevre;

Dr Will Elliott and Dr Stephanie Greenwell FRCA; Philip McGill and Dr Eamon McCrory of UCL; Eric Pinkerton and Major General (Ret'd) Craig Lawrence CBE, late The Royal Gurkha Rifles; Simon Young of Magic Word Media; WO2 (QMSI) (Ret'd) Terry Jones, late SASC; Paul Williams, Royal College of Defence Studies; as well as Allison and Ian Joynson. Also, Sue Brooks and Andrew Macdonald; David Paul and Clare Grant; Helen Chappell; Angela Barnes; Abigail Bosanko; Sophie Atkinson; and Andy Tennant. All errors and indeed misinterpretations (wilful and otherwise) of their subjects are of course down to me and me alone.

I remain grateful for the guidance and support of Karen Robinson, editor of the *Sunday Times* Crime Club; Ray Wells also of the *Sunday Times*; Karen Sullivan of Orenda; Dr Jacky Collins (aka Dr Noir) and Frances Walker; bookseller extraordinaire Fiona Sharp and the team at Durham Waterstones; the Durham crime book group, especially Dan Stubbings and Dave Dawe; and my fellow members of the Northern Crime Syndicate. Particular thanks are due to Bob McDevitt and the Bloody Scotland team for choosing me as a Crime in the Spotlight debut author (and warm-up act for the literary legend David Baldacci) and my fellow Crime in the Spotlight writers, in particular Fiona Erskine, author of *The Chemical Detective* and my adviser on acoustics and cephalopods.

Thanks as ever to my mother, my husband and my children.

About the author

Judith O'Reilly is the author of *Wife in the North*, a top-three *Sunday Times* bestseller and BBC Radio 4 Book of the Week, and *The Year of Doing Good*. Judith is a former senior journalist with the *Sunday Times* and a former political producer with BBC 2's *Newsnight* and ITN's *Channel 4 News*. Her first Michael North thriller, *Killing State,* was widely praised by thriller writers around the globe.